WHERE THEY FOUND HER

PRAISE FOR *WHERE THEY FOUND HER*

"Suspenseful. . . . McCreight is quickly rising into a league with the best purveyors of the stuff, from Jodi Picoult to Harlan Coben."

—USA TODAY

"I recently picked up McCreight's 2013 debut, and I could not put it down. . . . It's no surprise that McCreight's latest novel, *Where They Found Her* . . . is at the top of my to-read list."

—EW.COM (*ENTERTAINMENT WEEKLY* ONLINE)

"The way McCreight weaves the tale through three different perspectives will both haunt and shock you."

—GLAMOUR.COM

"While many books have been billed as the next *Gone Girl*, this mystery thriller definitely will intrigue fans of Gillian Flynn's bestseller. . . . Told in multiple views, the reader will have to decide what is truth and what is fiction in this heart-pounding read."

—INSTYLE

"Coiled as tightly as a spring, *Where They Found Her* begins with a small town's tragedy and doesn't relent until every secret, and character, is exposed. Kimberly McCreight has written another satisfying, dark page-turner that pounces off the page."

—MIRANDA BEVERLY-WHITTEMORE, *NEW YORK TIMES* BESTSELLING AUTHOR OF *BITTERSWEET*

"*Where They Found Her* is a fast-paced, intensely moving story filled with complex characters who drag you unresisting into their dark and tangled lives. It kept me guessing until the very last chapter."

—CHEVY STEVENS, *NEW YORK TIMES* BESTSELLING AUTHOR OF *STILL MISSING* AND *THAT NIGHT*

"Even seasoned mystery readers won't see the twists coming in this fast-paced read filled with unreliable narrators."

—CLEVELAND PLAIN DEALER

"McCreight . . . keep[s] us guessing right to the end."

—CHARLOTTE OBSERVER

"McCreight has done an excellent job of weaving a haunting story of expectation and loss."

—COLUMBUS DISPATCH

"Genuinely suspenseful and disturbing; McCreight delivers a provocative, timely novel that reminds us that sometimes the things that shine the brightest have the dirtiest underbellies."

—KIRKUS REVIEWS (STARRED REVIEW)

"*Where They Found Her* is the electrifying story about the power of secrets spilling from one generation to the next, growing larger and more terrifying until they swamp everyone in their path and sweep to a shocking, unforgettable end."

—CARLA BUCKLEY, AUTHOR OF *THE DEEPEST SECRET*

WHERE THEY FOUND HER

Kimberly McCreight

HARPER ● PERENNIAL

NEW YORK ● LONDON ● TORONTO ● SYDNEY ● NEW DELHI ● AUCKLAND

FIRST HARPER PERENNIAL EDITION PUBLISHED 2016.

The Library of Congress has catalogued the hardcover as follows:

McCreight, Kimberly.
   Where they found her : a novel / Kimberly McCreight. —First edition.
      pages ; cm
ISBN 978-0-06-222546-7 (hardcover)—ISBN 978-0-06-222547-4 (softcover)—ISBN 978-0-06-237042-6 (large print) 1. Murder—Investigation—Fiction. 2. Psychological fiction. I. Title.
   PS3613.C386444W48 2015
   813'.6--dc23

                                                                    2014038003

ISBN 978-0-06-256076-6 (Can.)

16 17 18 19 20   OV/RRD   10 9 8 7 6 5 4 3 2 1

For all the daughters, especially my own.

ONE CAN'T BUILD LITTLE WHITE PICKET FENCES
TO KEEP NIGHTMARES OUT. —Anne Sexton

WHERE THEY FOUND HER

Molly

The sky through our large bay window was just beginning to brighten when I opened my eyes. Not quite morning. Not the alarm, not yet. When the noise came again, I realized it was my phone vibrating on the nightstand. *Erik Schinazy* glowed on the screen in the darkness.

"Is everything okay?" I answered without saying hello.

In the five months I'd been working at the tiny but respectable *Ridgedale Reader*, the paper's contributing editor in chief had never once called me outside business hours. He'd had no reason to. As the *Reader's* arts, lifestyle, and human-interest reporter, I covered stories that were hardly emergencies.

"Sorry to call so early." Erik sounded tired or distracted. Or something.

I wondered for a second whether he'd been drinking. Erik was supposedly sober these days, but it was widely rumored that his drinking had gotten him fired from the *Wall Street Journal*. It was hard to imagine fastidious Erik, with his tall, rigid posture, swift military gait, and neat buzz cut, ever being sloppy drunk. But there had to be a better explanation for a reporter of his caliber landing at the *Reader*, editor in chief or not, than his wife, Nancy—a psychology professor at Ridgedale University—being tired of commuting to Ridgedale from New York City, where they'd lived when Erik was at the *Journal*.

Not that I was one to judge. I'd gotten the staff position at the
Reader thanks to Nancy being on the faculty welcoming committee. I didn't know how much Nancy had pressured Erik to hire me
or how desperate Justin had made my situation sound, but from
the exceedingly kind, almost therapeutic way Nancy regarded me,
I had my suspicions. And with only a law degree and a decade
of legislative public policy experience for the National Advocates
for Pregnant Women on my résumé, I was fairly certain that I
hadn't been the most qualified candidate for the staff reporter
position.

But Justin—now a tenured English professor, thanks to
Ridgedale University—had been right to do whatever it took to
get me a fresh start. And writing for the *Ridgedale Reader* had given
me unexpected purpose. I had only recently come to accept—after
much grueling therapy—that the grief, flowing from me un-
checked since the baby died, would continue until I forcibly turned
off the spigot.

"No, no, that's okay, Erik," I breathed, trying to get out of bed so
I didn't wake Justin. "Can you just hold on one second?"

It wasn't until I tried to move that I realized Ella was in our bed,
her body latched on to mine like a barnacle. I had a vague recollection of it now: her standing next to the bed—a bad dream, probably.
Ella always had the most vivid night terrors, often shrieking into
the darkness while dead asleep. I'd been the same as a child, but
I'd assumed it was a side effect of life with my mother. More likely,
the terrors were genetic, the pediatrician told me. But I could handle them better than my own mother did: earplugs, a lock on her
door, her most angry shout. So Ella regularly ended the night tucked
between us, something Justin had begun a gentle, but concerted,
campaign to stop.

"Okay, sorry, go ahead, Erik," I said once I'd managed to twist
myself out from beneath Ella and made my way into the hallway.

"I was hoping you could help with something," he began, his tone even more brusque than usual. Nancy was so warm by comparison. I often wondered how they'd ended up together. "I've had to leave town for a family emergency, and Elizabeth is on assignment in Trenton, and Richard is in the hospital, so that leaves—"

"Is he okay?" I felt a knee-jerk wave of guilt. I hadn't wished an actual illness on Richard, but in my darker moments I'd come close.

Elizabeth and Richard, both in their late twenties, covered the actual news for the *Reader*, though they weren't trying to compete with the national dailies or the twenty-four-hour online news cycle. Instead, the *Ridgedale Reader* prided itself on in-depth coverage with lots of local color. Occasionally, I got assignments from Erik— covering the new director of the university's prestigious Stanton Theatre or the celebrated local spelling bee—but largely, I pitched my own stories, such as my recent profile of Community Outreach Tutoring, a program for local high school dropouts generously run by Ella's kindergarten teacher, Rhea.

Elizabeth had been polite to me, at least, but Richard had made clear that he saw me as a washed-up mom unjustly handed a seat at the table. That his assessment was largely accurate did not make it more enjoyable.

"Is who okay?" Erik sounded confused.

"You said Richard was in the hospital?"

"Oh yeah, he's fine," he scoffed. "Gallbladder operation. You'd think he was having open-heart surgery from the way he's complained, but he should be back in forty-eight hours. In the meantime, I just got a call. Someone reported a body up by the Essex Bridge."

"A body?" It came out in a squeak I loathed myself for. "You mean a *dead* body?"

"That would be the implication." Erik sounded skeptical of me now. He probably had been from the get-go, but I wasn't helping matters. "I need someone to head out and see what's going on. And with Elizabeth at the Governor's Round Table and Richard out of commission—I'd do it myself, but like I said, I have this family emergency. I'm not sure when I'll be back."

"Is everything okay? With your family, I mean."

Why was I getting personal? Erik hated personal. When we'd arrived in town back in August, I'd been sure that Erik and Nancy would be our first friends. Justin and I hadn't socialized in a long time, and we needed to. Justin already had the professorial connection with Nancy, and I'd been instantly drawn to her warmth, even if it was partly attributable to her view of me as a prospective patient. Erik was a little prickly, yes, but he was also incredibly bright and extremely interesting.

However, Erik and Nancy had politely spurned all our advances: brunch, barbecues, concert tickets. All of which had been outside my comfort zone, anyway. Perhaps it was Erik's checkered history or Nancy's fertility problems—ones she talked about with an emotional frankness I envied—that kept them at a distance. Or maybe they just didn't like us. Regardless, it was as though Nancy and Erik were encased in very fine barbed wire, visible only upon close inspection. And my own skin was far too thin to risk pushing nearer.

"Yes, we're fine," Erik said with typical curtness. "Anyway, looks like you're on this dead-body story for now. Assuming you're up for it."

"Of course, I'll head out right now," I said, relieved that I sounded so calm and efficient.

But I was already nervous. To everyone's surprise, including my own, I'd done a pretty good job so far bringing my little corner of Ridgedale to life. Even Erik, once a prizewinning foreign affairs correspondent, had seemed impressed. But I'd never covered anything remotely like a dead body. In Ridgedale, those were a rarity. There hadn't been a single one since we'd lived there.

"Good," Erik said. There was still hesitation in his voice. "Have you, um, ever covered a crime scene?" He was being polite. He knew I hadn't.

"A crime scene? That seems to presuppose a murder. Do we know that?" I asked, pleased that I'd picked up on his jumping of the gun.

"Good point. I suppose we don't," Erik said. "Our source in the department was vague. All the more reason to tread lightly. Despite what they seem to think, the local police aren't entitled to any sort of special treatment from us, but they'll already be on the defensive with the university to contend with."

"The university?"

"The wooded area near the Essex Bridge is outside campus proper, but it's university property," Erik said. "It's my understanding that it was a Campus Safety officer who called in the body. As you can imagine, the university will be motivated to keep this quiet. Assuming any of this information is even accurate. There's always the chance that we'll find out the whole thing is a false alarm."

The door creaked as Justin came out into the hallway, squinting his hazel eyes at me. His shaggy brown hair was sticking up in all directions like a little boy's. *Who's that?* he mouthed, pointing to the phone with a furrowed brow as he crossed his arms over the Ridgedale University T-shirt hugging his triathlete's wiry frame. I held up a finger for him to wait.

"Okay, I'll be careful." Now I sounded so effortlessly confident that I was almost convincing myself. "I'll text you an update once I've gotten down to the scene. I assume you'll want something abbreviated for online, full-length for print tomorrow."

"Sounds good," Erik said, still hesitant. He was doing his best to buy into my confidence, but he wasn't all the way there. "Okay, then. Good luck. Call if you need anything."

=====

"Erik?" Justin asked sleepily after I'd hung up. He scrubbed a hand over his beard, which, despite early resistance, I now felt weirdly attached to. It covered up much of Justin's angular features, yet it managed to make him look even more handsome. "What did he want in the middle of the night?"

I looked down at my phone. It was a little past six a.m. "It's not the middle of the night anymore," I said, as though that were the relevant point. My voice sounded spacey and odd.

"Hey, what's wrong?" Justin pushed off the doorframe and put a concerned hand on my arm. Because I wasn't allowed to be spacey, not even for a second. Not anymore. That's what happens when you dove off the deep end: people got alarmed when you dared poke a toe back in the murky waters.

"Nothing's wrong. Erik just wants me to go out to the Essex Bridge for a story," I said. "They found a— Someone reported a body."

"Jesus, a body, really? That's terrible. Do they know what happened?"

"That's what I'm supposed to find out. Apparently, I'm the temporary substitute features reporter for the *Ridgedale Reader*."

"*You?* Really?" I watched Justin realize he'd stuck his foot in his mouth. "I mean, great, I guess. That seems weird to say if someone's dead."

The bedroom door opened wider behind us, and Ella padded out in her red-and-white-striped pajamas, brown curls twisting out in every direction like a bouquet of springs. She was squinting exactly the way Justin had, with her matching hazel eyes. Apart from her hair—which was a chocolate-hued replica of my own reddish curls—Ella was a miniature version of Justin. From her oversize eyes and full ruddy lips to the way she smiled with her whole face, Ella was living proof of the power of genetics.

"Sorry, sweetheart, I didn't mean to wake you." I reached down and hoisted a heavier-than-ever Ella up on my hip. "Let me put you back to bed."

"I don't want to go to bed." Ella pouted into my neck. "I want to be ready."

"Ready?" I laughed, rubbing a hand over her back as I carried her down the hall toward her room. "Ready for what, Peanut?".

"For the show, Mommy."

Shit, the show. A kindergarten reenactment of *The Very Hungry Caterpillar* in which Ella was to be that crucial "one green leaf." The show was at eleven a.m. There was no telling if I'd make it.

"You'll be too tired for the show if you stay up, Peanut. It's way too early," I said, pushing her door open with my foot. "You'll need more sleep or you'll forget all your lines."

Ella's eyes were already half closed by the time I was tucking her back under her pink-and-white-checked duvet and her massive, colorful menagerie of stuffed animals. Reading to Ella in that bed had always made me feel like the little girl I'd never been. And on a good day, it could almost convince me that I was the mother I'd always hoped I'd be.

"Mommy?" Ella said as she snuggled up against her huge red frog.

"What, sweetheart?" I smiled hard, trying not to think about how crushed she'd be when she realized that I wouldn't make her show.

"I love you, Mommy."

"I love you, too, Peanut."

Now that I was *finally* back—not perfect, not by a long shot, but much, much better—I did everything I could to avoid disappointing her. I was about to say something else, to apologize for missing her show, to make promises or offer bribes. But it was already too late to plead for forgiveness: Ella was fast asleep.

Justin was back in bed by the time I returned to our bedroom. I could tell he was not yet asleep despite his best efforts.

"Ella's show is at eleven today. It won't take long, fifteen minutes, maybe. Tape it for me, okay?" I headed for my bureau. Nice but practical, that was what I needed to wear. Or maybe professional but unafraid to tramp through the woods was closer to the mark. Yes, that was it: intrepid. "I didn't get a chance to warn her I was going to miss it. You don't think I should wake her up to tell her, do you? I hate to think of her being surprised that way."

I could feel Justin watching me move around the room getting dressed. I pulled on my nicest sweater—the pale blue cashmere that Justin's mother had bought me, that set off my eyes—then tugged on a pair of my best non-mom jeans.

"I have to teach at ten, babe," Justin said. When I turned, he was propped up on an elbow. "I can take Ella to school, but I can't do the performance. I'm sorry, Molly, but you know how the university president has been about professors missing class lately—he's on a personal crusade."

"One of us *has* to be there, Justin," I said with irrational force. I knew he couldn't miss a class unless there was a true emergency, and despite how I was feeling, a kindergarten performance didn't qualify. "I'll have to stay at the bridge until I have what I need for the story. Assuming I can figure out what that is. This may be an all-day thing."

"I agree completely," Justin said. "You need to go out there and report on this story to the best of your ability. This could be a real opportunity, Molly, and you need to seriously nail it. My guess is, Erik's not big on second chances. Today, you chasing this story is more important than even *The Very Hungry Caterpillar.*"

Because for me, this wasn't just a story, of course. Everything I did these days was another plank in the bridge to a better me. I had become what I once would have despised: the living embodiment of a self-help book.

"And what about Ella?" I felt panicky. I couldn't help it. *Letting her down again. Letting her down again.* It was playing on a loop in my head.

"Come on, she'll survive." Justin laughed, but not unkindly. "No offense, but this isn't her Broadway debut. And how many shows have you been to this year? Ten?"

I shrugged. "I haven't been counting."

Justin pushed himself up in bed and swung his feet to the floor. "You know as well as I do that we're not doing Ella any favors by giving her the impression that love means never being disappointed."

"I think she's already been disappointed plenty, don't you?"

"Come on, Molly." Justin stood and beckoned me into a hug. I shuffled over and wrapped my arms around his strong upper back. As he squeezed me tight, he smelled like the menthol he'd been massaging nightly into a torn right hamstring as he lamented the indignities of aging. "You're a good mom," he whispered into my ear. "You don't have to keep trying to prove it."

But Justin—with his doting parents and idyllic childhood—could afford to live in a world of value judgments and calculated risks. It had been part of what attracted me to him. But it wasn't easy to be someone's mother when you'd never really had one of your own. Even before I was depressed, I'd always relied on a single sure-fire parenting strategy: trying to be perfect.

"Okay, fine," I said. Because Justin was right. I knew that intellectually, even if I didn't *feel* it. "But you'll explain it to Ella when she wakes up, right? Why I can't be there? You'll prepare her that neither of us will be?"

"I'm on it, I promise," Justin said, kissing me. "Now go kick some writerly ass."

It was barely light, the world a muted gray as I drove through the center of Ridgedale. Around the manicured green downtown, the trendy boutiques and expensive coffee shops were locked and dark. The sidewalks were empty, too, apart from an old man walking a tall spotted dog and two women in fluorescent tops and coordinat-

ing sneakers, jogging and chatting. To the right was the wide stretch
of ivy-covered campus behind a tall iron fence, the sky burning orange at the horizon.

It was all so beautiful in the half-light. It was hard to believe how
much I'd resisted moving to town when Justin—whose specialty
was nineteenth- and twentieth-century American literature—first
mentioned the professorship at Ridgedale University. Twenty-five
miles north and a little west of New York City, Ridgedale was a
place we probably never would have considered living had it not
been for the university. I'd been afraid that leaving the city would
make me feel even more isolated and lonely. Not that Ridgedale
was some remote farming village. There was a Michelin-starred
farm-to-table restaurant and a dozen good ethnic ones, not to mention the world-class Stanton Theatre, an excellent university hospital, and two independent bookstores. The people in town were
an eclectic mix, too, with students and faculty from around the
world.

Things hadn't always been so sophisticated, or so I had been told.
The Bristol-Myers executive offices, relocated from downtown Manhattan to right outside Ridgedale three years earlier, had notably
increased the percentage of the town's wealthy liberals. Some long-
standing Ridgedale residents—in general, less affluent and more
conservative—were still bristling at the proliferation of soy lattes
and Pilates studios. They longed for the good old days when the
university students could shop only at the campus store or Ramsey's
pharmacy and when the dining options in Ridgedale were limited
to pizza, chicken wings, or all-night pancakes at Pat's.

It was a conflict that often played out in the spirited comments
section of the newspaper's online edition. These battles might have
little to do with the article they were appended to, but nonetheless they routinely mutated into personal attacks on reporters. At
least according to Elizabeth, who had cautioned me never to read

the comments on any of my articles posted online, even those that seemed innocuous. It was the one piece of advice she'd given me, and I had listened. I might have been ready to try my hand at this journalism thing, but I wasn't steady enough to weather being assaulted for it.

I made a left and a quick right, heading past all that majestic stone on the leafy western edge of Ridgedale University. From there, it was a quick shot to the Essex Bridge, which was far enough away that I was surprised it was university property.

When I came around the last bend, the sky had gone from gray to pale blue, the sun hidden behind the high hills in the distance. Even in the dimness, the patrol cars up ahead were impossible to miss. Three were sticking out into the road and a fourth was parked up against the trees, as if it had rolled to a stop there on its own. I had been preparing myself to arrive and find nothing, for it to have been a false alarm, as Erik had warned. But there were the police, and here was the bridge. And down below was Cedar Creek and, apparently, a body.

There wasn't a person in sight when I got out of the car, just the flashing of the blue and red lights between all those leafless trees. It was quiet, too, the only sound my feet on the pavement. It wasn't until I'd walked up to the car at the front of the line that I heard some voices floating up from the woods. I paused, noticing for the first time that my fists were clenched.

Tread lightly, like Erik had said, that was all I had to do. And yet that had seemed so much easier to execute before I'd gotten out of the car.

Hello, I'm Molly Sanderson from the Ridgedale Reader. *Would someone maybe have a minute to answer a couple questions?*

No, much too tentative. Not being obnoxiously overbearing made sense. Presenting my questions as though they were optional? Decidedly ill advised. I didn't need to be a seasoned reporter to know that.

Hello, I'm Molly Sanderson of the Ridgedale Reader. *I'd like to verify some facts.*

Much better. A little pushy but not appalling. It was also accurate: I did have the fact of a body I wanted to confirm. *Facts*, plural, was a bit of an overstatement. But I knew from being a lawyer that feigning a position of strength could be a prerequisite to success.

When I'd inched up close enough to see the water, I could tell right away what all those nervous weathermen had been worried about when they'd talked about late-winter snow followed by early-March rain. Flash flooding wasn't something you really considered in New York City. They mentioned it, but big dirty puddles were usually how it manifested. As I looked at the creek, though—more like a river as it bounced dark and fast over stones and swept up broken branches—the potential for destruction was clear. Already, a big chunk of the near bank was gone, caved in like the ragged edge of a cliff.

On the far side of the rushing water were half a dozen uniforms near the water's edge. A handful of others fanned out in the woods beyond, searching for something, though their procedure didn't seem particularly methodical. They were crisscrossing back and forth, kicking at leaves, poking with sticks, half seeming like they were merely pretending to be doing something useful.

There was something blue on the far bank, too, a plastic tarp cordoned off with yellow police tape. My breath caught—all that nervous energy sucked into the ether. Because there it was, down in those wet, rotting leaves, between all those skinny, leafless trees: the body. *Somebody's* dead body.

"If you ask me, they should flip the switch when they find the bastard," came a voice next to me. "And I don't even believe in the death penalty."

When I turned, I saw a young guy in a snug, bright yellow fleece and fitted black shorts. He had a radio strapped around his chest and a Campus Safety officer emblem on his shoulder. He smoothed a gloved hand over his fluffy blond hair and rested it on the back of his neck. He should have been good-looking. He had all the makings of it—cute face, muscular body. But he looked like an oversize child, as if he had gotten larger without actually maturing. It wasn't the least bit appealing.

"What happened?" I asked, opting not to identify myself, which probably violated all sorts of reporterly ethics. But then I wasn't technically interviewing him. He was the one who'd started talking to me.

He looked me up and down, eyes lingering on the expensive brand-new Sorel hiking boots I was wearing. A gift from Justin meant to get me excited for our new life in the "country." They presented an inaccurate, outdoorsy picture of me, but one that might be helpful in context.

Finally, the man looked back up, his eyes narrowed. "Who are you?"

"Molly Sanderson." I held out a hand. He hesitated before shaking it, squinted eyes locked on mine. "And you are?"

"Deckler," he said with annoying brevity. "You're not with the Ridgedale Police. I've never seen you."

"I'm a writer." It was more neutral than "reporter." "Someone from the police department contacted us."

Shit, why had I said that? Erik's contact was surely not public knowledge. It was probably the only thing more important than treading lightly: not exposing my boss's critical confidential relationships.

"Someone from the police department contacted *you*? To come here?"

"*Us*, I should have said. I don't personally know the details," I said, hoping he'd drop it. "You found the body?"

Deckler held up a hand and shook his head. "Don't think so," he said. "You want an official comment, you'll have to talk to Steve."

"And Steve is?"

"Down there." Deckler nodded toward the water. Standing in the middle of the creek in thigh-high rubber fishing pants was a huge man in a sharply pressed shirt. He had his muscular arms crossed, strong square jaw set as he stared upstream, glaring at the current as if willing a suspect to float down his way. "It's in his hands now."

"His hands?" I asked.

"Ridgedale Chief of Police," Deckler said, but with an edge. Like he didn't think much of him. "Campus Safety's here for support."

"They just come in and take over?" That had been his implication, and there was no telling what might pop out if I stirred the pot.

His jaw tightened. "Only on something like this." He exhaled in a puff of disgust. "Most campus crime stays on campus. There's a whole disciplinary process, with hearings, evidence, all that. We handle it all ourselves, confidentially. You know, to protect the students."

"To protect the students, right," I said, trying not to sound snide. Because all I could think was: *or protect the perpetrators.* "But not with something like this?"

He shook his head and looked back out over the water. "No, I guess not."

"And what is 'this,' exactly?"

Deckler shook his head and huffed again, seeming insulted that I'd asked the same question twice. "Like I said, you want details, you'll have to talk to Steve."

"Okay."

I smiled as I took a step toward the creek, already imagining myself at the edge, waving like an idiot to get Steve's attention. Even from this distance, he did not look like he'd appreciate that kind of thing.

"Whoa, hold up!" Deckler barked before I'd gotten very far. "You can't just go down there. I'll have to call him up."

"Oh, no, that's—"

Before I could get my objection out, Deckler had whistled loudly through his fingers, right next to my ear, as if calling a dog. When Steve swiveled his head in our direction, he did not look happy.

"Really, I can wait," I offered meekly, though it was already too late.

"Not here next to me, you can't."

Steve looked even more aggravated as he stalked to the side of the river. *Don't you think we've got more important things to do than waste our time talking to reporters?* I could already imagine him saying that as I watched him take the time to climb out of the water, put on his police hat, which he'd left on the bank for safekeeping, and start up the hill. It took an excruciatingly long time for Steve to climb in those boots that should have looked ridiculous on him but somehow didn't. It helped that he moved with a slow, strong surety. Like he already knew how things were going to turn out.

At the top of the hill, Steve nodded briskly in my direction before turning to Deckler. He was better-looking up close, the lines of his strong face offset enough to make his square features interesting instead of odd. Nothing like Justin's fine bone structure, of course. Justin was the kind of man women openly ogled. Steve was the kind they counted on for a rescue.

"There a problem, Officer Deckler?"

"This is Molly Sanderson." Deckler sounded pleased to be ratting me out. "She's a writer. Someone from your department told her to come here."

"I'm with the *Ridgedale Reader*." I reached out a hand and smiled at Steve, hoping we could breeze past the whole issue of who had called me. "I don't want to take up your time. I'd just like to confirm some facts." I motioned toward the tarp. "You found a body?"

Steve shook my hand slowly, eyes boring into me. "The *Reader*, huh? Are you new? I know that other fella. Robert, is it?"

"Richard," I said, feeling stupidly satisfied that he'd gotten Richard's name wrong.

"Someone from my department called you?"

"I don't know the details. My boss told me to come down here. Actually, I'm just pinch-hitting. My usual beat is arts." Little lost girl seemed as good a way to play it as any, especially when it didn't feel that far from the truth. And from the way Steve's face immediately softened, I could tell it had been the right call. "I really do apologize for intruding. You have a job to do, I understand that. But if you wouldn't mind helping me do mine, then I can get right out of your way."

Steve stared at me for what felt like an inordinately long time. I had to strain not to look away. "Because you're here and you're local, I'll tell you what I can," he said at last, crossing his arms. "Shoot."

It took me a beat too long to realize that he was waiting for an actual question. "Have you identified the victim?" I asked, hustling to maintain my composure as my heart beat harder.

But I could do this. I'd practiced the whole ride over. And being a reporter wasn't that different from being a lawyer. Not that, as a policy analyst, I had done a lot of interrogating. I hadn't really questioned anyone since mock trial in law school.

"No," Steve said, shaking his head as he turned to look at the water.

Okay, not as wordy a response as I had hoped. But that was okay, I had other questions. "Any leads on who it might be?"

"No."

"Male or female?"

"Female."

I felt a little thrill: an actual answer. A female victim. It wasn't much, but it was something. I was getting worried I'd have absolutely nothing when I went back to Erik. "Approximate age?"

"I wouldn't want to guess." Steve's eyes were back on mine but softer now. Sad, almost. "We'll need confirmation from the medical examiner."

I could feel Deckler staring at the two of us. Judging, was what it felt like. *You're not falling for his macho crap, are you?*

"Two more questions," Steve said. "Then you're going to need to clear the scene so we can get our job done."

"Did she die of natural causes?"

"Unclear," he said.

"Unclear?" I couldn't let him get away with that. "No indication?"

"Nothing I'm going to comment on without an official ME report."

Just then the radio on Steve's hip buzzed to life. "They're going to need a smaller bag down here," a crackly voice said. "You know, baby-size. Adult ones won't work. ME wants *us* to go pick one up."

Steve snapped the radio off his waist, his jaw tightening. His eyes were locked on the creek as he brought the radio to his mouth. "Then send someone," he answered through clenched teeth. "Now." He switched the radio off entirely before sliding it back into his belt.

He hadn't looked back at me. And I was glad, because the air felt thin as I wrapped my arms around myself. A baby? A *dead* baby? I was afraid I might be sick, right there on the chief of police's tall rubber boots.

I thought about Ella. How hot and alive she'd been, wriggling against me when they'd laid her on my chest that first time. How surprised I'd been that my body had actually worked, that she'd made it out in one pink wailing piece. I thought, too, of the next time, when my body hadn't worked the way it was supposed to. When I'd gone to the doctor for my routine thirty-six-week checkup and she couldn't find a heartbeat. And the trauma of the agonizing labor and delivery that had followed, for a baby everyone already knew was dead. Everyone, that is, except me. I alone held out hope that my second daughter would gasp and cough her way to life once she was free of me.

She did not. There had been only that awful clinical silence afterward, metal against metal, rubber gloves snatched off. And how she'd felt in my arms. Like she'd been emptied out and restuffed with wet tissue and sand.

No. I should not be letting myself do this—think of it, of her. I would not. I closed my eyes and shook my head. I was not in that delivery room. That was almost two years ago. Right now I was there on the side of that creek with a job to do. And I needed to do it. As if my life depended on it.

"It's a baby," I managed. It was a statement, not a question.

Steve was staring in silence down the hill, his face an unreadable mask. "Listen, I understand," he said with genuine, unexpected kindness. When he turned to look at me, his face was so sincere that I thought I might burst into tears and throw myself against his huge chest. "You're just trying to do your job."

"I am doing my job," I said, trying to remind myself. "That's exactly right."

But all I wanted to do was go back to my car and pretend this whole thing had never happened. That Erik had never called me, that I'd never taken the job at the *Ridgedale Reader*. That we'd never moved to town. I wanted to return home, crawl into bed, and pull the covers up over my head. I might have, too, if I hadn't known that this time there was no way I'd ever climb back out.

"I've got a deal for you," Steve said. "You run some kind of basic alert right now online—body found, details pending. Hell, I don't even care if you say it was on university property."

"Hey, I don't think that's a good—" Deckler fell silent when Steve shot him a look.

"You're here as a courtesy, remember?" Steve said.

Deckler pressed his lips together like a huge toddler trying not to scream. I was surprised he didn't stomp one big black-sneakered foot.

Steve went on, "You'll still have a big jump on the story. But I've got to ask that you keep that last detail confidential." As though the victim being an infant were a "detail" at all, like eye color or hair length. "It could compromise the investigation if you make it public now. And I'd like a chance to get our sea legs here before the word gets out. Not long, just a few hours. You do that, and I'll give you an exclusive interview."

"Okay," I heard myself say.

Steve checked his watch. "How about you meet me back at the station at ten a.m.?"

I wanted to say "No, thanks" or "Never mind." But that baby out there wasn't my baby. My baby was safe and sound at school. And she needed me to keep it the hell together. She needed me to keep on moving on. Something about turning away from this story—of all stories—felt perilous. As if, unbeknownst to me, I'd be letting go of the one thing holding my head above water.

"Sure," I somehow managed. "Sounds good. I'll see you then."

But already I regretted every word.

Sandy

Sandy wasn't asleep. But she wished she was, lying there on the stumpy living room love seat, eyes closed, especially when there was a knock on the front door. It wasn't a regular "hey, anybody there" knock, either. It was one seriously pissed-off *bang, bang, bang.*

Sandy had learned to tell the difference without asking who was doing the knocking. Motherfuckers looking for money would never leave once they knew you were home. Instead, they'd sit on your place all day and night, making a shitload of noise. That was their whole job: to make your neighbors hate you. Like that could make someone without money suddenly come up with some.

"Open the door, Jenna!" came a man's voice outside.

Sandy rolled over to face the front door. But she didn't get up. She wasn't scared he would kick it in or anything. They never went that far. He could have, though, no problem. Their front door was basically bullshit cardboard. Ridgedale Commons was the cheapest, shittiest place in all of Ridgedale, tucked way the hell in a corner of town, in the only two blocks of nasty for miles around. When they'd moved in eight months earlier, the apartment hadn't looked half bad, especially compared to some of the places they'd lived. But as it turned out, the okay part of Ridgedale Commons was paper-ass thin. The place fell to shit overnight.

"Come on, Jenna!" came the voice again, closer this time, sounding like his sweaty face—their faces were always sweaty—was pressed against the door. "I know you're in there."

Now, that right there? Total load of shit. There was no fucking way he, whoever he was, could know that. Sandy didn't even know that. She never knew for sure when she woke up whether Jenna would be home. Most of the time she was, but Sandy had learned a long time ago to sleep through whatever noises came in the middle of the night. She lifted her eyes toward Jenna's bedroom door. Shut, which must mean Jenna was home but not alone. Otherwise, she'd be sprawled out naked on top of her covers with her door open wide. She got lonely when she couldn't see Sandy out there on the couch.

If it had been up to Jenna, she probably would have left the door open even when she had company. But the men she brought home sure as hell wanted privacy. And thank God, because there were lots of things Sandy wanted to see in this world—the sun setting over the Pacific, the Grand Canyon, the Great Barrier Reef—but Jenna going at it with some liquored-up scumbag wasn't one of them. She'd already seen enough of that to last a lifetime.

Sandy pushed herself up off the couch, wincing. Her arm had scabbed over, now it looked even more disgusting and hurt like a son of a bitch whenever she flexed it hard. Her knee was a crazy shade of purple, too. Hard to forget something when your fucking body kept sending you news flashes. But she would eventually. She'd have to. And Sandy was good at forgetting things. She'd had lots of practice.

Sandy pulled her sleeve down over the huge scab, then grabbed a cigarette out of the pack Jenna had left on the coffee table. Sandy wasn't a huge smoker. Wasn't even sure she liked it. But there were times that called for a cigarette. Like now. She put a Parliament in her lips and lit it with the jewel-encrusted *I Love Tampa* lighter Jenna must have swiped off of somebody.

Sandy took a drag, glancing down at her see-through tank and low-rise sweatpants, the thorned stem of a rose tattoo wrapped around her arm, the flower tucked safely behind her shoulder blade. She twisted her long straight black hair into a knot at the back of her neck, then exhaled a long stream of smoke. There were worse things than this asshole being able to see through her shirt. A free peek might be her best chance to get rid of him. Ever since Sandy had gotten tits, they'd been the main thing she had going for her.

"Hold on!" she shouted so he wouldn't yell again. "I'm coming."

This asshole making noise was the kind of thing that Mrs. Wilson, their eighty-year-old neighbor, would get all bent out of shape about. Mrs. Wilson was a complaint-making machine—everything and everyone—like it was her fucking profession. But she hated Jenna and Sandy extra. Her face puckered every time Sandy ran into her, like she'd sucked on a rotten lemon. Mrs. Wilson wanted them out of the building, that was the bottom line. If they gave her an actual reason, she might just get her way.

Sandy took the three short steps to the door, then put her hand on the knob. She took one last drag before swinging open the door and exhaling into the air. "Jesus, take it easy," she said, calm and cool, chin tilted up as the last of the smoke escaped her lips. "I'm here, okay?"

The sun was barely up, the sky a suck-ass gray. It was earlier than Sandy had thought. Chance for this mess to pass and for the rest of the day not to be a total shit-show. Maybe. Sandy lowered her eyes to the man outside her door. He was skinny and short and weaselly, with some gross strands of hair combed over the top of his head. Disgusting. Guys like him always were.

"You're Jenna Mendelson?" He squinted skeptically at his clipboard.

"Who's asking?" Sandy took another drag and leaned against the door. No need to give up the full-frontal view of the ladies just yet. They might come in handy later.

"Well, Ms. Mendelson, you're three months behind on your rent." He ripped a notice off the top of his pad like a parking ticket and handed it to her.

Three months? That shouldn't be. They shouldn't be a single month late. But with the tutoring and everything lately, Sandy hadn't had time to get the money order herself, like she usually did. Who knew what the hell Jenna had done with the cash— drunk it, smoked it, given it away. Sandy could be so fucking stupid sometimes. Why the hell had she taken Jenna's word for it? She should have made sure the money had ended up where it was supposed to go.

Then again, considering everything, maybe it was a good time for them to be getting the hell out of Ridgedale. Not that Jenna would be easy to convince. About a year ago, she'd mentioned running into some guy from Ridgedale she "used to know" on the street in Philly. Then she'd acted like it was all a big coincidence that they'd ended up back there. But Sandy wasn't an idiot. Biggest surprise was how long it had taken once they'd moved to town for Jenna to tell Sandy the whole ugly story. Sandy would have sworn she knew every last one of Jenna's awful secrets, but there had been more. And knowing what had happened to Jenna in Ridgedale all those years ago didn't change how messed up she was. But it changed the way Sandy saw her. Made ditching Jenna—even now when she probably should have—a total fucking impossibility.

"We're not late," Sandy said. She'd been down this road before. Even if this guy was right, denial might buy them some time. "We're totally paid up."

"You got proof you've paid?" the greasy guy asked.

Sandy curled her body around the door so he could get a good view of her see-through top. She pulled her upper arms together as she leaned forward a little, pressing her tits together. "You could *say* that I had proof," she said, rolling her eyes up his pant leg. "Just for a couple days, give us some time, you know?"

The guy looked Sandy up and down, his eyes lingering on her breasts. Then he snorted and shook his head like Sandy was a disgusting piece of shit. "You've got twenty-four hours, miss," he said. "After that, the place'll get locked up. If I was you"—he looked at her boobs one last time—"I'd get packing."

Sandy took the wrinkled yellow ticket out of the asshole's hand, then watched him strut his stubby legs down the walkway and disappear. *Notice of Pending Eviction*, it read across the top. Goddamn, Jenna. Yeah, it was time to go, but did it have to be with a fucking gun to their heads? Thank God Sandy kept an emergency stash—a thousand dollars she'd saved up, in a box behind the couch. It wasn't enough for three months' rent, but it would hold them over for a few days someplace new. Somewhere far the fuck away from this place and all its bad goddamn memories.

Sandy stormed back toward Jenna's bedroom, the eviction notice crumpled in her fist. "Jenna!" she screamed at the door so loud it burned her throat. "Wake the fuck up!"

When there was no answer, Sandy kicked the door. It flew open, Sandy bracing herself for the sight of some naked, hairy ass diving for cover. But there was nothing. And no one. Jenna wasn't there. And from the looks of it, she hadn't been all night.

"Fuck," Sandy said quietly, her anger tightening into a ball at the bottom of her stomach. Where the hell was Jenna? Sandy went over to check her phone for a text, something like *Going to crash here. See you in the morning.* But there was nothing. Not a goddamn thing.

So much for that civics and econ homework Sandy was supposed to finish for Rhea and the algebra quiz she had to study for. Not that she should have been surprised. Going for her GED had been a stupid goddamn long shot. It was the kind of thing that other people did. But then Sandy had let herself get sucked in by Rhea. Found herself thinking: *Why* not *me?* Jenna, that's why fucking not. What a joke.

Where the hell are you? Sandy texted Jenna.

"Listen, Sandy, no one's perfect," Rhea had said at the end of that first meeting they'd had back in October, almost six months earlier. The sweet way she'd been smiling at Sandy had made her throat tighten up. "And anyone who pretends they're perfect is a liar."

It had taken a lot for Sandy to drag her ass into Ridgedale High School to the Community Outreach Tutoring Office. She hadn't been in a school since the spring before, when she'd finished up her sophomore year at that hellhole in northeast Philly. She hadn't even considered starting at Ridgedale High School when they'd moved there in September. Food, rent, coffee, all of it was a lot more expensive in Ridgedale. Sandy would have to work more to carry her own weight.

But then goddamn Rhea had come into Winchester's Pub for lunch when Sandy was working. And she had that nice smile and those kind eyes, and she'd asked Sandy all these questions. Caught off guard, Sandy hadn't had her usual lies at the ready. And so, by the time Rhea was paying the bill, she'd talked Sandy into coming down to Ridgedale High School to check out her Outreach Tutoring. "You might even be able to get your GED before you would have graduated," she said.

Sandy didn't tell Jenna about the tutoring. She wouldn't have tried to talk Sandy out of it; even Jenna would have known that would be fucked up. She probably would have cheered Sandy on. Told her to go for it, rah, rah, rah.

But then Jenna would have come up with all sorts of reasons for Sandy *not* to do the work: "Come to the movies with me, Sandy"; "Snuggle on the couch with me, Sandy"; "Share a beer with me." Jenna couldn't help herself. She just couldn't bear the thought of being left behind.

It hardly seemed to matter that Sandy hadn't told Jenna. When she was sure Rhea had been talking shit anyway. That she wouldn't remember Sandy when she finally showed up.

But then she totally did.

"I'm so glad you made it!" Rhea said, jumping out of her chair and grabbing Sandy into a hug.

By the second time they met, Rhea had a plan set up for Sandy. "I took a look at your old transcripts. With the courses you've taken and your excellent grades, I bet, with a little review, you could get your GED by the end of this year. That would be like graduating a whole year ahead of schedule." Rhea blinked her big blue eyes at Sandy. She was so pretty and healthy-looking. It made Sandy want to take a shower. "All you need is someone to supervise your progress and practice tests, which I'm obviously happy to do. And I'll arrange for a student tutor for the math and science."

"A student tutor?" Sandy felt sick. She couldn't deal with some rich asshole from Ridgedale looking down on her.

"Come on." Rhea laughed. "It won't be that bad. I get it, but it's not like you have to be best friends. You just have to let someone help you. Can you do that?"

"I'll try," Sandy said. She sounded like an ungrateful asshole, but she didn't want to lie. Especially to someone who was being so nice to her. "When do we start?"

"Right now!" Rhea said. "I'm going to go grab the books you'll need and the syllabus. Once we've got you going on all of that, we can talk about the GED honors program and college. I think you're the perfect candidate."

Sandy had played out this moment in her head a million times, imagining somebody like Rhea swooping in and rescuing her from the shit-show that was her life. But she hadn't counted on just how good it would feel. *Don't believe her. Don't believe her. Don't believe her.* But it was too late.

"College?" Sandy asked, feeling this dumb mix of nerves and delight.

Rhea winked and grinned as she stood. "Yes, college. They've revamped the GED. These days it can be about getting somewhere, not just making up for what you lost."

Rhea had barely stepped out the door when the first text from Jenna came through: *Where are you? Come home now! I have SUCH a good story to tell you. U won't fucking believe it.*

Be home in ½ hour, Sandy texted back.

Hurry. And bring Cheetos! xoxoxoxo

Fucking Jenna. Worst part was that Sandy felt guilty not being there. And that was sick. Sandy knew that. But its being sick didn't make it any less true.

When Rhea returned to the office, she dumped a stack of books and photocopies on the table in front of Sandy. "Okay, I've got a *great* tutor for you." Rhea handed Sandy a printout. *Hannah Carlson*, it said beneath an address, phone number, and email. "Hannah is such a sweetheart. Quirky, too, in a way not so many girls around here are. She's this amazing pianist, and she's on the math team. She's also a terrific writer. She even took English classes over at the university last spring as a junior."

Which meant she was a senior now. At least she was a year older than Sandy. Being tutored by someone younger would have been way too much.

"Sounds awesome," Sandy said flatly.

"Oh, I'm sorry. That was stupid," Rhea said. "Who would want Little Ms. Perfect teaching them anything?" She stuck out her tongue and pretended to gag. Then she leaned forward conspiratorially. "I'll let you in on a secret. Hannah's mom is a total b-i-t-c-h. With a capital B. So, you know, Hannah's got her own cross to bear."

"Cool." Sandy nodded, looking down at the girl's name. But she knew what this Hannah's mother being a "bitch" meant on the scale of actual problems: fucking nothing.

"Listen, I know this isn't easy. But don't give up before we've even gotten started," Rhea said, reading Sandy's mind. Her voice was different now, more serious. She put her hands on the pile of coursework. "These are your assignments. When we meet next week, I expect all of them to be finished. And you can do it. I have absolutely no doubt."

Sandy tried and failed to lift the heavy stack with a few fingers. "That makes one of us."

Rhea put her hand over Sandy's, squeezing it until she looked up. Rhea's eyes were glassy, her smile sort of sad but also weirdly hopeful. "I think you and I both know *this* is it, Sandy. *This* is your chance." Rhea made two fists in the air. "You're going to have to grab onto it with both hands."

When they were done, Sandy rushed out the side door of the school, praying she'd make it away before she started to cry. At least it was the middle of the school day, the parking lot dead quiet, the lawns all empty. Even the fancy track that looped around the perfectly green and neatly trimmed football field didn't have a soul on it. The only sound was Sandy's breathing when her phone chirped with another text: *WHERE R THE CHEETOS!!! I'm DIIIIEEEING HERE. Come home. Judge Judy is ripping into this chick with a hair salon. You should see her roots!*

Sandy slid her phone into her back pocket, then dropped herself against the cool brick of the school building so hard it scratched her back. "Fuck, ouch," she said out loud. Then she rested her head against her hands, rocking it back and forth. Why did her life feel the most fucked whenever she was trying to make it better?

"Want one?" someone asked.

When Sandy looked up, there was a kid about her age with messy blond hair, some freckles across his nose, and perfect teeth. He wasn't Sandy's type—too pretty. But he was cute, there was no getting around it. He knew it, too, which, annoyingly, made him cuter.

He was holding a cigarette out toward Sandy, a lit one in his other hand. "You look like you could use one."

Sandy looked around before she reached over and took it. What could they do, kick her out? Technically, she wasn't even *in* school. She leaned forward and lit it on the Zippo he'd flipped open, the kerosene bringing back unwanted memories of one of Jenna's old boyfriends. Sandy took a deep drag and felt her body steady on the exhale.

"I'm Aidan," the kid had said. She could feel him staring at the side of her face. Boys like him were always drawn to her: the slutty bad-news girl. The one who pissed off their moms. Sometimes that was fine. And sometimes it was annoying as shit. "I'm new here."

Sandy took another drag. She should go, get away from this kid. Get home to Jenna. Sandy knew that. So why hadn't she moved off the wall? "Cool," she said.

The kid had smiled, a troublemaker's gleam in his eye as he stepped closer to her. Close enough for Sandy to smell his shampoo or his cologne—something spicy and clean. Expensive. "You going to tell me your name?" he'd asked.

"Not yet," Sandy had said, pushing herself up. Because she needed to get home before Jenna's texts took their usual dark turn. And Sandy had known better than to want this kid, but that didn't mean she couldn't leave him wanting more. "But thanks for the cigarette."

Now Sandy looked around Jenna's empty bedroom, then went back out to the living room. She thought about texting Jenna a WTF about the rent. But Jenna would never come home if she thought she was in trouble. *Helloo???* Sandy texted her instead. A second later, the phone vibrated in her hand. "About fucking time," she muttered.

But the text wasn't from Jenna. It was from Hannah. For the three hundredth fucking time. Sandy wondered if Hannah ever pulled this stalker shit with guys, because it must get her ass blocked immediately. Sandy would have blocked Hannah, too, if she could have. It was too much of a risk, though. Who would Hannah text instead? And what would she tell them when she did?

Are you okay? Hannah's text read, like pretty much all of the other ones in the past week and a half.

Yeah. I'm good. You don't have to keep asking.

I'm just worried about you.

Nothing Sandy wrote back would make a difference. They'd been up and down this road a bunch of times. No matter what Sandy said, Hannah would send another text in a couple hours, asking the exact same thing. And it would go on and on and on until—what? Because there had to be an end to a thing like this. But as much as Sandy wanted Hannah's texts to stop, she was afraid of what it would mean once they did.

???? Sandy wrote to Jenna again, ignoring Hannah. If Jenna was passed out somewhere, sleeping it off, there was a chance that the noise from another text might wake her. *????????? Hello???*

Sandy looked around the filthy apartment. Their best option would be to walk out the door. Leave all their shit behind like the garbage it was. Except if they didn't have the money for rent, they sure as hell wouldn't have the money for new just-as-shitty shit. Wherever they went, they'd have to find new jobs, and that could take time.

That would be Jenna's best argument for staying in Ridgedale— and she would try to keep them there, for sure—that they both already had decent jobs. That wouldn't be why she really wanted to stay, but it was a much better story than the truth.

Where are you? Sandy typed to Jenna one last time.

She waited a minute more. Still nothing. Then she tried to call. An actual phone call was the official "911 I need you to save my ass now." Jenna's phone rang four times before going to voicemail. It was on, at least. That was something. And there was Jenna's smoky drawl on the greeting, the one she meant to be sexy. And it was. "I'm not here. You know what to do. Bye-bye."

"Where the hell are you? I've sent a million texts," Sandy said, trying to sound more worried than pissed off. "I need to talk to you. It's kind of— No, it *is*. It's an emergency. Call me back as soon as you can. Okay, Mom?"

The word "mom" felt swollen in Sandy's mouth and made of something hard. Her lips had to stretch to fit around it. It had been so long since she'd called Jenna that, longer still since it had meant anything. It was a shot in the dark, a grab at something totally out of reach. But there had to be a chance it would land. That it would settle inside Jenna and wake up some long-dead thing. That it would make her pick up the goddamn phone.

But what if it didn't? Sandy shook her head, tried to push away the thought. In her world, what-ifs were never fucking helpful. She had to focus. She had to get her stash of money and get the hell out of there and try to find Jenna. That was the only option. Because as much as she might like to pretend she'd leave town without her, Sandy couldn't. She'd never leave Jenna behind.

Sandy knelt on the couch and reached around the back, sliding her hand into the gap where she kept the thin box. She stretched farther when she didn't feel it. Her heart sped up as she kept rooting around. It had been a few days since she'd checked, but it had to be back there. Where else would it be?

Finally, Sandy's nails scratched against the cardboard. The box had gotten wedged farther away, that was all. But as soon as she yanked it out and reached in she could tell something was wrong. The envelope inside was too thin. Sandy's hands were trembling as she pulled out a short stack of one-dollar bills. She fanned them out: twenty-six in all.

Nine hundred and seventy-four dollars less than there was supposed to be.

MOLLY

Dr. Zomer. Sounds like a cross between a serial killer and an antidepressant. I'm glad she waited to bring up journaling, because I was barely on board with therapy to begin with. But that's not because of her. I like Dr. Zomer, with her huge brown eyes and warm, wrinkly face. She's nice and I can tell she wants to help.

But wait. I'm not supposed to be writing about Dr. Zomer in here. I'm supposed to be writing about me.

I think it makes Justin happy that I'm seeing Dr. Zomer. Just this morning he said that I seem more like myself. But sometimes I wonder if that person exists anymore.

Look, now I'm writing about Justin. Me. Me. Me.

Oh yeah, I didn't cry today! I never let myself cry in front of Ella—wait, that's such a lie. Why am I bothering to lie HERE? No one's going to read this.

For WEEKS after I lost the baby, I cried my face off right in front of Ella. Cried so much, I'm surprised she didn't wash away in a river of my selfish tears. But after Justin went back to work, I did keep my crying contained to when Ella was in day care, from nine to five. And then today, not a single tear.

Until right now. Because now I'm getting teary because I feel guilty that I didn't cry. God, sometimes I really do hate myself.

Well, look at that, Dr. Zomer. A whole page filled that you'll never read—no one will, so I don't understand the point. But it's filled all the same. Because that's what you asked me to do. And I'm trying to do the right thing here. I'm trying as hard as I can.

Molly

After fifteen minutes of erratic driving and careful square breathing, I reached the outskirts of Ridgedale and the lovely stretch of shops that included the *Ridgedale Reader* offices. The parking lot was nearly empty as I pulled in, the stores—the Knit Wit knitting shop, Ridgedale Antiques, and the Peter Naftali Gallery—starting to open for the day. I was parking when my phone buzzed with a text.

Tell me you have purple sweatpants? It was Stella. Her son Will was a plum in *The Very Hungry Caterpillar.*

Shit. Ella's leaf-green clothes. I'd even bought special lime-colored leggings for the occasion. I tapped Stella's message closed and wrote one to Justin. *Bring green clothes. On counter!! xoxo*

My phone vibrated right back in my hand, startling me. *On it!*

There was a picture, too. A selfie of Justin and Ella, already in her green outfit, flashing a thumbs-up and a huge beaming grin. I shouldn't have underestimated Justin. Sometimes I forgot how much he'd taken care of Ella by himself in the past two years.

After I lost the baby, Justin had taken a month's leave from his adjunct position at Columbia. His mother also came for the first couple of weeks to help. And thank God, because in those early days, Justin had to focus on holding me as I cried and cried. Once Justin's mother was gone and I was a bit better, he took over Ella's care. Despite never having been much of a hands-on dad before,

with ease and not a single complaint, Justin brushed Ella's hair and
cuddled with her and gave her long, silly baths. He paid all the bills,
dealt with our car being towed, did endless laundry, and cooked all
our meals as though the key to our survival lay in his successful
completion of household chores. In between, he kept on holding me
as much as he could. He didn't go back to work until he was sure
I'd be okay getting myself and Ella through the day. I did get there
by week six, but I couldn't possibly have returned to work at the
National Advocates for Pregnant Women. No matter how much I
had loved that job, I could never again have spent all day talking
about pregnancy.

I closed Justin's message and returned to Stella's. *No purple sweats.
Sorry!* I wrote back.

Shit. I totally forgot.

Me too.

It was typical of Stella to forget the sweatpants—she always forgot things—and to think that someone else might have some lying
around. Luckily, she didn't wear her maternal shortcomings like a
badge of honor. Growing up as I had, I was always irked by that.
But Stella wasn't embarrassed by her imperfections either. A gorgeous former stockbroker five years my senior but who looked much
younger, Stella hadn't returned to work after the Lehman crash had
left her unemployed. Instead, she'd gotten pregnant with her son
Will, now five. Her older son, Aidan, was a junior in high school.

Shortly before Will was born, Stella's husband, Kevin, had
dropped thirty pounds, rented a glossy pied-à-terre in Chelsea, and
found a twenty-seven-year-old yoga instructor for a girlfriend. Stella
and Kevin had divorced not long after, when Will was six months
old. According to Stella, Kevin had wanted out so badly that he'd
acceded to even her most absurd financial demands. He was on his
third girlfriend—Zumba this time—and visiting the boys only on
occasional weekends.

Maybe that was why Aidan was struggling so much. Recently kicked out of St. Paul's, the area's most prestigious private school, he'd quickly found trouble at Ridgedale High School. He'd been suspended twice already. Still, I liked Aidan, probably because he shared Stella's outsize spirit and take-no-bullshit bluntness.

Fuck. Will is going to kill me.

My phone rang then, startling me. *Erik Schinazy.*

"I was about to call you," I lied. It was amazing how calm and authoritative I sounded, especially considering how I'd rushed away from the creek in a panic. "I'm just stepping into the office now."

"Didn't mean to jump on you, but I'll be unreachable for a bit," Erik said in a way that begged for me to ask why. "Wanted to touch base before I left."

I unlocked the door to the office, balancing the phone to my ear. It was dark inside except for Erik's office light, left on in the back as though he'd dashed out in the middle of the night. Everyone besides Erik sat in the central open-plan space, where four desks were arranged in a square—one for each of the three of us on staff and an extra for a fourth writer, gone since the advent of the Internet. I headed for my pristine desk, which looked pathetically unbroken in, compared to Elizabeth and Richard's stacks of research files, tacked-up notes, and piles of printouts.

"Well, there is a body," I began as I dropped my things on my desk. I sucked in some air. Time to say it out loud without my voice catching. "And it's a baby."

"Shit," Erik said quietly. He sounded genuinely troubled. "My source didn't say anything about a— That would have been— Obviously, I would have—"

"I don't have any more details yet, apart from the baby being female," I said, trying to get past Erik's fumbling to be kind without admitting what he knew about me and my lost baby. "But I agreed to wait a few hours before running that it's a baby. Technically, I overheard that part."

"Overheard?" He did not sound pleased. "What does that mean?"

And here I'd been thinking the "overheard" part would make me seem resourceful. But it did sound vaguely sleazy now that I'd said it out loud.

"I happened to be standing with Steve Carlson, the chief of police, when an officer on his radio mentioned a baby," I went on. Because it hadn't been inappropriate, it was fortuitous. "He offered me an exclusive interview in exchange for holding off on disclosing that detail. I'm supposed to meet with him again at ten a.m. In the meantime, Steve's fine with us running a basic story about the body."

"Oh, *Steve's* fine with it, is he?" Erik asked sharply. "You do realize we don't work for Ridgedale's chief of police. *We* decide what we report on, not Steve."

"Right." My cheeks felt hot. I was glad Erik was on the phone so he couldn't see how embarrassed I was. "I suppose I was trying, as you suggested, not to alienate him."

Erik wasn't wrong. I hadn't given much thought to my obligations as a journalist. Largely because I hadn't given much thought to *myself* as a journalist.

"Just remember with something like this, everyone you talk to is going to have an angle—police, parents, university officials. Anything they tell you willingly is going to be in support of a self-serving narrative. That's not because they're bad people. It's human nature. And it's your job as a journalist to weave these biased threads into some semblance of the truth."

It sounded so noble. The truth: I wanted to be a part of that. A part of finding out what had happened to the baby and making sense of it for people.

"You're right," I said. "It won't happen again."

"Listen, it isn't fair, dumping you into this with hardly any guidance. Do you want me to put a call in to Richard? See if he can

ance. Do you want me to put a call in to Richard? See if he can handle some of this from home?"

I felt a wave of panic. I did not want the story being taken away from me. That couldn't happen. "No," I said, and perhaps too vehemently. "I can absolutely handle it. I want to."

"Good, then." Luckily, Erik sounded impressed instead of troubled. "And, Molly, I know better than anyone what it's like to try to reinvent yourself. Hang in there. You know, one day at a time."

"Thank you. That's good advice." It was, and so why did it make me feel so ashamed?

"We'll go with your basic announcement online for now and include an update after your exclusive. That'll be fine," he said, and more gentle than I'd ever heard him sound. "As soon as you have that first piece, email it to me. I'll post it right away."

"That sounds great," I said. Then I waited for him to close off the conversation. But there was only a long silence, followed by some odd rustling. I wondered whether he had dropped the phone or forgotten I was still there. "Hello?" I asked.

"Yep, I'm here," he said abruptly, as if trying to hide whatever he was doing on the other end. Was someone there with him? I hoped not a woman or a purveyor of liquor. What kind of emergency was this? "I'll brainstorm some questions for Steve and send them your way. Use them or not, it's your story. But I've found with high-stakes interviews, it helps to have twice as many questions as you'll need."

"Yes, any suggestions would be great."

"No problem," Erik said. "Believe it or not, I do remember what it was like starting out in this game. It's a steep learning curve, but it's mercifully short."

After I'd written a quick piece for online posting—two sentences about the body; there was virtually nothing to say—I had enough time before my meeting with Steve to do a little online research into crime rates in Ridgedale, background for the longer print article I was formulating in my head.

I was surprised by the amount of minor crime in Ridgedale—simple assaults, automobile thefts, robberies—but there had been only two murders in the past twenty years. Esther Gleason had shot her elderly husband in apparent self-defense, and an ex-convict from Staten Island had been killed in an off-campus student apartment, a Ritalin deal gone wrong. It was in reading about the second case that I came across the mention of another death, this one accidental, near the Essex Bridge.

Simon Barton was a high school student who'd died when he tripped and fell during a high school graduation party just south of the Essex Bridge. Now there were four dead bodies in twenty years, and half of them had been found in the same spot? *Simon Barton*, I wrote at the top of my pad.

My phone buzzed with a text. *Package delivered*, Justin had written. *She's more than fine, I promise. Now get back to work.*

I was looking at my phone when the door to the office swung open. When I looked up, Stella was standing in the doorway in a short white tennis skirt and matching fitted sweatshirt. Her dark brown hair was in a high ponytail, and her regal face—strong jaw, long elegant nose—looked beautiful, as usual.

Stella strode into the office, pausing to eye the darkness. She stepped back toward the panel of switches for the overhead lights, flicking them on all at once with a hard swipe of her palm. "Why the hell are you sitting here in the dark?"

Stella was more flamboyant than my friends typically were, but she was exactly what I needed these days: someone to forcibly drag me out when I said I'd rather stay home, someone to make me talk when I was convinced I couldn't breathe a word. We'd known each other since Justin and I had moved to Ridgedale in August, not even a year. But it felt like we'd been friends much longer.

"Oh, I guess I forgot to turn on the lights. What are you doing here, Stella?"

"I saw Justin at drop-off. He seemed stressed."

I shrugged. "He can't miss class."

"He said that you got called in on some big story. Then I was driving by—because now I have to go to Target to buy a stupid purple sweatsuit—and I saw your car. Thought I'd try to get you to come to *The Very Hungry Caterpillar* with me. You know how I hate to face the mommy brigade alone." She looked over at the papers covering my desk. "Not happening, is it?"

"Can't, sorry," I said. "I have an interview in half an hour."

"All right, I won't stay and distract you." But instead of heading for the door, she started fishing through the pencils in the cup on my desk, sorting out the dull ones, discarding one that was missing an eraser. "Provided you tell me what the big story is."

I raised an eyebrow at her.

"You know, people used to trust me to keep secrets worth millions." She shrugged nonchalantly. "Discretion is one of my strengths."

Though Stella loved to gossip, so far, she had seemed to know better when anything important was involved. I'd trusted her enough to tell her about the baby, my depression, even what had sent me to Dr. Zomer. She'd handled all those confidences respectfully, with a comforting nonchalance: *Hey, we're all crazy, honey.*

"They found a body up by the Essex Bridge, a baby," I said. "But, Stella, you really can't tell anyone about it until my story is posted. The police will kill me."

"Oh my God." Stella's eyes got instantly huge. She teared up as she clasped a hand over her open mouth. "That's horrible."

"I know," I said, feeling a little thrown by the intensity of her response. But had I really expected her to make it *less* bad by laughing it off? A dead baby was a dead baby, even when you'd never had one of your own. "It's completely awful."

She closed her eyes and reached forward, grasping my hand. "Are you okay? Of all the stories for you to get."

"I've got to be honest, it's not great," I said. I regretted telling her. Already, I felt worse. "I'm hoping it might be therapeutic."

Stella raised an eyebrow. "Are you sure about that?"

"No, but every time I think about passing it off, I feel worse. *Much* worse."

Stella frowned, considering. "Then you should stay on it." She turned toward Elizabeth's desk and began plucking the dull pencils out of her cup, too, leaning over to use the electric sharpener. I watched her jam in each pencil until it was ground to a bright point. I was pretty sure she'd start sharpening her fingers if I didn't get her to stop. I reached forward and tugged the remaining pencils from her grasp. "Stella, what's going on?"

"Shit, is it that obvious?" she said, her voice cracking. Then she dropped her face into her hands and began to sob.

"God, Stella." She was not a woman who cried. "What's wrong?"

"Jesus, I'm sorry. I don't even know where that came from," she said with a teary, manic laugh. She sniffled and sat upright, wiping her eyes. "Aidan got into some fight yesterday at school. An actual fight, with his fists." Aidan was big on threats; he wasn't usually big on making good on them. "And then I had this absurd run-in with Cole's mother, Barbara, at drop-off this morning."

Barbara was someone I avoided. She was the supermom to end all supermoms, and after a year and a half of profound maternal subsufficiency, I was fighting hard just to be a decent one.

"About what?"

"I told her Will didn't like going to other people's houses. And Barbara said in that judgmental-bitch way of hers: 'Well, that's just not normal.' Like she's some almighty arbiter of psychological stability."

"That is kind of mean," I offered tentatively. Because it wasn't the nicest thing for Barbara to say, to be sure, but Stella was also overreacting.

Stella wiped her nose with the back of her hand. "Christ, what does a girl have to do to get a damn tissue around here?"

"Oh, sorry." I grabbed a box off Elizabeth's desk.

Stella snatched a handful of tissues, wiped her face, then pressed her lips together. "This is what teenagers do—turn you into a sobbing lunatic. But what the hell *does* Barbara know about normal?"

"Nothing," I said, and that much was true. "People are only wound that tight when they're about to fly into a million pieces."

"See, I knew you would make me feel better," Stella said with a smile. She wiped at her eyes as she stood, then pulled me into a hug. "Now I'll leave you alone so you can go win that Pulitzer."

I parked just off the lower end of the green near the old stone city hall. To the right, in a smaller but equally quaint colonial building, was the police station. I stood on the edge of the square, staring at it, unable to get myself to move. It had been a long time since I'd been inside a police station.

But the Butler, Pennsylvania, police department had once been like a second home. It was the place where I'd had my first soda, an orange Crush, sitting barefoot in my faded unicorn nightgown at the desk of a friendly, chubby police officer named Max while two other officers interviewed my mom.

They'd found us walking along Route 68 in the middle of the night, trying to find my father. He was off—as he was so often in the months before he filed for divorce when I was ten—with Geraldine, his then girlfriend, now wife of twenty-five years. Her house was two miles away, and my father had taken our only car.

"You can't stop us from taking a walk," my mom shouted to the officers before they were out of their car. Her voice already had that familiar tremble. Soon it would rise and explode into a million furious pieces. "There's nothing criminal about a walk." She might have convinced them had it not been for my nightgown and bare feet.

"She do this a lot, your mom?" Officer Max asked me that night.

My mother did most of the things a mom was supposed to do. She went to her job every day as an administrator at the Butler Department of Buildings, and she collected her decent paycheck. She paid the mortgage and kept our house in good living order. She cooked my dinner and sent me to school with money for lunch. But she was enraged by all of it.

After my father divorced her, the true work of my mother's life became hating him. Making sure he knew it took up most of her time (and therefore mine) right up until she died of a heart attack while pulling weeds in our backyard the summer before my sophomore year in college. By then my dad had three-year-old twins with Geraldine, but he dutifully took up the mantle of sole surviving parent, at least financially. He also called on birthdays and invited me for holidays with an "I'm sure you already have plans" casualness. I hardly ever did, but I never went. Instead, I lived on as the orphan I had always really been. Right up until I met Justin.

"Does my mom do what?" I'd asked Officer Max that night, because there had seemed infinite possibilities.

"Take you out in the middle of the night looking for your dad?"

"No," I'd said, staring down at my hands. "It was a one-time thing."

That was a lie. Not my first about my mother and not my last. Because I was only nine, and already I knew there was one worse thing than having my mother. And that was having no mother at all.

When I stepped inside the Ridgedale Police Station, the floor was sloped and creaky, the carpet worn. The air had a decidedly musty but not unclean tinge. I would have thought I'd stepped inside the Ridgedale Historical Society were it not for the portraits of uniformed officers on the wall. Seated behind a small polished wood desk was a woman with spiky gray hair, a forearm full of gold bangles, and a beaming smile.

"Can I help you?" she asked brightly, her bracelets jangling as she straightened the wooden nameplate on the counter in front of her: *Yvette Scarpetta, Civilian Police Dispatcher.*

"I have an appointment with the chief of police?" My voice rose at the end as if it were a question. Dammit. Enough with the nerves. "My name is Molly Sanderson. I'm a reporter with the *Ridgedale Reader.*"

Better. Not perfect, but I could live with it. I'd have to.

"Have a seat." Yvette pointed to a row of antique-looking wooden chairs along the wall, then picked up the phone. "I'll let Steve know you're here."

Question #5: Do you have enough resources to handle the scope of this investigation? Or will you have to rely on neighboring jurisdictions? That question was Erik's, and it was a good one. Most of his questions never would have occurred to me, and I was grateful to have them.

"Steve's right through that door straight to the back," Yvette said after a brief phone exchange. "You can head on through."

When I knocked on Steve's office door, he was standing, talking on the phone. I hesitated, but he waved me in, pointing to the chairs in front of his desk. He was older than I'd realized out at the creek. At least early forties, with a face that looked like he'd been standing out in the elements most of that time.

Steve nodded again after I sat, and his blue eyes locked briefly on mine before he turned to face the windows. Outside was a full view of the green, the gray sky breaking blue. With his back to me, Steve tucked his one free hand under his other arm, which made his strong shoulders look even broader.

That guy could kick my ass, I imagined Justin saying of Steve. He liked to freely admit this whenever we were in the company of much larger men, which was fairly often. Naturally, the admission had always served to make Justin seem utterly invincible.

It was cold in Steve's office, and I slipped my hands into the pockets of my coat as I waited. I felt the little slip of paper then. One of Justin's notes. I knew without even having to look. He'd started leaving them for me again in the past few weeks. It had been something he'd done all the time when we started dating, back when I was finishing up law school and he was in the middle of his Ph.D. Quotes from poems, usually about love, tucked romantically somewhere for me to stumble upon. If I hadn't already been in love with Justin when he started giving them to me, they would have surely done the trick.

I couldn't remember exactly when he had stopped, but it had been gradual and natural, relegated—like so much spontaneous sex—to birthdays and anniversaries and then not at all. Now that Justin had started up again with the notes, finding them gave me a little thrill, as if I were cheating on my damaged self with the new, steadily improving me. And the notes felt like Justin's way of welcoming me home. I smiled, rolling the scrap of paper between my fingers in my pocket.

"Yes, well, unfortunately, that's it for the moment," Steve said into the phone. "I'll call you back if there's anything new. Yep." Silence. "Yes, sir."

Steve exhaled loudly as he hung up, then rubbed an exasperated hand over his face as he sat down. I wanted to ask who it had been on the phone, the mayor, the governor? But asking a question like that—one I'd never get the answer to—would only undermine my credibility.

"Thanks so much for taking the time to meet with me," I said as if the interview weren't a little bit of extortion.

"If anyone should have the story first, it's our local paper," Steve said. "I know I can trust the *Reader* to present what's happened in a fair and reasonable manner."

A throwaway comment, calculated to make me feel obligated not to disappoint him. An agenda. Erik was right. Steve was smoother and more practiced than I'd anticipated, but then Ridgedale was hardly a one-horse town.

"I'll do my best," I said, holding Steve's stare. "So the body is a baby?"

"Yes, a female infant," Steve said with clipped efficiency.

"How old was she?"

"Medical examiner will need to confirm her age," he said, then seemed to realize he would have to give me something in return for my silence. "I would estimate newborn."

"Do you have any idea who she is?"

"Not at the moment," he said. "We're pursuing all leads. But if anyone has any information about the identity of the baby or the baby's parents, I'd ask that they contact the Ridgedale Police Department. I'll get you a number to include."

"Was the baby stillborn?"

I'd been preparing over the past hour for that particular question. For saying that one word out loud. *Stillborn*. I'd been afraid I wouldn't get it out. After my petite pregnant-herself doctor had held my hand and told me that my baby's heart was no longer beating, I'd convinced myself that all I had to do was never say that word, and I could alter the history that had already been written.

"That's the obvious question," he said. "And the honest answer is we don't know yet. Given the condition of the body, an official determination on cause of death isn't going to be easy."

"What was the condition of the body?"

"You saw for yourself where she was found. And with the weather we've been having? Freezing, then warm. Something like four inches of rain in two days, and that's just this week. I'll leave it to you to imagine what that might do to complicate things."

"How long was she out there?"

There was a knock at the door, and a slight red-haired officer with a face full of freckles leaned in.

"We're in Interview One, Chief," the officer said in a voice that was much deeper than his small body would have suggested.

"Great, thanks, Chris," Steve said. "I'll be there in a minute." When the officer was gone, Steve turned back to me. "To answer your question, we don't know how long she was out there. That'll be for the medical examiner to determine, too."

"Do you think the baby is connected to the university?" I asked. "Given where she was left?"

Steve frowned and shook his head. "There's no reason to suspect a connection to any of the students at the university."

"Would the university tell you if there were?" I asked. "My understanding is that Campus Safety handles a lot of criminal matters on their own."

"Not without keeping us informed, they don't." Steve leaned back in his chair and crossed his arms. His mouth turned down. The university question had been one step too far, though his defensive posture had done nothing to assuage my curiosity. "Now, I'm afraid we'll have to leave it at that for the moment. I have another meeting to get to. I'll give you an hour to get a story online before we issue an official statement. That sound fair?"

I thought about my long list of other questions, all the ones I hadn't asked, including my zingers about resources and Steve's experience with this kind of complex investigation. But they all seemed premature or unwisely hostile now. "Can I ask one last question?"

"Can't promise I'll answer it," Steve said tiredly. "But you can ask."

"I came across an incident in my research, a death in town years ago. It happened in virtually the same spot where the baby was found." I looked down at my notes. "A high school student named Simon Barton?"

Steve nodded grimly. "I wouldn't read anything into the location. That area near the Essex Bridge is secluded. Even back then, there weren't many places in Ridgedale that out of sight. Kids have always partied back there."

"Is that who you think left the baby? Some partying kids?"

He shook his head, frowning down at his desk. I waited for him to seem annoyed, but he looked genuinely sad. "No, ma'am. I don't think any party anywhere ends that way. At least I sure as hell hope not." He narrowed his eyes at me, as if appraising the kind of person who would suggest such a thing. "You're new to town?"

I was caught off guard by his shift in focus. My throat felt suddenly dry. "Yes, my husband just got a position with the university. He's an English professor. We moved here with our daughter at the end of August."

"A daughter, that's great." Steve's face brightened. "How old?"

"Five." I picked up my bag from the floor as my mind tumbled forward. Was there any reason I didn't want Steve to know these personal details? I didn't think so, not that I had a choice anyway. "She's in kindergarten."

"At Ridgedale Elementary?" He smiled wider. "My son, Cole, is in kindergarten there, too."

Cole. Which meant Barbara was his wife. I felt nervous remembering how I'd listened to Stella bad-mouth her. I'd even agreed with her.

"Actually, I think Cole's in class with Ella," I said, hoping I didn't sound guilty. "I've met your wife, I think. Barbara?" Better to get it out on the table, hope he wouldn't be able to tell I didn't like her.

"Yes, well, Barbara is—" He hesitated, then nodded. "She saves my ass, is what she does. I couldn't do what she does with the kids. No way." He looked self-conscious. I wasn't sure why. "Anyway, welcome to town. I've been here a long time, and it's a great place to live. Despite this." He frowned as he motioned to a folder on his desk. When he looked up, he seemed angry. "But I can assure you, we will find out what happened to this baby, Ms. Sanderson, and that person or persons will be held accountable. *That* I hope you do print."

RIDGEDALE READER

ONLINE EDITION

March 17, 2015, 9:12 a.m.

Unidentified Body Discovered

BY MOLLY SANDERSON

The unidentified body of a deceased female was discovered in Ridgedale this morning shortly after 5:00. The body was spotted during a routine patrol by Campus Safety in a wooded area near the Essex Bridge.

Police remain on the scene and the investigation is ongoing. No further details are available at this time.

COMMENTS:

Samuel R.
10 min ago
"No details." That's it!?! A body?!! Was somebody murdered or something?

Christine
9 min ago
How can they post something like that without giving us any details? It's obviously going to make us panic!

AYW
7 min ago
I agree. It's tabloid journalism. Where's the personal responsibility? Why don't they actually get out there and try to report on something rather than dropping a bomb in the middle of our town and walking away?

Anonymous
5 min ago
*Because they're lazy a-holes, that's why. All they want is to sell ad space.
What the hell do they care what happens to the people who read their
garbage? And that's what this is: Total garbage. The whole point is to
freak us out. So that we come back here and click, click, click away for
more!*

firstborn
3 min ago
*Or, you know, maybe they printed that because that's all they know. Not
everything is some conspiracy.*

Anonymous
Just now
Or maybe you're just too dumb to realize that it is.

Barbara

Barbara knocked once, then again, on the classroom door. When there was no answer, she opened it and slid quietly inside. She was just going to drop off the curriculum materials for Rhea and then slip back out. Barbara wanted to do it now, while there was time for her to stop at the dry cleaners and get back in time for Cole's role as butterfly in *The Very Hungry Caterpillar*. He was so excited about wearing the wings Barbara had made for him. So she'd leave the pages for Rhea with a Post-it: *Something to consider?* She didn't want to seem confrontational. It was only an educated suggestion, *not* a criticism.

Because Barbara liked Rhea. She was a perfectly nice woman and clearly a committed teacher. Otherwise, Rhea never would have spent all her spare time supervising the Outreach Tutoring at the high school. A little strange, if Barbara was completely honest, that Rhea didn't have children of her own. She was married and had to be pushing forty. But that oddity notwithstanding, Rhea was consistently kind and supportive and warm, at least according to Barbara's seventeen-year-old daughter, Hannah, one of Outreach's volunteer tutors.

Barbara kept smiling—a smile could head off so many misunderstandings—as she watched Rhea and the assistant teacher at the far back of the room, surrounded by the children. Rhea's long white-blond hair swung back and forth as she explained how they could put on their own coats by placing them on the floor, putting their arms inside, and pulling them capelike over their heads. As usual, Rhea was dressed in black leggings and a snug knit top that accentuated her toned, curvy figure and very muscular thighs.

Rhea loved to exercise. And she loved to talk about it with the children—the miles logged, the races registered for. Cole had told Barbara *all* about it. It was cute and inspirational for the children, if a tiny bit funny to hear Cole sounding as though he were Rhea's workout partner instead of her student.

Barbara turned back to the children, with their puffy faces and awkward bodies, wide eyes locked on Rhea as though she were performing a magic trick. Barbara felt weepy watching them. She'd been that way ever since Steve had called to tell her about that poor baby. He didn't know much yet, only that there was a baby. A little girl. Her tiny body left out there in the woods to rot away with the mulching leaves.

Steve had made clear there was no reason to suspect it was some random thing, a killer on the loose. There were no reports of missing pregnant women in the area, which meant the baby's mother must—Barbara's words, not his—be responsible. And in a place like Ridgedale, with all that money and all those endless options? Disgusting, really. Never mind that there was one surefire way to make sure you didn't have a baby you couldn't care for: Don't have sex. Or, for heaven's sake, why not use birth control?

Barbara thought of Hannah and Cole. How light they'd been as newborns. How breakable. The thought of a little baby like that out there alone, crying and crying until it could cry no more. Worse yet, what if someone had stopped her from crying on purpose? The thought made Barbara positively nauseated.

"Was she born alive?" Barbara had asked. "I mean, she wasn't *killed*, was she?"

"We don't know yet," Steve had said, his voice rough.

"You mean it's possible someone could have—"

"I sure hope not," Steve said. "But with the condition of the body—let's just say I think the medical examiner will have his work cut out for him."

He was sparing her the most gruesome details. Ironic, given that, between the two of them, Steve was the far more sensitive.

"What do you mean, the condition of the body?" she asked.

"I don't think—"

"Steve, please. I need to know."

He was quiet for a minute. "The water and the cold, I guess they complicate things. Looks like the baby started out buried, and then the creek gave way in the rain. There's a lot of damage to the body. Some of the bruising and lacerations look postmortem, that's the one bit the ME could say for sure. But the broken bones and the fractured skull could be the cause of death. On that, the ME wouldn't make a guess yet. Made clear he might never know. Sounds like that's the way it can be with real little babies."

Barbara winced. Newborn heads were so very soft. How many times had she feared crushing her own children's heads, slipping down the stairs as she held them, and now someone could have done that on purpose?

There was a loud round of giggles at the back of the room. Barbara wiped her eyes, fully teary when she smiled up at the children. So precious. So little. So fleeting. They were kindergartners, but soon they'd have lengthened, lost their babylike lisps. They'd be full-fledged children with opinions and well-formed arguments, and they'd spend more time rushing away than snuggling close.

Barbara had already been through that with Hannah. It had been bittersweet, but healthy in its way. Especially for Hannah, who'd always needed to be a little more independent. Barbara still missed her daughter being a little girl, of course, would have kept her that way forever if she could have. Seventeen already, with friends Barbara didn't love and fashion choices she would never understand— did Hannah really have to dress every day in yet another sweatshirt?

She'd even be driving soon. But such was the nature of motherhood, holding them tight in order to let them go.

At least Barbara had time left with Cole, a good deal because of the gap between the children. After that early miscarriage before Hannah and then the years of trying to conceive again after she was born, Barbara had resigned herself to the reality that she would never have another baby. But then there she was, pregnant again. It had been something of a shock to have a newborn and a twelve-year-old, but Cole was always so easy. Food, sleep, cuddling, and he was the picture of contentment. So much easier than Hannah had ever been with all her "sensitivities"—the temperature, the tags in her T-shirts, the slightest change in Barbara's tone of voice. With Hannah, Barbara could never do anything right.

Barbara spotted Cole at the far back of the group in his dark gray caterpillar-body sweatsuit, a hand cupped near his mouth, whispering to his friend Will. Whatever he said made Will giggle. It was nice, the boys' friendship. And Will was very sweet. High-energy but very, very sweet. He wouldn't necessarily be the boy Barbara would have chosen to be Cole's friend, but that was more because of Will's mother.

Barbara didn't even dislike Stella, she just found her so confusing. It wasn't simply that the two of them were different either. Despite what some people seemed to think, Barbara didn't pick her friends based on whether they made the same life choices. She did tend to steer clear of women with "big" careers. But that was because they so often made her feel as though talking about her children meant she was a less worthwhile (and significantly more stupid) human being.

The worst part about Stella—who had said she used to be a stock-broker so many times that Barbara sometimes wondered if she had Tourette's and waved her divorce around like a bra on fire—wasn't her swollen résumé, it was her unpredictability. Stella could be bla-tantly inattentive in certain ways, wildly overprotective in others. It turned scheduling a simple playdate into a minefield. The latest was

Stella's claim that Will didn't like going to other people's houses, that it made him nervous. It was obviously a lie. Will was the least nervous child Barbara had ever encountered.

Barbara had always gone into every conversation with Stella hoping they would find common ground, only to walk away feeling as though she'd stepped on Stella's toes again. It was silly, really. The fact that Stella and Barbara would never be friends—and there was no question about that—hardly seemed reason for them not to be *friendly*. These days, Barbara would have settled for civil.

When the children had gotten their coats on, Barbara watched them shuffle single-file toward the door. She wiggled her fingers in Cole's direction, but he didn't see her as he headed toward the steps to the side yard. Barbara drifted to the windows to watch them spill outside. Most of the children ran for the playground equipment, a few clinging to the edge of the building as if they'd been turned loose in an unfriendly prison yard. Cole moved fast, sprinting alone for the back fence. He didn't stop until he'd reached it, linking his fingers through the wires as he stared across the empty, muddy fields that stretched behind the school. Watching him made Barbara's heart ache.

She felt such love for both her children, but Cole was much more like Barbara: simple, straightforward. Her love for him was, too. Hannah was like Steve, a big bleeding heart. Between Hannah's tutoring and Steve's police work, it was as if they were trying to save the world one needy stranger at a time. Deep down, Barbara knew that their compassion was their strength. But in her experience, all that caring for strangers came at a cost. The only question was who would pay.

There were benefits to Hannah's sensitivity though. She never wanted to disappoint. So she didn't drink or do drugs or anything like that, and there were no tattooed older boys sniffing around. There were no boys at all to speak of yet. Barbara had made clear that girls who ran around having sex in high school had no self-respect. And Hannah, being Hannah, had listened without Barbara ever having to repeat herself.

Barbara squinted in the direction of Cole, still staring across the field. What on earth was he looking at?

"Oh, Barbara," Rhea said, startling her from behind. "I'm so glad you're here. I was going to call you later today."

"Call me?" Barbara asked, feeling caught off guard. "Why?"

Rhea smiled and motioned toward two small chairs. "I was hoping we could match notes about Cole."

"Cole?" Barbara pulled in some air through her nose, hoping it might slow her heart. Silly that it was already beating so hard when she didn't know what was wrong. "He isn't being picked on, is he? I've been worried about that ever since the class picnic. He doesn't always hold his own around some of the higher-energy boys." Barbara didn't say Will's name. She didn't want to go that far, but that was whom she was thinking about. Inevitably, boys like Will had a dark side.

"No, Cole isn't being picked on." Rhea's smile shrank. "I'm afraid he's the one doing— But 'picking on' isn't the term I'd use."

"Excuse me?" Barbara felt her face flush. "I'm afraid I don't understand what you're talking about."

"Well, there have been several things in the past couple of days." Rhea's tone was cautious now, which made Barbara more nervous. "Things that are totally out of character for Cole."

Barbara dropped down hard onto a chair. *Don't be defensive*, she told herself. Even if Rhea was wrong—which she was, Barbara had never been called in to speak about her children—she clearly believed what she was saying. She was trying to be helpful. And jumping on her wouldn't be persuasive.

"I'm sorry, exactly what is it you think Cole did?" Barbara asked, trying to sound merely interested.

"Not listening, talking back, being disruptive." Rhea ticked them off as though they were the tip of a much more ominous iceberg. "He wouldn't sit for morning circle on Thursday, and then he left the classroom on Friday without permission. He was standing right outside the door when I followed him out, but it took several minutes to get him back inside. I got worried I'd have to physically carry him. With another child, I might not think much of any of it—at least not any one incident. But now it's something of a pattern, and Cole is always so sweet and well behaved. He's the one I count on being helpful when everyone else is falling apart."

"That's certainly the Cole I know," Barbara said, glad they were in agreement on that point.

"Could there be maybe— Has there been, perhaps, something going on at home? A job change or a death in the family, some stressor of some kind?" Rhea's mouth was open, her lips parted in an O. She blinked her doe eyes a few more times before looking down into her lap. "For someone as sensitive as Cole, I'm not sure it would take—"

"Cole's not sensitive," Barbara snapped. She couldn't help it. What Rhea was suggesting sounded an awful lot like a personal attack. It would make anyone defensive. "Anyway, there's nothing 'going on' in our home."

The worst part was that there *could* be something: the bureau. More specifically, her and Steve's silly fight about it a few weeks earlier.

"How could you just forget?" Barbara had shouted when Steve got home that night. Barbara's dad, Al, had been threatening to move an old bureau on his own for weeks, and Steve was supposed to make sure that didn't happen. "You promised, Steve. He'll have another heart attack if he moves that bureau!"

Steve hung his head, eyes closed. "You're right. I'm sorry," he'd said quietly, hands raised in surrender. "It completely slipped my mind."

Forgetful, that was her husband. Ever since Steve had taken over as chief of police six years earlier, things had been slipping his mind. Barbara sometimes even wondered if Steve was using the promotion to spend less time with her. He was always kind, and they rarely argued, but lately he was so much more passionate about his work than about Barbara.

Now, of course, Barbara worried that Steve's distraction had nothing to do with his job. She was worried it was about *her.*

Barbara had been sure she was imagining it the first time she'd spotted the woman downtown. Barbara had followed her for seven blocks to be sure she *was* imagining it. But no, Barbara wasn't seeing things. It was definitely her, returned after all these years, still looking like an overused prostitute. And how long had she been back in Ridgedale? Weeks, months? Festering out of sight like a nasty staph infection. Barbara hadn't mentioned her to Steve. Nothing good would have come of that. But it had been weighing on every interaction she'd had with him since.

"I sent you two texts today, reminding you about that stupid bureau!" Barbara had shouted, feeling angrier and angrier.

Even after twenty years of marriage, it was amazing how fiercely you could argue without having to admit what you were really angry about. And that was in a good marriage, with a husband you loved. Because Barbara did love Steve so very much. More than anything.

"I'll go right now," Steve had said, picking up his keys.

Not yelling back, not looking angry. Like he was some beaten-down manservant instead of a man who loved his wife. It only made Barbara angrier.

"Right now?" Barbara had pointed at the clock. "It's almost ten p.m., Steve. My parents are asleep. *If* my father's not already dead!"

"Who's dead, Mommy?" Cole had asked from the doorway. He had his stuffed dinosaur tucked under his arm like a briefcase. He hadn't seemed upset, though, only mildly curious.

And that argument couldn't have anything to do with Cole's behavior now. He hadn't seemed like he'd remembered it the next morning. More to the point, that had been three weeks ago. What Rhea was describing was recent, the past several days.

"I'm sorry, I didn't mean to suggest——" Rhea shook her head, smiled awkwardly. Barbara was glad she was uncomfortable. She couldn't go around throwing out accusations about people's families and expect there not to be consequences. "Perhaps it's best to focus on a plan of action."

"A plan of action? Isn't that a bit extreme?" Barbara squinted at her. "This behavior may be out of character for Cole, but it's hardly outside the bounds of normal."

"This morning Cole shoved Kate off a chair."

"An accident," Barbara said. "Obviously."

"Kate is okay, thank goodness," Rhea went on like Barbara hadn't spoken. "Nothing some ice and a Band-Aid wouldn't fix. But it could have been much worse. She was standing on the chair, trying to reach a book, which she shouldn't have been doing. But if she'd fallen in the other direction?" Rhea put a hand to the back of her head, as if imagining the blow to Kate's head. She shuddered.

"Cole wouldn't do something like that unprovoked," Barbara said, though she couldn't imagine him doing it period. "The children must have been having some kind of argument."

"They honestly weren't. I saw the whole thing. Cole just walked right up behind her and . . ." Rhea looked out into the distance, her face empty and stunned, like she was seeing it happen in front of her. "He just pushed."

"No," Barbara said. She meant that unequivocally. "That's not possible."

Rhea was looking at Barbara sadly. Almost like she felt sorry for her. Barbara's face was hot as she crossed her arms tightly. "Why is this the first I'm hearing of this?"

"I didn't want to upset you unnecessarily. As you know, these things often pass. Especially with a child like Cole. But now, unfortunately, the situation has changed."

Barbara pulled her chin back sharply. "What does that mean?"

Rhea took a deep breath and stiffened in her chair. She met Barbara's eyes reluctantly. "With an incident like this with Kate, we have to consider the safety of the other children."

"*Safety?*" Barbara laughed. But she could see from the look on Rhea's face that she wasn't joking. "I'm sorry, but this is absurd. I've seen some of the other boys in class. And you're worried about Cole? Will, for instance—he's the one who's out of control."

Barbara hadn't meant to mention anyone by name, certainly not Will. The last thing she needed was Stella getting wind of that. But Will was something new in Cole's life. He'd been over to Will's house several times in the past few weeks, each time, at Stella's insistence, without Barbara. Barbara had probed for details afterward. *What did you eat? Where was Will's mother? What did you play?* But Cole was only five. God knew what he'd left out.

"Barbara, I know this is confusing and unexpected. But there's no need to panic. I'll speak to Kate's parents, let them know what happened. They're very sweet. I can't imagine them wanting to pursue the matter." There was such unbearable pity in Rhea's voice. It was making Barbara light-headed. "For now we'll just take some basic precautions."

Precautions? Like Cole was some kind of *animal*. As though people should be getting inoculated. This made no sense whatsoever. A child could not go from being essentially perfect to dangerously disturbed, not overnight. Barbara knew that. But right now she just needed some air. She went to stand. "If you'll excuse me, I think I—"

Rhea reached out and put a hand on Barbara's arm. She tilted her head to the side and smiled warmly. Barbara stared down at Rhea's fingers pressed against her skin. How had she become this woman, this mother in need of a steadying hand?

"Watchful waiting is our best approach," Rhea said. "These things do so often pass, vanish as quickly as they cropped up. But if you feel you need to *do* something in the meantime—and sometimes I feel that way—I have the name of someone." Rhea stood, then walked over to her desk, returning with a business card pinched in her fingers. Barbara took the card reluctantly. *Dr. Peter Kellerman, Developmental Child Psychologist.* "He comes very highly recommended."

Barbara didn't breathe again until she was halfway down the hall, the business card crushed in her fist. Then she felt a wave of heat followed by cold. Worried she might pass out, Barbara ducked into the girls' bathroom at the end of the hall.

Locked in one of the narrow stalls, she squatted fully clothed on the small toilet. Under the stall next to her, she saw a girl's feet shuffle back and forth in worn pink sneakers. They were the glittery kind Hannah had begged for in elementary school and Barbara had always refused to buy. She could no longer remember precisely why.

Barbara stared down at her own much bigger shoes in front of that small toilet. What was she doing, getting so upset? So what if there was something Cole needed to work on? Sooner or later, each child had a weakness. Besides, like her own mother had always said, a mother needed happy children, not perfect ones.

But there was still a loud sob creeping into Barbara's throat. She clamped a hand over her mouth so it couldn't make it all the way out.

Barbara waited until the girl in the pink sneakers had washed her hands and left before she pulled her hand off her face. When no sound came, Barbara forced herself to her feet and tried to smile a little. But there was still that sucked-out feeling at the bottom of her stomach.

When she stepped out of the stall, Barbara smoothed her blond hair, cut these days into an elegant bob, and straightened her crisp white blouse. Then she caught sight of her reflection in the long bathroom mirror. She smiled, but her face looked so ashen and afraid in the fluorescent light. Like someone she no longer recognized. Like someone she didn't even want to know.

Q: Have you spoken to your father about what happened to the baby?

M.S.: You're joking, right?

Q: I wasn't, no. That would be a joke, talking to your father?

M.S.: We barely know each other. And before you go off on a tangent, no, I don't blame him for that. Okay, maybe I blame him. But I just—I don't care anymore. Or I don't care now. After we lost the baby, he sent me a sympathy card and made a donation to my work—or my old work—like we asked people to. But there's only so much that a stranger can do in a situation like this.

Q: And that's okay with you? That your sole surviving parent is a stranger?

M.S.: What difference does it make whether I'm okay with it? It's the way things are. I have enough problems right now without dredging up ancient history. I had a rough childhood and a cold, angry mother who died when I was eighteen. I can't change any of that now.

Q: But you could acknowledge that not having parents makes this harder for you.

M.S.: Because feeling sorry for myself is going to make me feel better?

Q: It might. And what about Justin's parents? What's your relationship like with them?

M.S.: Justin's mother came and stayed for two weeks right after. I don't know what we would have done without her help.

Q: But it doesn't sound like you're exceptionally close.

M.S.: Are we supposed to be? Justin's parents are just— They're intimidating, I guess. His mother told me once that I was different from Justin's other girlfriends. More spirited, that's what she said. I think she meant it as a compliment, that I kept him in better line than his other girlfriends or something. But it made me feel like a horse. That's what they're like: well-intentioned, but always off somehow.

Q: Have you and Justin spoken about trying to have another baby?

M.S.: How could I have another baby? I can't take care of the one I have.

Q: I didn't mean now. Eventually. Sometimes making plans like that for the future can be helpful.

M.S.: I can't do that. Not yet.

Q: Have you told the NAPW that you're not coming back?

M.S.: Yes, I told them. They said I could have more time off, as much as I needed. But I don't want more time. I want to know that it's over. That I never have to go back there.

Q: What will you do if you don't go back to work?

M.S.: Try to survive. Right now that feels like more than a full-time job.

Molly

I headed straight from the police station to the Black Cat Café on the far side of the chilly green. Gray had overtaken the sky, turning it from the front edge of spring back into the tail end of winter. I pulled my coat tighter around me and lifted my bag on my shoulder.

I was glad I'd brought my laptop with me. There wasn't much time before everyone would have the story, which meant I'd have to go for basic in my second post. I'd save my crime statistics and the background on Simon Barton. As it was, I would have barely anything to add in the print follow-up. I'd already called the ME's office and, as expected, I had gotten a curt "No comment pending our official results."

Despite my initial vertigo, I was no longer conflicted about staying on the story. I wanted to, needed to write about it, and with an intensity that even I had to acknowledge was somewhat disconcerting. I could only imagine what Justin would say if he knew what I was feeling, which was why I didn't plan to tell him.

Can you have coffee? Justin texted before I'd gotten all the way across the green. He was checking up on me. Acting like he was sure I'd be fine, but wanting a peek with his own eyes to be sure.

Great. Black Cat? Thirty minutes?

By then I'd be done with the Web update.

Wouldn't miss it.

It was warm inside the rough-hewn Black Cat, the air rich with the ten varieties of free-trade coffee beans on offer. It was my favorite café in town, the place I went when I didn't want to write at home, which was most of the time these days. That was the thing about not being able to get out of bed for weeks on end. Once you finally could, you developed a real phobia of being at home.

The Black Cat was a true university hangout—professors and students—complete with wobbly wood tables, faded concert posters, and bathrooms that didn't lock properly. The moms in town all went to Norma's around the corner, which had brightly hued art deco throw pillows on its long benches and lavender soap in the bathroom. It also had an organic juice bar, two kinds of vegan muffins, and wine from four o'clock. Meanwhile, the Black Cat didn't serve decaf and refused to stock skim milk or artificial sweeteners. The first time Stella came in with me, she got lippy when they scoffed at her request for stevia. The argument between her and the barista got so heated, I thought for sure he was going to throw his skateboard at her.

But I liked the Black Cat. It reminded me of the unapologetic cafés around Columbia that Justin and I had frequented when we first started dating.

I ordered a full-fat latte and sat in the window. In fifteen minutes, I had a decent draft. It was short, under a hundred and fifty words. My interview with Steve had been exclusive because it was first. That didn't mean he'd given me much new to say.

I read through the post one last time. Satisfied, I emailed it off to Erik with a note: *Extended print story to come.* But extended how, exactly? I was pondering how I'd flesh it out as I headed to get another latte. I ran smack into Nancy on her way out the door.

"Oh, hi, Molly," she said, smiling, but with none of her usual ease.

Her face was drawn and her eyes were puffy. Her long dark blond hair was pulled back in a ponytail that looked slept on. She seemed very much like somebody in the midst of a family crisis.

"It's terrible what's happened with that baby," she said, sadness and sympathy flicking across her face. "Erik told me that you're covering it."

I couldn't tell whether Nancy was upset for herself or concerned for me. We'd never spoken about the baby I'd lost, but I could tell she was thinking about it. And after all she and Erik had been through—three miscarriages, followed by two rounds of unsuccessful IVF, one larcenous surrogate, and an already arduous and still unsuccessful adoption process—a dead baby must have triggered all sorts of strong emotions for her, too. I wanted to ask if she was okay. But everything I thought about saying felt presumptuous and awkward.

"I'm trying," I said, feeling myself well up. It was that caring look in Nancy's eyes. It did it to me every time. "It's terrible. I feel terrible for—well, everyone involved."

Nancy nodded, then mercifully looked away, toward the Ridgedale town green. But she lingered while I waited in line, as if she wanted to say something else. After a while, it started to feel uncomfortable with her standing there, not saying anything.

"I hope everything is okay with your family," I said, compelled to fill the void.

Nancy turned sharply in my direction. "What do you mean?"

Dammit. Why had I said anything? There I'd gone, hooking myself on all that invisible barbed wire again. What if Erik was off somewhere on a bender or something that Nancy didn't know about? Elizabeth told me once that she'd spotted Erik at Blondie's, a dive bar downtown. But she added that she'd been very drunk herself—"totally wasted," as if she were sixteen instead of twenty-six—so I hadn't taken it seriously. But judging from the look on Nancy's face, there was something complicated going on.

"I'm sorry, I thought Erik said he had to go out of town for something family-related. I may have misunderstood. This story has me pretty distracted."

"No, no, you're right," Nancy said quickly. She smiled again, even less convincingly. "It's Erik's cousin. There was a fire at his house, bad wiring. No one was hurt, but the family lost everything. Thank you for asking." She looked around as if searching for someone or something to grab on to, but she came up empty-handed. She checked her watch. When she looked back at me, her eyes had softened, filled with compassion, not pity. She squeezed my arm. "I should probably be going. You take care of yourself, Molly. And don't work too hard."

"I won't," I said, turning away so she didn't see the tears that had rushed crazily to my eyes. "Thanks, it was nice to see you."

I watched Nancy's tired face disappear past the front windows and Justin appear in her place. I scrubbed my face with my hands, trying to rub away the incriminating weepiness as Justin stepped inside. He was wearing jeans, Vans, and an untucked, slightly wrinkled button-down—a young literature professor's uniform.

"Hey there." He wrapped an arm around my waist and leaned over to kiss me. "Everything okay?"

"Yes." I tried to smile. "And no."

He nodded sympathetically. And he didn't know the half of it yet. "Why don't you go sit? I'll get your coffee for you," he said. "A latte?"

I smiled. "Sure."

I went back and sat down, watching Justin's quick back-and-forth with the girl behind the counter. She had a plain square face and an athlete's sturdy frame. She laughed too loudly at whatever Justin said as he motioned to the baked goods. Preternaturally charming— men, women, old, young. Justin couldn't help himself.

I'd known that since the day we met. I was at the Hungarian Pastry Shop, an old-school no-frills café near Columbia, studying constitutional criminal procedure, listening to Justin a couple tables away, chatting up the sixtysomething man sitting near him. Apparently they shared an intense interest in collecting. In the older man's case, it was mechanical banks; for Justin, it was bottle caps.

"Do you collect anything?" Justin had asked me once the man was gone.

"No," I said, trying not to notice just how good-looking he was.

"Me, neither," Justin said.

"I just heard you telling that man—"

"See, I knew you were listening," he said with a sly smile that made him even better-looking. "Anyway, no. No collecting. I was just making conversation."

"So you were lying," I said.

According to my law school friend Leslie, a cheerful guy's-girl soccer player who never had a shortage of boyfriends, this was why men never called me for a second date: I was a hard-ass. Too serious, too exacting. Humorless. I needed to let some of their harmless male bullshit flow over me; men didn't want to be called out for every little thing. It wasn't the first time I'd heard this. My whole life, friends—men especially—had been telling me how much luckier in love I would be if I'd lighten up. Sometimes I wanted to defend myself, to ask how many of them had grown up like me. Because the truth was: I would choose alone any day over angry like my mother.

As it turned out, Justin fell in love with my sharpest edges. He genuinely valued my willingness to call him out on his particular brand of bullshit.

"I'd say I was just being friendly," Justin had said that day in the café. "But I guess that depends on how you see the world."

And as much as Justin valued the clarity of my black and white, I'd been intoxicated by his world of grays. By his fearlessness and his freedom and his very modest sense of entitlement. Justin had never believed that he needed to be right 100 percent of the time to be a decent person; he didn't need to be perfect to be loved. As it turned out, I wanted to feel that way also, much more than I'd ever let myself believe.

No doubt it had been easier for Justin with Judith and Charles, his generous parents, celebrating every milestone big and small in his picture-perfect house in New Canaan, Connecticut. With his accomplished and loving sister, Melissa, at his side, Justin had played lacrosse and swum competitively. He spent summers on the Cape and winter holidays in Vail. He had a golden retriever named Honey. And thank God for the relentless optimism those things had given Justin. Without that, I never would have had the courage to forge ahead with him on a family of our own.

"Not everything about where you're headed, Molly, has to be about where you've been," he'd told me once when we'd been deep in the throes of debating getting pregnant the first time.

And I'd believed him, proof of just how much I'd loved him.

"It's a baby," I blurted out when Justin returned with our coffees. So much for playing it cool. He hadn't even sat down.

"What?" Justin looked confused.

"The body they found," I said. "It's a baby."

His face was stiff as he lowered himself into the chair across from me. "Well, that's a completely upsetting turn of events."

"Tell me about it."

He turned his coffee cup in his hands. His face was tighter. He was trying hard not to overreact, but he was worried. It was obvious.

"Do they know whose it is?"

I shook my head and willed my tears back. "Somebody terrified, I'm sure."

I knew that much from my years at NAPW. I'd never handled the criminal side of things; my focus had been on legislative change, drafting amicus briefs and working with lobbyists. But I had spoken to colleagues who had clients with pregnancies that had ended in tragedy. Almost always, the women had been abused themselves or worse. They were usually poor and alone, always terrified and overwhelmed. Assigning blame in these circumstances wasn't nearly as simple as some people liked to believe.

Justin reached forward and put a hand over mine. "Are you okay?"

I shrugged, then nodded and again tried hard not to cry. Because as much as I wanted to pretend I was upset about what the poor mother of this baby might have been through—assuming she was responsible—I was thinking more about myself. I was thinking about what *I* had been through. What I was still going through, at least enough that I wasn't ready to contemplate trying for another baby. I wasn't sure I'd ever be ready for that. But I had to be careful. If I seemed like I was slipping under again, Justin wouldn't let me out of his sight.

"Obviously, it would be better if it weren't a baby," I said, trying to smile. It didn't feel convincing. "But I can handle it."

Justin closed his eyes and took a deep breath. He was quiet for a long time, then turned to stare out the window. "Are you sure you should do this story, babe?" He had this expression on his face when he looked at me again: tragic, as though *I* were the tragedy. "I know it's an opportunity, and that's important. But maybe it's not worth it."

"I have to do it," I said, probably too forcefully. I smiled weakly, trying to claw back some credibility. "It feels—I don't know, connected somehow. To what happened to us."

"But it's not." Justin eyed me seriously. If he was trying to hide his alarm, he was not succeeding. "You know that, right? This has nothing to do with what happened to us."

"Of course I know that, Justin." And I did. Didn't I?

"I just, I don't want you to . . ." He looked more than worried. He looked petrified. "Where's Richard, anyway? Shouldn't he be back soon?"

Justin loved me and wanted to help. But there was a difference between protecting me and making me feel irrevocably damaged.

"This is my story, Justin," I said, wishing I hadn't phrased it quite that way. "It's my responsibility. And I have the expertise—both personally and professionally—to handle it. I'm not going to 'give' it back to Richard because it's a little 'uncomfortable' for me. Life is uncomfortable. I can't hide from it."

My phone buzzed with a text, saving me from further interrogation. I braced for it to be from Erik, Nancy having told him that I'd seemed too unstable to be trusted with such an important story. But it was Stella. *Can you meet me at Univ. Hospital? Please?*

"Who's that?" Justin asked, pointing his chin toward the phone.

"Stella," I said, wondering how worried I should be.

"What is it this time?" he asked tightly.

"She's at the hospital. Aidan, I'm assuming."

"And let me guess," Justin said. "It's an emergency."

From the start, Justin had pegged Stella as a drama queen, which she was. But he'd always tolerated her with good humor. Lately, though, she and her late-night calls seemed to be grating on him. Justin was probably wary of Stella dragging me back down in a blaze of unbridled nuttiness.

"She's entertaining, I get that," Justin had said when we got home from the first—and one of the few—dinners the three of us had eaten together. If it had been up to Stella, we would have done it much more often. She was utterly unfazed by being a third wheel. But Justin always demurred. "From ten miles off, Stella's batshit crazy. You've got to see that."

I'd laughed. "'Batshit'? That's a tad melodramatic, don't you think?" We were standing side by side in our huge sparkling-white bathroom with its polished double sinks. Yet another benefit of Ridgedale living—clean, wide-open spaces.

"Be friends with her if you want, I don't care," Justin said through a mouthful of toothpaste. He spat into the sink. "But I've known a bunch of girls like Stella in my time, and—"

"Eww, please. Must we do a 'who I've slept with' walk down

memory lane?" Justin had not been a monk before we met, and he'd never pretended otherwise.

"I'm just saying, women like Stella are fun to be around. Until they're really, really not."

But I didn't care if Stella's scalding sunshine came with a little extra drama on the side. That was a price I was willing to pay.

Please? came another text from Stella. *Quick as you can?*

"It's okay," Justin said, probably reading the tension on my face. "Go check on your crazy friend." He reached forward to squeeze my hand. "As long as you can look me in the eye and promise me you'll be okay on this story."

"Come on, you know me." I smiled playfully as I stood, then leaned over to kiss him. "When have I ever *really* been okay?"

Stella had directed me to a room on the second floor of the hospital. When I arrived, she was sitting in a chair next to the far bed. Her arms were crossed, her elegant face bunched and gray. I looked past the empty bed closest to the door, bracing myself to see Aidan lying in the bed against the windows—face smashed, some terrible tube helping him breathe. But there was a dark-haired woman lying there, pretty and young—twenties, maybe. Or she would have been pretty if her face hadn't been swollen and bruised about the eyes.

"Oh, Molly." Stella jumped to her feet and rushed over. "Thank you so much for coming." She wrapped me in her warm embrace and pressed her smooth, cool cheek against mine. Her perfume smelled of flowers and citrus.

The woman in the bed raised a hand in something like a wave. "Hi," I said, smiling back politely. I had no idea who she was.

"Rose was in a car accident this morning, the poor thing," Stella said, going over to put a protective hand on the woman's arm.

"That's terrible," I said.

Stella was talking to me like I was supposed to know Rose. But Stella didn't have any local relatives, and the girl looked too young to be a friend. I wouldn't have put it past Stella to show up at the hospital room of a woman she didn't know, but I gathered from the equally warm way the young woman reached out and put her IV'd hand over Stella's that they did have some kind of genuine relationship.

"A truck driver texting," Rose said. Her voice was hoarse, and it seemed to be taking great effort for her to talk. "But I'm fine. It's only some stitches and a lot of ugly bruises."

"What is that Zen saying of yours, Rose? 'Let go or be dragged'? I think we should find that driver and drag him."

"I love you for loving me, Stella." Rose smiled. "But I'm pretty sure that's not how the phrase was intended."

"And now Rose would like to go home." Stella rubbed the woman's arm some more. "No one can give us a legitimate medical reason why she can't, but for some insane, incompetent reason, they *still* will not discharge her. I thought maybe you could, you know, mention that you're from the local paper. See if we could get them to snap to it. Nothing like fear of a little bad press to get someone's attention."

This was why Stella had wanted me there? To throw my very meager weight around? I felt simultaneously flattered and insulted. I smiled at Rose through gritted teeth. "Stella, can I talk to you in the hall for one second?"

"Oh, sure," Stella said, turning back to Rose. "I'll be right back, honey. Do you need anything else? You're sure you don't want a trashy magazine while we wait for these jerks to get it together?"

"No, no, I'm fine," Rose said, squeezing Stella's hand. "You've done way too much already."

"Who is she?" I whispered when we were out in the hall, the door to the room easing shut.

"Rose," Stella said at full volume, pulling her chic cranberry-hued cardigan closed. Her saying the woman's name a second time did not make it more familiar. "I'm telling you, Molly. There's definitely something weird going on here. First they said they needed to wait for more test results; now they're saying there's some problem with Rose's insurance. And that's definitely not true, because she's still on her parents' insurance. It's the *one* thing they help her with. Anyway, Rose called and checked. Her insurance is fine. The hospital is making up one excuse after another."

"But Stella, who is Rose to *you*?"

"Oh, Rose cleans my house." Stella looked confused and maybe a tiny bit appalled. "You *have* met her, Molly. Don't you remember?"

Now that Stella mentioned it, I did have a vague recollection of one occasion, right after Stella and I had met, when I'd been at her house and her cleaning woman had passed through the kitchen. Stella had told me about her afterward in hushed tones—a straight-A psychology student at Ridgedale University, planning to work with autistic children like her younger brother, until her parents cut her off financially and she had to drop out of school. Criminal, according to Stella. Absolutely criminal.

The story had not surprised me. Most people Stella knew came with some kind of hard-luck history—even me.

"I didn't recognize her with the bruising," I lied.

"I know," Stella said, making a disgusted face. "Horrible, isn't it? She's in agony, too, the poor thing. And she won't take any pain medicine because she's one of those crazy all-natural types. You know, raw food, meditation. Especially now, with the nursing, she's definitely not taking anything."

The nursing. There was a pull in the pit of my stomach. *For some insane, incompetent reason, they will not discharge her.* Surely the police had alerted the hospital to be on the lookout for mothers of missing babies.

"Rose has a baby?"

"Yeah, *just* had a baby three weeks ago," Stella said. "She shouldn't be back working. But I guess that's what happens to people on the margins. Her parents are such assholes."

Rose hadn't been visibly pregnant when I'd seen her, but that had been nearly six months ago.

"Stella, *where* is Rose's baby?"

"What do you mean, where is her—" I watched the lightbulb finally go on for her. "Oh my God. They think it's *her* baby they found?"

"I'm assuming," I said. "It would explain why they're not letting her go."

"That's insane." Stella crossed her arms, but she didn't sound that sure. "I mean, I'm sure Rose's baby is at her apartment."

With whom? A nanny? How many "people on the margins" could afford that? It didn't sound like Rose had family helping her out, and it wasn't like Ridgedale was overflowing with affordable day care options. Most people in Ridgedale didn't need affordable.

Before I could press Stella on this substantial hole in her theory, a doctor came up, pausing to grab the chart outside Rose's door. He had a full head of thick gray hair and large glasses that obscured his eyes. He was trying hard not to make eye contact with us, as though by not seeing us, he could make it so we weren't seeing him.

"Oh, hi," Stella said, stepping into his path. "Did you just come on shift?"

"Yes," he said, but not very pleasantly. His eyes stayed locked on Rose's chart.

"We're friends of Rose's. Well, technically, she works for me," Stella said. "And Molly is a reporter with the *Ridgedale Reader*."

And there went Stella, doing whatever she wanted. Not that I thought this doctor would be bothered by an implied threat about my cutting investigative journalism. Except, from the way his eyes shot up from Rose's file, it appeared he did care.

"A reporter, huh?" he said unpleasantly. "You'll need to talk to the communications office if you're looking for a comment."

A comment? There was some kind of story, then. Because he'd seemed awfully prepared with that retort. As though he'd already been briefed about reporters turning up. Even in Ridgedale, that didn't happen for routine traffic accidents.

"It's quite simple," Stella began, calm but firm. "Rose wants to leave right now. And there's no earthly reason why she shouldn't be allowed to. Discharge her immediately, or Molly here will be stuck hanging around the hospital, and who knows *what* kind of stories will catch her eye. Didn't you just have another case of MRSA after that boy lost his hand last year?"

I turned and glared at Stella. This was so her—unsure of Rose's innocence and yet willing to throw herself (and me) headlong into the fray. The doctor was glaring at me through his big glasses. I smiled as he pushed open the door to Rose's room.

"A MRSA story, huh?" he asked. "And your paper approves of this sort of thing? Extortion?"

I just stared at him and kept on smiling. There wasn't much else I could do. That was exactly what Stella had been suggesting. I just had to hope that he wouldn't report back to Erik. If Erik had questioned the ethics of my allowing Steve to dictate our reporting, I could only imagine how he'd feel about extortion. Finally, the doctor shook his head in disgust and stepped inside Rose's room, letting the door slam shut behind him.

As soon as he was gone, I turned wide-eyed to Stella, waiting for her to apologize. She was staring at Rose's door, oblivious. "Maybe the father of Rose's baby had something to do with what happened. I mean, *if* something happened to her baby, which I'm not conceding."

"What are you talking about, Stella?"

"Rose told me how she got pregnant. Not the specifics. And she didn't use the word 'rape,' but it sounded to me like that's what it was."

"Who's the father?"

"I don't know. A university student, I assume. An entitled asshole, no doubt. And you know how universities like Ridgedale can be. Cover up first, ask questions never." Stella shook her head. "Rose was so excited for the baby, though, despite how she'd gotten pregnant." When Stella looked at me, her eyes were wide and shiny. "I'm telling you, none of this makes any sense, Molly. No sense at all."

RIDGEDALE READER

ONLINE EDITION

March 17, 2015, 10:25 a.m.

Update: Unidentified Female Infant
Found Near Essex Bridge

BY MOLLY SANDERSON

Police have confirmed that the unidentified body found on campus property beneath the Essex Bridge is that of a female infant.

According to police sources, the infant appears to be approximately newborn. However, the infant's age cannot be confirmed until the findings of the medical examiner are released. The cause of death at this time is also unknown.

Chief of Police Steve Carlson has asked that anyone with information relating to the identity of the infant or her parents please contact the Ridgedale Police Department at 888-526-1899.

There have been only two murders in Ridgedale in the past twenty years. In 2001, Esther Gleason shot her husband in an incident determined to be self-defense. Five years later, a man was fatally shot during a drug transaction in an off-campus apartment. The Essex Bridge was the location of another death twenty years ago. Simon Barton, a Ridgedale High School senior, died of brain trauma when he slipped and fell at a graduation party. Alcohol was a suspected contributing factor.

COMMENTS:

sarahssutton

4 hours ago

Oh my God, I am so sad for that poor little baby! She was left outside? Who would do something like that? It's disgusting. There are so many people here who would be more than willing to care for an unwanted child. It just breaks my heart.

abby

3 hours ago

Personally, I wish I felt more like praying. Because all I want to do is get my hands on whoever did this and leave them for dead somewhere, too.

msheard

3 hours ago

There should be some test for moral decency and kindness before people are allowed to procreate.

Carla Shrift

3 hours ago

I for one am not going to be comfortable assuming that it was the baby's parents until someone shows me more than random statistics to prove it. Until then, I'm going to be dusting off the old alarm system and learning to sleep with one eye open.

sssuzy

2 hours ago

Personally I'm sick of having to climb over all those teenagers who hang out in front of the 7-Eleven. I know this is politically incorrect, but doesn't it make sense to think the parents of this baby are probably some of those kids from Ridgedale Commons who are always hanging out downtown? Where are their parents?

FSH

2 hours ago

I'm not going to guess at where they're from, but only a teenager would be stupid enough to leave the baby right where anybody could find it. Why even have the baby? Abortion is legal.

realdeal

2 hours ago

Maybe she was waiting for the daddy to propose. Isn't young love grand?

Eric

2 hours ago

I know it's not popular to bring up religion in this bright blue town, but some people—myself included—believe that life starts at conception.

Maureen

2 hours ago

So it's better to kill a newborn than have an abortion? Is that seriously what you're saying?

Dawn D.

1 hour ago

I just want to say, if we act afraid, our children will be afraid. Kids absorb everything.

246Barry

1 hour ago

THEY SHOULD BE AFRAID.
FIND HIM.
BEFORE HE FINDS YOU.

Kara

57 min ago

"Before he finds you"? You have got to be kidding me, right? I know that this is an open forum, but I'd seriously expect people to rise to the occasion under the circumstances. I haven't been thrilled with a lot of what's been said here, but this is a new low.

Piper Lee

42 min ago

Another Ridgedale murder?? Is anyone else freaked out that there was another murder in the EXACT same spot? I don't care how long ago it was, that seems like a crazy coincidence.

Harry S

40 min ago

HELLO!!!??? The article says DEATH, not murder. Sounds like it was an accident.

KellyGreen

37 min ago

Or so they think. They could be wrong. Maybe the person who did it was in jail or something. That happens all the time, a serial killer stops because they go to jail for something totally unrelated.

JENNA

The Captain finally said hi to me today. I know: fucking crazy.

But it seriously happened. There I was, walking down the science hall, the part where there are no lockers and that whole group of them is always hanging out. And he was with a couple of guys from the team. I think there might have even been a few girls there. Anyway, the Captain looked GORGEOUS, as usual. That hair and those eyes. He looks just like Rob Lowe. Just like him. Actually, he looks better than him. The Captain is the most perfect-looking boy I have ever seen. And let's face it, I've seen my share of boys.

Plus, he's so smart. I never would have thought that smart could be so hot, but it TOTALLY is. I've never talked to him myself. But when he recited the Gettysburg Address from memory at the Presidents' Day assembly a couple years ago—Jesus! Totally masturbated thinking about it later. (Sorry, Jesus, for writing that so close to your name, but it's true.)

So there I was, walking down the hall, and the Captain and I do that thing we've been doing for a while now where we stare and stare at each other in the middle of a crowd like it's just the two of us. The thing that totally makes me feel like all I want to do is give him a BJ in the bathroom.

But I don't want to do that, not this time. This time I'm going to try for something else. Something like other girls have. Who says I can't have a regular boyfriend?

Anyway, this time, instead of looking away when I got close like he usually does, the Captain raised a hand in a kind of wave. And he said it: Hi. Out loud. I thought Tex's girlfriend was going to barf on her shoes.

Sandy

In the end, it was the pain in Sandy's thighs that helped the most. The harder she pedaled, the more her legs ached, the less she thought about anything—Jenna, Hannah, what had happened the last time she'd been out on the bike. That sick feeling of her body flying one way and the bike flying the other, like two halves of an exploding bomb. Or the vicious-ass burn of the concrete ripping a long strip of skin from her forearm.

For two hours, Sandy rode everywhere in town she thought Jenna might be: Sommerfield's (the only bar other than Blondie's that Jenna could stand), past the park up on Stanton Street where Jenna had had at least one hookup (the details of which she'd seen fit, as usual, to share with Sandy), and that shitty dump on Taylor Ave. where Jenna bought pot sometimes. There was no sign of Jenna or her car anywhere. Sandy was panting, her throat on fire, by the time she turned in to the parking lot of Blondie's, where Jenna worked.

Blondie's was the least fancy place in the fanciest part of downtown Ridgedale. It had a faded green awning and frosted glass windows. Inside wasn't much better, with stained carpeting, cracked leather benches, and St. Patrick's Day decorations up year-round. The bartenders were as old-school as the decor. Monte, with his big belly and tight white crew cut, had owned the place for thirty years. He worked there most nights with his son Dominic, a thinner, younger version of himself. Both Monte and Dominic were big, sweet guys, the kind Sandy wished Jenna would fall for. But they'd always treated Jenna way too nice to be the least bit interesting to her.

For decades, Blondie's had been a favorite of blue-collar locals, people just like Jenna. But in the past few months, the bar had gotten popular with kids from Ridgedale University. Some campus blog had called the usual student hangout, Truth—a bar with a small dance floor, oversize chaises, and a "mixologist," whatever the hell that was—"cheesy poser bullshit." After that, the university kids wanted someplace "real" to get loaded. And Blondie's was it.

"You know what one of those kids said to me tonight?" Jenna had told Sandy as they were driving home one night after Jenna's shift bartending and Sandy's waitressing at Winchester's Pub—avoiding the bike for the past week had meant getting rides from Jenna. "That Blondie's is ironic. What the hell does that mean?"

"That they're dicks," Sandy had said, slipping her shoes off in the passenger seat. Her feet always ached so much at the end of her shifts that she could feel them pulsing.

"Ha, that's funny." Jenna had laughed hard, smacking the steering wheel. "You're right, baby. They are dicks. Every last one of them."

Sandy tucked her bike into the sliver of an alleyway next to Blondie's. Her phone chirped as she headed up the steps. Jenna, it had to be. Pulling it out by the skin of her teeth at the eleventh hour, like she always did.

Are you okay? I'm worried.

Hannah, not Jenna. Jesus. Sandy took a deep breath and blew it out hard. But she couldn't lose it on this girl, no matter how bad she wanted to.

I'm fine, Sandy typed, her fingers banging hard against her phone. *I promise.*

Are you sure?

The texts were making the whole thing worse. They might have been the worst part of the entire situation. Actually, no, they weren't. They were bad, but they weren't the worst part. Not by a fucking long shot.

The first time the two of them had met to study, Hannah had picked the Black Cat.

Sandy got there ten minutes late and totally out of breath. She'd had to haul ass on her bike to make up the twenty minutes she'd spent sitting around thinking she might not go meet Hannah after all. That she might bag the whole GED thing, honors or not. But then she'd remembered how Rhea had looked at her: that hope. No one had ever looked at Sandy that way. Like they had expectations.

She spotted a girl she thought might be Hannah, sitting there in the window with books spread out in front of her. She was tall and real pretty, with shiny shoulder-length brown hair and bright blue eyes. Her long legs were folded kind of awkwardly under the little table, and she was wearing an oversize Yale hoodie. She was smiling a little, too, like she was enjoying some kind of funny private joke.

"Sandy?" Hannah had asked, standing as she made her way over. "Are you okay?"

Sandy was sweating and still breathing hard. Her face was probably beet-red. "I'm fine," Sandy said, dropping herself down into the chair. She thought about mentioning her bike but decided against it. Hannah had probably gotten there in a chauffeur-driven limousine.

"Oh, okay," Hannah said, but she looked a little worried still as she shuffled around her books and papers. "Should we start with the math? Maybe that would be fun." Sandy must have made a face, because she watched Hannah's smile sink. "Sorry, it's not fun, I know. None of this is fun. I'm just nervous. I've never tutored anyone. I can try to be less annoying."

"That's okay," Sandy had said, smiling for real. Because it was kind of funny, the way Hannah had said that. Maybe she wouldn't end up hating this girl after all. "Anyway, what do I know? I've never had a tutor."

Before they could start, Hannah's phone rang. She stared at the screen, smiling in a way that made her seem the opposite of happy. "Sorry, hold on just a second." She answered the phone, sticking a long finger in her ear to block out the sounds of the café, even though it wasn't that loud. "Hi, Mom."

Her voice went all high, like a little girl's, and she said "Uh-huh" a lot. "Sorry, I forgot," she said finally. "Okay, yeah. Okay. Mom, *stop*. Okay, yes. An hour." After she hung up, Hannah kept smiling, but she seemed sad. "Sorry about that."

"Everything okay?" Sandy asked. And she was curious. She always wanted to know what kids like Hannah—good, regular kids— fought with their moms about. She was always the one riding Jenna for screwing things up. She couldn't imagine it being the other way around.

Hannah looked embarrassed. "My mom's just kind of, you know"—she shrugged—"intense sometimes."

"About what?" Sandy needed details to be able to picture Hannah's regular-girl life. "What did you forget?"

"To clean out my junk drawer."

Sandy's eyebrows lifted. "What the hell is a junk drawer?" There was no end to the things other kids had that Sandy did not.

"You know, where you keep all your—" Hannah moved her hands around, as if trying to figure out how to describe it.

"Shit you should throw out?" Sandy offered.

"Yeah." Hannah had laughed. "I guess you're right."

"That's intense."

Hannah looked confused. "Having a junk drawer?"

"Your mom hunting you down to bitch you out about it." For the first time ever, Jenna calling Sandy all the time and begging her to come home because she missed her didn't seem so bad.

"I guess. Sometimes it feels like I can't do anything right," Hannah said. Then she shrugged and smiled like she was over it completely. "But I know that's just the way my mom is. She likes things a certain way."

Sandy had laughed for real. "Don't they all, sister. Don't they all."

Blondie's was dark and mostly empty when Sandy got inside. There were two old guys at the far end of the bar, listening to one of Monte's loud stories. Straight ahead was a younger guy with his back to the door. He had longish brown hair and was wearing some kind of suit jacket and a big expensive-looking watch. It was the watch that stood out. It wasn't the kind of thing you saw in Blondie's, not even on those ironic assholes. He was good-looking, too, Sandy could tell even from behind. It was the way he was sitting—like he owned that stool.

"Hey, kiddo!" Monte boomed, heading over to meet Sandy. "What are you doing here?"

Sandy loved when Monte called her "kiddo." Men never treated her that way anymore: like a kid. Monte always seemed so happy to see her, too. Suddenly, there were tears at the back of Sandy's throat, trying to break free. *Don't cry. Don't cry. Don't cry.*

"Have you seen Jenna?" Sandy asked.

Monte frowned and shook his head, wiping the bar with a white cloth that looked tiny beneath his huge hand. "She's not on the schedule this morning, kiddo." His brow wrinkled. "You know how she bitches about the crap tips on the day shift. And you know, there's only so much of Jenna's bitching any one man can stand."

"Yeah." Sandy forced a laugh. It didn't even sound like her voice.

"There something wrong, Sandy?"

Monte only called her Sandy when he was worried. Like that time he gave her a talk about staying away from strangers as if she'd been five years old. There had been a lot about puppies and candy. Totally useless and totally sweet.

"I can't reach her, that's all. Her phone's probably dead or something," Sandy said. "I just thought I'd check here for her."

"Hmm." Monte narrowed his eyes, then ran his tongue around the inside of his cheek. His antennae were already up. He waved Dominic over. "Hey, Dom, you seen Jenna today?"

Dom shook his head, his fleshy cheeks trembling. He looked worried, too. "No, why, Pop?"

Dom and Monte knew Jenna was messed up. Lots of people did. It didn't take a genius to figure that out. But they were the only men in her life who'd never tried to take advantage of it.

"I'm sure she'll be home soon," Sandy said. "But I— Our landlord called and this thing came up and I need to ask her something." That was almost sort of true, and it sounded a lot better than them getting thrown out on their asses.

"The last time I saw her was at close last night," Dom said.

"Did she say where she was headed?" Monte asked.

"Nah, she was talking to some friend of hers," Dom said. "I told her she could cut out a few minutes early."

Dom was being polite. Most of Jenna's "friends" were the kind she took home for only a night. But there was a chance Sandy could track him down, whoever he was. "What did he look like?" she asked.

"*She*, not he," Dom said. "And I didn't look at her real close." Which meant she wasn't pretty. "You could try asking Laurie. She was in last night. I saw her talk to them for a minute."

Laurie, a senior at Ridgedale University, was the only student who worked at Blondie's. Laurie came from nothing, needed the job to pay for tuition. So far, it was taking her a couple extra years to make it through. She was twenty-three and a few credits away from graduating, but she swore she would. Sandy believed her, and it gave her hope. Laurie was proving it could be done even when you started at less than zero. Laurie lived in an apartment a few blocks away with her roommate, Rose, who was in Blondie's all the time, even lately, when she was super-pregnant. People gave her crap about it—pregnant and in a bar—never bothering to notice that all Rose ever drank was water.

"Okay, thanks," Sandy said. "If you see Jenna, could you tell her to call me?"

"Of course we will, kiddo," Monte said. "And if she doesn't turn up soon, you come back here, okay? We'll help you find her."

"Okay," Sandy said, though she already knew she wouldn't. Asking for help never ended up being worth the humiliation.

As Sandy headed for the door, she got another text—not from Jenna. But at least it wasn't from Hannah. It was Aidan. *Meet up after lunch?*

Don't you have class? Sandy wrote back.

Nah, that's in the fuck-it bucket.

That bad?

Worse. Come on. Hang out with me. I'll let you share my bucket.

Sandy laughed a little. Even with everything else—Jenna being MIA, getting kicked out of their apartment, and, well, that most-fucked-up thing she was working real hard to forget—Aidan had made Sandy laugh. That was why she liked him so much. It was right after Sandy met Aidan that she'd started thinking about tomorrow and even the day after that. It was a fucking risk for sure. But it was nicer than she'd thought it would be.

Not like Sandy and Aidan were Romeo and Juliet or some shit. Sometimes it even felt like there was this huge hidden canyon between them. Like one wrong step to the left and one of them would disappear forever. Because it was one thing when your fuck-it bucket was filled with stupid, worthless crap like Sandy's, but if she'd had even a quarter of everything Aidan did—the house, the money, the perfect future—she wouldn't have ever joked about trashing it.

Sandy had no idea how different their lives were until she went over to Aidan's house for the first time. It was like not knowing you'd stumbled into a foreign country until you couldn't understand a fucking word.

"Come back to bed," Aidan had said that day.

He was lying naked on the bed, hands tucked behind his head against the pillow, a woven bracelet on his wrist and a faint tan, both souvenirs from his family's summer in Nantucket. He was watching Sandy walk around his room in just her panties and his plaid shirt. She was checking out all his fancy kid stuff: trophies for basketball, swimming, tennis, the books on his shelves, the pictures and certificates tacked up on his bulletin board.

"Super-sporty, huh?" she asked, like it was something he should be ashamed of.

Really, she was jealous. Ever since she'd bought her bike at the Salvation Army and had it tuned up, Sandy had seen this glimmer of what might have been. She was fast as shit on that bike. And strong. And that was without any training or the right kind of gear. Who knew what she could have been if she'd had all the opportunities that Aidan did? And there he was, shitting on them. She reached forward to finger a frequent-customer card from Scoops, the local ice cream shop, tacked to Aidan's bulletin board. It was half filled with stamps but faded and wrinkled. "Really holding out for that free cone, huh?" Sandy asked.

Her eyes moved on to a postcard from Barcelona signed *Much Love, Aunt Eileen*, and three pictures of some boys jumping off a dock into a lake, then huddled in a smiley pile under a bunch of towels. Aidan was in the center, with the biggest smile of all.

"My dad and I go there when he visits," Aidan said. His voice sounded weird. Weird enough that Sandy turned to look at him, but he was staring up at the ceiling. "It's been a while."

"Oh, that sucks," Sandy said. And now she felt like an asshole.

She wasn't trying to make Aidan feel bad about his deadbeat dad. She could be too casual about dads in general. It was because she'd never had one of her own. He'd been a marine Jenna had dated for a few months before he died in a car accident on his way back to his base. Jenna didn't find out she was pregnant until after the funeral.

"Whatever," Aidan said. "Fuck him."

"Yeah," Sandy said. She wanted to make it better, but she had no idea how. "Listen, I should go. Your mom's going to be home soon."

"Whatever. Fuck her, too."

"Easy for you to say. I'm the one she'll bitch-slap."

But it wasn't what Aidan's mom would *do* that worried Sandy. It was the way she'd look at her. Like she was a piece of shit. People looked at Sandy that way a lot. That included the men who wanted to fuck her and the women who wanted her to go fuck herself. Hard to say which was worse.

"Why do you care what she thinks?" Aidan said.

"Right, and you don't? Seems like you want me to stick around just to piss her off." Sandy hoped that wasn't what Aidan was doing. She'd been trying to stop herself, but she'd already started liking him. "Tell me something. What the hell's so bad about all of this?"

Aidan had surveyed his room for a minute. "Looks can be deceiving," he'd said finally, his face serious when he turned back to her. "You should know that better than anybody."

Sandy read Aidan's text again. He wanted to meet, but seeing him wasn't what she needed right now, no matter how much easier it would have been to pretend that it was.

Stay in class, Sandy wrote back. *Text me when you're done.*

"Terrible, isn't it?" someone said.

When Sandy looked up from her phone, the guy with the fancy watch was looking at her, his brown eyes catching the light from the front windows. He wasn't as young as she'd thought, but she'd been right that he was good-looking. In a dickhead kind of way. The look on his face as he stared at Sandy made her want to take a shower. "What did you say?" she asked.

"I said it's terrible, isn't it," he repeated, nodding toward the TV over the bar.

Sandy looked up. Police cars on the midday news. Maybe a car accident? Sandy told Jenna all the time not to drive when she'd been drinking, but she did it anyway. Jenna did so many dangerous things. And their car was such a piece of shit. The brakes had been making this fucked-up noise for weeks, and they didn't have the money to get them fixed.

"You need something else, friend?" Monte asked, appearing out of nowhere.

He didn't like strange guys talking to Sandy. Anytime anyone tried to chat her up in Blondie's, Monte would turn up like magic. That was usually enough. He was a huge guy. He had a way of scaring people away without saying a word.

The dickhead seemed to get the message loud and clear. He held up his hands and ducked his head. "I'm good, thanks," he said. "I was just about to leave."

Sandy turned back to the TV, to the police cars in front of all those tall trees. Suddenly, the camera panned backward to the Essex Bridge. And Sandy felt the earth beneath her give way. She wrapped her hands around the brass bar rail to steady herself. "What happened, Monte?" she asked.

"Ah, they found a baby in the woods up near Cedar Creek." Monte looked up at the TV and shook his head. "Poor thing. The world is filled with goddamn animals. That's why you got to be careful, kiddo. Like I told you."

"Hey, Pop!" Dom called to him from the other side of the bar. "Come here for a sec."

"You call us if you need anything, kiddo," Monte said, then glanced in the direction of the dickhead. "You know you're like a daughter to us. No, you *are* a daughter to us. And we take care of family."

"Thanks," Sandy managed, her eyes moving back to the TV as soon as Monte headed back to the other end of the bar. She wanted someone to turn the volume up. Wanted to hear exactly what they were saying. The dickhead said something once Monte was out of earshot, something Sandy caught only a piece of: "like her."

When Sandy looked away from the TV, he was swallowing the last of his beer and dropping some money on the bar. Finally, he pushed himself off the stool, straightening his jacket as he stood. "I guess I *should* be going," he said to no one in particular.

"What did you just say?" Sandy asked, wondering if she'd imagined it.

"That I've got to be going."

"No, what did you say before?"

"Oh, that." He took a step closer to Sandy, then leaned in to whisper in her ear. "You look just like Jenna."

Frat Chat

Here are the chatters in your area. Be kind, follow the rules, and enjoy the ride! And if you don't know what the rules are: READ THEM FIRST! You must be 18 to Chat with the Frat.

I think it's Sadie Cresh. She's been getting seriously round in the belly.

Fat, I didn't even think of that. Why don't they just round up all the fat girls and test them or something?

1 reply
Because there ARE too many!

What about Ellie Richards and Jonathan Strong? They'd definitely kill a baby before they'd risk not going to Harvard together.

2 replies
Jonathan Strong is totally gay.
He grabbed my ass in the locker room.

You guys, it's Harry Trumble with the candlestick in his mom's room. Have you seen her? She's hot as shit.

You are all disgusting pigs.

3 replies
I agree. I can't believe I know you people.
Pretentious bitch.

You are some sick shits. Funny as hell but sick as shit.

You know you're supposed to be in COLLEGE to be on this thing.

1 reply
Fuck off, loser.

I think it was Aidan Ronan. His baby. He killed it.

9 replies
I heard he did some fucked-up shit in his old school.

And have you seen his mom? I heard she fucks everybody. That probably messed him up.

I saw him last week with some skanky bitch downtown.

I've seen him with her, too. Total crack ho.

I heard he once tried to kill his little brother.

I heard that, too. Choked him so hard he had to go to the hospital.

That's bullshit. He'd be in jail.

Not bullshit. His parents lie for him all the time.

I heard he got kicked out of St. Paul's for bringing a hunting knife to school.

MOLLY
APRIL 17, 2013

Justin and I had our first argument today. The first since we lost the baby. It was stupid, about dinner plans for our anniversary that I don't even care about.

Lost the baby. Lost the baby. Lost the baby. I'm supposed to keep writing that in here. Not supposed to—Dr. Zomer never tells me what I'm "supposed" to do. But she says I need to normalize the experience.

But how to make killing your own baby normal? Because I know what happened is my fault. Who else's fault could it be? I was the one who was supposed to keep track of how often she was moving. I was the one who was supposed to notice the second she stopped.

And I didn't. I didn't notice a thing. And I let myself get so stressed out the night before. That whole weekend. So stupid when I think about it now. The doctor made a point of telling me that none of that mattered. That it wasn't my being upset that made her heart stop.

But how can they know that for sure when they don't know why it DID stop?

The saddest part about my fight today with Justin was how relieved he seemed. So happy to have a regular old fight. Like the ones we had before. Before we lost the baby, before we had Ella, before there was even really an us. Because that's where we are: a place where a fight is the best hope we've got.

Molly

When I arrived at Ridgedale University's main administration building, I spotted Deckler, the Campus Safety officer from down at the creek. He still looked weirdly muscular, now in a long-sleeved lemon-yellow spandex shirt and the same snug black bike shorts. He was standing next to the building's front steps, hands on his hips, like he'd been expecting me. Or maybe he'd just been expecting someone like me. There were several news vans parked around the green, and I'd seen notepad-carrying people milling around in town, pointedly avoiding eye contact. Like if they pretended they were the only one covering the story, they'd beat everyone to the headline-grabbing punch. Surely this was only the beginning. How big the story became depended entirely on how salacious the details.

"I wondered when you'd get here," Deckler said.

"Oh, hi," I said, hoping I sounded glad to see him even though I was not. "Deckler, right?"

"Yes, Molly Sanderson from the *Ridgedale Reader*," he said in this odd robotic way that was maybe supposed to be funny but was extremely creepy.

"Yes, that's right." I forced myself to smile. "That's me, Molly Sanderson. And what did you mean that you wondered when I'd get here?"

He shrugged. "You're a reporter who's going to cover all her bases. Campus property and all that."

That wasn't it. He'd meant something else that he wished he hadn't hinted at. He was wrong anyway. Coming to campus hadn't been my idea. Erik had suggested it after I'd updated him about Rose.

Univ. student in the hospital. New mother. Hospital refusing release, I typed away, wanting to tell someone, not fully considering the implications. *Might be related.*

Okay, came Erik's quick reply. *Follow up on campus. Get her story. Try dean of students. He usually comments without referring to Communications Department.*

As a reporter who'd stumbled onto a lead, I knew that was the natural thing to do: follow up. But I did feel conflicted. It had been easy to say that I wanted to find out what had happened to the baby, to get at the truth. But what if that truth implicated the baby's mother? And what if she'd been one of those desperate terrified women I knew all about? Not to mention that it felt wrong pointing a finger at Rose when I didn't know for sure that she was an official police suspect. That was one thing the arts beat had going for it: no moral complications.

But asking a couple questions about Rose on campus was hardly the same thing as running a headline calling her a baby killer. It seemed likely that the police already knew about her, and soon others would, too, including the press. I could at least poke around, see what there was to find out, and commit to reporting whatever it was, if and when the time came, with great care.

"I'm surprised they let you leave the creek," I said, trying for friendly chitchat with Deckler, even though there was something about him—the weirdly intense way he had of looking at me, perhaps—that made me genuinely uncomfortable. "With all that ground to cover, I'd think they'd want every available set of hands."

"*Let* me leave?" Deckler asked. "*I'm* surprised they didn't run me over with one of their 'cruisers.' " His fingers hooked the air dismissively. In the Ridgedale Police's defense, I found it hard to take Deckler seriously, with that baby face and tight bike-cop outfit.

"Sounds like you don't think much of the local authorities."

Deckler shrugged. "It's a club, and some of them have been in it a long time." He stared at me pointedly. "They treat all of us on campus like we're second-class citizens, even though we've had the same training and passed the same damn tests. Plus, we get paid about twice as much and get free housing."

"Sounds like a good deal to me." *So why do you seem so pissed off about it?*

"It is," Deckler said, eyeing me like he was trying to figure out if I was mocking him.

"Okay, well." I took a step past him toward the building. "The dean of students' office is in here, right?"

"Why?" Deckler asked protectively.

Why, indeed. I shouldn't have mentioned where I was going. It had been something to say, an excuse to leave. "I have some questions about a former student."

"Who?"

Why did I keep saying things that led to more questions? I wanted to tell Deckler that it was none of his business, but there was a chance I might need his cooperation later. A change of subject seemed a better tactic than confrontation. "Actually, there's something I was hoping I could clarify with you first."

"Oh yeah?" Deckler looked intrigued. "What's that?"

"You mentioned there were some crimes that you dealt with entirely on campus. Did you mean they don't get reported to the local police?"

I suspected whatever gap there was between Steve's assertion that all crime on campus got reported to the Ridgedale Police and Deckler's implication that the opposite was true had everything to do with the enormous chip on Deckler's shoulder. But I did wonder

whether Rose Gowan, whose last name Stella had given me somewhat reluctantly, could have been sexually assaulted by the father
of her baby—maybe *the* baby—and whether Campus Safety would
have a record of it even though the police did not. Ridgedale certainly wouldn't be the first university to prioritize the confidentiality
of an accused student over a full and fair investigation.

"Life on campus can be complicated that's all. These are all just
kids," he said, and with this look like I was supposed to get what he
meant. "But if you want details about our procedures, you'll have to
talk to our director."

"You must know what happens when you're the reporting officer,
though. From what you said before, it sounded like there are all sorts
of procedures in place. Is one of those calling the local police?"

Deckler narrowed his eyes at me. "Listen, I don't know what
you're looking for, but if you think I'm going to be the one to start
speaking on behalf of the university about a thing like this, then
you must think I'm as dumb as Ridgedale's finest do."

Guess where I am? I texted Justin as I waited inside the dean of
students' suite for his bulldog of a secretary to see whether he was
available. It had occurred to me that I should have warned Justin
that I was on campus, headed to speak with the dean of students, or
at least trying to. Justin didn't report to him, but this dean probably
had a close relationship with the dean of faculty and the university
president, both of whom Justin did report to.

There was no response to my text. No ellipses signaling an answer
on its way, either. I checked the time. I was pretty sure Justin was
in the middle of office hours. If he was in a meeting with an advisee,
he'd never notice his phone.

I tried again. *On campus. Interviewing dean of students.* Waited. Still
no answer.

"Ms. Sanderson? I was told you wanted to speak with me?" When I looked up from my phone, there was a long-haired man standing in front of me in a sport jacket. He had a hand outstretched. "I'm Thomas Price, the dean of students."

He was *much* more attractive and younger than I'd been anticipating. Dashing, that's how I would have described him. My thinking that would have made Justin gag. He didn't like Thomas Price very much. He'd mentioned that more than once. Seeing Price, I understood why. In general, Justin wasn't fond of dashing men, found them too precious and pretentious. In addition to being good-looking, Thomas Price had an air of easy sophistication—an excess of money and education that probably went back for generations. I always thought Justin and his family were so fancy until I met someone like Price, who was actually fancy.

"Yes, thank you so much for seeing me." I reached out to shake his hand. "I imagine you're incredibly busy."

"You are correct," he said with a warm but tired smile. He wasn't wearing a wedding band. I felt a guilty thrill that I'd noticed. It had been a long time since I'd been capable of registering such a thing. Price waved me toward his office, checking his watch: large and silver and expensive. "I have a meeting soon, but I have a few minutes."

Thomas Price's office was spacious and bright, a large, paned window filling most of the back wall. Through it was a view of the athletic center and the hospital beyond and, in the very distance, the woods that led to Essex Bridge.

"Please, have a seat." He pointed toward two red wing-back chairs facing his desk.

"Thank you," I said, admiring the floor-to-ceiling shelves of books. "Your library is amazing."

"And thank you for not immediately dispensing with common courtesy. You're not the first reporter I've spoken with today, but you are certainly the most pleasant," he said as he sat behind his beautiful mahogany desk. "I suppose it's the nature of this situation, but I don't recall reporters ever being this aggressive. You wouldn't believe the number of people who have threatened to park themselves on campus if they don't get answers immediately. Answers we don't have. Answers I don't believe anyone has yet. In any case, if even a small fraction make good on their threats, it will be quite crowded around here."

"Well, I bet none of the other reporters has a husband who's a brand-new professor here," I said. "Having your spouse's livelihood hanging in the balance tends to encourage good behavior."

"Sanderson, of course," Price said, pressing a palm to his forehead. "You're Justin's wife, right? He told me that you were going to be working at the *Ridgedale Reader*. Welcome to town. I know you weren't convinced about leaving the city—and that's understandable—but Ridgedale is a wonderful place to live. I've only been back for a few years, but I also lived here when I was in high school; my father was a professor in the English Department. I apologize for not making the connection immediately. It's been an extremely long day."

"All the more reason for me not to take up too much of your time."

"Yes, the university president just called to summon a group of us to discuss the problem of the police being on university property." Thomas Price took a deep breath, his body sinking into the chair as he rubbed his hands over his face like someone trying to rouse himself from sleep. He seemed so genuinely overwhelmed that I felt disarmed by the intimacy it had given our conversation. "How exactly he expects *us* to make this very big, very bad problem go away is another matter entirely."

"That sounds stressful." And it did, but the words came out awkward, canned.

"Stressful, indeed." Price smiled at me, holding eye contact for an extra beat as if he were noticing something for the first time. What was it? That I was pretty? Once upon a time, men had often responded to me that way. Maybe they had never stopped even though I'd certainly stopped noticing. Price added, "I'm sorry, here I am complaining, and you came to ask me questions."

"There was a student here named Rose Gowan," I said, stumbling to get back to the reason I'd come. "Do you know why she withdrew this past year?"

He frowned. "This is connected to the baby?"

"It's part of a broader set of circumstances we're investigating."

Good. That didn't expose Rose unnecessarily, and it wasn't a lie. It was simply what I hoped would be true.

"In other words, you don't plan to tell me?" he asked, eyes locked on mine.

"No, I don't." I held his stare.

"Fair enough," he said, smiling a little, as if enjoying our push-and-pull. "I suppose that would be inappropriate. I'm afraid it would also be inappropriate for me to answer." Thomas Price narrowed his eyes, considering, then turned to face his computer. "But because you have been so nice, and because you are part of the university family, as it were, let me see what I can find out for you here." He turned to point a finger at me. "This is off the record, however. I'll claim you broke into my office and rifled through my files before I admit to having told you."

"Understood," I said. Erik probably wouldn't have agreed to "off the record." But what choice did I have?

We sat in silence for a minute as Price clicked through various screens on his computer. "Ah, here it is. VW," he said finally. "Voluntary withdraw. That doesn't tell you much, I'm afraid; it could be for personal reasons, socioeconomic, almost anything. But it does mean that Ms. Gowan would be welcome back at Ridgedale University anytime. She wasn't asked to depart for academic or behavioral reasons."

"And is there any record of her filing any complaints against another student?" I asked.

"Not here," Price said. "But there wouldn't be. This is solely her academic record. Complaints like that are handled confidentially. The security office would have those records, not that they should be disclosing them."

I waited for him to ask why I wanted to know. He didn't. Instead, he looked down at his watch. "And now, unfortunately, our time is up. I assure you, I'd much rather stay and chat with you, but the president is expecting me." He held my stare again, long enough that I felt another little twinge. He was . . . well, not quite flirting—noticing me. Price smiled almost bashfully, as though he knew I'd noticed his noticing. "Feel free to send an email with more questions."

Respectful, too. Not come *see* me again. Because that would be inappropriate. He knew I was married.

"I definitely will. Thank you," I said as he showed me out.

"Good," he said. When he shook my hand, he held it for an extra second. "And send my best to Justin. The three of us should get together. I used to live in the city, too. We could reminisce."

When I came out, Deckler was waiting for me in the hall.

"The director of Campus Safety will see you now," he said, as if we'd had a whole conversation about my wanting that very thing. "Ben LaForde. His office is right there."

"Meet with me about what?"

Deckler was blocking my way, pointing to an office a few doors down from Price's. I did need to speak to LaForde. Still, I had the distinct impression that I was being sent to the principal's office.

"You had questions about campus crime reporting. He's the one who should answer those. He's waiting for you."

Indeed, Ben LaForde seemed to be. He jumped right up when I peeked in his open door. A small man in his sixties with a thick head of salt-and-a-little-pepper hair and a trim matching mustache, he made his way over with an outstretched hand. He had a decidedly unfancy way about him.

"You must be Ms. Sanderson," LaForde said. "Come, have a seat. Deckler said you had some questions for me?"

"I just wanted to confirm the university's procedure when there's a crime on campus, particularly how these crimes are reported to the local police."

I braced myself for a defensive "Why?" or "What are you suggesting?" But LaForde's face remained relaxed.

"When the victim comes to us?" he asked, as though he wanted to be sure he'd gotten the question right so he could be as helpful as possible. "Because they can go directly to the police if they want. That's always their right. They'll come to us if they want the incident reported as a disciplinary violation in addition to or instead of a crime. Students are entitled to confidentiality, however. We report the crime to the police as a courtesy, but we don't disclose the students involved. In the case of a sexual assault, no such disclosure would be made at all unless a student requested it."

"'As a courtesy' sounds as though it isn't legally required."

"It's not mandated, but we do typically let the Ridgedale Police know about crimes on campus in real time. Can I promise that it happens with every single missing-iPhone report that later turns out not to be a theft? No, and I'm sure the local police wouldn't want that." The procedure sounded a lot more vague than he was making it out to be. "There are federal reporting requirements as well. Some things are so serious that we also handle them as a disciplinary violation even if they were only reported to the police. And in some circumstances, the police are going to get involved regardless of what we do—like this situation with the baby. Confidentiality, though, is always critical. Students need to feel protected."

Especially the guilty ones, I wanted to add, but didn't.

"There was another death on that same part of campus years ago, is that right?" I asked instead. It was too early to be getting that aggressive no matter how much I would have liked to. "A high school student?"

He shook his head. "It was a real tragedy. An accident, not a murder, just to be clear, but a terrible coincidence nonetheless. A shame for the boy's parents if that gets dragged back up."

"Did campus police participate in the investigation?"

He nodded. "Teenagers drinking. It's always a recipe for disaster." He paused, then reached behind him and picked up a pamphlet, slid it across the desk toward me. "If you want to know more about our procedures, they're all set out in the university charter, which is a matter of public record. Not sure you want to comb through all that. This booklet here is what we give to students; it'll probably tell you everything you need. But the two-minute version is that there is an involved procedure—an investigation, a hearing before a panel, a verdict—we call it a finding. Finding has to be by majority."

"Who's on the panel?"

"Five people appointed by the dean of students. Two professors, one administrator—which would be me at the moment—and two students. We've all gone through extensive screening and sensitivity training. The students change every year. The professors do five-year stints. Right now that's Miles Cooper, who's an English professor, and Maggie Capitol, biology. They're both at the end of their five-year tenure. The dean of students presides."

"And who investigates complaints?"

"Campus Safety officers."

"Like Deckler?"

"Yes." LaForde's face tightened at the mention of Deckler. "Among others. There are ten officers on staff, plus supervisors. It's all in the pamphlet."

"Did a student named Rose Gowan ever make a complaint of any kind?"

"Does this have something to do with the baby?"

Lie. This time there was no question in my mind. "No," I said firmly. "It doesn't."

"Oh." He frowned and looked confused, but also concerned. "Regardless, Ms. Sanderson, I can't comment on a specific student's complaints. I'd like to be helpful, but my hands are tied. Confidentiality, I'm sure you understand. The only thing I'd be able to respond to would be a subpoena. And you'd know better than me, but I'm not sure they're in the business of giving those out to reporters."

When I came out of LaForde's office, I caught a glimpse of Deckler, some distance down the hall. He was just standing there, staring in my direction, like he was waiting to see me again. I waved when he kept on staring, then darted for the door, hoping I could avoid him. I didn't slow down until I was walking through the front gates of the university.

On the sidewalk, I pulled out my phone to check how much time I had before I needed to pick up Ella. A small scrap of paper fluttered to the ground—Justin's note. I'd forgotten to read it after feeling it in my coat pocket when I was in Steve's office. I knelt to pick it up, and sure enough, there was Justin's jagged script.

In order that two imperfect souls might touch perfection. E. M. Forster

I smoothed my fingers over the words, feeling the grooves Justin's pen had left in the paper. He must have slipped it into my pocket that morning before I left the house, or maybe the night before. Did he wonder why I hadn't mentioned it at the Black Cat? Did he think I'd read it and not cared? I wouldn't have said that I needed one of Justin's notes right then, but it suddenly felt like the only reason I was breathing.

I was going to send Justin a text, thanking him for the note, when I checked the time: past two thirty, barely enough time to pick up

Ella. I also had an unread text from Stella, sent a half hour earlier. *You were right*, it read. *Police are holding Rose for questioning! Call me ASAP!*

Tuesdays were always a light day at school pickup because many of the students went on to an after-school swimming program. Barbara and Stella weren't there, only a dozen or so parents whom I knew by sight but not by name. Waiting in the hallway for Rhea to finish the afternoon meeting, I glimpsed Ella through the little window in the door. She was sitting in the circle with her hand raised, still dressed in her bright green outfit, eyes eager and wide. Whatever Ella said when she was finally called on made Rhea clap her hands and laugh loudly, which sent Ella into a fit of giggles.

She *was* a happy little girl. Justin was right. However much I had failed her in my darkest moments, I must have done something right.

"Mommy!" Ella shouted when Rhea opened the classroom door.

I crouched down as she ran at me full speed, jumping hard into my open arms. I buried my face in her mass of loopy curls and squeezed. She smelled like blueberry shampoo.

"Hi, sweetheart," I said. "How was the show?"

"It was great, Mommy!" I waited a beat for the *but*—but you weren't here, but I missed you, but I was sad. Instead she just squeezed me back, so hard it was difficult to breathe. "I'm so glad to see you!"

"Me, too, Peanut." I took a deep breath. Already I felt so much better, the thoughts that had been weighing on me—the baby, Rose, Stella, my *other* baby—already floating up and away as if someone had pushed open a vent. "How about you and I go to Scoops and get some ice cream?"

It was past four by the time Ella and I arrived at Ridgedale's picture-perfect ice cream shop, which sat on a sunny, tree-lined stretch facing Franklin Street and the university. Scoops had homemade flavors like Cocoa Conniption and Strawberry Slalom, and kids could churn their own ice cream on Saturdays using the shop's famed bicycle ice cream maker. It was the kind of magical place I couldn't have imagined as a child.

"What do you want, Ella?" I would have bought her everything in that store if she'd promised to keep on smiling.

"Vanilla!" Ella shouted like she'd never heard of a more thrilling flavor in her entire life. "In a cone!"

"*Just* vanilla?" I laughed. "Are you sure? No sprinkles, nothing?"

"Nope," she said, rocking back on her heels as she gripped the edge of the counter. "Vanilla is the best!"

As the sweet-faced teenage girl behind the counter set to work digging out the ice cream, I put my hand on Ella's head, marveling at how perfectly it still fit in my palm. Through the etched front window, the late-afternoon sun lit up the university gold. The moment was so beautiful and perfect—Ella and the ice cream and the sun. But it didn't feel like it belonged to me, not in any permanent sense. Happy was my adopted country, not my native land. I was still bracing to be expelled without warning.

I was about to turn from the window when I saw Steve Carlson walking quickly in the direction of the station. He nodded to someone going the other way, but it wasn't until they'd exchanged brisk pleasantries that I realized the other man was Thomas Price. Neither seemed to want a real chat, understandable under the circumstances. Depending on how things progressed, they could easily be forced to turn against each other.

"Here you go," said the girl behind the counter, handing a wide-eyed Ella her cone and winking at her. "I'm with you, vanilla is the best."

We found our way to a bench in front of the shop, where Ella took a huge bite of ice cream with her teeth, which made me shiver. As we snuggled against each other, I felt my phone buzz in my pocket. A voicemail, not a text. And from a number that I didn't recognize.

I tapped on the message and put the phone to my ear, twisting my fingers through Ella's curls as she pumped her legs back and forth under the bench like she was reaching for extra height on a swing.

"Molly Sanderson, this is Officer Deckler," the message began. "Just checking to be sure you got everything you needed on campus today." Deckler paused, breathed loudly into the phone. My stomach tightened. How did he even have my number? Had he looked it up in Justin's file? "If you, you know, have other questions, you can, um, call me. This is my cell. Okay, bye."

The second part of the message had been rushed and nervous, like he'd realized halfway through that he shouldn't have called. And he was right. Deckler was hovering like someone with something to hide.

"Mommy?" Ella asked as I slipped the phone back in my pocket. She paused to take another lick.

"What, sweetheart?"

"What's a slut?"

I coughed, choking on my own saliva. "My God, Ella, where did you hear that word?"

"From Will," she said with a shrug as she took another bite. Like where she'd heard it was the least interesting part and also should have been obvious. "His mom said it to Aidan."

"She called Aidan a slut?"

Stella was bound to lose it on Aidan eventually—it was hard to blame her. But it was weird that she hadn't mentioned some big fight. Stella confessed compulsively to me. Why not this? Had the argument escalated further? Had something even worse happened, something so terrible that Stella didn't want even me to know?

"Come on, Mommy. Tell me."

"Tell you what?"

"What's a slut?"

"Oh, Ella," I said, trying not to sound too horrified. But the way the word kept popping out of her innocent little mouth was making me feel sick. "Please don't say that again. It's not a nice word."

"Then why did Will's mommy say it?"

"Oh, maybe she was really tired when she said it to Aidan," I offered. "People sometimes say things that aren't very nice when they're tired."

"You never do that. And she didn't call *Aidan* a slut, Mommy," Ella went on, saying it again as if I hadn't just asked her to stop. She was focused on licking the edges of her cone, catching the drips. "She called his *girlfriend* a slut."

A girlfriend? I'd heard about Aidan's drinking and drugs and stealing money. I'd heard about the time he got arrested and how Stella fantasized about leaving him in jail. These were not good things that Stella had told me, and yet she had done so willingly. Now she was leaving out something innocent, like Aidan having a girlfriend? Why? *Who* was the girlfriend?

"And then she broke his phone," Ella added.

"Stella broke Aidan's phone?"

"Boom!" Ella imitated an explosion with her chubby little hands. "That's what Will says. But when Daddy's phone broke, it didn't blow up like that. I think Will is lying. He lies a lot."

Except Stella *had* complained—with great annoyance—about having to replace Aidan's broken phone. "What's Aidan's girlfriend's name?"

Ella shrugged. "Will calls her the flower girl," she said, then rolled her eyes. "But I know that's not her *real* name. No one's named that. He's lying about that, too."

Rose: the flower girl.

RIDGEDALE READER

ONLINE EDITION

March 17, 2015, 5:03 p.m.

Baby's Cause of Death Still Unknown

BY MOLLY SANDERSON

The medical examiner has declined to comment on the cause of death of the female infant found at the Essex Bridge. However, police have confirmed that the condition of the infant's body makes it impossible to rule out homicide at this time.

Once again, the Ridgedale Police Department asks that anyone with information regarding the infant's identity or cause of death contact their office as soon as possible at 888-526-1899.

COMMENTS:

Mae Koeler
37 min ago
I have a friend who works in admin at the University Hospital. She said that there's some woman up there who the police were talking to about her missing baby.

Eastern Elijah
36 min ago
Some woman with a missing baby? Are you serious? Isn't that exactly the kind of the thing the police should be telling us?

Darren C.

30 min ago

Some university kids trashed my car when it was parked overnight on Franklin Avenue last week. I complained to campus security: total runaround. It's like the NSA over there—everything is one giant cover-up.

Cara Twin

15 min ago

I agree. I have a friend whose son went to Ridgedale and he said that break-ins were rampant on campus. I don't know if they're ever reported to the police. Just because they haven't told the police doesn't mean the university doesn't know what happened.

246Barry

12 min ago

YOU'RE NOT GETTING ANY WARMER
OPEN YOUR EYES AND FIND HIM
BEFORE IT'S TOO LATE

James R.

10 min ago

Knock it off, 246Barry. Everyone's had enough of you. You better hope we don't find out who you are. People in this town don't take harassment lightly.

Colleen M.

8 min ago

What is WRONG with you 246Barry? If you actually knew something you'd go to the POLICE. You don't, so leave us alone.

JENNA

The Captain sat with me during lunch! I was eating out in the courtyard with Tiffany and Stephanie when he came out all by himself. And like he was LOOKING for me!

Thank God Steph and Tiff took off when he came. They did it real subtle, though, like they just had somewhere to be.

They still think the Captain is a dick and that he's fucking with me. But now that they've said their piece, they're not going to stand in my way. Because, unlike my parents, those girls actually care about me.

All my parents have ever cared about is "bettering themselves." Especially now that my dad is the brand-new night manager of the Stanton Hotel, which my mom acts like is the same as president of the United States. And after my mom got that office job at her church? Forget about it. We've got to be this picture-perfect family so we can keep "getting somewhere in the community."

Or really, I've got to be perfect. Because my parents already think they are. And if their idea of me being perfect—quiet, girlie, sweet (none of which I am)—makes me feel like crap? Oh well, too bad so sad for me.

But the Captain doesn't judge people just on the surface like that. Because he isn't pretending to be something he's not.

After Tiff and Stephanie were gone, the Captain and I talked for a while. He said his history paper was kicking his ass, which is kind of hard to believe considering how smart he is. I liked that he talked to me about school. Guys always think that all I can talk about is getting wasted and maybe music or something. But I'm interested in lots of things and it shows how smart the Captain is that he can tell I'm pretty damn smart myself.

And that was it. For a whole thirty minutes. Nice, sweet. And at the end the Captain said: Good talking to you. See you around.

I hope that means soon.

Barbara

"Hello?" Barbara called for the kids as she stepped inside.

No one answered—no Hannah, no Cole. But they weren't technically late yet. Hannah picked up Cole on Tuesdays after swimming,
and they'd be even later because Barbara hadn't canceled his stupid
playdate with Will afterward. Really, she should have brought Cole
home when *The Very Hungry Caterpillar* was finished. She'd been
right there, it would have been easy enough to do. It wasn't as if he
would have missed something critical. He was only in kindergarten.
But Cole loved school, and he loved routine. He would have been
upset about leaving without some kind of explanation. It seemed
absurd now, but Barbara had also been worried about Cole being
disappointed—missing swimming, missing his playdate. That had
seemed so much more important a few hours ago. It had felt like the
only thing that mattered.

Barbara looked out the kitchen windows toward the row of bare
trees ringing the small backyard. The sun had already sunk out of
sight, a wide swath of pinks and purples marking the place where it
had gone. It would be dark before long.

"I'm sure Cole's fine," Steve had said when she'd called him from
the Ridgedale Elementary School parking lot after her meeting with
Rhea and after she'd had to return an hour later to suffer through
The Very Hungry Caterpillar. "Rhea means well, no doubt. But that
doesn't mean she's right. All kids act funny sometimes. Even the
totally normal ones are mostly weirdos."

Steve was trying to lighten things up, but it was hard not to feel like he was also searching for the fastest way off the phone, so he could get back to what he really cared about: work. "I hope you're right," Barbara had said, not persuaded in the least.

"I'm sorry, Barb, but can we talk more about Cole when I get home? I've got my hands full here at the moment."

After what had happened to that poor baby, she could hardly blame Steve for being distracted; surely he was overwhelmed by the investigation. Assuming that's where his mind really was. And Barbara refused to let herself speculate about the alternatives. Nothing good would come of it.

"Sure, I guess, okay," she'd said, trying to be supportive. It was the right thing to do. Even though she really wanted to beg Steve to come right away. "But when will you be home?"

"As soon as I can. But really, Barb, try not to worry about Cole," Steve had said. "He'll be fine. He's a tough nut, just like his mom."

Finally, Barbara heard a key in the side door.

"Hi, guys!" she called—too cheerfully, probably—smiling wide as the door opened.

But Barbara's chest seized the second she saw them. Hannah looking stunned and pale as she clutched Cole, his face buried in the shoulder of her long Brown University sweatshirt.

"What happened?" Barbara asked, rushing over and grabbing him. "Cole, what's wrong?"

He felt leaden in Barbara's arms. He wasn't crying anymore, but from the look of the puffy little scar under his eye, he'd been outright bawling. Cole buried his face in Barbara's neck but didn't answer her.

"Hannah, what on earth happened?" Barbara snapped. She'd tried to keep the accusatory edge from her voice, but it was no use. All

Hannah had to do was pick him up. Was it that much to ask that she manage it without him getting hysterical?

"I've asked him at least a hundred times, but he won't tell me." Hannah sounded like she might cry, which was hardly helpful. "Will's mom said they were playing LEGOs and Cole just freaked out."

"Freaked out?" Barbara snapped. "Hannah, I'm sure she didn't say that."

"But she did." There were tears in Hannah's eyes now. "She said it exactly like that. That's kind of mean, isn't it? For a mom?"

Barbara took a deep breath and rocked Cole back and forth in her arms. *That's because Stella's not a regular mom*, Barbara wanted to say. *She's an oversexed narcissist who probably cares more about finding a new boyfriend than her own children.* Stella was exactly the reason Will was so out of control. Look at Will's brother, Aidan. One messed-up child could be a fluke; two was a pattern that could be traced right back to the parents.

"Oh well, I'm sure she didn't mean to say that," Barbara said, rubbing a protective hand over Cole's head. *Yes, she did, that thoughtless bitch.* "Don't worry, Hannah." *Even though you were probably too worried about pleasing Stella to stand up for your brother.* "Cole will be fine, honey. He's just tired. Now, why don't you go ahead upstairs and get started on your homework?" That way Barbara wouldn't be tempted to say something to her daughter that she truly might regret. "Dinner will be ready soon."

"Are you sure he's okay?" Hannah asked, drifting closer to Cole.

Instinctively, Barbara held him tighter, swallowing the irritation that was clogging her throat. "I'm sure, honey."

She was willing to overlook whatever role Hannah might have had in allowing Cole to get upset. But she would not tolerate her daughter getting upset herself. Sometimes all of Hannah's "sensitivities" seemed an awful lot like self-involvement.

"Your physics midterm is tomorrow, isn't it?" Barbara had Hannah's entire exam schedule committed to memory. More proof that whatever was going on with Cole wasn't some oversight on Barbara's part. She *paid attention*—it was what she did. "You need to stay focused on your classwork, Hannah. Acceptance letter or not, Cornell will look at your final grades."

"Okay," Hannah said reluctantly, like she was afraid something worse might happen the second she stepped from the room. She tried to meet eyes with Cole, but his face was still buried in Barbara's neck. "I'm sorry you're upset, Cole." She waited a second for him to look at her.

When he didn't, she finally drifted away. She was barely up the stairs when the doorbell rang.

"My goodness, now what?" Barbara singsonged into the side of Cole's head, hoping she sounded more amused than worried. She put him down on one of the kitchen chairs. "Stay here, honey. I'll be right back. Don't move."

Not that it looked like Cole was going anywhere ever again.

Barbara tried to stand taller as she headed to the front door. *Not perfect, only happy. Not perfect, only happy.* Except how was that supposed to make her feel any better, when Cole did not seem remotely happy?

Through the squares of glass beside the front door, Barbara could see her own mom, Caroline, standing on their front stoop. It was Tuesday, the day her parents joined them for dinner each week. Barbara had completely forgotten. She loved her mother dearly, but having her parents there today, of all days, wouldn't make anything easier.

Barbara forced the corners of her mouth up. "It starts with a smile!" That was Caroline's second favorite saying, right after "Not perfect, only happy." The truth only matters as much as you allow it, that was Caroline's point.

"My word, that took a long time!" Caroline called when Barbara finally opened the door. Her round cheeks looked especially rosy against her red coat, but her new chin-length hair was making them seem puffier than usual. Barbara worried that her own shorter hair-cut was doing the same thing—inflating her. Caroline shifted the casserole in her hands and pressed a squishy cheek against Barbara's much stiffer one. There was never a kiss, only the cheeks.

"How many times did you ring? I only heard it once." Barbara was already on the defensive. But she needed to relax. Not take everything so much to heart. Her mother didn't mean anything. Everything in her head just came right out of her mouth. Besides, with Caroline, reacting only served to draw attention to her most vulnerable spots. "I was with Cole in the other room."

"Let me guess. That terrible SpongeBob blotting out the world again."

"Cole doesn't watch SpongeBob, Mom," Barbara said, nipping at the bait anyway. "The TV wasn't even on. Where's Dad?"

"Oh, his back is acting up again." Caroline waved an aggravated hand. "It's all that leaning over the cars all day. I keep telling him to leave it to the boys. That's what he pays them for, and too gener-ously, I might add. But you know your father; he treats that business like some precious orchid in need of constant attention. They're *cars*, for heaven's sake."

"Well, I'm glad you made it," Barbara said, though she wished she could send her mom home to take care of her dad without of-fending her.

As Barbara turned back to the kitchen and Cole—whom she really needed to be worried about—a sudden shakiness nearly overwhelmed her. She had to press a hand against the wall to keep herself upright.

"Oh my, what's wrong, dear?" Caroline stepped closer, clutching the casserole between them. "Have you not eaten today? You know how woozy you get when you don't eat."

Barbara forced herself to take a deep breath and pushed herself up off the wall. She'd already left Cole out there too long. "I'm not hungry, Mom," she said as she headed toward the kitchen. "It's Cole. There's something— He had an off day. It's all been a little stressful. Maybe I'm just tired."

"An off day?" her mom called after her. "What on earth does that mean?"

Back in the kitchen, Barbara poured herself a glass of cold water, gulping it down, trying to ignore the way Caroline was hovering inside the kitchen door, peering at Cole.

"Well, is he hurt?" Caroline sounded concerned but a little disgusted, too. To her, physical pain was the only legitimate justification for any kind of outburst.

Barbara knelt down in front of Cole, smoothing the hair out of his eyes. He'd found a rubber band somewhere and was wearing it around his wrist, snapping it over and over against his skin. Not hard, but Barbara put one hand over the band so he'd stop, then lifted his chin with her other hand. Finally, Cole looked at her. His brown eyes, wet and pink-rimmed, glowed. Barbara wiped her thumb over his cheek, stained gray where his tears had turned playground dust to mud.

"Can you tell me what happened, Cole?" she asked. "With Will?"

Cole's lower lip started to shake. Then he squeezed his eyes shut and started to rock, clamping his hands over his ears as if blocking out some horrible sound.

"Cole, stop that!" Caroline cried, rushing closer, still with the stupid baking dish in her hands. "What on earth?"

Hands over his ears, Cole dove into the crook of Barbara's arm. She thought she might be sick. It was so awful. All of it.

Barbara wanted so badly to smack his hands down. To shout at him to stop. But she wouldn't do that to Cole. Whatever this was, it wasn't his fault. *Something* had happened to him. *Stella* and her house of horrors, that's what. Barbara took a breath and covered Cole's hands with her own, rocking him gently against her. She heard Caroline's voice in the distance, but she needed to focus on her son. And he was so stiff in her arms. It was like holding a rusted metal coil. Barbara pressed her nose into Cole's hair. At least he smelled right: of salt and sand and sweat. Like any other normal little boy. She put her lips against his clammy cheek and kept on rocking. Because Cole *was* normal, that much she knew.

"It hurt my eyes," Cole mumbled finally. "And my ears. It was hurting my ears."

"What hurt?" Barbara asked, trying to keep her voice calm and gentle. But all she wanted to do was scream. And all she could think about was how she was going to let loose on Stella. That woman could raise her children in whatever substandard fashion she saw fit, but how *dare* she let the consequences of her casual neglect injure someone else's. "Did Will do something to you, Cole?"

"It was the way he was looking at me," Cole whispered.

"For heaven's sake, *what* way he was looking at you, Cole?" Caroline shouted, angry now.

Barbara tried not to bristle. Caroline didn't mean to sound so harsh; she lost her patience when she was worried. She couldn't help it. And Cole did look and sound absolutely crazy.

"How was Will looking at you, Cole?" Barbara asked him quietly.

He pulled back to look at her. Eye contact was progress. But then Cole shook his head. "Not Will." Great. What did that mean? Aidan? Some strange boyfriend Stella had over? Barbara sucked in a little mouthful of air. "Do you know who it was, Cole?" she asked, lifting her voice, hoping that would make it sound less afraid. "Who was looking at you?"

Cole just shook his head some more.

"This is ridiculous, Barbara. How can he not *know*? He's just not saying," Caroline said sourly. Then she really yelled: "Cole, tell your mother exactly what happened this instant!"

Cole flinched and tucked himself back into Barbara's arms. She thought about asking Caroline to leave. Imagined telling her mother that she could not speak to Cole in that tone. Not in her house. Barbara would not tolerate it. If Caroline didn't stop, she wouldn't be welcomed back in their home. Not ever.

Or Barbara could do much less. She could signal to Caroline to be more gentle. She could politely ask her mother not to raise her voice. But Barbara already knew she wasn't even going to do that. She wasn't going to do anything.

"It's okay, sweetheart. Don't worry," Barbara whispered into Cole's head and went back to rocking him. "You're safe now. You're here with me. Everything will be just fine."

Barbara held Cole like that for so long, rocking him gently. The whole time she could feel Caroline's eyes burning into the back of her head, clearly dying to tell Cole to go get a tissue, to tell Barbara to make her son get out of her lap already. Mercifully, she didn't say a word.

At last Cole's body loosened so much that Barbara was about to check if he'd fallen asleep, but then he pushed himself up and wiped his nose on his sleeve. "Can I watch *Bob the Builder* now?" he asked, as if they'd been in the middle of discussing that very thing.

"Okay," Barbara said reflexively. Though they were ordinarily a no-TV-on-weekdays household, she would have said yes to anything. "But only for a couple of minutes."

"All right, Mommy!" Cole cheered as he jumped up and raced happily toward the living room.

Caroline laughed harshly once he was gone. "That's one way to be sure he'll pull *that* stunt again. TV as a reward for a tantrum. Now, there's a parenting strategy we didn't have back in my day."

Barbara couldn't look at Caroline. She loved her mother. She did.

But Caroline needed to go away right now, just for a few minutes. Until Barbara could pull herself together. Claw back a sense of humor and maybe some semblance of patience.

"Mom, can you go out and get us a loaf of French bread?" Barbara asked as she stared down at the kitchen floor.

"Of course," Caroline said, sounding delighted as she rested her casserole on the counter. She loved nothing more than a job to do. "While I'm gone, put this in at three-fifty for twenty minutes. And why don't you fix yourself a snack, some almonds and raisins, maybe. Something with protein. Or a glass of milk. You need to balance your glycemic index." She pulled her car keys out of her purse. "Back in ten minutes!"

"Take your time, Mom."

Absurdly, Barbara did drink a glass of milk once her mother was gone, but it instantly nauseated her. She could hear *Bob the Builder* in the other room as she put her glass in the sink. It was a comfort to think of Cole safely secured in front of the TV. Maybe Barbara needed a distraction, too. Just while Caroline was gone and Cole was occupied, a sliver of space in which to pull herself together.

All day she'd wanted to see what kind of news there was about the baby. Nothing could put your own living child's problems into perspective like thinking about someone else's dead one. Barbara would eventually know much more from Steve about what was going on, but there were unexpected tidbits one could pick up from the news online, not to mention the chatter of regular people. If nothing else, the citizens of Ridgedale could be counted on to have opinions and to insist on sharing them.

Barbara grabbed her laptop off the counter and sat down at the kitchen table. A quick Internet search brought up several stories about the baby, but it wasn't until Barbara found her way onto the

Ridgedale Reader's site that she found anything to pique her interest. Already there were quite a few comments on the articles about the baby. As usual, many from crackpots who just wanted to hear themselves talk. But there were remarks that gave Barbara pause. It was true that someone could have murdered the mother and the baby, like that one commenter suggested, and maybe the mother's body was yet to be discovered. Though Steve had dismissed that possibility out of hand, Barbara was no longer convinced.

But it wasn't until Barbara was skimming the comments on the second story that she saw a post that stopped her dead in her tracks.

FIND HIM.
BEFORE HE FINDS YOU.

The hairs on the back of her neck lifted. What the hell did that mean? Was it some kind of liberal nonsense, like someone had suggested? Except there was something so chilling about the words: menacing, almost. As though someone—a killer, for instance—was taunting all of them. Barbara was squinting at those few words when something came to rest on her shoulders. Something heavy and warm. A pair of large hands. Barbara jumped up, her chair falling back and smacking the ground as she whipped around.

"Whoa!" Steve said as Barbara was about to bolt for the living room and Cole. His hands were raised like he was trying to corral a spooked colt. "Take it easy."

"Dammit, Steve! Why are you sneaking up on me?" Barbara clutched a hand to her chest. The surge of adrenaline made her heart feel like it was going to burst. "Why didn't you text when you were on the way? And why didn't you come in through the garage?"

"I'm sorry, I wasn't even thinking—battery died in the Taurus,

battery died in my phone. Been that kind of day." Steve shook his
head as he dropped his hat on the table. He looked completely exhausted but handsome in his dress uniform. He must have been
meeting with someone important—the mayor, the press. "I got a lift
in a cruiser. I really didn't mean to scare you."

Barbara took a couple more breaths until her heart slowed. She
felt bad for yelling at him. Surely, it had not been an easy day—it
had not been easy on anyone.

"No, *I'm* sorry. I really didn't mean to snap like that. I was just
reading this—" But that eerie post wasn't going to make Steve
happy. It would just get his mind back on work, and she needed him
here with her now. She'd mention the post to him later, or maybe
she wouldn't. It was all nonsense anyway. "God, what a terrible day.
You must be exhausted."

"Amen to that," Steve said. He leaned over and kissed Barbara
on the forehead—the forehead again, the forehead always—then
righted her chair so she could sit back down.

"Can I get you something to drink?" Barbara offered. But he
shook his head and frowned as he sat down at the kitchen table
across from her.

The volume on the TV out in the living room got loud, than sank
just as quickly back down.

"TV on a Tuesday?" Steve asked with a tired smile. He supported
Barbara's rules, took them on as his own, especially in front of the
children, but they were always Barbara's rules.

"Like I said, it's been a rough day all around."

Steve nodded, then got up for the drink of water he'd refused. He
stood at the sink with his back to her, filling a glass from the tap.
Barbara watched him there at the counter, so steady and strong. The
man she'd always known would step up and take care of her. The man
she would do anything to protect. No matter what. For the third time
in one day, Barbara felt like she was going to cry. It was ridiculous.

"Hey, what's wrong?" Steve asked as he turned back to her.

"Oh, it's just this whole mess with Cole and that conversation with Rhea and then—" The words shot out like a breath Barbara had been holding. Steve came back over and rested a firm hand on her shoulder. "And then just now, when Hannah picked him up from Will's house, Cole was hysterical. He even had this—I don't know, this *episode* right here." She gestured to the kitchen floor, the scene of the crime. "It was horrible. Just awful, Steve. There is something wrong, really wrong. For all we know, he was abused over there. *Molested.*"

"Molested?" Steve pulled his chin in. "Where'd that come from?"

"When kids start acting out, sometimes it's because something has been done to them. Between that woman and her boyfriends and her older son and whoever—"

"Wait, what woman are you talking about?"

"Stella! Come on, Steve, I've been telling you. Have you not even been listening?" This was their son they were talking about. Steve needed to pull it together and pay attention. The rest of town would just have to get in line.

"Hold on and back up," Steve said firmly, sitting across from Barbara. At least he seemed focused. "Cole had a bad day. I get that, but everyone's entitled to one of those, right?"

"But that's not—"

He held up a hand, silencing her. "One thing at a time. Do you have any proof that's not all this is? That this isn't going to be like Hannah with the bridges? You remember that? One day out of nowhere, we can't drive anywhere over water without her screaming her head off. *Screaming*, in case you've forgotten. Then one day she's fine again. You have proof that this isn't just like that?"

Barbara stared into Steve's clear bright blue eyes. There was so much feeling in them, so much caring. Sometimes it aggravated her that Steve was more emotional than she was; always it mystified her.

He certainly hadn't gotten his overactive heart from his mother. A widow who died of breast cancer, Wanda was always cold as a corpse. And yet there was Steve, all mushy under that hard masculine exterior. God love him—and Barbara did, every last ounce of him—but Steve could be too trusting and too generous in general. Still, his being so emotional did make it seem like he understood things Barbara didn't. And right then she needed to believe he was right. Steve stood up and came around behind Barbara, putting a hand on her neck and kneading the knots at the base of her skull. Slowly, her shoulders lowered.

"You're right, I guess," she said, letting her eyes slide closed.

This could be just like Hannah with the bridges. Barbara had forgotten all about that. At Cole's age, Hannah was always having an episode about one thing or another. She was still high-maintenance, but she was well within the range of normal for a teenager. Maybe none of this was as serious as Barbara was letting herself believe. Maybe she did need to calm down. She tried to focus on Steve's fingers on her neck, the sensation of her muscles unraveling.

"Wait, what's that?" Steve asked, the sleepy warmth suddenly gone from his voice. When Barbara opened her eyes, he was staring at her open laptop. *"Find him. Before he finds you?"*

She'd forgotten all about the *Reader* comments. Steve hardly needed another thing to worry about. And now she'd lose him again to the investigation. He'd be gone for the rest of the night without ever leaving the house.

"Someone trying to make some stupid point," Barbara said. It was so obvious to her now that the message was not some well-calculated threat. It was a stupid prank. She really was letting herself get too wound up about everything. "You know this town: God knows what their point is, but you can be sure they think they have one."

"What is it?" Steve's voice was sharp as he stepped closer to the computer. "Where is it from?"

"Oh, they're comments on the articles from the *Reader*," she said. "You know how people *love* to comment on there. They find a way to go at each other about the annual Turkey Trot."

"Great, just what I need, somebody causing a panic." He shook his head in disgust. "Are there other comments like that?"

"Not that I've noticed, but I haven't had the chance to get through them all." Barbara dragged her finger across the touchpad, scrolling down. "Can't you just contact the *Reader* and make them take it down or trace the email or something?"

He shook his head. "First Amendment. They're not actually threatening anybody, and you have a constitutional right to be a jerk. Besides, the *Reader* isn't going to crack open its computer records to the police, not for something like this." He ran a finger down the screen, blowing out some air. "Dammit. I looked at the articles. There was nothing to them. These people really can make a damn mountain out of a molehill."

"They're just worried," Barbara offered because it felt like Steve was talking about her. And that part *was* understandable. "It makes them feel better to yammer on about it. Like they're in control of something."

"Wait, stop." Steve tapped the screen.

Another Ridgedale murder?? Barbara had known as soon as they found the baby near the Essex Bridge that Simon Barton's death would come up eventually. But she was surprised it had happened so soon.

I don't care how long ago it was, that seems like a crazy coincidence.

"Seems this Molly Sanderson is just dying to make something out of nothing," Barbara said.

"I think the problem is she really believes what happened to Simon *is* something," Steve said quietly.

"Well, tell her it's not."

"I did." His eyes were on the computer screen.

"Then tell her again and make her listen, Steve," Barbara snapped.

She wasn't going to tolerate some reporter adding to their troubles by bringing up something upsetting from years ago. "You *are* the chief of police. Who is she?"

"Actually, you know her, or she knows you," he said. "They just moved here last fall. Her daughter is in Cole's class."

"You're kidding me." Ella's mother, it must be. Ella was the only new child in the class. Barbara had exchanged niceties with her mother, but that was it. Molly was friends with Stella, and that was all Barbara needed to know to get her to steer clear. "Well, this is a hell of a way for her to make new friends."

Steve stayed quiet. He'd been staring at the computer longer than it could have taken for him to read the rest of the comments. The muscle in his jaw had lifted like a walnut. "Print those out for me, will you?" His voice was so low it didn't sound like his.

"You weren't even a police officer back then," Barbara said. Because there he went again, responsible for everyone and everything. He probably felt like he should have kept Simon from getting so drunk that night. Steve had never been much of a drinker himself. "We were all upset about what happened to Simon. But whatever should have or could have been done at the time—it really has nothing to do with you."

She did realize that might be easier for her to say. Barbara had been way on the other side of the woods that night, near the circle of logs where the girls hung out, at least the ones who weren't off hooking up with boys in the wet leaves. The logs were the only place they could sit without getting filthy. The boys, meanwhile, were always taking off into the woods to play something they called "drunk obstacle," seeing who could scramble the fastest over a pitch-black course of branches and logs. Dumb high school jocks: Everything's got to be a competition. Steve had never wanted to talk about the details of that night—it upset him too much—but he and some of the other boys had seen Simon slip.

Steve nodded. "Just print them out, okay?" He straightened up and headed for the steps. "What I really need now is to wash that creek off me. I've got it coming out of my pores."

"Okay, but try to be quick," Barbara said tentatively. She had no choice but to warn him. "My mom's coming back in a few minutes. For dinner. It's Tuesday, remember?"

Steve paused on the stairs. His head dropped as he rested a hand on the banister. "Okay," he said, looking up at Barbara and forcing a smile, obviously steeling himself. "Okay."

As he drifted up the steps, part of her wished he'd demanded that she cancel dinner with her parents. Because, lately, his doing what she wanted seemed in inverse proportion to his affection for her.

After Steve was gone, Barbara went out to the sitting room. Cole wasn't in front of the TV, a sure sign she'd left him out there far too long. Instead, he was sitting at his small table, tucked in the corner. His back was to Barbara. From across the room, she couldn't see what he was doing, but the closer she got, the more it looked like he wasn't doing much of anything. Except sitting there, staring once again, at nothing.

"Cole, honey," Barbara called, slowing halfway across the room. She was afraid of startling him. She raised her voice, hoping he'd snap out of it before she got too close. "Bob's not so interesting today?"

Cole didn't answer. And he didn't move—not an inch, not a twitch. Barbara couldn't even tell if he was breathing.

"We have Nana's lasagna for dinner, Cole." Barbara made her voice louder but cheery as she made her way over to him, her hands clasped so tightly they had started to throb. "With no green things in it, just the way you like."

She saw the markers then, the short, chubby ones. All fifty were scattered across the table and on the floor, most of their caps off, as though someone had tossed them into the air and let them rain down. Why would he do that? Cole was a neat, particular kid. He worried about things like markers drying out. Barbara was a couple feet behind him now. She reached out a hand as a hole opened up in her stomach.

"Bob the Builder, can we fix it?" Bob and his friends sang from behind her.

"Cole," Barbara said more loudly. Her fingers stroked the air. "Cole, please. Look at me."

She was right behind him now. She was right there. But he hadn't moved. And she was so afraid to touch him. Afraid of what he might do—that was it. She felt afraid *of* her son. And why? It made no sense, but it was true. And she hated herself for it.

"Can we build it? Yes, we can!"

Cole was at least breathing, panting. "Honey?" Her voice was high and choppy. "Are you okay? Please, Cole, say something."

There was only his breath, *puff, puff, puff.*

And then Barbara was close enough to see it. There, on the table. The drawing Cole had been working on. It was rough and childish, all jagged lines and out of proportion, like all of his drawings. But there was no pretending it was anything other than what it was.

A picture of a boy with his arm cut off.

(Audio Transcription, Session Recorded with Patient Knowledge and Consent)

Q: Do you think you're ready to talk about what happened that night?

M.S.:   You mean the night I lost the baby? We've talked about that a couple times. We can talk about it again if you want.

Q: I mean after that. The night that brought you to see me the first time.

M.S.:   You're making it sound more serious than it was.

Q: Justin had to call an ambulance.

M.S.:   He did call an ambulance. He didn't *have* to call an ambulance.

Q: What happened that night, Molly?

M.S.:   Justin panicked. I'm not blaming him, but that's what happened. It was five stitches. I didn't need an ambulance.

Q: I think it's important that we talk about it. You've made good progress here. But I don't want to overlook the fact that we've been treading lightly around some pretty significant issues.

M.S.:   I dropped a glass. It broke. Then I slipped when I was cleaning it up.

Q: You slipped on your arm?

M.S.: Yes. That's what happened.

Q: And Ella?

M.S.: I didn't realize I was bleeding until Justin came home. I never would have picked her up. If I'd been trying to kill myself, do you really think I would have done it when I was home alone with her?

Q: You wouldn't have?

M.S.: No. I would have waited until I was by myself. And then I would have been sure to finish the job.

Molly

From the sitting room, I heard the front door open. Justin. I listened to the familiar sounds of him dropping his bag, hanging up his jacket. I looked past my laptop to Ella, sound asleep on the couch next to me. Justin wouldn't approve of my having let her fall asleep here instead of taking her up to bed. Admittedly, I was our weak link in the sleep department. But I couldn't bring myself to say good night. I'd needed Ella's warm little body pressed up against me. I thought about picking her up and hustling for the steps to hide the evidence, but before I could move, I got a text from Erik. *Any word on that former student in the hospital?*

Police holding her for questioning, I replied. *I'll need official confirmation before I report.*

The more I thought about it, the less comfortable I was covering Rose's part in the story. And that was unlikely to change after I had confirmation she was a suspect. She was probably like so many of those women I had worked on behalf of for years—scared, alone, traumatized. Not thinking clearly. That was something I certainly knew all about. How could I possibly add fuel to the police fire? I wished Stella had never called me, that I'd never met Rose. Especially after what Ella had told me. Had Stella invented the story about Rose's sexual assault to protect Aidan? It was hard to believe that even Stella could be that good an actress or that calculated.

Hold off mentioning her until we see where it goes, Erik wrote back. *We don't want to jump the gun with something like this.*

Okay, I wrote back, glad to be off the hook, but surprised by the sudden caution, at odds with Erik's usual take-no-prisoners approach. *Any idea when you'll be back?*

Soon, I hope. Helping with uncle's funeral arrangements.

Your uncle?

Yes, elderly. Long illness.

Sorry to hear. My sympathies to your family.

Thx. Be in touch soon.

Nancy had said Erik's cousin's house had burned down. Now it was a dead elderly uncle. It was possible Nancy had gotten it wrong. Possible but unlikely. From the beginning, Erik's abrupt disappearance had been suspicious. Now I felt sure that whatever Erik was doing had nothing to do with a dead uncle or a house fire.

I held a finger to my lips when Justin appeared in the doorway to our small sitting room, then I gestured guiltily toward Ella. He smiled—no hint of the irritation I'd expected—looking especially handsome in the suit he had on. The faculty cocktail party, I'd forgotten all about it. He must have come home to change after I'd seen him at the Black Cat. It was only then that I looked at the clock: almost eleven p.m. I'd gotten so wrapped up in fruitlessly searching for a connection between Rose and Aidan that I'd lost track of time.

There were no photos of Aidan on Rose's Instagram account (dormant for days) and no mention of Rose on Aidan's sparse Facebook page, wide open for the world to see with its absence of privacy settings. I'd come across Rose's raw-food blog, which included mentions of her roommate, Laurie, and a handful of photos of her friends. But no mention of any boyfriend.

Justin motioned for me to follow him toward the kitchen as

he loosened his tie. When I'd slid carefully off the couch without waking Ella and made my way to the kitchen, Justin had his back turned. He was pouring two glasses of Scotch, his twice the size of mine.

"Rough day, huh?" I asked.

"Not the best I've had." His voice was low and heavy.

"Want to talk about it?" I asked, crossing the room to him.

"Feels stupid on a day like today," Justin said, shaking his head and gesturing toward me—the baby they'd found, he meant. "Different university, same old politics. That's all. Not very interesting." He took a long swallow of his whiskey, so long that it verged on a gulp.

"Wow, it must be bad." I pressed my body against Justin's back, hooking my arms under his. "Come on, talk to me."

I wanted him to tell me everything. It had been so long since I'd been able to be there for Justin, to listen to his problems, no matter how trivial, relatively speaking. It was nice to think of our marriage regaining the equilibrium I'd once prided myself on.

"It's just hard to compete when you're the new kid on the block. Miles Cooper doesn't have half my publications, but the president of the university was his professor at Yale. And he plays basketball every Wednesday with the dean of students."

"You could play basketball," I offered, kissing him on the neck. "You're good at basketball."

"I think you'd be a better way to curry favor with Thomas Price," he said. "He was there tonight. Seems you made quite the impression."

"I'm sorry I didn't give you more warning than a text two seconds before. Talking to him was very last-minute."

Justin turned around to look at me. He smoothed the hair out of my face. "I hope you made Thomas Price uncomfortable under the weight of your incisive questioning."

"I'm afraid it was all awfully polite." In retrospect, maybe too polite. I probably should have pressed Price more about how the university handled student complaints, about sexual assaults especially. "And what do you mean, 'impression'?"

"He found you 'absolutely charming.' Those were his exact words—who even talks like that? Anyway, I think he might have a crush on you."

I felt a rush of juvenile delight. This was what happened when you spent months locked away from the world: you regressed. Briefly, I imagined a scene in which Justin and Thomas Price fought for my affections. I'd end up with Justin, of course. But that was hardly the point.

"Oh, please," I said. "He was just being polite because I'm married to you."

"A crush, I'm telling you." Justin smiled, then took another huge swallow, finishing his drink. "If only we could get Thomas Price's crush on you to somehow turn into the university president's crush on me."

"Thanks for the note, by the way," I said, laying my face in the warm crook of his neck. "It really— I needed it."

"I never should have stopped giving them to you." His voice was serious. "Never."

"Yeah, well, I think we both have plenty of things we wish we'd done differently."

Justin set the empty glass on the counter, then put his hands on my face, running a thumb over my cheekbone. "I'm so glad you're back, Molly Sanderson," he said, smiling at me in that way of his that always made me feel like some miraculous, unearthed treasure. "Promise me I'll never lose you again. No matter what."

"I promise," I said, staring straight back at him.

He was still worried about my ability to handle the story. But he was wrong. It would be good for me, even if I wasn't sure how.

Justin leaned forward, sliding his fingers to the back of my neck and pulling me to him. He kissed me hard, the way he had before he was afraid I might shatter. And I let myself get lost in it, in a way I hadn't for a long time. Suddenly, I needed us to disappear into each other. I needed everything else to fall away—the past, the future. All my mistakes and shortcomings. All the ways I had failed Justin and Ella and myself. The ways I had failed *her*, my baby who never was. I needed to know that we had done better than survive. I needed to believe that we were reborn.

Justin kicked the kitchen door closed as he peeled off my shirt and I tugged at his jacket. A second later, my pants were off and I was naked up against the kitchen counter, unbuttoning Justin's pants as he slipped his fingers under the edge of my bra. I pressed my open mouth against his neck to keep my sounds from waking Ella. As Justin pushed inside of me, I watched us move together in the reflection of the kitchen window.

We lay on the floor afterward, Justin's crumpled suit between us and the cold tile floor, giggling and panting, our bodies threaded together like our much younger selves. My head was resting on Justin's damp, naked chest.

"Do you remember the first time you spent the night?" Justin asked, his voice vibrating against my ear.

"How could I forget?" I adjusted my cheek until I found a softer nook under his collarbone. "It's not every day you get the pleasure of sleeping with your head jammed up against a refrigerator."

"It was a small apartment, wasn't it? I remember waking up in the middle of the night, and there you were, pulling on your clothes."

"It was six a.m., not the middle of the night, and I wanted to slip out before you fed me any lines," I said. "I liked you. I wanted to keep it that way."

"But my irresistible charm convinced you to stay."

"Pancakes early on Saturdays, that was supposedly your thing. Except you had no idea what was open at that hour."

"Yes, and you pointed out that I'd been lying, while eating the delicious pancakes I did eventually find for us."

"Did I?" I laughed. "I was a hard-ass. Leslie was right. I'm surprised you wanted to see me again."

"Come on, Molly, you know I've always loved that you're straight-shooting."

"Lucky for you I've mellowed with age."

"You're going to make an amazing reporter, too, I have no doubt." Justin took a deep breath, which rocked my head up and down. "Just not on this story, okay? I want you to ask Erik to reassign it, Molly. Do it for me."

I lifted my head to look at him, but he was staring at the ceiling. It was such a bomb, I was assuming I must have misheard him. "What did you say?"

"I'm too worried about what this will—how much this is going to dredge up for you," he said, meeting my eyes. "Things have been so good lately, Molly. I don't want to lose what we have back."

This was my fault. I never should have gotten so emotional at the Black Cat. I'd probably seemed like I was about to go right off a cliff again. I felt so much steadier now. The story was just that: a story. One that meant something to me, yes. But it wasn't *about* me.

"I was caught off guard at first that it was a baby. It's true," I said. "But I'm okay now. The story actually feels like it will bring—"

"Closure," he said, finishing my sentence. "Yeah, I know. That's what you said before. And that's exactly what's worrying me."

"That's not what I said before." I hadn't, had I?

"No, you're right," he said, his eyes sad as he stared at me. "You said it was 'connected' to what happened to us."

He was right, *that* I had said. All I could do was stare at him. I didn't have any defense.

"We've gone over this all before, Molly—there's never going to be closure. Not for what we lost. And you're just going to have to learn to live with that. We both will. Give the story back to Richard, Molly. He's the news reporter, not you."

"I'm not *giving* the story to anyone, Justin," I said, feeling an unexpected flash of anger. I didn't care if Justin was well intentioned. What he was doing and the way he was doing it were wrong. He was my husband. I needed him to support me. "I have to do this. I know it doesn't make sense to you, but if I can find out what happened to this baby, maybe I can make sense of . . ."

How had I started down *that* path again? I did sound delusional. Every road kept leading back to me and my baby. Justin let my unfinished sentence hang there, proof of his point.

"I understand you want to do this story, and I even understand why," he said finally. "But what if you're wrong about being okay? What if you're not the best judge of how you're feeling?"

"That's insulting." I jerked my shirt on, then pushed myself off the floor. "You're talking about me like I'm—like I have some sort of permanent affliction. I was depressed, Justin. And for good reason, I might add. I'm not anymore. End of story."

"I'm asking you not to do this *one* story, Molly," Justin said, angry now, too, as he tugged on his own shirt. "Haven't I earned the right to ask for that much?"

"Earned the right because you took care of me?" My chest felt raw as I moved away from the spot where we'd been lying. "Are you seriously going to use that as a bargaining chip? You think that's fair?"

Justin pressed his lips together as he stood. "You know what's really not fair, Molly?" His voice was calm and deliberate. He knew better than to forfeit his credibility by losing his patience. "You trying to turn my caring about you into me being an asshole."

"Well, I'm sorry if our dead baby didn't roll right off my back the way it did yours." My voice was too shrill and too loud. But I wanted to hurt him. "That actually doesn't make you a better person, you know. It just makes you lucky."

Justin stared at the floor, frowning, shaking his head. "I'll see you upstairs," he said. He didn't look at me again as he stepped toward the door. "But first *I'll* put Ella to bed."

After he was gone, I stood there alone in the kitchen in my T-shirt and underwear, furious and filled with regret. Wanting to apologize and go after him and fight some more. I was saved from having to choose when my phone rang. A number I didn't recognize. I hoped it wasn't Deckler again.

"Hello?" I barked.

"This is Chief of Police Steve Carlson, Ms. Sanderson. Sorry to disturb you so late."

"That's okay." I tried to soften my voice. "What is it?"

"You were at the hospital this afternoon?"

Ugh. I did not like where this was starting, much less where I knew it was headed. "Um, yeah, my friend's cleaning woman was in a car accident. She wanted moral support." Why had I said it that way? That made Stella sound involved. "Or company, that's a better way of putting it. My friend can be a little dramatic, even in situations that don't involve her."

Oh, great. Dramatic? What was wrong with me? Just because it was true didn't mean it was something I should be saying to the police. And not saying Stella's name didn't make it any better, no matter what I was trying to tell myself.

"What time did you leave the hospital?"

"Probably around one p.m.," I said. "I went to the university for an interview."

"Okay. Could you please call me if you hear from Stella?"

No, I will not. That was what I wanted to say. And why should I go around reporting on the whereabouts of a friend? But refusing seemed awfully confrontational under the circumstances.

"Sure," I said hesitantly. "Can you tell me why?"

"Rose Gowan is gone," Steve said. "And so, it seems, is your friend Stella."

I dreamed of babies. Dead ones. One of them was mine. But I didn't know which, in a roomful of little caskets. I startled awake, bolting upright in the darkness. I could see the outline of Justin, sleeping on his side next to me. I put a hand on him to check that he was breathing, then curled up tight behind him, pretending we hadn't argued earlier. It seemed such a silly waste now. And with those kinds of dreams, it was hard to maintain that the story wasn't having an effect on me.

When I awoke again, it was almost seven a.m., and Justin was already gone. He'd left a note: *Conference at Columbia; back late.* There was another one of his little notes, too. I felt a pang of guilt about our fight the night before.

"Hope" is the thing with feathers—That perches in the soul—Emily Dickinson

I rolled over and picked up my cell phone off my nightstand and sent Justin a text: *I know you're just trying to help. Sorry about last night. xo.*

I didn't expect him to answer, but he did. Right away. *I'm sorry, too. And I do believe in you, Molly. More than you'll ever know. xo.*

I felt relieved as I headed downstairs. Glad that Justin and I were no longer technically in a fight. Glad also that there'd been no overnight text from Stella, angry that I'd talked to Steve. Ella had even slept later than usual, leaving me time for a quiet cup of coffee before we got swept into the morning routine.

But as soon as I stepped into the living room, I was unnerved by something out of place. There was a small cardboard file box sitting a few feet inside our front door. Some kind of gift from Justin? Except the closer I got, the more it seemed an odd box for a present. Also, *Molly Sanderson* was written in large black letters across the top, and it didn't look like Justin's handwriting.

I pulled my phone out of my sweatshirt pocket and sent Justin another text, hoping to catch him before he lost a signal when the train went into Penn Station. *Is the box a peace offering?*

What box?

Come on. The box by the front door?

I'm all 4 peace offerings. But I don't know anything about a box.

I took the stairs two at a time. *Someone had been in our house. Someone could still be in our house.* Maybe Ella wasn't asleep. Maybe something had been done to her. I threw open her bedroom door so hard that it banged against the wall.

Ella jerked up from a dead sleep. "Mommy!" she shouted, bursting into terrified tears.

But she was okay. She was fine. That was the most important thing. I sucked in a mouthful of air—okay, Ella was fine. Now I had to pull myself together and get the two of us out of the house, just in case whoever had been in the house was still there.

"It's okay, sweetheart," I said, trying to stay calm as I pulled Ella out of bed and into my arms. I sounded out of breath. I probably looked scared to death, too. Luckily, Ella was still half asleep. "I thought we could go out for pancakes. You know, a special treat."

"But I'm tired," Ella whined, rubbing her eyes as she wrapped her legs around my waist. "I don't want breakfast. I want to go back to sleep."

"I know, Peanut, I know." I rubbed her back as I headed down the steps.

I paused only long enough to grab my car keys and purse. Not long enough to notice it was pouring outside, much less to grab an umbrella. I rushed down the front walkway toward the car, with Ella in her Hello Kitty pajamas, trying to shield her from the deluge, relieved to see that I was at least in yoga pants and a sweatshirt and not naked.

Getting soaked, I buckled Ella into the car seat smoothly and slowly, smiling the whole time as though that might convince her she'd imagined all of our racing around. Once I'd climbed in the driver's seat and locked the doors tight, I wiped the rain off my face, grinning at her in the rearview. But she just turned her sleepy, grumpy face to the side as I backed slowly out of the driveway. It wasn't until I'd driven three streets away that it felt safe to pull over. I turned off the wipers, and the drumming rain quickly blurred out the windshield.

When I looked up at Ella in the rearview again, she was clutching her blanket and sucking her thumb, sound asleep.

"Steve Carlson," he answered on the first ring. He sounded like I'd woken him. In bed with Barbara, surely. And yet it was so hard to picture.

"This is Molly Sanderson. I'm sorry to bother you so early," I began. "But I—I had your number in my phone from last night. And I wasn't sure who else to call. I think someone was in my house."

"Are you inside your house now?" he asked, serious, official, coplike.

My heart picked up speed again. I'd been so prepared to be dismissed out of hand. "No, I'm in my car a few blocks away with my daughter. Someone left a box in my living room while we were asleep. I'm sure I'm overreacting, but—"

"Stay where you are for now," Steve said. "Give me your address and I'll check it out."

By the time Steve had called me to return home, it was barely misting.

He was leaning against an unmarked car—maybe just his car—when I arrived, looking much younger in jeans and a long-sleeved T-shirt. I parked behind him, quietly unbuckling my seat belt and leaving the car running as I got out, hoping Ella would stay asleep.

"Morning," he said, nodding at me, then flicking his eyes disap-
provingly in the direction of my humming car.

"I was hoping Ella would stay asleep in there," I explained.

Steve nodded, but his brow stayed furrowed. "Well, there's no one
in your house."

"That's a relief," I said. "I was home with Ella alone; my husband
left early. And when I woke up, there was this strange box sitting
inside our living room. I guess I kind of panicked."

"Did your husband leave the door unlocked when he left?"

"Maybe," I said. Because entering without breaking in wasn't a
big a deal? Except someone had still invited him- or herself into
my *home* and left God knows what. *A baby*, my crazy brain jumped
there. *A dead baby in a box.* I was lucky Justin couldn't read my
mind. "We lock the door at night. And when we go out. But when
we're home during the day . . ."

No one in the suburbs ever locks their door, I wanted to say. *That's the
whole point of living here.*

"In the future, I'd keep it locked, always. Ridgedale isn't a big
city, but reasonable precautions make sense anywhere." He nodded
toward my car. "I also wouldn't leave a sleeping child unattended in
a running car."

"Right, of course," I said, fully mortified. "Did you, um, check
what was inside the box?"

"Just enough to see that it's some kind of papers." He held up his
hands. "Didn't read what's on them. Don't want to be accused of
interfering with the press. My guess is someone put them inside to
keep them out of the rain."

We didn't have any overhang, and it had been pouring. The box
would have gotten soaked. And so the person just went ahead and
opened our door? Steve was presenting it like a normal thing to do.
But it wasn't normal. Not even in Ridgedale.

"What happens now?"

"That's up to you. Happy to open an investigation. But you should know we'll need to keep the box, mark it as evidence."

"That hadn't occurred to me."

"That's why I mention it. I'm not trying to discourage you from pursuing this. That's entirely up to you. But this kind of thing happens. Years ago, during some mayoral campaign, somebody put a dead rat in Jim McManus's mailbox—he was the *Reader's* editor in chief at the time." Steve shook his head. "Man, was his wife bent out of shape. Anyway, my guess is this has something to do with your articles. Isn't that what you people want? A reaction?"

Steve was aggravated about something I'd written. That was obvious. "'You people'?"

"Meaning your editors." He rubbed his forehead. He still looked aggravated. But also like he didn't want to be. "Nothing personal, but they must like that you're willing to stir the pot. That's all I meant. It must sell papers or get you clicks or whatever it is you all want these days."

But my articles had been far from controversial.

"Is there something specific I've written that you're taking issue with?"

"Just pointing out the facts. And the fact is, you've riled people up. This 'find him, he's out there, another Ridgedale murder' nonsense. People are going crazy in the comments to your articles."

I felt a queasy twist in my stomach. I didn't even want to know those comments existed. Between that and the files and the pressure from Justin, I might beat a hasty retreat from journalism after all.

"I wouldn't know about that," I said, and I didn't like the feeling that Steve did. "I don't read the comments on my articles."

Steve frowned and looked uncomfortable. He wasn't frustrated with me, I was realizing. He was just frustrated.

"So what'll it be with the situation here?" he asked, looking at his watch.

I didn't much want to see what was in the box, but I couldn't imagine letting the police take it without looking through it first. What if it was something important?

"I don't think I'll pursue investigating. But thank you so much for coming." I did appreciate the way Steve had rushed over, no questions asked.

He nodded, pushed himself off his car, and turned toward the driver's door. "Not a problem. Call me if anything else comes up."

"Before you go, is there any news about the baby?" I asked.

"You're interviewing me *now*?" Steve raised an eyebrow as he stood in his open car door. "Seriously?"

"You're here." I shrugged. "And you did say I could follow up."

He shook his head and exhaled. "You don't give up, do you?"

The old me did not. It was good being reminded of her. Justin was wrong about this story. It was exactly what I needed. "No, I don't."

"ME says it'll be another couple days before we have an official cause of death."

"Does that mean he's still having a hard time determining it?"

Steve's face tightened. "It means it's going to take another couple days."

"But it could still be a homicide?"

"It hasn't been ruled out. All the more reason we need someone to come forward. And *that* I hope you do write: Someone out there knows who this baby belongs to, and we need to hear from them."

My phone vibrated with a text. I pulled it out, thinking it was Justin needing further reassurance that Ella and I were okay after my first cryptic text about some anonymous box.

Coffee after drop-off?

Stella. Shit. Did she seriously have to text me with Steve standing right here, staring at me? He'd specifically asked me to contact him if I heard from her. I'd have to say something. I couldn't lie for her, not that much. I'd just say as little as I could.

"Stella." I held up my phone. "I guess she's back." Why had I made it sound like she was on the run? "Or here. I don't know that she ever left."

"Yes, I spoke with Stella late last night," Steve said. "She claims she doesn't know where Rose is. Was surprised as anyone to hear that she had disappeared."

"You don't sound like you believe her."

Steve had a hand on the door and one leg in the car. He looked back at me. "Would you?"

RIDGEDALE READER

Print Edition

March 18, 2015

Body of Deceased Female Infant
Discovered Near Essex Bridge

BY MOLLY SANDERSON

The body of a female infant was discovered early yesterday morning by Ridgedale University Campus Safety in a wooded area near the Essex Bridge. The cause of death and exact age of the infant remain unknown, pending the release of official findings by the medical examiner.

The grim discovery of the baby's body has come as a shock to many in the community.

"I can't believe something like this happened here," said Stephanie Kelsor, a mother of two who has lived in Ridgedale for seven years. "What a tragedy."

Others saw the situation differently.

"People here like to pretend they're perfect," says Patrick Walker, owner of Pat's Pancakes. "But they've got the same problems as anywhere else. They've just got more money to cover it up."

Historically, crime rates in Ridgedale have been very low, with minor property crimes the most common offense. Serious crime is all but nonexistent in town. In the past two decades, there have been only two murders and six reported rapes.

However, these numbers may not reflect all crime that occurs on the university's campus. While there are federal reporting requirements, offenses involving students will often be handled exclusively as a violation of the university's disciplinary code.

The Ridgedale Police Department has asked that anyone with information relating to the infant's identity or cause of death contact them as soon as possible at 888-526-1899.

JENNA

We hung out after school today in the woods near the Captain's parents' house. He got some beers and I was going to say no thanks, so he didn't think I was some drunk loser, but then I thought if he was drinking, too . . .

He asked me about my parents and told me about his. They sound kind of uptight and whatever, but he said that they would really like me.

Did you hear that? HIS PARENTS WOULD REALLY LIKE ME??!! What guy talks about you meeting his parents unless he's seriously into you?

He asked me about Tex, too. "That dude would ditch his girlfriend in a second for you," that's what the Captain said. And it sounded like they're not even that good of friends, which is strange, because I thought they were. But who knows? Guys are weird.

I told the Captain the truth: I like Tex as a friend, but just a friend.

And what's not to like? Tex is always saying how amazing I am because I'm a spitfire instead of a wack job inappropriate nutso, like my parents think. Too crazy, too loud, too wild—my voice, my clothes, my friends, my thoughts. I embarrass them. That's the bottom line. Always have. Always will.

And so, yeah, I like that Tex gets me and that he's sweet and nice and tries to watch out for me (even when he's getting in the way). But he doesn't DO anything for me (even if I sometimes kind of wish he did). Not in that way, not at all. And you can't make a fire by pretending there's a spark.

And you know what the Captain said when I told him that Tex and I are just friends? He said: "Good." And then he kissed me soft and sweet and slow. And so you know what I did?

Gave him a BJ! Best one of my fucking life.

Sandy

It was early, a little past nine a.m., as Sandy waited on the front steps of Laurie's building. She'd already rung the buzzer three times. There hadn't been an answer, just like there hadn't been any of the five previous times she'd come by in the past twenty-four hours. But Sandy had kept coming back because Laurie was the last person who'd talked to Jenna. More important, she'd talked to this so-called friend of Jenna's who might have been the very last person to see her.

In between coming by Laurie's, Sandy had kept riding around looking for Jenna and calling and calling and calling. Late the night before, the calls had started going straight to voicemail. Sandy had been waiting for that to happen. Still, it hit her hard, like some kind of nail in Jenna's coffin. Monte had called Sandy, said he was going to start driving around, looking for Jenna. Sandy wanted to say no, that she didn't need his help. But she did need it. Jenna did, too.

Sandy closed her eyes there on Laurie's steps, tilted her face to the sun, wishing it would light her skin on fire. At least then she might feel something again. Because she was slowly going numb—first her toes, then her feet and legs. Now the deadness was creeping up her arms.

Her phone buzzed in her pocket. By now, she knew better than to get her hopes up. Sure enough, it was a text from Hannah. *I need to see you. Please.*

This girl was *literally* killing her.

Can't right now. Meeting someone. I'll text when I'm done.

Okay. But as soon as you can.

Or I'll tell someone: That was the threat, sitting there, just out of reach.

Sandy started down the steps, wondering what she should do or where she should go next, when Laurie's door finally swung open.

"What the hell do you want!?" Laurie shouted before she'd even stepped out, her face all screwed up and red. "Oh, it's you." She blinked at Sandy. Then she exhaled and slumped against the doorframe. Her square white-blond bob was perfectly smooth, and she was wearing a short kimono-like robe that was too small for her wide hips. "Sorry, Sandy, I thought you were the goddamn police again. The intercom's broken, so I've had to come down four stupid flights every time they've shown up, which has been at least six times. I started ignoring it. But they just keep coming and coming."

"Police?" Sandy couldn't help thinking it had something to do with Jenna.

"They're looking for my roommate, Rose, and they think I'm lying about her not being here, so they keep coming back and coming back, ringing my damn doorbell at all hours. Like if Rose is hiding upstairs, she's all of a sudden going to forget and answer the door."

Sandy wondered how many of these supposed "visits" from the police had been her ringing Laurie's buzzer. "Why do they want Rose?"

"They won't tell me. They'll harass the crap out of me, but won't tell me why. Who knows, maybe Rose's parents put them up to it. You know I love that girl. I was even willing to put up with a *baby*—longest goddamn three weeks of my life—but between the police and her parents and her stalker, I think she needs to find a new place to live. Assuming she comes back."

"You don't know where she went?"

"Not a clue. She left two days ago with the baby and some of her stuff. Said she was going to see a friend." Laurie rolled her eyes. "You know me, I don't like to ask questions."

"And who's her stalker?" *Blond woman?* That's what Sandy was thinking.

"Real tall guy, buzzed hair, super-intense. I thought at first he was some kind of cop or, I don't know, a soldier or something. Way uptight. Erik, that's what he said his name was. For all I know, he's Rose's baby daddy. She never would tell me who that was. For her sake, I hope not, because he was old as shit." She rolled her eyes again. "But that hippy-dippy crap of hers makes her do some weird stuff sometimes. Anyway, what are you doing here?"

"I'm looking for Jenna," Sandy said, feeling even more stressed. Because this was it. Laurie was pretty much her only hope. After her, it was all dead ends. "Monte said you were talking to Jenna at the end of her shift the night before last."

Laurie's face screwed up. "No, I don't think—" Then a light-bulb went off. "Oh, wait, yeah, I was," she said, nodding, seeming half surprised at the memory. "I did talk to Jenna for just a min-ute. I would have hung out with her for longer, but that friend of hers?" She whistled quietly and shook her head. "I'm sure she's a nice person and whatever, if she's your mom's friend, but there was just something about her. Not to be rude, but she was kind of a bitch."

"Do you know what her name was?"

Laurie shook her head, made a disgusted face. "Blond hair, puffy cheeks, bad jeans. Nothing like Jenna, that's for sure. Drank club soda, too. Weird, I'm telling you, the two of them hanging out. But you know Jenna. Maybe she was working some angle. That's why I love Jenna—she's always got an angle."

"And they left together?"

"If that's what Monte said." Laurie checked her watch. "I got distracted by some idiot. Same idiot who won't get the hell out of my bed right now and get his ass back to campus."

"If you hear from Jenna, can you tell her to call me?"

"You got it, sweetie. But don't you worry about her." She waved a hand. "Jenna will come rolling in any minute with a wicked headache and some crazy-ass story to tell. She always does."

Sandy stood across the street from the police station, airing out her hands so they wouldn't feel clammy if a police officer shook one. Last thing she wanted was to go inside, into the lion's den. But she was out of options. She was even kind of hoping Jenna might be there, safe and sound and sobering up on some little cot.

"Hey."

When Sandy turned, there was Aidan, silhouetted by the sun. She lifted a hand to her eyes so she could make him out better in the glare. She hated how happy she was to see him. Her heart skipped an actual stupid beat. And she was the one who'd been ignoring Aidan's texts and then his calls since yesterday, freezing him out on purpose. What she and Aidan had was fun and whatever, but Sandy wasn't dumb enough to think he had any role in this actual, real-life situation.

"What are you doing here?" she asked. "And why do you look like such shit?"

Aidan was pale, with dark circles under his eyes, and his hair was a mess. He crossed his arms in front of him, tucking his hands under the opposite armpit. "Kind of hard to get a good night's sleep when your girlfriend is trying to break up with you."

"Girlfriend?" Sandy laughed. Because she really thought he was joking. But he was staring straight at her, his eyes glowing in the sun like polished amber. "So you just happened to see me here?"

"If by 'happened,' you mean that I've been driving around looking for you ever since that last text you sent—you were supposed to meet me after I stayed in class, remember?"

"So you've been stalking me?"

"I prefer 'search and rescue.'"

Sandy turned away. Already she could feel herself caving, giving in to temptation. She should have said: *Fuck you, I don't need a rescue.* Because she didn't. But she did want to let go, to let all of it crash over and wash her away. She couldn't tell Aidan the worst of it—she couldn't tell anyone that—but maybe she could tell him something. And then, for one second, she wouldn't be alone with all of it anymore.

"There's just a lot of shit right now," she said.

"Like what?"

"Like we're getting evicted from our apartment." Sandy stared right at Aidan, daring him to screw it up by looking shocked and appalled. He didn't blink. "And now I can't find Jenna."

"What do you mean?" He looked worried, but not in a bad way.

"That I can't fucking find Jenna. I've looked everywhere for her, and I've called her a million times. Last time anyone saw her was at work a day and a half ago."

"Did you tell the police?"

"About what?" Sandy felt a guilty twist.

"Um, about your *missing mom.*" He looked at Sandy like maybe she was being dumb on purpose. "They should be out looking for her or whatever."

"I'm thinking about it." She nodded in the direction of the police station. "But what if she's high out of her mind somewhere? It's not like your mom being gone."

"Yeah, I don't think my mom's the police's favorite right now, either."

"What are you talking about?"

"The police showed up looking for her last night." Aidan pulled out a cigarette and offered one to Sandy. She waved it off, too nervous to smoke. "My mom loved it, too, wouldn't shut up about it afterward." He made a face, imitating her. "'The police are so stupid, they'll believe anything.' She's full of shit anyway. She just wants to pretend she knows something that somebody might care about."

"*About* what?" It felt like he was avoiding telling her.

"That baby they found, I think," he said quietly. He seemed embarrassed. "Like I said, she doesn't actually know anything."

They stood in silence for a minute longer, facing the police station.

"Let me help you look for your mom," Aidan said finally.

Sandy could feel him staring at the side of her face, but she kept her eyes down. Her throat felt thick. "No, I don't think—"

"Come on, give me a chance not to be the asshole everybody thinks I am. You won't *owe* me anything, if that's what you're thinking. I want to help."

What Sandy really wanted right then more than anything was someone to help her. To take care of her. She wanted a mom. That was the truth, even if she didn't want to admit it. And not Jenna, no matter how much she wanted to find her. What Sandy wanted was a real mom. A regular one. But what she had was Aidan. And maybe he was something.

"Okay," Sandy said, because letting him help wasn't the same thing as needing him to. "For now."

Relax, Sandy told herself inside the musty old police station. She was alone. Going in with Aidan would have been too suspicious. She'd sent him to check the hospital for Jenna. She'd been avoiding that, too.

The creaky floor and stale air reminded her of a place she'd gone on a field trip as a kid back when they'd lived for a year in South Jersey. Some colonial house where the kids were taught how to churn butter, except no one had gotten it to work. Only difference here were the flags lined up against the wall and the pictures of all those friendly fellas in uniform who could easily arrest her anytime they wanted.

Keep it the fuck together.

"Stapler, stapler, stapler," a tall guy behind the desk was muttering, half to Sandy and half to himself. "You'd think finding office supplies wouldn't be the hardest part of this job, but I tell you, sometimes . . ." He reached forward and grabbed something. "Ah, here it is."

He stapled the pages, then looked up at Sandy. Fucking instantly, he looked suspicious. And she hadn't even opened her mouth. A teenager alone in the police station? Of course he was wondering what her deal was. But the more he looked at Sandy, the more it felt like he was trying to see right through her. Like maybe he already had.

"Can I help you?" he asked.

It was too late to run. Her only choice was to calm the hell down. "Um, yeah," she said softly. "I'm looking for my mom. She didn't come home the night before last. She was with some friend right before she left work—or I don't really know if she was a friend. The people my mom works with think she was . . . some woman with blond hair, they said. She was the last person to see my mom, I guess, but they didn't get her name, so I have no way to find her." Now that Sandy had gotten herself talking, she could not shut up. "And she— Well, my mom isn't always the most dependable person, but she always comes home, you know, eventually."

"Hmm." The police officer's brow furrowed. He looked less suspicious and more concerned. "How long since you last spoke to her?"

"The night before last," she said.

"And how old are you?"

Shit. Child Protective Services—Sandy hadn't thought of that. But she couldn't lie now. Too big a risk that she would get caught. She just had to hope that leaving a kid her age alone wasn't some kind of crime.

"Sixteen. But I don't want to get her in trouble or anything. She's a great mom, really."

Except Sandy had already said that Jenna wasn't that dependable. Why had she said that? The police officer stared at her some more, squinting now, like he was trying to figure out where he'd seen Sandy before. But no one *had* seen her. She was sure of that much. He reached over the desk and held out his hand. "I'm Steve," he said. "What's your name?"

"Sandy."

"Okay, Sandy. Lucky for you, I've got a soft spot for daughters." He waved for her to follow him into the next room. "If I put your mom in the system, there's a chance this will end up getting bounced to Social Services, and that could make a mess of things for both of you when your mom shows up an hour from now. Why don't we start with a quick off-the-record search, just to make sure she hasn't been in an accident or anything."

"Thanks," Sandy said. "A lot."

"No problem," Steve said, leading the way to his office.

Sandy sat in the chair in front of Steve's desk as he hunted and pecked his way across the keyboard, finally getting to a screen filled with numbers and blank lines. Then he reached for some reading glasses, peering down his nose through them at the screen. At this rate, Sandy could be there for hours.

He turned to her and smiled. "As you can see, I don't do this much."

And judging from his big office, Steve wasn't a regular police officer. He was *the* police officer, the one in charge. Sandy looked up at the bookcase over his head: a couple of framed certificates, a diploma, and a trophy with a basketball player on top. On the second shelf, she noticed the pictures. Dozens of family snapshots. Her eyes settled on one in the middle: a family of four, clustered together on the beach, all smiles and lit up by the sun. And right there, in the center, a face she fucking recognized: Hannah.

Jesus Christ. That would have been something nice to know. You know: *Hey, FWIW, my dad's the chief of police.* But it wasn't like Hannah had lied. They'd never talked about their dads, only their moms. Always their moms.

"Wait, your mom wouldn't let you *what?*" Sandy had asked a month or two into their sessions, choking on her coffee. Hannah had been telling another insane story about her mom—they seemed extra insane because Hannah seemed to think they were totally normal. At least Sandy *knew* Jenna was screwed up.

They'd been studying at the Black Cat again. Hannah always wanted to go there, said she felt more comfortable around the college kids, though Sandy always felt like Hannah was waiting to see someone. Like maybe she had a crush on a barista or something. Sandy even asked once whether there was someone, and Hannah had blown her off with the usual "You know I don't date yet."

"My mom wouldn't let me wear sparkles," Hannah said.

"Sparkles? What are you, Dora the Explorer?"

Hannah started laughing so hard that her face got all red. "I mean when I was *little*," she said when she'd caught her breath. "I always wanted to wear those sneakers that are all covered in glitter. You know?"

"No, I don't know," Sandy said. Like the junk drawer, glitter sneakers: another of life's mysteries. "But I gotta be honest, they sound ugly as shit."

"Yeah," Hannah said this time with a forced laugh. But she looked kind of sad as she turned to look out the window. She was so pretty in the light. Delicate and soft in a way Sandy would never be. As Hannah's smile sank, Sandy watched her try to lift it back up. "They were ugly, I guess. But I cried for so long when she said no. I couldn't stop crying, which only made my mom madder." Her eyes got wide, remembering. "Like she really, really hated me."

I'm sure she doesn't hate you, Sandy thought about saying. But she didn't like it when people said that kind of bullshit to her. As if them thinking the world was always so perfect and right would make it so.

"That's messed up. What did you do?"

"Do?" Hannah blinked at Sandy. "With my mom, there's nothing to do except try not to make her mad the next time. I'm always trying to do that. To be the person she wants me to be."

"Is it working?"

"Not really." Hannah shook her head. Her eyes were glassy.

"Don't you ever just want to say fuck off instead?" Sandy asked. "I mean, no offense, but isn't she supposed to be the person who loves you no matter what?" Even Jenna did that.

"I think about it sometimes—a lot, even," Hannah said, looking down. She was quiet for a while before she looked up. "But that would just make her hate me forever."

"Maybe it wouldn't. Maybe it would make her change." Sandy wasn't sure who she was talking about: Hannah's mom or Jenna.

"No," Hannah said softly, picking her pencil up and focusing again on her schoolwork. "My mom will never change."

"Yikes," Steve said. When Sandy snapped her eyes down from the pictures, he was pointing toward the scab on her arm. "What happened there?"

Shit. Sandy had let her sleeve ride up. "Oh, I fell off my bike." She wrinkled her nose like a little kid—you know, "these things happen." But her heart was pounding. *Breathe. Fucking breathe. It's just a question. One that anybody would ask, not just a cop.* "At least my bike's okay."

"I don't know about that." Steve shook his head. "Bike can be replaced. You can't. Hope you're not riding around at night without reflective gear. I'm telling you, there are more bicyclist fatalities that way. Got to be careful out there."

"Yeah. I mean, no. I mean—" Sandy shook her head, feeling sick. "I have reflectors."

"Good, good. Okay, now I'm ready here with this system. Spell your mom's full name for me?" Steve was leaning over his computer again, fingers raised above the keyboard.

"Jenna Mendelson. M-e-n-d-e-l-s-o-n."

Steve didn't type. Didn't move. He stayed frozen like that, hands floating over the keys. Sandy could feel her stomach pushing up. Was Jenna already dead, and Steve knew it? Did the mention of her name click the pieces into place? Slowly he turned to look at Sandy, peeling off his glasses. The friendly-dad look on his face was totally gone. Now there was a full-on cop there. And it was scaring the hell out of her.

"I think maybe we should start again. At the beginning," he said, staring dead at her. "When exactly was the last time you saw your mother?"

MOLLY

What I told Dr. Zomer was not the whole truth. I didn't even tell Justin that. But I think he knew. Of course he did.

I did drop a glass and I did slip and cut my hand a little when I was trying to clean it up. That's all true. But when I saw the blood on my hand, I didn't feel upset or worried. I felt relieved. Like the world had been rebalanced.

I don't even remember picking up the piece of glass that I cut my arm with. But I did. I must have. I do remember being careful not to cause any real damage, in my nonexpert medical opinion. Because I could have if I'd wanted to. I could have done so much more.

And then Ella started to cry—one of her night terrors. And so I ran to her without thinking, because I could do that by then, comfort her after a bad dream. I didn't realize how much that small cut was already bleeding.

I had Ella in my arms when Justin came home a few minutes later. As soon as he saw us, he started yelling: Where's she bleeding? Where's she bleeding? It wasn't until I looked down that I saw Ella's head was covered in blood.

A second later, I passed out. Luckily, Justin caught me—and Ella, thank God—as I fell. Next thing I knew, the paramedics were lifting me into the ambulance. Halfway to the hospital, they realized that the cut to my arm wasn't serious. That I'd passed out not from blood loss but from the sight of it all over my daughter.

Justin lied and told the paramedics that he had been there, seen the whole thing. That it had been an accident, me and the broken glass and my arm. And watching Justin do that for me, lie like his life depended on it, like my life depended on it—and it might have, they could have hospitalized me against my will—I have never loved him more.

And so when he'd insisted the next day that I go see Dr. Zomer, I went. It was the least I could do.

Molly

"I got you a latte," Stella said when I got to the Black Cat. She was at a table by the window, two coffees already in front of her. "Full-fat milk, of course. Because that's *all* they serve in this godforsaken place." Her nostrils flared. "Honestly, I don't understand why you like it here."

"It reminds me of the city," I said as I sat down across from her, trying not to think of the box of files I'd had Steve leave in our living room. The box that was left by some stranger. A reader, maybe, but an angry one? A happy one? Who was to say? Thinking of it still inside my house filled me with dread. I wasn't sure that I'd done the right thing, not reporting it as a crime.

I'd gone back inside after Steve left, but only long enough to get Ella dressed and to change out of the yoga pants I'd slept in. I'd deliberately avoided looking at the box. After Ella was safely at school, I'd planned to go home and look inside. Except now I was doing my damnedest to avoid the house. I was so stressed about the whole thing, I was even tempted to tell Stella. But that box was exactly the strange turn of events she lived for. She'd have us rushing back to my house to go through every last page.

"Cockroaches would remind you of the city, too, you know," Stella went on. "But that doesn't mean we need to start importing them. Oh, wait, I didn't tell you, did I?" She leaned forward conspiratorially. "Zachary and I are having lunch after my lesson today."

"Really?" I was relieved to be talking about something silly like Stella's endless—but largely halfhearted—pursuit of her thirty-one-year-old tennis coach. It gave me an excuse not to ask the questions I had about Rose and her baby and Aidan. I wasn't sure I was ready for the answers.

I startled when my phone buzzed on the table.

"Wow, jumpy much?" Stella asked, intrigued. "Who is it?"

Richard Englander. I was surprised it had taken Richard all the way until nine thirty to call me again. It was his third call. There had also been a couple of texts. He was back in the office and wanted in on the biggest story that had hit Ridgedale in years. In fairness, it would have been his if he hadn't been out. His first message, the night before, had been nice—just checking in to see if I needed any help. But each one had gotten more insistent. I let his call go straight to voicemail, fairly certain I'd never listen to the message. And absolutely sure I wasn't giving him the story back. Not unless and until Erik made me.

"So you were saying: lunch with Zachary?" I turned back to Stella. "Really?"

"Wait a second, don't try to change the subject." She pointed a finger at me. "What's wrong? Who was that?"

"It was just that guy, the other reporter from the *Reader*. The young one."

"The asshole?"

"Yes, him. He's the news reporter. The baby would have been his story if he hadn't been out sick," I said. "He wants me to hand it over."

"Screw him," Stella said. "You're doing a great job. I read that piece of yours this morning about—what's it called—neonaticide. It was really . . ." She searched for a word. "Impassioned."

"Yeah, well, it would definitely make Justin happy if I let Richard take over."

"Oh yeah?" She paused, pressing her lips together. I could always see Stella bracing to pounce whenever I complained about Justin, which was why I never did. She loved to bitch about husbands—ex, current, prospective, it didn't matter.

"He's worried I'm going to have some kind of breakdown because it's about a baby."

Stella stared at me for a long time, her expression unreadable. "Are you?" Her tone was matter-of-fact. As though, yes, a calamitous mental breakdown was *always* a possibility, just an utterly unremarkable one.

And that was why I loved her.

"No," I said. Not only did I mean it, but it felt true. "I'm really not. I know it doesn't make any sense, but I actually feel better than I have in years."

"Then, as your friend, I say you need to do it," Stella said with unusual seriousness. There was an unfamiliar look on her face, too—sincerity. "Regardless of what makes sense. And notwithstanding what Justin wants."

"Right, screw the damn husband," I said with a gentle smile. I didn't think that was what Stella meant, but she could be flip about marriage.

She looked wounded. "I'm just saying sometimes there are things you need to do, no matter what anyone says about it."

"So what ended up happening with Rose?" I asked, knowing it was time to change the subject. And I needed to clear the air. My suspicions were surely ridiculous; they felt ridiculous. But a little proof would be nice. "You know, the police called me looking for her. And you."

"Yes, apparently I needed permission to take my aunt to the Philadelphia Flower Show." Stella didn't seem the least bit surprised or concerned. "Anyway, Rose took off. I told the police that. And can you blame her? They will eventually figure out that it wasn't her baby, but in the meantime, why should she stick around while they harass her? Anyway, I don't think that's why she left. I think it was the baby's father. She told me she wasn't on her way to work when she got into that accident. She was leaving town. She wouldn't tell me details, but I think she was scared."

"How can you be sure she's okay? Have you spoken to her?"

"Are you saying you think I lied to the police when I said I didn't know where she went?" Stella asked with exaggerated offense. "Working on this story has made you awfully suspicious, Ms. Sanderson."

"I'm just saying, what if the baby's father came and took her from the hospital?"

"That's what you're worried about, Rose's safety?" Stella asked. She could tell I wasn't convinced Rose was in the clear. Stella was hard to manipulate. "*That* baby is not Rose's baby. Didn't they say it was a newborn? Rose's baby was at least three weeks old. And she wasn't a small baby."

"Approximately newborn," I clarified. "I don't think they know for sure."

"Well, well, you've certainly drunk the Kool-Aid," Stella said. "You sound just like them, Molly. And I don't mean that as a compliment."

Before I could defend myself—and it would have been a lame defense—Stella was distracted by a text.

"Great," she said. Then she spoke aloud at an annoyed clip, the contents of the response she was typing. "Why aren't you in school, Aidan?" She shook her head and looked up at me. "You'd think he'd know enough not to text me when he's supposed to be in class. Aidan's crappy behavior might bother me less if it didn't always make him look so damn stupid."

"Sounds like things are the same with him, then."

Aidan. The flower girl. I could still hear Ella's little voice: *What's a slut, Mommy?* There was surely an explanation. I just needed to hear it. And I needed to figure out a way to get Stella to tell me without having to ask her outright. Because I liked Stella, and I wasn't sure our relationship could survive that kind of direct accusation.

"Things with Aidan never change." She shrugged, frowned. "I just have to accept that I have no control over what he does. Maybe Aidan will end up fine, and maybe he won't. That's terrifying, but it's also reality. I can't drive myself crazy waiting to see how he'll turn out."

"Maybe he needs a girlfriend," I said. "You know, somebody to keep him in line."

"Bite your tongue," Stella said. "The one thing—probably the only thing—we have going for us is that Aidan doesn't have a girl-friend."

When I got home, I stood in the open door, staring down at the box, afraid to open it. Finally I crouched down and jerked off the lid as if ripping off a Band-Aid. My pulse was racing when I looked in, but Steve had been right, just some ordinary files.

I pulled one out at random. It was for a girl named Trisha Campbell from 2006. Inside were photocopies of a hodgepodge of Ridgedale University records—transcripts, dorm information, food-plan data. Trisha had been a good student, a double major in English and history who'd studied in Spain her junior year. I had Trisha's file open in front of me as I pulled out another, this one from 2007. A girl named Rebecca Raynor. Inside was a slightly different mix of records. Rebecca had been a biology major with less impressive grades but several awards for music achievement. I put Rebecca's file next to Trisha's. Then I saw a name I recognized: Rose Gowan, 2014.

When I looked back at Trisha's file, sure enough, there it was: VW, in the middle of her senior year. Rebecca had voluntarily withdrawn as well. As it turned out, every one of the students in that box—six, all female—had withdrawn voluntarily from Ridgedale University. One in 2006 and two in 2007, the remaining three from 2012 to 2014. The only obvious connection I could find was between the three girls who'd withdrawn in 2006 and 2007: They'd all taken the same American studies class, taught by a Professor Christine Carroll. Otherwise, the remaining girls' schedules and backgrounds were completely different.

I rushed out of the house, gripping the box of files, intent on confronting Director of Security Ben LaForde. But as I drove toward campus, I began to wonder what I was confronting him about. A series of improperly investigated sexual attacks on campus that led half a dozen women to leave school—that's what I was thinking. I felt sure that Ben LaForde was hiding something. But what proof did I have?

Six young women had withdrawn from Ridgedale University in about a decade. What was an average rate at any university? Perhaps many male students had withdrawn as well. There was no note in the box of files, nothing to explain what their assemblage meant. My theory was based largely on the fact that Stella suspected Rose Gowan had been raped on campus and then withdrawn. It was something of a leap to assume that the box implied that the same bad thing had happened to all the other girls.

By the time I'd reached campus, it had occurred to me that I would at least need some evidence the assaults happened before I started making accusations. Instead of parking and heading for LaForde's office, I circled back toward home, taking the long way past the Essex Bridge.

I was struck with unexpected sadness when I saw only a single police car parked along the road near where the baby had been found. As though everyone else had already given up. Forgotten. Moved on. I slowed as I rolled past, but the officer in the car didn't look up, his eyes locked on a cell phone. When I was a few yards past him, I noticed the driveway across the street, tucked between a couple shaggy trees. It curved right, to a run-down ranch house with a clear view of the road and the near side of the creek.

I jerked my car left and into the driveway. Surely the police had interviewed whoever lived there. But that didn't mean I couldn't also.

The house was more decrepit up close, the edges of the foundation disintegrating into the lawn, a rusted gutter unhinged, a garage window cracked, a lopsided shutter. The lawn was all crabgrass and tall weeds, mostly brown from winter, with a crumbling flagstone path leading up to the front door. There was a threadbare flag beside the front door. Even the house numbers had shifted, revealing rusty shadows in their wake.

I knocked hard, rattling the screen. I waited a minute with no response, then counted to twenty before knocking once more. There was a truck in the driveway, but that didn't mean anyone was home. I took a couple steps to the side, thinking about heading back to my car, when suddenly the front door opened.

"Hello?" an angry-sounding man shouted through the screen door. "Who's out there?"

He was big, tall and heavy if not quite overweight, with a head of straggly gray hair and a very large face. He was wearing pajama pants and a snug black T-shirt with a big Nike swoosh on the front. It hugged his big belly like a fabric sack.

"Oh, hi," I said, stepping forward so he could see me, even though I wasn't sure I wanted him to. "I'm Molly Sanderson, a reporter with the *Ridgedale Reader*, and—"

"A reporter, huh?" He sounded intrigued. "What do you want?"

Nothing, I thought of saying. *So I'll just be going now.*

"I'm working on a story about the baby they found across the street," I began. What if he'd had something to do with it? It wouldn't be the smartest thing in the world to dump a dead body across the street from your house. Then again, he didn't seem like the most thoughtful fellow. "I was hoping I might talk to you for a minute."

He narrowed his eyes, then pushed open the door with one meaty hand. "You coming in or not?" he asked when I didn't move forward.

"Oh, yes, thank you," I said, stepping inside.

Since when was it safe for me to go into the house of a huge man I did not know, an angry, possibly unstable man who, despite his age, could have easily overpowered me? Was this really the best use of my rediscovered moxie? For all I knew, that baby belonged to some poor woman this guy kept locked in his basement.

Fueling my fears was the overwhelming smell of rot, which smacked into me the second I stepped inside the house. Cat feces mixed with garbage, maybe? Hopefully, in fact. That was much better than the many other options that had jumped to mind, like death. I tried to breathe through my mouth so I wouldn't gag. But the filth in the air was palpable. I could feel it gathering in a sour blanket over my tongue.

It was dark, too. The curtains were pulled shut, the only light from a single standing lamp in the corner. Not dark enough, unfortunately, to hide the mess. There were boxes overflowing with clothes and papers and dusty Christmas decorations, and stacks and stacks of old magazines. In the open kitchen beyond, I could see dirty dishes and open food packages covering every available surface. An orange tabby cat was sitting in the center of the cluttered stove next to half a dozen industrial-size bottles of moisturizer. There were three more cats in a circle on the floor. I would have missed them if one hadn't switched its tail. They were staring up at two parrots in a cage hanging from the ceiling, waiting for their chance at a tasty treat. When one of the parrots ruffled its feathers, all the cats sprang to life, circling below like sharks. I waited for the man to shoo them away, but he didn't seem to notice.

"*Hannity* starts in ten minutes," he said, stepping around me to his recliner. "So you'll need to make it quick." He dropped himself down and jerked out the footrest in one practiced motion. He pointed at a couch that was either heavily patterned or very dirty or both. "Have a seat if you want."

"Oh, okay, great," I said, feeling my way carefully, praying I wouldn't trip and end up facedown on the revolting carpet.

"Sorry it's so dark," he said, motioning to the curtains. "Got to keep them closed. Otherwise, when the drones come, they'll be able to take pictures of everything. A couple shots of me looking long in the tooth, and"—he snapped his fingers—"like that, they'll convene a death panel."

Naturally: death panels and drones.

"I understand," I said. *That you're delusional.* "With the curtains closed, I guess you couldn't have seen anything related to what happened to the baby?"

"Who said that?" He sounded defensive again. "Damn police. Because I won't talk to those numb-nuts doesn't mean I don't know things. I just don't think it's my job to do *their* job by spying on people. I believe in personal liberty: every person's right to do as they wish."

"Including leaving a baby out in the woods?"

"Who the hell am I to judge?" He shrugged.

His beliefs seemed mostly random and nonsensical, but there was a thread of extreme conservatism. I hoped if I pulled at it, something interesting might unfurl.

"But if we don't hold people accountable for their actions, what kind of world will we have?" I asked. "A welfare state."

"You got that right." He narrowed his eyes at me. Then he nodded as though he'd come to some conclusion. "Come on, let me show you something."

He waved me down an even darker, more cluttered hall, where he could be planning to house me. I hesitated before following. I'd been out of shape for a long time, but I'd have to hope that I'd retained some kind of muscle memory if he charged at me.

"Did you see what happened to the baby, Mr. . . ."

I pulled out my phone as I walked behind him, quickly texting Justin the man's address with no explanation. If I didn't come home, it would at least give him a place to start. He was going to love hearing why I'd sent it, when I was forced to explain later.

"I didn't see what happened to the baby," the man said, turning in to the laundry room to the left of the door out to the garage. "But I seen something."

Inside, there was a telescope pointed out the window. He walked right over and placed a satisfied hand on it, as though it were the answer to all my questions. I stared at it, unsure what to say. The telescope made me feel better and worse—better about the possibility of this man having seen something useful; worse about the kind of person he was.

"What did you see?" I asked, my voice a quiet rasp.

"You believe in ghosts?"

No. But that wasn't the answer he wanted to hear. "Sure, I guess," I said. "Why?"

"Because I saw one." He leaned over to peek through his telescope. "Late one night, couple weeks ago."

"What did you see?"

He looked back at me and nodded gravely. "It *looked* like a girl," he said meaningfully. "Crawling out of the creek. She was covered in something, too, like war paint. Dark, you know, like that camouflage."

"Camouflage?" *Curious, not skeptical. Inquire, don't challenge.*

"Yeah, all over her face." He demonstrated how she might have applied it.

"And you saw her climb out of the creek?"

"I saw her twice. This time she came out of the creek and threw up. And she had the war paint. Last time, no paint. And she was running, in a red dress."

"This time?" And I'd been so hoping he'd say something that would prove him less delusional than he seemed.

"Yep, this time she climbed out and threw up." He shrugged. "Bent over the yard down there. Drunk, maybe. Then she took off, ran that way along the trees. With the paint on her face."

"When was the other time?"

"Oh, *long* time ago—fifteen, twenty years. Long, long time. It was the night that kid fell down and hit his head at that party."

"But it was the same girl?"

"Yep."

Great.

"I went outside with my camera, so I could get proof this time. You know, send it into one of those ghost-hunter shows. But by the time I got out there, she was gone. Disappeared." He clapped his hands together. "Just like that."

"So you don't have any pictures?"

"Nah, but I do got one thing. If I can find it." He started yanking open the drawers in the laundry room, which hadn't been used to launder anything in God knew how long. "It's in here somewhere. Hold on. Ah, wait. Here it is." He had something hidden in his fingers. I opened my palm, bracing for something damp and disgusting to be placed there. "It was hers. I found it in the street after I seen her here the first time."

Luckily, it was just cool and heavy. When I looked down, it was a small silver bracelet with words engraved on the inside: *To J.M. Always, Tex.*

"I'm telling you. It was the same girl. A goddamn ghost."

*The Legal Insufficiency of the Infanticide
and Neonaticide Paradigm*

AN ESSAY BY MOLLY SANDERSON

The body of a newborn female infant was discovered in Ridgedale less than thirty-six hours ago, near the Essex Bridge. The medical examiner has not yet released an official cause of death, and the baby remains unidentified.

Many have concluded that the infant's parents are responsible. Indeed, national statistics may support such assumptions. Children under the age of two are twice as likely to be murdered as they are to die in a car accident. According to recent Bureau of Justice statistics, in murders of children under the age of twelve, 57 percent of the perpetrators are the victim's parents. Further, in those cases, women account for 55 percent of the defendants. Meanwhile, women account for only 10.5 percent of all murder defendants.

At the same time, our understanding of maternal psychological disorders is continuing to evolve. Once thought of as a disorder that struck women only immediately after birth, postpartum depression is now known to be far more disparate. Women can suffer from birth-related mood disorders as early as their first trimester of pregnancy; likewise, symptoms can first surface long after labor and delivery. Contrary to previous assumptions, maternal depression can also manifest in a myriad of ways, many far different from what some might consider traditional depressive symptoms, including psychosis, obsessive-compulsive disorder, and other anxiety disorders.

In the tragic event that a mother does take her newborn's life—neonaticide— maternal depression, whether pre- or postnatal, often fails to meet the strict definition of insanity required by a court of law. Thus, expert testimony regarding the mother's mental state will often be barred. However, even if insanity is not an appropriate defense, juries and judges could still be allowed to consider evidence of a mother's mental state as one issue of fact to be weighed. This compromise alternative remains largely unexamined by our justice system. There are few areas of criminal law as unsettled as neonaticide. Often the severity of the crime is determined purely according to prosecutorial discretion; charges ranging from murder to illegal disposal of a corpse are common. Such inconsistency only serves to further complicate already volatile legal and emotional terrain.

There may be no crime more tragic than a mother taking her child's life. But we cannot allow our fear about what the murder of a baby says about us as human beings to relegate it to the unexamined provenance of monsters. Because those monsters are somebody's daughter or sister. They were once somebody's mother.

COMMENTS:

JoshuaSki2
57 min ago
Speak for yourself, Molly Sanderson. No woman I know would ever kill her own baby. No way, no how. You know who does that? Animals. That's who.

SaraBethK
55 min ago
Why are you trying to make this kind of behavior okay? "Anyone" could kill a baby?? Really? Lots of people have unexpected pregnancies and

go on to raise happy babies or they give them up for adoption or they raise them to be unhappy—but they don't KILL THEM!!! Why are you defending this mother when you don't even know what happened?

MommaX

52 min ago

Lack of money=lack of education=fewer options and higher stress. 22% of American children live in poverty in the U.S., with the rates among minority children much higher. Maybe there are people who really are just evil. Or maybe there are people who are forced by circumstance to make awful choices.

WyomingGirl

50 min ago

Did any of you hear about that case in Newark where they found a dead baby and then a long time later they found out the mother was dead? She was murdered also. For all we know they just haven't found the mother's body yet.

Anniemay

45 min ago

Personally, I prefer to stay sold on the idea that it was some scared kids. But it would certainly be helpful if the police told us something more . . .

Gracie55

37 min ago

This whole thing sounds like a witch hunt to me. Why don't we just round up everyone in Ridgedale who makes less than a certain dollar amount because unwanted pregnancies are more common in that group. Just because something is effective doesn't make it right.

ariel.c

28 min ago

I've been biting my tongue here, but if no one else is going to say it I will. Absentee parenting. None of this ever would have happened if teenagers weren't left unsupervised. I'm not saying it needs to be the mom. But it needs to be SOMEONE for God's sake.

tds@kidsrus

25 min ago

Ariel, are you seriously blaming this baby's death on working parents? We don't even know who the baby belongs to! Grr.

HeatherSAHM

21 min ago

Okay, maybe Ariel could have said it better, but I get her point. The parents who abandon babies are usually young. And only a parent who is really out of touch—or simply out of the house—would not notice that their own child was pregnant.

246Barry

11 min ago

HE IS STILL OUT THERE. FIND HIM.

Barbara

"Should we stop and get some ice cream, Cole?" Barbara called brightly as Steve drove them home. But she hardly felt lighthearted. Ever since she'd seen Cole's terribly violent drawing—all the blood and that missing arm—Barbara had been frantic. Quietly, though. She'd been doing her very best to keep her worry to herself, or at least away from her son.

Cole's appointment with Dr. Kellerman, a slight man with unnecessarily unkempt hair and saggy brown eyes, had been a real disappointment. It wasn't much more than a glorified playdate. And it had been so traumatic being in that little observation room, watching Cole through the one-way glass as if he were some kind of animal. Barbara had kept promising herself that she wouldn't get wound up afterward. But that was easier said than done.

"At this point, it doesn't make sense to press Cole on exactly why he did the drawing," Dr. Kellerman had said after his forty-five minutes of games and puzzles (and hardly any talking to Cole) were finished. "It's unlikely that he even knows."

"How can you possibly be sure?" Barbara had all but shouted. Unwise, obviously, unless she wanted to be blamed for everything. She couldn't help herself though. "You barely *asked* Cole anything."

"Trying to compel Cole to explain himself at this juncture would be both ineffective and counterproductive." Dr. Kellerman's voice had stayed calm, soothing, as if Barbara were the patient. "It would likely only add to his anxiety."

"So that's it?" Barbara asked.

"At this immediate moment, what triggered Cole to do that particular drawing isn't nearly as important as managing his anxiety. That's what's behind both his acting out in school and the drawing." The doctor went on, "With some careful assessment, we may find that his anxiety has been going on for quite some time, and these incidents represent some kind of peak. Sometimes it's possible to notice certain sensitivities only in retrospect."

"Cole isn't sensitive," Barbara had snapped. And that was that. She wasn't listening to Dr. Kellerman anymore, and she didn't care if he knew it. "He never has been."

Besides, Barbara already knew exactly what was going on. Cole had heard something he shouldn't have or seen some kind of violent video game or some bit of a terrible R-rated slasher movie, and it was haunting him. And there was only one place that could have happened: Stella's house. It was that older son of hers, probably, or maybe some fly-by-night boyfriend of Stella's. That was the best-case scenario: a movie, a game, something two-dimensional and not real-life.

Because Barbara had seen enough of Stella to know that there might be no end to the inappropriate nonsense that went on in her home.

"Honey, did you hear me about the ice cream?" Barbara called again.

When Cole still didn't answer, she craned around, bracing herself to see him sitting there in his car seat, staring out the window in that awful zombified way. Mercifully, his head was tipped forward in his sleep. He looked so peaceful and perfect like that. The way he'd always been. It made Barbara want to cry. How could he have fallen apart so quickly and so completely?

"Home," she whispered to Steve, motioning toward the backseat.

Steve glanced in the rearview at Cole sleeping, and nodded. He made a left onto Rainer Street, taking the back way, under the canopy of bowed beech trees on Mayfair Lane. Those trees had always seemed so magical and mysterious when Barbara was little, riding in the back of one of her dad's Al's Autobody pickups. Now they just looked ugly and evil.

She turned to look at Steve as he drove on. He was trying to seem relaxed, unconcerned, but she could see the worry gathered at the corners of his eyes. He'd actually seemed off ever since he came home to bring them to the appointment, even though he'd been fine that morning. Barbara hadn't asked what had happened in the intervening four hours at work. She wasn't going to, either. She didn't care about any investigation right now, not even one about some poor baby.

What Barbara cared about was *her* baby. She would have preferred that Steve hadn't gone into work at all that morning, but that was her husband: Duty calls, he goes. And now here he was, distracted again. She especially hated this particular faraway, worried look. She'd seen it before, and nothing good ever came of it.

Barbara had never liked the parties in the woods. Too out of control for her taste. Of course, that was what most of the other kids in Ridgedale High School loved about them. Sometimes as many as a hundred kids spread out all over the place—couples hooking up, boys playing their stupid game, girls gossiping in their cliques. Everyone drunk on the beers and whiskey they'd stolen from or been given at home. It was impossible to find any of your friends, and even when you did, everyone was too messed up to have an actual conversation. Barbara put up with the stupid parties, though, because Steve thought they were fun, especially "drunk obstacle," not that he was ever allowed to play. He was never drunk enough.

Steve hadn't proposed yet, but she knew he was planning to once they'd graduated. Sometimes she wondered if he'd already talked to her father about it. There was tension between Al and Steve whenever they were in the same room. But that might have been because the two men didn't really like each other. Al had built the lucrative Al's Autobody from the ground up, and he'd been looking forward to Barbara marrying someone to take over the family business. Instead, she had fallen in love with Steve, whose father had been a police sergeant killed in the line of duty back in Houston when he was six. Raised by the forever-frosty Wanda, who'd come to Ridgedale for a fresh start—a second cousin had offered her a good job at his insurance agency—Steve had always wanted to be a police officer like his father. He wasn't going to give that up for Al's Autobody, no matter how easy the money.

Even with a proposal in the works, Barbara knew she shouldn't keep Steve on too short a leash. They'd be grown-ups before long, and Barbara didn't want Steve to have regrets. And it was their senior year and, as Steve kept reminding her, their last chance to have fun. So she'd learned to bite her tongue and go to the parties in the muddy woods where she always ended up getting some piece of clothing smudged or torn. She tried to pretend to have fun sitting around on those soggy logs, talking to girls who'd been her friends for years but who she wouldn't miss after graduation. And she let Steve go off with his teammates to play their stupid game and forget about her for an hour or an entire evening. Because he always came back when he was ready, every single time.

It wasn't as easy to let him roam, though, once *she* started buzzing around, talking to Steve about her perfectly nice family who didn't like her or the boys she loved who didn't love her back or the boys who (naturally) dumped her once she'd lifted her skirt. Jenna had no shame, either. She couldn't have cared less that Steve belonged to someone else. Not that Barbara was worried, because honestly, how could you take a girl like that seriously—garbage is as garbage does. And Steve knew better than to fall for Jenna's bells and whistles. He loved Barbara. They complemented each other perfectly. Barbara was their head. Steve was their heart. He was just too nice to turn his back on some pathetic whore with no self-respect. And that might not have been a nice thing for Barbara to think, but that didn't make it any less true.

By that last Saturday in May of their senior spring, Barbara had had enough of the parties. Still, she'd gone out to the woods again to make Steve happy, even though she'd had a splitting headache. Her only request was that they leave early. But when she wanted to go, she couldn't find Steve anywhere. She looked for him for at least twenty minutes before she spotted him—not with the other boys, like she'd thought. Instead, there he was, at least a five- or ten-minute walk down the creek, sitting on a rock. *With* Jenna.

There was plenty of space between them, their hips weren't even close to touching, and all they were doing was talking. But it was the *way* they were talking that made Barbara's heart feel like it had been cleaved in two. Worse was the way Steve looked at Barbara as he tried to explain on the way back to his truck. His eyes were so filled with regret, not about what had happened but about what was *going* to happen. What Steve was helpless to stop.

"It's okay," Barbara had said, smiling hard and waving his explanations away like she didn't have a care in the world. "You're trying to help her, I know."

Because the last thing in the world she wanted was for him to make *excuses*. She didn't want to hear how much thought he'd already put into the whole situation.

"I do feel bad for her," Steve had said once they reached his truck. And then he paused. There was a "but" there. *But that's not . . .* Barbara had no interest in hearing the ending.

"Because you're a nice guy, Steve." She leaned over to kiss him before he could say anything else. "And that's why I love you."

As Steve carried Cole up to bed, Barbara sat down at the kitchen table with her coat still on. Their morning coffee cups were on the table, and there was unopened mail on the counter, and the pile of unfolded laundry and scattered toys. Ever since that meeting with Rhea, Barbara had been too distracted to worry about housework. After just a day of inattention, the house was falling into disarray. The mess couldn't be helping Cole. Maybe it was making things worse.

Barbara jumped to her feet, snatched up a mug in each hand, and marched toward the sink, where the caked breakfast plates were piled up. Underneath were their dinner dishes from the night before in several inches of brownish, foul-smelling water. It was revolting. All of it. But she'd barely made it through dinner with Caroline after seeing that drawing—a drawing Cole seemed not to fully remember doing—never mind doing the dishes afterward.

She'd left it to Steve to get them an appointment with Dr. Kellerman in the morning. No matter what it took, she'd said before taking Cole up to bed. Steve surely had to pull strings, maybe throw his status around, to get them in so quickly. She was grateful he hadn't felt the need to tell her about it.

Barbara was staring down at the disgusting filth when Steve came back downstairs.

"Well, he's out cold," he said with forced cheer, as usual trying to pump her up so he could sneak out the door. "If nothing else, that Dr. Kellerman sure knocks him out. Reason enough to go back."

"I'm never going back there." Barbara jammed her hands into the crowded sink. "And neither is my son."

Why had she let herself think about that stupid party all those years ago? Because now here she was, about to have yet another fight with Steve without him knowing what they were actually fighting about. But she was suddenly so *angry* at him. Furious. All that history, he was responsible for every last page. Maybe if Barbara hadn't been so distracted by *her* being back, she would have been paying more attention to whatever was happening with Cole.

As Barbara tumbled her hands around the sink, a glass stacked on top of one of the dinner plates slid off to the side. She grabbed for it, but it slipped through her fingers and shattered, the pieces vanishing into the grimy water below.

"Dammit!" Barbara yelled as she jerked off her coat and threw it on the floor. Then she grabbed the edge of the sink and started to cry.

"Whoa, hey," Steve said as he came up behind her. She waited to feel his hands on her arms, but he didn't touch her. "It's going to be okay. Cole is going to be okay."

Barbara turned around and pressed her face against his chest so she wouldn't start screaming at him. Because everything seemed like his fault suddenly. She stayed there for a long time, until Steve finally patted her shoulders.

"You should get back to work," she said, when he still hadn't hugged her. Because that was what he wanted, wasn't it? To get back to the job that Barbara was beginning to wonder if he might not love more than her. Anyway, if he stayed, she couldn't be sure what she'd say. "I'll be fine, really. I'll be even better when I see you on the news announcing that you've arrested the person responsible for what happened to that poor baby."

"Yeah, well, I wouldn't hold your breath." Steve shook his head, then scrubbed his hands over his face.

Barbara took a breath: *Make nice, ask about it.* Steve hated it when she was cold, absolutely hated it. He didn't ever *say* that, of course. Steve was never one to criticize, but he'd draw right back into that shell of his. And once he was tucked in there, it was impossible to pry him out.

"What about that girl in the hospital?" she asked.

He shook his head. "There's something not right with that situation, given the way she took off," he said. "But *her* baby isn't *that* baby. Midwife swears she gave birth three weeks ago to an eight-pound baby. The ME isn't ready to make an official announcement yet, but he's sure the baby wasn't that old."

"But she ran away."

"Who knows? Maybe your friend Stella put her up to that." He was joking, that was clear. "Apparently, Stella really likes drama."

"Drama? Who told you that?" Serious or not, he'd gotten the idea from somewhere.

"Oh, her friend Molly—Ella's mom. The reporter for the *Ridgedale Reader*."

"Did she mention Will or Cole? What did she mean, 'drama'?"

"No, no, no." Steve waved a finger back and forth. "I shouldn't have even mentioned Stella. There's no reason to think that she has anything to do with what's going on with Cole."

"But he heard or saw something somewhere, Steve. And it wasn't here."

"First of all, you're deciding that's true. That's not what Dr. Kellerman said."

"I know it's true, Steve. Something happened to Cole when he was with Will. At his house."

"Barbara, you *can't* know that. Even Dr. Kellerman said it could be some kind of preexisting—"

"Steve, stop it!" Barbara shouted. "Stop making excuses so I won't get angry at some woman you have no proof is innocent and who you don't even know!"

His jaw set. He was losing patience with her. But that was it. That was as mad as he'd get. Soon he'd disappear, retreat. Off to work, into his precious shell. Sometimes Barbara would have done anything for him to start screaming at her.

"I'm not trying to protect her," he said, the picture of reason. "But focusing on her instead of Cole isn't going to help anything."

He picked up his keys. Because he was going to go anyway, of course, whether or not Barbara needed him to stay.

"Promise me you'll leave it," he said. "That you'll drop it with Stella."

"Sure," she said. And if he believed that—the way she'd said it—he was even more distracted than she'd thought.

"Did they help Cole?" Hannah asked the second she got home from school, looking around downstairs like she was trying to find him.

"Cole's fine, honey," Barbara said, specifically not answering Hannah's question. "He's tired and a little stressed, that's all. How was the AP calculus practice test?"

Hannah shrugged. "Okay, I guess. It was kind of hard to concentrate."

"'Okay, I guess.'" Barbara mimicked Hannah's shrug and her tone of voice. There were better ways to handle Hannah's worry about Cole's worry than mocking her. But Barbara wasn't perfect. She'd never pretended to be. "Cornell may have accepted you early, but they won't be very impressed if you don't pass those APs you've promised them."

"Sorry, I didn't . . ." Hannah looked wounded. "I think I probably did okay enough. Thanks for asking."

"Wait, it's Wednesday, isn't it? Do you have tutoring today?" Barbara hoped not. She'd been counting the minutes until Hannah got home so she could leave.

"She couldn't make it," Hannah said, blinking up at Barbara guiltily. She probably felt responsible for that girl's bad choices, too.

Barbara shook her head and exhaled. "It'll hardly be your fault when that girl doesn't get her GED."

"Mom, that's mean." She recoiled when Barbara's eyes shot over to her. "I just— Sandy tries really hard."

"Trust me, Hannah." Barbara laughed, trying not to let her annoyance get the best of her. But *mean*? Really, how dare she? "Girls like that never know what's good for them."

"But you've never even met her," Hannah said. And there she went, defending some girl she barely knew. Just like her father. God help her. The heartbreak that lay ahead for that bleeding heart of hers.

"Oh, honey, someday you'll understand. I don't need to have met her to know what kind of girl she is." Barbara smiled angrily as she grabbed her keys off the counter. "Cole is napping, and I need to run out for a little. Don't wake him—he was just so exhausted—but if he does get up, have him watch TV. I need him to stay calm."

It wasn't until Barbara had pulled the car out of the garage that she realized she'd forgotten her purse on the kitchen counter. She left the car running as she dashed back inside, afraid something might stop her from leaving again. Sure enough, as she crossed the kitchen from the side door, she heard a strange, soft murmuring coming from the living room. Hannah talking on the phone, maybe? But the conversation was oddly one-sided, and Hannah's voice was strangely high. Barbara inched around the corner to see what she was doing out there.

Hannah was sitting on the couch with Cole's legs stretched across her lap, the rest of him tucked warmly into the crook of her arm. Hannah must have woken him the second Barbara left the house— exactly as she'd told her not to do. She was reading to him, too, from *The Missing Piece*, her favorite book when she was little. For years, Hannah had slept with it under her pillow every night.

Barbara swallowed the urge to snap at Hannah for defying her. Instead, she clenched her jaw and forced herself back out to the car. So she could find the person she really needed to be snapping at.

Fifteen minutes later, Barbara was pulling up Stella's long curved driveway toward the huge mansion at the top of the hill—a new-made-to-look-old structure set deep in the woods. With a stone facade and rambling wraparound porch, the house was big enough for a family of seven, maybe more. And yet there poor, husbandless Stella lived with all her money and her Botox and her two measly messed-up children.

Barbara forced herself to take a deep breath, pasting a smile on her face as she headed up the polished stone walkway, which went on forever before turning toward the front steps and two absurdly huge red doors. Stella wasn't going to admit that something had happened to Cole in her home. Barbara would need to ease her into it, charm her a little. She took another breath and smiled harder before she rang the bell.

A teenage boy opened the door, Aidan, presumably. He had shaggy surfer hair, a freckled nose, and large golden-brown eyes. Barbara had once asked Hannah what he looked like. She'd said, *Cute, I guess*, unimpressed in that way Hannah always was by boys. But even Barbara had to admit Aidan was a good-looking kid. She could only imagine the piles of broken hearts he'd left in his wake. What a stroke of luck that he'd answered the door. She was much more likely to get something out of a cocky kid like Aidan—too arrogant to be careful—than Stella.

"You must be Will's brother, Aidan?" Barbara smiled so hard it made her cheeks ache. "My son, Cole, is in class with Will."

"Yeah?" He looked past Barbara, staring vacantly as if trying to process Cole not being there behind her. Was he high, or slow, or something? Was that what Stella was hiding? Barbara had also asked Hannah what Aidan was like, but she didn't know. He was new to school and a year younger and didn't really hang out with anybody, she'd said. Certainly not, Barbara suspected, the group of popular kids that Hannah counted as her closest friends. Hannah did say there were rumors that Aidan had gotten into trouble at his last school, and he'd already gotten into more than one fight at Ridgedale High.

"Well, Cole's not here right now, Aidan," Barbara went on, tilting her head a little to the side to make eye contact. "But Cole has been spending a lot of time here lately. Do you maybe know if the boys saw something here that they weren't supposed to? Like a TV show or a video game or something?" *Or, you know,* you *doing something horrible.* Barbara stepped closer and tried to soften her expression. But her face felt like it was made of rubber. "We don't think for a second *you* did anything wrong, Aidan. I'm sure whatever happened was an accident."

"An accident?" He looked angry all of a sudden. Really, really angry. Like someone who had something horrible to hide. "Seriously, lady, what the hell are you talking about?"

There was a voice then, coming from inside the house. Stella, surely. Shoot. Just when Barbara was getting somewhere. With his hand on the doorknob, Aidan turned to shout back. "Cole's mom!" And then, annoyed: "How would I know? Why don't *you* ask her?"

A second later, Stella appeared in the doorway, shooing Aidan off until he disappeared into the house behind her. "Excuse me, Barbara." She crossed her long, muscular arms. Her cheeks were flushed, eyes aglow. "But can *I* help you?"

So much for charm. At least Barbara could cut to the chase now.

"I need to know what happened to Cole, Stella."

"Have you lost your mind, Barbara?" Stella looked her up and down. "Are you seriously *accusing* us of something?"

"Cole said that something happened here that scared him." That might as well have been the truth. "He's too afraid to tell me exactly what, but he's positively traumatized."

"So you thought it was appropriate to try to traumatize *my* son by interrogating him outside of my presence?" Stella worked her neck like a teenager. "What are you, Barbara? The Mommy Gestapo?"

"I'm just trying to help Cole," Barbara said, her voice cracking unexpectedly. She couldn't get emotional, not now. Not in front of Stella. She'd go right in for the kill. "If it was Will who was traumatized, I'm sure you'd be asking the same questions."

"Listen, Barbara," Stella said, her voice trembling. She checked over her shoulder to be sure that Aidan had gone. "I think I've been pretty patient with you and your husband, but I've had just about all the bullshit accusations I can take for one week."

"I'm here as a mother who's worried about her son, Stella. I'd think you could have some compassion. I just want to restore calm to my household." Barbara should leave it there, she knew. But there was that *look* on Stella's face—so smug. "Maybe it's hard for you to understand, but not everybody lives for drama."

"Drama?" Stella snorted. "I'm sorry, is that some kind of dig? You don't even know me, Barbara."

But Stella's best friend, Molly, did and it was she who'd said that Stella was a drama queen. Barbara wanted so badly to rub that in Stella's face, but Steve would have killed her.

"Let's just call it an educated guess."

Stella batted her eyelashes, then smiled unpleasantly. "I'm sorry your son is struggling, Barbara." Her voice was so cool and composed suddenly. It was unsettling. "I can imagine that would be extremely difficult for someone like yourself, who really values what's 'normal.'" Stella's fingers hooked the air. "But nothing happened to Cole here. Not under my roof. And now I'd like for you to get your bony, judgmental ass the fuck off my porch."

And with that, Stella stepped back and slammed the door.

By the time Barbara made it down to Ridgedale Elementary School and was walking down the hall to Cole's classroom, it was past four o'clock. Luckily, she saw through the small glass window, Rhea was still there, seated at one of the tables writing out some kind of card.

After their run-in, Barbara was absolutely convinced Stella knew more than she was telling. Otherwise, why would she be so defensive? But Barbara needed one last piece of proof before presenting her case to Steve: that nothing could have happened to Cole at school.

Barbara knocked on the door and kept her face near the glass. Rhea frowned as soon as she looked up. She was probably about to leave for the night and didn't want to get hung up. Slowly, Rhea closed the card, then slid it into her bag. After forever, it seemed, she waved Barbara inside.

"What can I do for you, Barbara?" Rhea asked flatly, gathering her things. She hadn't even looked at Barbara. There was something wrong. Rhea wasn't at all her usual bubbly self.

"I wanted to talk some more about Cole," Barbara began carefully. "If you have a minute."

"Yes, I heard about some of your *concerns*." Rhea's voice was coated in ice and pointy things. "At length."

At length? Barbara blinked at her. And then it occurred to her with a creeping unease. Barbara had stopped by the PTA office to talk to some of the mothers there, and she *may* have said a thing or two about Rhea in anger. And she *may* not have been careful about who was around listening. Had it been one of Rhea's fellow teachers? Or, God forbid, Rhea herself?

"I'm only trying to do what's best for my son," Barbara said. She wasn't about to *admit* to saying anything specific, not if Rhea was going to be vague. "I'm sure you understand."

"My shirts are too tight?" Rhea said, crossing her arms over her— precisely the point—very clingy top. "Oh, and I wear too much makeup. That's right, it's all coming back to me. Enlighten me, how is either of those related to my teaching ability?"

"Well, that's taking what I said quite out of—"

Rhea held up a hand. "On second thought, I don't even want to know." She walked over to a short stack of papers on a nearby table, brought them back, and slid them into her bag. "Now, what is it? I'm on my way home."

"We had Cole evaluated by that doctor you suggested," Barbara offered. It was something of an olive branch.

"Really?" Rhea looked genuinely taken aback. Because Rhea was judging Barbara, too: stubborn, inflexible know-it-all. She'd heard it all before. "What did he say?"

"That Cole's behavior is the result of a trauma." A small lie with a noble purpose.

Rhea's eyes were wide. "My goodness, what trauma?"

"We're trying to figure that out. We were hoping you could help."

Rhea's face tightened. "Nothing happened to Cole here, Barbara. If that's what you're suggesting *again*. I thought we already discussed this."

But Barbara needed to push. She needed to be absolutely sure before she went to Steve. Otherwise, he'd never listen. "Well, I'm sure that you didn't mean for it to. But there are *nineteen* children, Rhea. Surely you can't have your eye on every single one of them all the time."

Rhea hung her head and let her shoulders drop. She took a deep breath before she looked up. "Listen, Barbara, I understand how difficult this must be for you and your family," she began, as though she had mustered the very last of her patience. "It's so painful for a parent to watch a child suffer. I know what you're feeling and—"

"Wait, I'm sorry, what did you just say?" Rage flashed in Barbara's gut. "*You* know what *I'm* feeling? Excuse me, Rhea, but you don't even *have* children. How *dare* you say you know what I'm feeling?"

Rhea looked like she'd been slapped. But that wasn't a judgment, it was a fact. Rhea didn't have children. It wasn't Barbara's fault if Rhea was the kind of person who could be unaware of the gaping hole that created in the center of her life.

"To each his own, of course," Barbara went on, just to clarify. Because she wasn't suggesting that everyone *needed* to have children. Only those people who wanted to claim they knew what it was like to be a parent. "Not everyone was meant to have a family."

Rhea nodded, frowning with exaggerated thoughtfulness. But now there was hate in her eyes. "You know, Barbara, all these years, I've been wondering: Why me? Why did *I* have to have a hysterectomy when I was only twenty-six?" Her voice quaked. "And here you had the answer all along: I just wasn't meant to have a family."

Barbara's eyes went down to Rhea's perfectly flat midsection. Well, how was she supposed to know? "I didn't mean to suggest . . ."

But there was no point. They both knew exactly what she'd meant. And Rhea was already reaching for her coat.

"I am genuinely sorry that Cole is hurting. I care about him very much." Rhea was all business as she crossed the room and opened the classroom door. "But if something happened to him, it didn't happen here." She waved a hand toward the hall, ushering Barbara out the door. "And now, Barbara, you really do need to go."

RIDGEDALE READER

Print Edition

March 18, 2015

Essex Bridge: An Area Marked by Tragedy

BY MOLLY SANDERSON

The woods behind Essex Bridge were long known to be a place where Ridgedale High School students congregated on warm weekend evenings. When the parties got too raucous, neighbors would inevitably summon the Ridgedale Police. Students would be sent on their way, the intoxicated occasionally having their keys confiscated or being driven home in the back of a police car.

There were never any arrests. The general view among residents and local law enforcement was that these were good kids, out to have a good time.

In the spring of 1994, Simon Barton was enjoying the end of his senior year at Ridgedale High School. An accomplished athlete as well as an honor student, Simon's biggest concern was whether he should enroll in Duke University or play basketball for the University of Virginia, where he had been offered an athletic scholarship.

The only child of Sheila and Scott Barton, Simon was born at Ridgedale University Hospital and had lived in town his entire life. He died after slipping in the woods and suffering a traumatic head injury.

Despite evidence of heavy underage drinking that night, there were never any arrests in connection with his death. In place of accusation or prosecution, there was a collective outpouring of grief. Simon Barton's funeral was attended by more than 900 of Ridgedale High School's 1,000 students. Within weeks, there had been more than half a dozen fund-raisers to establish a scholarship in Simon's name.

Twenty years later, there has been another death in those same woods. As of today, there have been more than 200 posts on a social media site called Frat Chat. Intended for use by university students, Frat Chat has in Ridgedale—as in many other towns—been overtaken by high school students. The vast majority of these posts accuse various students of being responsible for the baby's death.

Despite the proximity, the police believe the two incidents are unrelated. Police have yet to identify the baby's mother or father and continue to ask for the public's help. If you have any information, please contact the police at 888-526-1899.

M.S.: Why don't we ever talk about the baby? We talk about everything else—my job, Ella, Justin. My mother, who's been dead for almost twenty years.

Q: You don't think she's relevant?

M.S.: No, I don't. I'm afraid I'll turn into her, of course. But other than that, no, I don't think she's relevant.

Q: Turn into her how?

M.S.: She was destroyed because my father left her. And because she was destroyed, she was a terrible mother.

Q: Do you think you're destroyed? That you'll end up a terrible mother?

M.S.: End up? It's already happened. I've been a terrible mother for months. I have to get over this. I have to get better. Or, yes, I'll end up just like my mother. I can live with almost anything but that. So how am I going to get over it?

Q: I think we need to address your guilt.

M.S.: The baby was inside me. Of course I feel guilty.

Q: What was happening in the days before you found out the baby's heart had stopped?

M.S.: The days before? I don't know. I don't remember much. What difference does it make?

Q: The fact that you can't remember suggests to me that it might matter very much.

M.S.: The usual things. I was finishing a draft of a piece of proposed legislation before maternity leave. And we were trying to potty-train Ella, and she kept peeing on the carpet, which sounds funny now. But it wasn't funny then. All I kept thinking was that we were going to have to get the carpets cleaned before Justin's family came to see the baby.

Q: And what about Justin? Was he busy, too?

M.S.: So busy. He'd taken over a class for a colleague, and he was presenting two different papers at two different conferences in the three weeks before the baby was due. We were both really busy. That's life, right? Everybody's busy.

Q: I've never heard you be frustrated by that.

M.S.: That Justin was busy? After how much he's given up to take care of us since? How could I possibly be irritated by that? Besides, I was the one carrying the baby.

Q: And so he bears no responsibility?

M.S.: He has *responsibilities*, yes. He helped with Ella afterward. And before, too. But he was working all hours. That wasn't his fault. He had a job to do.

Q: You seem very frustrated now, though.

M.S.: I am frustrated. With *you*. Listen, our problem wasn't who folded more laundry or unloaded the dishwasher or who last took out the garbage. Our baby is dead, that's our problem.

JENNA

It finally happened!!! The Captain and I had sex! I'd call it making love, if that wasn't so gross. But that's what it felt like: love. Everything about it was so perfect. His parents were away, so we had the house to ourselves and I lied and told my parents that I was staying at Tiff's house.

And it worked like a charm. For once, they didn't even call Tiff's mom to check. Otherwise, they would have found out that her family was away at a wedding in Philadelphia.

The Captain actually COOKED dinner for me first. Like he was my husband or something. It was some kind of spaghetti that was kind of gross, but I never tasted anything better in my whole entire life.

And it was amazing. Didn't hurt at all like Tiffany said it would. The Captain was so sweet and gentle. And he didn't even know it was my first time. (I didn't want him to be freaked out, and anyway it's not like it's that big of a deal. I've done A LOT of other stuff with A LOT of other guys.) He didn't tell me he loved me afterward—I wouldn't have wanted him to.

It was so much better when he just held me like he did.

Sandy

At least there weren't any cars in the driveway when Sandy got to Hannah's house. Her heart was still beating hard, though, as she jumped off her bike.

Sandy never would have gone to Hannah's if she'd had any choice. After making it out of the chief of police's office, the last place she wanted to go was his *house*. But it was the way Hannah had sounded on the phone when she'd given up on texting and started to call Sandy—like she was sliding down to the bottom of a well. Sandy had thought: *This is it. This is the end.* The whole time Hannah had been a house of cards. And finally, those motherfuckers had started to slide. Maybe right into the hands of the chief of police.

He'd been nice enough to Sandy, had said he would look for Jenna and all that. But there was something about the way he acted after Sandy said Jenna's name. Like it had changed everything for him. For sure Hannah's dad at least knew of Jenna, had heard her name before. Maybe that could be a good thing, but Sandy sure as hell wanted to get in and out of his house before it turned into a bad one.

"I'm so glad you're here," Hannah said when she opened the door. She gave Sandy a teary, worried smile, then pulled her into a tight hug as she dragged her inside. "It's so good to see you. I've been really worried."

"But you *really* don't have to worry," Sandy said. Even though she already knew there was no point. Nothing she said was going to get them out of this wack-ass country they'd gotten lost in. "I'm all right, I promise."

"Do you want a drink or anything?" Hannah asked, leading Sandy toward the kitchen. "God, you look tired. Did you ever end up seeing a doctor?"

Barely in the door and there Hannah went. Sandy had been hoping Hannah wasn't going to do this—make them have this conversation face-to-face. Seemed stupid now, but Sandy had actually thought she and Hannah would never talk to each other again after that night. That Sandy would never have to talk to anyone about what happened. And after a while—a long time even—it would be like it hadn't. Looking now at Hannah's worried face, Sandy could see just how wrong she'd been.

"I'm all good," Sandy said. "Like I said a bunch of times. *Totally* fine."

The truth was she felt like crap. She hadn't slept in two days, and she didn't think she'd ever be hungry again.

"Sorry to drag you over here," Hannah said. "But I have to watch my brother. He hasn't been . . . he's not feeling well. He's okay right now, but my mom had to go out and, well, I didn't know when I was going to get the chance to get out again."

"Listen, can we go upstairs? Just in case your parents come home, I don't want to be sitting here, right near the front door."

Really it was that Sandy could hear the TV in the other room, where Hannah's little brother must have been. And it was giving her bad flashbacks.

"Sure, come on," Hannah said, smiling as they headed for the steps like she was eight and Sandy was there for a sleepover. "We'll go to my room."

It wasn't the first time Sandy had felt like a little girl around Hannah. It was part of why Sandy had liked hanging out with her. She felt like a regular kid when they were together, gossiping about stupid, regular shit.

"You've *never* had a boyfriend, ever?" Sandy had asked during one of their last tutoring sessions. She'd been telling Hannah about Aidan, which felt dumb. It wasn't like he was her boyfriend. "How's that possible? You're, what, seventeen? And look at you. I don't believe you."

It wasn't like she and Hannah had known each other long, but lately they had been talking about all sorts of stuff that had nothing to do with Sandy's coursework. Hannah had suggested it the first time. You know, *if* Sandy wanted to hang out after. And it was nice, Hannah wanting to do that, because it wasn't like she was hard up for friends or something. Unless what Hannah wanted was a friend as messed up as Sandy, to feel good about herself by comparison. But Sandy could live with that. Everybody needed something.

"What do you mean, you don't believe me?" Hannah had laughed a little. "I'm serious, no boyfriend ever. It's true."

"Fine, whatever, but for the record, I don't believe you." Sandy had waved a pencil in Hannah's face. "You're too pretty and nice and smart— Wait, are you gay?" That felt like it might explain a lot. "I mean, I don't give a shit. But in this particular situation, I think that would count as lying. Girlfriend, boyfriend, same thing."

"I like boys," Hannah had said with a shrug. "But it's complicated. They're not worth the trouble right now."

"Maybe you've been with the wrong guys. Usually, it's the ladies who overcomplicate shit."

But maybe Sandy was the one getting things wrong. When guys really wanted you—all of you—it probably was a shitload messier. Maybe Sandy's relationships with boys had always been simple because they weren't relationships at all. Guys wanted one thing from Sandy: sex. And she knew after a lifetime of watching Jenna that it was stupid to give it up to them as easily as she did. But for some reason, it had always felt more stupid to snap on a chastity belt. Only an idiot would think doing that would change the way things were going to turn out for her.

"I'm not saying the *guys* are complicated." Hannah rolled her eyes.

"It's a bunch of other things. My mom, for one. If you think she's uptight about glitter shoes, imagine what she'd be like about boys. Anyway, it's not just her. I think maybe I want to save myself until marriage. And don't bother making fun of me. I already know you'll probably think that's 'fucked up' or whatever."

Hannah always sounded so weird, swearing. Like she didn't know what the words meant.

Sandy shrugged. "Is that what *you* want? To wait until you're married? And I mean you, not your mom."

Hannah looked up then. "Yes," she said quietly. "It is what I want. When I'm with someone finally, I want it to be someone who likes me for me, you know. All the boys I know, usually, it feels like all they care about is themselves."

What the hell did Sandy know? That was probably exactly what Hannah should do: wait for someone more mature. It was probably exactly what Sandy should have done.

"If that's what *you* want," Sandy said, "then there's nothing fucked up about it."

"I can't tell you how good it is to see that you're okay," Hannah said again once they were upstairs. She motioned for Sandy to sit on the bed while she pulled out the desk chair and turned it around. Hannah did look relieved now, happy almost. "I mean, you look tired, like I said. But I was picturing—I don't know, worse."

Sandy needed to pull the trigger—end this in a way that hopefully wouldn't make Hannah freak. Then Sandy needed to back the fuck out of this mess, slow and steady. No big movements.

"Yeah," Sandy said. "So listen, I'm glad I came, too. Because I needed to tell you that I'm going out of town. I might be pretty hard to reach for a while."

Not moving out of Ridgedale, though, that would be too much. Just a trip, an excuse for Sandy to be out of touch. People like Hannah went out of town all the time—long weekends, summer vacation—it was a regular thing they did.

"Oh?" Hannah looked worried as she rocked her hips back and forth, tucking her hands beneath her thighs. "Where are you going?"

Crap. Sandy hadn't worked that out. That was another thing people like Hannah did: They planned an actual place to go instead of driving around randomly, like the last time she and Jenna had gone on "vacation" and ended up at a Courtyard Marriott in Camden.

"Washington, D.C.," Sandy said. First place that jumped to mind. And it was somewhere regular people went. "For a few weeks. Maybe a month."

"A month?" Hannah blinked at her. "That's such a long time."

Shit, it was. Sandy shouldn't have said a month. She should have started small, hoped for the best. But what did any of this matter? A week, a month. At the end of the day, Sandy wouldn't be able to control what Hannah said or who she said it to once she was gone. All the more reason for Sandy to go for real. To go far. And to go forever. But for that, she'd need Jenna.

"Yeah, it is kind of a long time," Sandy said. "But my mom wants to stay for a while, so . . ."

"Won't you have your phone?"

Shit. Why hadn't she thought of that either? "Uh, my mom won't let me bring it. She wants to, you know, unplug."

"Oh, okay," Hannah said. She seemed satisfied. Only she, with that mother of hers, would believe that bullshit. "Well, thanks for coming over. I just, I couldn't— I needed to actually see you to know that you were okay. It was— I couldn't sleep, thinking about it. Also, I wanted to make sure that you don't blame yourself. Because it was an accident, the whole thing."

Sandy nodded, afraid of saying the wrong thing when she was so close to getting out the door. "Yeah—I mean, no. Definitely don't blame myself. Thanks for checking. But I do kind of have to go now. My mom will be waiting for me. Can I just use your bathroom before I take off?" She wanted to splash water on her face, wash her hands. She'd been on her bike for hours.

"Yeah, sure, of course. It's right down the hall on the left."

Sandy stared at her reflection in the bathroom mirror. Hannah was right. She did look like shit. But it wasn't like she was going to start looking better anytime soon. When she made it home to their empty apartment, she'd never be able to sleep.

The medicine cabinet caught Sandy's eye then. Maybe there was a chance she could *feel* better for a while. Or maybe she could just forget a little bit. At this point, she'd settle for that. For temporary. Seemed about fucking time Sandy cut herself a break. And yeah, it would be better if it wasn't the chief of police's medicine cabinet she was about to swipe some bottles from. But it wasn't like he'd know she'd been there. Besides, maybe Aidan had the right idea all along. Maybe what she needed was a bigger fuck-it bucket.

Sandy opened the medicine cabinet; there were more than half a dozen little amber bottles with all sorts of different names. There had to be something in there that would work. That would wipe out the world. She grabbed a couple of the older bottles from the way back (one of Barbara's, one of Steve's—faded, nearly expired, less likely to be missed) that had the telltale *Danger, Controlled Substance. Illegal to Dispense Without Prescription.* Tranquilizers, painkillers, what difference did it make? One of them was bound to do the trick. Sandy shook the bottles, and something rattled inside. Not now, though, not yet. Only if she really couldn't fucking take it anymore—the looking for Jenna, the remembering. Sandy shoved the bottles in her pockets. She was pulling her shirt down over the lump in her jeans when there was a soft knock on the door.

"You should go now, Sandy. Out the back door," Hannah whispered from the other side. "My brother just woke up and he's really upset. My mom's on her way home."

Sandy saw the notice—bright yellow and taped across her apartment door—as she was coming up the steps of Ridgedale Commons. Even from that distance, she could see the padlock, too. The guy had said twenty-four hours. He'd probably even given her an extra few.

"Shit." Sandy stopped and leaned against the wrought-iron railing, feeling her throat squeeze tight. She just couldn't keep it all in anymore. Couldn't take one more goddamn thing. "Shit!"

She yelled it so loud that her throat vibrated as she slid down the wall. She curled up on the ground, arms wrapped tight around her knees, mouth pressed against them. And then she started to bawl. Once she'd started, it was like she was never going to stop. Her body shook and she couldn't catch her breath. Her face was a snotty mess. She jammed her lips harder against her knees until she felt like her mouth might tear. She wanted it to.

Sandy was still crying when she heard Mrs. Wilson's door open. A second later, she heard the old lady come out, felt her staring down. *Fuck.*

"Good Lord," her neighbor said. "What in heaven are you doing?"

Perfect. Exactly what Sandy needed: to have Mrs. Wilson rip in to her. Sandy shouldn't have yelled. Not right outside Mrs. Wilson's door. She knew better. Sandy tried wiping her eyes, hoping it would help her stop crying. But that only made it worse. She felt like she was melting beneath her fingertips, like her tears were washing away her skin.

"Such a goddamn mess, all of this, all the time," Mrs. Wilson muttered, coming closer. Sandy could see the old woman's wiry bare feet, her toes painted a bright orange. She wondered for a second what it would feel like when Mrs. Wilson kicked her. She braced herself for it.

When the pain didn't come, Sandy looked up. Mrs. Wilson was standing there in a teenager's pink sweatsuit, her eyes shiny brown marbles in her bony old-lady face. She had a hand on her hip and a look of disgust on her face. "You hurt or something?" she shouted, like the problem was Sandy's hearing. "One of these bastards do something to you?"

Sandy shook her head, but Mrs. Wilson looked up and down the walkway as if trying to find someone to blame. Then her eyes set on Sandy's front door. She turned her orange-polished toes in the direction of the door, then padded down for closer inspection. She lifted her pointy chin to squint at the ugly yellow sticker, then poked her nose in close to the padlock that was bolting shut the door.

Mrs. Wilson marched back toward her own apartment, muttering more angrily as she disappeared inside. Sandy waited for her to slam the door. Instead, Mrs. Wilson reappeared, a crowbar gripped in her hand.

Hoisting it against her hip, Ms. Wilson headed to the apartment on the far side of hers. Every step looked like it might topple her skinny body. She rested the crowbar on the ground before pounding on her far neighbor's door.

Two young guys lived there. Shady for sure, but not dealers, as far as Sandy knew. Otherwise, Jenna would have found her way over there a long time ago. Stolen electronics, maybe, or counterfeit something or other. From the constant stream of people in and out of their door, they were definitely selling something.

"Hey, I know you're in there!" Mrs. Wilson shouted when they didn't answer right away. She banged harder, this time with her whole forearm. "I just heard your TV through my wall! Open up the damn door!"

A second later, the one with the scruff of hair on his chin filled the entryway. He was wearing a 76ers jersey and a baseball cap backward over a tangled brown ponytail. There was a gold chain on his right wrist. The guy didn't say anything, just stared at Mrs. Wilson like a startled elephant, not angry, only confused.

"Here." She shoved the crowbar at him. He blinked down at it but didn't take it. "Go on," she scolded. "What are you waiting for?"

Finally, he reached forward. In his big fingers, the crowbar became a weightless matchstick. He stared down at it, surprised and even more confused.

"Now," Mrs. Wilson said, "you take that and go open that door."

"What?" His voice was nicer, more polite, than Sandy would have expected.

"You heard me. Go open that door for this girl." Mrs. Wilson hooked a thumb toward Sandy's apartment. "It's locked."

"What?" Now he sounded like a whiny teenager. "Why?"

"Because I said so," she snapped, crossing her arms. "You boys are lucky someone hasn't called the police on you. And *someone* still could."

The guy heaved a loud sigh and lugged himself out of his apartment. As he headed for Sandy's door, he tossed the crowbar higher in his huge hand. He paused at Sandy's door to read the notice, turning back to look at Mrs. Wilson.

"Oh, please, don't act like you care about the law." She flapped a hand at him. "Just do it."

He looked over his shoulder once more to see if anyone was watching—something he'd definitely done a hundred times before when breaking in elsewhere—then snapped the lock off in one easy movement. It fell to the ground with a thud. He walked back toward them, eyes on the ground. He rested the crowbar against the wall next to Mrs. Wilson and disappeared inside his apartment without saying another word.

Sandy pushed herself to her feet, heart pounding. She had to get in and out of that apartment now. Who knew what would happen when you broke open a lock like that? They arrested you, probably, and Sandy seriously did not fucking need that.

"Thank you," she said to Mrs. Wilson, her voice still hoarse from crying.

Mrs. Wilson shook her head and stepped closer to Sandy, looking her hard in the eye. "You get in there and take what you need," she said. "But then you *go*. Because you are the only person in this world who's going to take care of you. The sooner you realize that, the better off you'll be."

Inside the apartment, Sandy moved fast. She grabbed a couple of the boxes they'd used to move in months earlier, then went around scooping up their personal crap that mattered: Jenna's jewelry box, Sandy's grandparents' pictures, her school records. She opened and closed cabinets, eyes darting around for anything important. There wasn't much. Their stuff that mattered barely filled a single box.

Sandy filled a second box with some basic kitchen crap: couple plates, some bowls, and a handful of silverware. She also grabbed the stuff Hannah had given her that night for safekeeping. She couldn't imagine ever seeing Hannah again—she hoped to God not—but it felt wrong to leave it behind. Sandy couldn't take much else. They'd just have to replace the rest of their cheap shit with new cheap shit. As it was, she didn't know where the hell she was going to put these two boxes; it wasn't like she could ride away with them on her bike.

They'd need some clothes, too, an outfit for each, and she'd have to go with spring because there wasn't time to cover winter. It wasn't until then that Sandy noticed Jenna's coat hanging on the back of the door. It had been cold the night before last, frost on the grass in the morning. What if Jenna was outside somewhere? What if she'd frozen to death?

Sandy tried to shake off the thought as she went back to Jenna's room for one last pass. Though she was trying not to hope that she'd find her money somewhere, she was still disappointed when she didn't.

There was one last place Sandy could look, the place girls like Jenna always hid their secret stash. Sandy grabbed the mattress with two hands and pushed. She was almost glad when it pitched to the left and crashed against Jenna's bureau, taking everything on top—cheap bottles of perfume and small glass tchotchkes—down with it.

When Sandy looked back, she couldn't believe it, but there was something fucking there on the box spring. Not her money. She'd never be that lucky. It was a small black book. Sandy picked it up, bracing herself when she flipped it open. Sure enough, there were her mom's bubbly girlie letters and a date on the first page: February 15, 1994. Shit.

Sandy tucked the two boxes under the building's stairs in a dusty cobwebbed corner she was pretty sure no one would check. In her backpack, she'd shoved what was left of her cash—eighteen dollars now—Jenna's journal, a couple clean pairs of underwear, two T-shirts, and her toothbrush. She didn't know where the hell she was going to stay, but it wasn't here, that was for sure.

The last thing Sandy was about to drop in the bag were the pills she'd stolen from Hannah's house. She would take them only if she got desperate, and then she'd take one pill. Maybe two. Except at this point, with the way she was feeling, Sandy wasn't sure she could trust herself. Just in case, she should keep only a few and get rid of the rest. She cracked open the bottles and dumped the contents of both together into her palm.

When Sandy looked, there were a few different-shaped pills and a silver chain—broken at the clasp—with a silver moon charm, an aquamarine stone set inside.

It was Jenna's necklace. The one she always had on. The one that meant so much to her, though even Sandy didn't know why. Because for all the many secrets that Jenna wouldn't keep from her daughter—about the drugs she took and the men she slept with—who gave her that necklace was the one thing she refused to tell.

It was dark by the time Sandy got on her bike. Her hands were trembling against the handlebars and her heart was pounding. There was no good reason for Jenna's necklace to be in one of those bottles. There was only one bad reason for Jenna and her necklace to be separated in the first place: Jenna was dead. How the necklace had ended up in Hannah's house in a goddamn old pill bottle, Sandy didn't have a clue. Had Steve taken the pills off Jenna? No, they had his (or his wife's) name on them. None of it made any sense. Not good sense, anyway.

It wasn't until Sandy was pulling out of the parking lot that she noticed the police car parked across the street from Ridgedale Commons. *Don't look guilty. Don't give them a reason.* All Sandy had to do was keep going, real easy, like she wasn't worried about a damn thing. Like all teenagers in Ridgedale rode their bikes around in the dark.

As Sandy passed the patrol car, she lifted her eyes just a little above her arm. Could've been anyone in that police car, sitting there for lots of reasons. Except once she got a better look, she saw that it wasn't just anyone. It was Hannah's dad, Steve. The same guy who seemed to know all about Jenna the second Sandy mentioned her name. The guy who had Jenna's most prized possession in his medicine cabinet. Hannah's dad was *that* guy. And right now *that* guy was staring dead at Sandy. Like the person he was really looking for, was her.

MOLLY

Justin made it to the final round for the job at Ridgedale University! He's so excited and I really am happy for him. He gave up so much in the past year and a half to take care of us. In a weird way, the whole terrible thing brought us so much closer. And it's definitely his turn. I want us to focus on him and what he needs for a while.

But it's so hard to think of leaving. And I know she never even lived in our apartment. But she died here. Inside me. As I slept. As I walked. As I breathed.

What will become of her if we leave this place behind?

RIDGEDALE READER

ONLINE EDITION

March 18, 2015, 5:23 p.m.

NEWS ALERT

Police Schedule Community Meeting

BY MOLLY SANDERSON

The Ridgedale Police Department will hold a community meeting this evening at 7 p.m. at the Ridgedale University Athletic Center. The meeting will provide an update on the investigation of the deceased infant found near the Essex Bridge. Topics to be discussed will include the department's planned voluntary DNA testing.

The meeting is open to the public. A question-and-answer session will follow a brief presentation.

Molly

When I got to Winchester's Pub, Justin was sitting in one of the worn wooden booths near the front, the ones with the initials of university students from decades long past carved into the now-polished surfaces. With his scruffy face and beat-up jeans, Justin could have passed for a good-looking graduate student, if there hadn't been two actual students with him—a boy with bad acne and a huge Adam's apple, and a girl with a pixie face and spiky black hair with green tips—both of whom looked about twelve by comparison.

When I'd texted him, he'd said he was back from the conference, grabbing dinner with some advisees if I wanted to come by. And I did. I needed to see him. I'd felt shaken ever since I'd left Harold's house with that bracelet in my pocket, turned over in exchange for an old box of CDs I happened to have in my trunk.

Speaking to Steve afterward hadn't helped, either. I called him as soon as I'd driven a safe distance from Harold's and pulled into an empty driveway.

"I think you should consider speaking again with the man who lives across the street from where you found the baby," I'd said, trying not to sound pushy or judgmental. "I think he may have seen something the night the baby was left."

"Harold told you that, did he?" Steve had taken a loud breath. "Did he also tell you that he's a convicted felon—aggravated assault—with a history of mental illness and a record of filing false reports?"

"No," I'd said, feeling reprimanded and embarrassed again. "He didn't mention that."

"My personal advice is to steer clear of Harold," Steve had said. "Nothing you'll get from him could possibly be worth the risk of sticking around long enough to find it out."

Justin grinned and waved when he saw me. I was about to head over when my phone rang. I paused on the side of the bar: *Richard Englander*. I dropped my phone right back into my pocket and let the call go to voicemail again. I'd gotten several more texts from Erik, including one praising my essay about infanticide, but none had said a word about Richard. Erik was due back in a day or so, he'd said. If Richard had an issue with my being on the story, he'd have to take it up with Erik when he got back.

"Guys, this is my wife, Molly," Justin said when I'd made my way over to their table, which was covered with half-empty plates and glasses. They'd long since finished eating. "Tamara and Jeff are in my nineteenth-century fiction class. They were just telling me that the dean of students has shot down the Animal Rights Committee's plan to lock themselves in cages in the middle of the quad to protest factory farming."

"Factory farming is totally disgusting," the girl said, glaring at me as if I had a bunch of baby cows jammed in cages in my backyard.

"Yes," I said, because I was kind of scared to disagree. "Absolutely awful."

"I promise I will do what I can to help plead your case. But I'm afraid right now I'm on borrowed time with the wife," Justin said, winking at me. "Can we pick this up later, guys?"

"Yeah, sure," the boy said, grabbing his stuff and digging in his pockets for cash.

"No, no, Jeff," Justin said. "It's on me."

"Thanks, Professor Sanderson." Jeff elbowed the girl. "Come on, Tam."

The girl was still squinting at me.

"Tamara, we'll work it out," Justin said. "Don't worry."

"Okay, Mr. Sanderson," she said before pouting out the door.

"Wow, she's quite the ray of sunshine," I muttered.

"Hubris of youth." Justin shrugged, watching them go. "Someone needs to keep on fighting the good fight now that we're too old and decrepit to care about anything but getting a good night's sleep."

"They're, what, freshman? They look like babies."

"That's because they *are* babies. They're extension students from Ridgedale High School—juniors and seniors." His brow wrinkled. "Speaking of which, I'm pretty sure they aren't supposed to be joining the clubs, much less protesting anything on campus. But I may let Thomas Price handle that. He supervises the high school exchange program. Anyway, they're good kids. The boy is really sharp, more insightful than a lot of the actual freshmen."

"And the girl?"

"Hmm, not so much. Being angry may be taking up a lot of her mental energy," Justin said, which made me laugh.

"Well, if she's pissed about factory farming, her head is going to burst when she hears about the police department's DNA dragnet."

Steve had briefly mentioned the planned community-wide voluntary DNA testing when we spoke about Harold. He'd asked me to post an alert about the community meeting, where he would be making the official announcement.

"'Dragnet'? That sounds daunting," Justin said as I sat across from him and started picking at his leftover french fries.

"I think it might be," I said. "Can you get Ella on your way home? She's at Mia's house, having dinner."

"Sure," Justin said. "Everything okay?"

"I just need to cover the community meeting so I can be there to record the town's collective conniption when the police announce this thing."

"In their defense, it doesn't sound very constitutional," he said. "Oh, and by the way." He pulled out his phone and showed me the text I had sent earlier. "What is this? It looks like an address."

He could tell it wasn't innocuous. Wasn't a mistake. And it didn't seem wise to lie. If I wanted him to trust me, I needed to be trustworthy.

"I had to do an interview." I shrugged. "The guy made me nervous. It seemed best if someone knew where I was. Just in case."

"Just in case?" His eyes were wide.

"Excess of caution. Isn't that what you wanted?"

"Hmm." He was trying not to argue. Neither one of us wanted to go back down the bumpy road we'd traveled the night before.

I felt the slip of paper in my coat pocket then, the one I'd found there that morning. Though this one was hardly a slip. Nearly half a page, it was folded into a square. I pulled it out. "This is one of my favorites."

"I know," Justin said. "I remember."

and this is the wonder that's keeping the stars apart
i carry your heart (i carry it in my heart) E. E. Cummings

The waitress came and handed Justin the check. He pulled out some cash and tucked it into the hard leather check holder.

"Wait, you're not going to help publicize their fascist dragnet, are you?" Justin said, looking suddenly aggravated, as though the thought had just occurred to him. "I can't believe you'd be okay with something like that. It goes against everything you've always believed in."

Regardless of how old and decrepit he liked to proclaim himself, he could get pretty wound up about social justice.

"I'm reporting on its existence, not endorsing it," I said, feeling defensive. Justin was probably taking this as yet another sign of my fundamental instability. "Besides, I think they're hoping that they won't have to go through with it. That the threat will be enough to make someone come forward."

"And in the meantime, they want to use you as their propaganda machine?" Justin asked as if it were some kind of personal affront. "I'm not trying to be an asshole, Molly. And I heard you last night about needing to stay on this story. Loud and clear. I just don't want to see you get used in the process. I hate to say it, but you might be a bit of an easy mark."

"Well, gee, thanks for that," I said, but mildly. He was agreeing to drop his objections to my staying on the story. I had to be grateful for that and take the passive-aggressive swipe. "You're all about the compliments these days."

"I'm sorry," he said. I tried not to notice how sad he seemed. "I just— I'm trying to look out for you, that's all."

"I know." I put a hand on his face. "Maybe look out for me a little less, okay?"

"Are you sure?" He smiled. He seemed melancholy still, but less so. "Because I'm so good at it."

"Yeah, except, lucky for us," I smoothed my thumb over his cheek, "you're good at lots of things."

Halfway to the Athletic Center, I realized I should have driven and parked in the gym's easily accessible and brightly lit parking lot. I hadn't really been thinking when I'd parted ways with Justin on the green. It was night, but unusually warm, and I'd figured the walk would do me good. So I'd left my car parked on Franklin Avenue and blithely strode headlong onto campus.

It hadn't occurred to me, though, how empty and how dark it would be. The dorms and student center were all in the opposite direction, and so, it seemed, were all the people. The language lab, the art studio, and the theater were bright, but a distance away, and the largest academic buildings—Rockland Hall, Barry Hall, and

Sampson Hall—were all pitch-black at that hour. The deeper I went into the darkness, the more nervous I became, so that by the time I was halfway across campus, even the sound of my own heels on the path—loud and echoing—was making me jittery.

I texted Justin as I walked. *Please tell me campus is safer than it feels.* I held the phone in my hand, waiting for him to respond. But he was probably inside Mia's house getting Ella, his phone left behind in the car's cup holder.

I walked faster, feeling even more vulnerable with the unanswered text in my hand. I checked over my shoulder to be sure that no one was following me. When that didn't make me feel any better, I did it again and again. Until I was doing it every couple steps, feeling more wound up with each swivel of my head. There was no one behind me, at least no one I could see, and yet it felt like someone *was* there as I followed the path down the hill toward the Athletic Center and through a short tunnel of trees.

I was relieved when the sidewalk rose on the other side, the Athletic Center in sight, lit up a welcoming gold. There was a small crowd clustered near the door. Probably not close enough to hear me if I called out, so I picked up the pace, my heels louder as I headed across the last stretch of concrete.

I was about to step onto the tail end of the sidewalk hugging the circular drive when there was a noise to my left. Something in the darkness. The wind, hopefully. That was my best-case scenario. I was looking in the direction of the sound when I bumped right into something—someone. My phone slipped out of my hands and cracked to the ground.

"Oops," Deckler said, as though I were so silly for throwing my phone around. He bent to pick it up, inspecting it, then wiped the screen over his sleeve before handing it back to me. "Good as new."

He was out of his snug yellow-and-black Campus Safety bicycle uniform but was even less appealing in his sweatshirt and jeans. Why was he always everywhere, watching me?

The files. A campus security officer would have had plenty of access to each and every one of those girls. And the power to bury their complaints. Not to mention Deckler's menacing vibe and his apparent willingness to startle a woman walking alone in the dark. He didn't maintain appropriate boundaries, at least not with women. He knew I had those files, and he wasn't happy about it—I was convinced of it. He was hanging around waiting to see what I was going to do about them, and then, if necessary, he would pounce.

"Thanks," I said, taking my phone back. Had he somehow come from the left, where I'd heard that noise? "Are you here for the meeting?"

"Nah," he said with unsettling vagueness. "Just checking things out."

"Okay, well, great." I smiled, no doubt unconvincingly. "I should probably get going. Someone's saving a seat for me inside."

Deckler needed to know I was meeting someone, that I would be missed. Even if it wasn't true. I expected to see Stella, but we'd made no plans to meet.

"By the way, did you get what you needed on that student?" he asked, looking off into the distance like he was—you know—just curious. "Rose, was it?"

Except I hadn't told Deckler that.

"Yes, I did." I smiled, backing toward the building and out of Deckler's reach. "I have all the information I need now."

"Let me know if there's anything else I can do to help." His voice was flat and affectless. It made the hairs on my arms stand on end.

"I will, definitely. Bye!"

I spun on a heel and raced for the building without looking back, bracing myself for Deckler to grab me.

When I dove inside unimpeded, my heart was drumming against my rib cage. Steve was at a podium in the center of the gym floor. Next to him were Ben LaForde and Thomas Price, who kept checking his big watch like he had someplace he would much rather be. Anywhere else, probably. It was hard to blame him. It had been savvy PR, though, for the university to host the community meeting— Thomas Price's idea, I suspected. Instead of distancing itself from the baby's death, the university was letting itself be drawn further into the fray. Only an institution convinced of its innocence would do such a thing. But after my run-in with Deckler, I thought that confidence seemed woefully misplaced.

The meeting had gotten quite a turnout. People filled the bleachers on both sides. Folding chairs had been set up at each end. Many more were standing.

"I'm Ridgedale Chief of Police Steve Carlson. Thank you all for coming." It wasn't until then that I noticed the flyers making their way noisily around the room. "The purpose of this meeting is to update you on the status of our investigation into the death of an approximately newborn female infant found Tuesday morning near the Essex Bridge. There will be an opportunity for questions after a brief announcement. The infant remains unidentified, and we are still awaiting an official cause of death from the medical examiner. We do not believe this death is related to any other death." That was in response to my story about Simon Barton, but I stood by its newsworthiness—anything *that* serendipitous was worth investigating, even if all I had was hysterical Harold as proof. "We are proceeding with an innovative program of voluntary DNA testing that we hope will expedite the identification of the baby."

Well, that was carefully worded—as though the baby would be

identified by the DNA samples of good, innocent people. In reality, the only person whose test results would matter would be the guilty party.

"As discussed in the flyers being distributed to you now, the test is painless and quick, takes less than five minutes. Nonmatching DNA samples will be discarded immediately and confidentially. To reiterate, they will not be kept in any kind of database. Details of where and when the DNA collections will take place are on the handout. We hope that you will all consider lending your help."

There was rustling as people took the sheets, then a long pause as they read, probably having a hard time—like I was—digesting it. Especially galling was the fact that high school and college students were clearly intended to be included in the sweep of all Ridgedale residents age twelve and over. An asterisk provided that minors would be tested only in the presence of and with consent from their parents or guardians. A moment later, a bunch of hands shot up, and so did the amount of noise. People's faces had darkened, along with the mood.

"You there," Steve said, pointing at a squat man on the right side of the bleachers in an expensive-looking pumpkin-colored sweater. He was in his late forties, with thinning hair. By the time he stood, the sound had grown to a roar.

"Excuse me! Please," shouted Thomas Price, an unexpected savior, but probably the only possible one. "We'll all have to be quiet if anyone is going to hear!" Watching Price, I could see why the university had appointed him its unofficial spokesman: calm, authoritative, appealing. As a bonus, they could always claim he wasn't an official university spokesman if things went badly. The volume dutifully dropped. "Thank you, everyone. Now, go ahead with your question, sir."

"There are about a thousand ways a DNA sweep is one of the worst ideas I've ever heard." The squat man looked wide-eyed around the crowd. "No one is going to consent, you know that, right? At least

they shouldn't. Trust me, I'm a lawyer. Don't do it. At least talk to
your own lawyer first. You'd be forfeiting your constitutional rights.
Just because they're saying they won't keep the samples, there's
nothing to stop them." He nodded back at Steve. "No offense. I'm
not saying you personally. I mean in general."

Steve glared at the man until he sat back down. Then he stayed
quiet, eyes moving slowly over the crowd, letting the silence grow
uncomfortable.

"No offense taken," Steve said finally, working his jaw to the
side. "And to be clear, you are all absolutely free to consult your
attorneys or your accountants or your spiritual advisers before deciding whether or not to help. You can look inside yourselves and
decide that having a Q-tip wiped across the inside of your cheek
or your kid's cheek is wrong on principle. It's a free country, and
that's the meaning of voluntary: You get to choose." The crowd
was utterly still now. "But I would say this: When we found the
baby floating in a creek like a piece of trash, she was stuck there,
her neck hung up on a stick. I pulled her out myself, weighed almost nothing." He was quiet again, this time like he was trying
to gather his composure. "*Principles* are a luxury that baby's never
going to have."

It was good theater. Impassioned, persuasive. And genuine. Steve
obviously believed what he was saying. Of course, that didn't make
it true. The dragnet did sound unconstitutional, or at least poten-
tially so.

Nonetheless, Steve's speech had—as intended—succeeded in silencing public opposition. For an hour and a half afterward, people
steered clear of queries about the DNA sweep. Instead, someone
wanted to know more about Simon Barton. As he had with me,
Steve dismissed the connection out of hand. Others wanted to know
about some men on the local sex offender registry. Someone else agi-
tated for precautionary fingerprinting in the schools, and another for

an investigative neighborhood watch, focusing—it seemed—largely on Ridgedale Commons, the apartment complex that was the town's de facto low-income housing. Thankfully, several others dismissed that idea as appallingly discriminatory. Steve brought the hammer down on it anyway. Dangerous and irresponsible vigilantism, he called it. And not long after that, he called a stop to all of it.

"Looks like we'll have to wrap this up for now." Steve's voice was hoarse from all the talking as he pointed to a huge clock high on the wall. "University was kind enough to let us use their facilities, but I did promise we'd be cleared out by nine p.m., and we've already gone twenty minutes past that."

There was some displeased grumbling as people stood and slowly began to disperse. Some didn't get very far, settling into large pods dotted across the gym floor, presumably to exchange theories and complaints. Others shuffled toward the doors. I turned to make my way over to Stella, whom I'd spotted in the distance, embedded with a group of high school moms and dads. I was hoping she'd give me a ride to my car. I wasn't going to cross back over that dark campus alone, not with Deckler lurking out there.

"Stella!" I called as she and her group started to drift toward the door. She kept on chatting with a mother as she walked on; she hadn't heard me. A second later, she had disappeared, lost to the crowd.

"Molly Sanderson," someone said then. "Nice to see a friendly face."

I was relieved to see Thomas Price walking toward me with a hand clasped around the back of his neck. He looked absolutely exhausted.

"Oh, hi," I said, wondering how I could ask Price to walk me to my car without seeming needy or ridiculous. "How are you?"

"I've been better." He motioned to the dispersing throng. "I wish the university president were here to see this—all these people.

Maybe then he'd understand that this isn't going anywhere anytime soon." Price shook his head. "Anyway, other than that, I am very well, thank you. Yourself?"

"Okay. But can I ask you a question?"

"For you, anything," Price said, then glanced away as though he'd inadvertently shown his hand. But when he met my eyes a second later, his expression was so guileless I wondered if I'd imagined it. "However, do consider yourself forewarned: my actual answers seem in maddeningly short supply today."

"I ran into one of the Campus Safety officers on my way here— Officer Deckler?" How to accuse Deckler of sexual assault *without* accusing him, that was the question. Because not even Rose had put it in such distinct terms, and the files weren't proof of anything in and of themselves; they were merely a compelling clue. A strong opening salvo. My strongest evidence was my overwhelming instinctual suspicion, exacerbated by Deckler's incessant creepiness—hardly incontrovertible, either. "Deckler seemed overly interested in my conversation with you about Rose Gowan and the status of my investigation in general. Do you know why that might be?"

"Wait, Deckler was on campus tonight?" Thomas Price looked uncharacteristically alarmed. "Where did you see him?"

"Outside the Athletic Center, walking on the path toward the main campus." My stomach tightened. I had been so sure Price would tell me what a great guy Deckler was. "He wasn't in uniform. I don't think he was on duty."

"No, he wouldn't have been." Thomas Price was looking toward the doors as though making some kind of calculation. "Deckler was suspended earlier today. He was also barred from campus, pending an investigation. Which means he shouldn't have been here at all."

Deckler hadn't been off-duty. He was off the job.

"What is he being investigated for?"

"Let's just say overzealousness." Price shook his head and exhaled. "Among other things."

"What does that mean, 'overzealousness'?" I could hear myself sounding panicky. I couldn't help it. It sounded like a euphemism for something far more ominous.

"The details are confidential, I'm afraid. Our internal investigation is ongoing. Running afoul of employment law by making a premature allegation to the press about an employee with a contract will not win me any points with the president."

"I'm not asking as a reporter," I said. "I think Deckler might be— Right now I'm concerned about my safety, my family's. I have some information and I—well, I don't even know what it means yet. But I need to know how worried I should be about Deckler."

Thomas Price's face softened. He nodded but crossed his arms. "Between us, there have been complaints from female students. Deckler made a number of them uncomfortable, on more than one occasion. He's unnecessarily persistent."

Just like he had been with me. Just like he probably was with Rose Gowan.

"I know Deckler's been here for a while. But do you know if he worked here back in 2006? Or if he left for a time between 2008 and 2012?" It was one piece of the puzzle that I could confirm. Deckler's absence during that period of time would explain the substantial gap in the files.

"I don't think so. I don't know his résumé by heart," Price said, "but I'd be likely to remember those years. They match my tenure here exactly."

Boom, boom, went my heart in my ears. "Oh yeah?" I made myself smile. "You left Ridgedale University and came back?"

"Yes, I came as an American studies professor in 2006—to take over for Christine Carroll for a year while she underwent chemotherapy. It ended up being two years; the treatment was more complicated than anticipated. But when she returned for the fall of 2008, I departed for Wesleyan. I didn't come back to Ridgedale University until a few years later, and then it was as a dean." He looked confused.

But I wasn't. Not anymore. Not only did Price's tenure match the files; he'd taught the first three girls in the only class that connected them.

"I'm sorry, I believe I may have lost the thread on our discussion here. What does this have to do with Deckler?"

JENNA

Tex cornered me today on my way to Spanish. Totally sketched me out. Kind of pissed me off, too. It's been nice having him be like this secret big brother to me—especially after that liar Todd Nolan started telling everybody that we had sex in the boys' locker room. (He felt me up. And that was ALL.)

But I think Tex has gotten the wrong idea. First of all, he HAS a girl-friend, so I don't know why he's bothering me. Especially because I HAVE a boyfriend. Maybe not officially yet. But that's what the Captain and I are: TOGETHER. And I've told Tex a million times that he ISN'T my type—or maybe I didn't tell him that flat out. I didn't want to be a bitch or whatever. Besides, what I said should have been enough.

But then today Tex got me all up against the wall and was like "Be careful." And I was like "About what?" And he was like "You know." And I was like "Hey, no, I don't." After like ten minutes of that shit, he was like "The Captain, be careful of the Captain."

And so I'll admit it, I got totally mad and I said something to Tex I shouldn't have. Something so mean I'm not even going to write it here.

I felt kind of bad after because I don't think Tex is trying to be a jerk or whatever. But he's wrong about the Captain. And he's confused about us. But that's not even his fault. It's probably because his tight-ass girlfriend won't put out.

Barbara

Barbara was sitting on the living room couch. Waiting. With each passing minute, she was getting more aggravated that Steve wasn't home yet. She wasn't afraid to admit it: She couldn't handle the situation with Cole on her own. But when she checked the clock on the cable box, she saw it was only 9:34 p.m. The community meeting surely had gone past nine, with Steve held up by questions afterward. He would come home as soon as he could after that. Assuming that his phone wasn't dead or he wasn't so distracted that he hadn't noticed how many times she'd called. In any case, how many more messages could she leave?

A second later, her phone rang. Barbara leaped for it, telling herself not to snap at Steve. No one wanted to do the right thing and then have his head bitten off for being late. But it was a blocked number. Dr. Kellerman, Barbara presumed—psychiatrists knew better than to call you from a number you could call them back on. So nice of him to *finally* get back to her after Barbara's *fourth* page.

"Hello?"

"This is Dr. Kellerman." He sounded annoyed.

"Thank you so much for calling me back." *Finally*, she wanted to add, but didn't.

"Yes, Mrs. Carlson, what seems to be the problem?"

The hell of their afternoon poured out of Barbara in an unstoppable rush. By the time she'd gotten home from Ridgedale

Elementary—and a stupid "quick stop" at the grocery store, which had stretched out because she'd been so hopelessly distracted by her miserable exchange with Rhea—Cole had completely fallen apart. Hannah had been in the kitchen, frantically trying to convince him that the red light on the smoke detector meant only that it was on, not that there was a fire.

But Cole wasn't buying it. "I don't think so," he said, shaking his head back and forth and back and forth. He didn't even seem to notice that Barbara had come home.

"Mom, he's not okay," Hannah whispered, looking terrified.

"Why don't you go upstairs, Hannah," Barbara said. Because Hannah either needed to hold it together or get out of Barbara's way. "Do your homework, listen to some music. Do something to distract yourself. Because Cole is fine, honey. He is just fine."

"Mommy, please put it off," Cole whispered once Hannah had headed reluctantly for the stairs. He was pointing at the red light on the smoke detector.

Oh, and did Barbara rise to the occasion. She was a virtual model of motherly calm, smoothly taking the battery out of the smoke detector and handing Cole its lifeless shell. He was better after that, for all of about ten minutes. Until Barbara turned on the stove to make dinner. One look at that blue flame flickering under the pot and Cole had jumped right out of his skin again. At least Hannah had stayed up in her room—she didn't even come down for dinner. It was true, Barbara didn't go up to get her, either; Hannah knew what time dinner was served. Instead, she decided to be grateful for small mercies.

After dinner was finished, Barbara spent at least a half hour trying to convince Cole that a Wild Thing couldn't possibly fit behind his bookcase. And while he was brushing his teeth, Cole asked her at least a dozen times whether a "cat burglar," which he seemed to think was an actual cat, was going to crawl in the window as he slept.

No, was Barbara's answer each time. *No, Cole. Of course not.* All the while she prayed she'd keep it together. And she did, but barely. It wasn't easy to sit by and watch your child lose his mind.

"I can make space for him tomorrow morning," Dr. Kellerman said when Barbara had finished recounting their terrifying evening. He sounded so irritatingly matter-of-fact. "We may need to consider medication to stabilize him."

"Medication?" Barbara snapped. "Wait, so things aren't bad enough to see him right away, but they *are* bad enough to *drug* him?"

"That's *one* possibility, Mrs. Carlson, and only on a temporary basis. But it is important we keep an open mind." *We*, as though Cole were his child. As though they were really in this together. "Bring Cole by at ten a.m., Mrs. Carlson, and we can discuss all our options. In the meantime, try to stay calm."

"Stay calm? And what if we can't wait that long? He's not okay *now*, Doctor."

"At this hour, our only option would be the hospital, and I don't think that's where Cole belongs, under the circumstances. Where is he now, Mrs. Carlson?"

"He's asleep at this exact moment, but—"

"Then at this exact moment, the issue is really *your* anxiety, isn't it? It's completely understandable. This is an extremely stressful situation. Nonetheless, you'll need to find a way to manage your anxiety for Cole's sake. If you'd like, I can give you the name of someone to see on your own."

"On my own?" Barbara asked. "The only problem *I* have right now is Cole. I don't mean that—*Cole* is not a problem. His *problems* are my problem, that's what I meant."

"Yes," Dr. Kellerman said, but not like he agreed. And then he was quiet for a long time in a way that Barbara didn't want him to be.

"Fine," she said, because she needed to get off the phone before she said something she would regret. "But I'm going to call you back if anything changes. Otherwise, we'll see you tomorrow at ten a.m."

"Absolutely call again if Cole's situation deteriorates. In the meantime, try to get some rest, Mrs. Carlson. It may take some time and hard work to get through this, but Cole will be fine. Children are extraordinarily resilient."

Barbara tried to go to bed after she got off the phone; 9:42 p.m. and *still* no sign of Steve, and it was making her angrier and angrier with each passing minute. Did he really need to answer *every* last stupid question? Or was he not even *at* the meeting anymore? Was he somewhere else entirely? His only excuse would be that he hadn't gotten her messages.

When Barbara got upstairs, she saw Hannah's light glowing in a thin strip beneath her door. Barbara thought about going in, telling Hannah to get to bed. But as soon as her hand was on the doorknob, it felt like a terrible idea. What if Hannah got worked up about Cole again? It would end badly between them, very badly. Barbara was sure of it.

And so she walked on, past Hannah's room, heading to her own bedroom, hoping not to open her eyes again until morning, when Steve would be there and it wouldn't be long before they could see Dr. Kellerman.

When she got into her room, she found her night table drawer a little ajar. It was where she'd tucked Cole's drawing. She hadn't let Dr. Kellerman keep it—especially when, at the time, she hadn't planned for them to ever go back. But she couldn't bring herself to throw it out, as Steve had suggested. Instead, she'd slid it in the drawer where she kept all her important papers. Had Cole been in her room? Had Hannah been snooping around? Barbara hoped not, but her daughter could be so maddeningly insistent. After the afternoon they'd had, maybe Hannah had been intent on finding out everything there was to know about Cole. Then again, maybe Barbara had left the drawer open herself. She couldn't recall, but she had looked at the picture more than once since hiding it there.

It took Barbara forever to get herself to sleep, and when she had just started to doze off, she was startled awake by a noise. When she snapped her eyes open, there was Cole, looming in the darkness right next to her face.

"There are bad things in my brain," he breathed. "Get them out, Mommy. Please."

He had a bad dream, that's all, Barbara told herself. And bad dreams were okay. They were normal kid stuff.

"It's okay, honey." Barbara pulled him into bed and curled her body around his. "Come here to me."

"But I'm still scared, Mommy," Cole whispered, sounding worried that the confession might get him in trouble. "I keep having the same bad dream."

"Oh, Cole, you're not even asleep yet," she said. "You can't be having a dream."

"But I just did, Mommy," he whispered. "And it was so, so bad."

What to say to that? To a little boy's bad dream that goes on long after he's opened his eyes? There was nothing *to* say. And so she rubbed Cole's back, and eventually, he fell asleep. Around the same time, Barbara became convinced she might never sleep again.

She managed to slip out of the bed without waking Cole. In the hallway, she could see that Hannah's light was *still* on. She was *still* not asleep. And Barbara *still* could not bring herself to go in and comfort her daughter. She simply had nothing left to give. And maybe that made Barbara a terrible mother and a bad person, but it was the truth. She could only do what she could do. Dr. Kellerman had been right: She needed to focus on keeping herself—and Cole—calm.

Downstairs, Barbara checked the clock on the wall again: 10:23 p.m. Steve was not at that meeting anymore, that was for sure. "Dammit, Steve," she said quietly as she looked out the living room windows toward the dark driveway. Where *was* he?

Soon, Barbara would have to call the station. She didn't like to do that. The chief of police's wife having to track him down? It didn't reflect well on either one of them. But what choice did she have? Before she could dial the number, there was a buzz from the opposite side of the room. Hannah's iPhone vibrating on the side table. Hannah wasn't one of those teenagers who was attached to her phone, but it was odd that she'd left it downstairs. When Barbara picked it up, the text came through a second time: *I'm sorry. I should have said that before. For everything.*

The text was from Sandy, the girl Hannah had tutored. What was Sandy sorry for? Missing her tutoring? Barbara felt a queasy tug in her gut. *For everything.* No, missing the tutoring wasn't it.

Barbara typed in Hannah's password—her knowing it was a condition of Hannah having a phone—then opened the text messages between her and Sandy, scrolling up to those that had preceded the new one. Barbara recognized many of the back-and-forths between the girls; from the beginning, she'd monitored them regularly. She had her concerns, of course, about Hannah socializing with the kind of teenagers served by Outreach Tutoring, and she wasn't ashamed to admit it. But the girls' exchanges had been so routinely uninteresting, about scheduling their tutoring or where to meet or the assignments. It had been obvious they weren't real friends. Not like

Hannah's other friends, who—let's be honest—came with their own Corona-swilling problems.

Are you okay? Hannah had written to Sandy about a week earlier.

Yeah. Was Sandy's whole response.

Are you sure? Hannah had pressed. *You should go to a doctor. That was really bad.*

A doctor?

To check you out. Make sure you're okay.

I AM okay.

Barbara's heart had started to pound. What was *really bad*? More exchanges followed, all essentially the same. Hannah asking if Sandy was okay. Sandy assuring her that she was. Hannah asking again. Over and over and over. Hannah was obviously worried about Sandy. But why? Barbara checked the dates of these very different texts. They had started nearly two weeks earlier. Right about the time the baby had probably been . . .

Barbara bent over as the room began to spin. She was going to be sick. Her head was ringing.

That Sandy girl had been in their house. Could she have had her baby there? *Oh my God: Cole.* Had Hannah been lying all this time to protect Sandy? Had she chosen some worthless white-trash stranger over her own brother?

All Barbara felt was rage as she charged for the steps, Hannah's phone gripped in her hand. Then there was a sound, the front door *finally* opening. Steve. Barbara didn't care anymore why he was late or where he had been. She was just so very glad he was there now. She sprinted toward him, diving into his arms and pressing her face against his chest. She didn't realize she was crying until she tried to speak.

"What is it?" Steve asked. But she couldn't get any words out. He pushed her back. Shook her once, hard. As if trying to wake her. "What's wrong, Barbara? Talk to me. Is it Cole?"

"The baby," she said, waving the phone at him. "It belongs to that girl Hannah has been tutoring. I think Cole saw something. I think whatever happened to the baby, Steve, I think it happened here."

"Barbara, what are you talking about?" His voice was raised—angry, alarmed, disbelieving.

Barbara didn't want to believe it, either. Didn't want to believe their daughter could be so unfeeling and cruel. Hannah had been acting upset about Cole, and this whole time she knew exactly what was wrong with him; worse yet, *she* was the one responsible.

Steve took the phone, his finger moving up and down the screen. His face hard and still. Finally, he took a deep breath and exhaled, rubbing a hand over his mouth. "Where is Hannah now?"

"Upstairs," Barbara said.

The look on his face was sharper now, the tired tinge gone from his eyes. He was in charge, a police officer on the case. Barbara felt such an enormous sense of relief. Steve was there and he was going to handle this. Her anger at him felt like such a silly, distant memory. Because they were in this together. They were in everything together. They always had been and they always would be.

"Wait here." Steve took a breath. "I'll be right back."

Barbara was glad he hadn't insisted she go along. Things with Hannah were always so much better without her.

Steve turned back at the steps. "This—Cole, Hannah, all of it—it's my priority to get us through and make sure the kids are okay," he said, staring at Barbara in such an unsettling way. "But once we get this all figured out, you and I will need to talk."

He didn't mean a casual chat.

"Talk? About what?"

"I think you know, Barbara."

Barbara stayed there, rigid on the couch, holding her breath. Trying not to think about what Steve had meant. All of that—*if* that's
what he was even talking about—hardly mattered anyway, certainly
not now. She listened hard for Steve's raised voice, for the sound of
Hannah crying, although she couldn't imagine Steve ever yelling at
their daughter, even now.

She braced herself for Hannah to come flying down the stairs, to
run for the front door. To race off into the night. Barbara thought for
a second about running out into the darkness herself. Disappearing.
Because she was overwhelmed now by the most terrible dread. As
though something, an actual thing—heavy and dark and hot—had
crawled up her back and attached itself to her neck.

A minute later, there were heavy, fast footsteps on the stairs. And
then there was Steve, his face tense and wide-awake as he moved
swiftly across the room for his keys. "When was the last time you
saw her?"

"What? Who?"

"Hannah, Barbara!" he shouted. "When was the last time you
actually saw her?"

"I—I don't know. I don't remember. I was too busy trying to
keep Cole together." She scrambled to recall. It had been before dinner, at least. But she wasn't going to tell Steve it had been that
long. He would never understand how overwhelmed she'd been by
Cole. "Maybe she went out for a walk. She does that sometimes, you
know."

"Without her phone?" He pointed to the counter where Hannah's
keys sat. "Or her keys? Her jacket's over there, too."

Steve seemed so angry, and *at* Barbara. Absolutely furious as he
grabbed his jacket off the back of the chair.

"Steve, where are you going?" she called as he strode for the door.

"I am going to do what you should have done hours ago: find our
daughter."

Frat Chat

Here are the chatters in your area. Be kind, follow the rules, and enjoy the ride! And if you don't know what the rules are: READ THEM FIRST! You must be 18 to Chat with the Frat.

How are we going to get Aidan kicked out of our school before he brings a gun or something?

> **3 replies**
> *He told me he had a gun in his bag last week.*
> *He did. I saw it.*
> *You guys are so bullshit.*

Anybody who could do that to a baby could definitely shoot a bunch of high school kids.

> **1 reply**
> *Kill Aidan Ronan before he kills us!*

Someone should tell the school.

Anybody seen the girlfriend? Maybe she's dead too?

> **2 replies**
> *I saw her once, it would be hard to tell the difference.*
> *Dead or not, she's still hot.*

Somebody should call the police and tell them.

3 replies

My mom told me the police already talked to his mom.

My mom can't stand his mom. She's a be-yatch.

My mom says HIS mom hits on MY dad. And my dad is totes disgusting.

Everybody send anonymous messages to the police today! Get Aidan before he gets us!

Molly

When I got home from the community meeting, Justin was asleep, a copy of *Tender Is the Night* open on his chest. I'd raced up the stairs, intent on telling him about Thomas Price. But once I was standing there, watching him sleep so peacefully, it occurred to me that he might not be thrilled to hear how I'd felt threatened enough that I'd fled Price in a panic. Or that I had been especially petrified, because of how utterly charmed I'd been by Price. He'd reeled me right in, just as he must have reeled in all those young women. And I wasn't young. I should have known better. God, I'd actually been flattered that he was flirting with me. I felt nauseated, thinking of it again, my hands still trembling as I lifted the book carefully from Justin and set it on the nightstand, then switched off his light.

On my way downstairs, my phone vibrated in my pocket: *Erik Schinazy.*

"Hi, Erik," I said, relieved it was him.

"Oh, hi, Molly." He sounded surprised, as though I'd called him. "I'm on my way back to Ridgedale, driving now. Just wanted to check in about the community meeting. Anything new?"

He also sounded nervous. Or maybe I was just projecting. "Most of it was about the community DNA sweep they're planning. As you can imagine, people in town are not happy about it. I can't say I blame them."

"No other updates? No mention of that woman they were holding in the hospital?"

"No, there really wasn't anything new. There would have been nothing to talk about if they hadn't had the DNA testing. The woman in the hospital is still missing, as far as I know. I think they've probably ruled her out as the mother of the baby, though, or they soon will. Her baby would have been several weeks old." I pulled in some air, preparing to deliver the rest. It was going to sound insane. "But I do think there's a chance that she was sexually assaulted by Ridgedale University's dean of students. That maybe her baby is *his* baby—it's just not the one they found."

"What?" He sounded shocked, as I'd expected.

"I know, it sounds— It was surprising to me. But I think it's true."

"That's a serious allegation, Molly. Where's it coming from?"

He sounded as skeptical as he had when he'd put me on the story about the baby. Actually, he sounded more skeptical now. And he didn't even know that I was basing much of my theory on a box of files anonymously dumped in my living room, by Deckler, I was now assuming. My low opinion of Deckler hadn't magically changed. So why was I willing to believe what he wanted me to now? Like Erik had said: Everybody has an agenda. It was definitely too much to unpack for Erik on the phone—stories at the *Wall Street Journal* probably never started as inauspiciously as breaking and entering. Before I laid it all out for him, I needed my ducks in a much tighter row.

"It is a serious allegation, you're right," I said. "And I won't know for sure until I make some more calls. Rose might be the best place to start. Come to think of it, she was a psychology student before she withdrew. Maybe Nancy knows her."

"I doubt it, it's a huge department," Erik said sharply. As though he wasn't going to bother his wife with my absurd theories.

"Okay, well, there's my friend Stella. She may have heard from Rose by now."

"Fine, follow up with her. And I'm not trying to be negative, Molly. It sounds like you have the start of something. I just don't want to make a libelous accusation against the dean of students without clear evidence. Once we have that—a comment from Rose or someone else, as you said—then we'll go after him full force. I promise, I'll be leading the charge." He sounded regretful now. I heard him take a breath. "And thank you, Molly. For all your hard work on the baby and whatever this turns out to be. You've done an excellent job with all of it. By any measure."

Once I was downstairs, I spread the files out on the floor, looking for connections between Price and each one of the girls. The first three were easy—he'd taught the American studies course as a last-minute replacement for Christine Carroll, the professor listed on their fall schedules. It took nearly an hour of cross-referencing various university sources, but soon I had linked each of the other young women to Price in one fashion or another. Jennifer Haben (2012) had been an intern for the dean of students' office, and Willa Daniela (2013) had worked in Student Services, in the office adjacent to the dean of students. Rose Gowan (2014)—whose name Thomas Price had convincingly pretended not to know—had sat with him on a seven-member student advisory committee that had met weekly for the past two years.

I was studying the remaining files when my phone buzzed, making me jump. I took a deep breath, not that it helped much. A text from a blocked number.

Find Jenna Mendelson.

That was the whole message. Who the hell was Jenna Mendelson? I turned back to the folders spread across the floor, wondering if

I'd somehow missed a Jenna Mendelson. There was Jennifer Haben, but no Jenna and no Mendelson.

Who is Jenna Mendelson? I texted right back, even though I felt conflicted about engaging. The last thing I needed was another mystery to solve. But already those three little ellipses had appeared, an answer on its way.

She's missing.

Then contact the police.

The police are WHY she's missing.

Who is this?

I waited for the ellipses. But this time, nothing.

I was still staring at the phone when I saw something move out of the corner of my eye, on the far side of the room. When I jumped and whipped around, there was Ella, standing at the bottom of the steps, gripping her blanket and trying not to cry.

"Ella, what are you doing?" I shouted, way too loud and angry. I closed my eyes and pressed a hand to my chest, trying to slow my heart. Then I heard a sniffle, followed by a squeak. When I opened my eyes, Ella was full-on bawling.

"Oh, Ella, I'm sorry." I rushed over and scooped her up in my arms. "I didn't mean to yell. You just surprised me. What's wrong?"

She pushed back my hair to whisper in my ear. "The bugs. They're everywhere."

One of her bad dreams, at least I was hoping. "All over where?"

"My bed."

A bad dream, definitely. "Come on, Peanut. You're safe. Mommy's here," I said, lifting her against me as I stood. "Let's go upstairs and get this sorted out."

A half hour of lying in Ella's bed, rubbing her back, and she was finally back to sleep. I made my way downstairs, wondering if it was possible that I'd imagined the blocked texts. But the conversation was still on my phone, my last question—*Who is this?*—still unanswered. And now *I* wanted to know who Jenna Mendelson was and what it meant that the police were "involved" in what had happened to her.

Why should I try to find her if I don't know who she is? I tried again, hoping they'd answer me now. *Or who you are?*

An instant response this time. *Because we know what happened to the baby. Find her and we'll tell you.*

How do I know you're telling the truth?

Baby was found with her head crushed. No one knows that but the police. And me.

I didn't know whether that was true. Steve hadn't told me those details, but it would fit with his reference to the "condition of the body." It would also fit with how disturbed he'd seemed.

OK. What do you want me to do?

There was no answer.

According to Google, there were—unhelpfully—many Jenna Mendelsons, and none appeared to be in Ridgedale. I spent close to an hour clicking through all those other Jennas. It wasn't until I was so completely bleary-eyed that I accidentally typed a new query into my email search bar instead of Google's that I stumbled on something: an email from Ella's teacher, Rhea, one of several we'd exchanged back when I'd done the profile on her tutoring program.

> Subject: Follow-up Interview Questions
>
> Hi Molly,
> Just wanted to get back to you with the names of some students from the program you might want to contact. The student I really think you could do an entire piece on is Sandy Mendelson. She's so smart and hardworking. I have such high hopes for her. She's really the poster child for this whole program.
> All the best!
>
> Rhea

Rhea had given me Sandy's phone number, too. I remembered leaving several messages for her at the time, but she'd never called back. I'd run the piece with comments from two other students Rhea was tutoring.

I dialed the number and held my breath, gambling on the fact that it was Sandy texting me about Jenna—her sister or maybe her mother. I hoped I wasn't going to be the one delivering upsetting news.

"Hello?" came a wide-awake voice.

"Is this Sandy Mendelson?"

There was a long pause. "Yes," she said finally.

"This is Molly Sanderson. I think you were trying to reach me?"

In the morning, I found Justin in the bathroom, already back from his run. He was standing at the sink, wrapped in a towel, neatening the edges of his beard with a razor.

"I think Thomas Price may be—or has been—sexually assaulting girls on campus," I said. I leaned forward and wiped the steam off the mirror with the back of my hand, so I could see his face in the reflection.

"Really?" He stood motionless, razor hovering in midair, head tilted to the side as he eyed me in the mirror—concerned, wary. "Where's that coming from? This has something to do with your story about the baby?"

He was probably worried about getting fired from his hard-won beloved job because I was rushing around making possibly groundless accusations. It would be understandable.

"I don't think it has to do with the baby, but I don't know. Right now it's more of a hunch anyway." Why was I downplaying it for Justin? I might not have been in a position to write a front-page story, but I wasn't pulling it out of thin air. Pretending otherwise wasn't going to help either of us. "No, it's more than a hunch. I'm pretty sure it's true. I just don't have enough evidence to do anything about it."

Justin shook his head in disgust, then leaned closer to the mirror and went back to shaving. "I don't want to say I told you so. But you know I never liked that guy."

"I'll warn you before I do anything. I know that my making that kind of allegation against Price could be disastrous for you. To be honest, I'm trying to figure out the right thing to do."

"Well, don't worry about me." He looked almost offended. "If what you're saying is true, Ridgedale University isn't going to want to defend him. And even if they do, I'll support you, Molly, whatever you decide."

RIDGEDALE READER

ONLINE EDITION

March 19, 2015, 8:27 a.m.

At Ridgedale Community Meeting
Police Announce DNA Testing

BY MOLLY SANDERSON

Police officials held a public meeting last night at the Ridgedale University Athletic Center to discuss the ongoing investigation into the death of the infant found near the Essex Bridge. Chief of Police Steve Carlson answered questions for over an hour. The baby's cause of death has not yet been determined, and she remains unidentified.

In an effort to assist in identification, the Ridgedale Police Department is to begin voluntary, community-wide DNA testing. It will take place at the Ridgedale Police Department over the next three days. Hours of testing, as well as a detailed explanation of procedures are available online at www.ridgedalenj.org. David Simpson, Esq., a criminal defense attorney and Ridgedale resident, has invited anyone concerned about the legal implications of DNA testing to contact him for a free consultation.

COMMENTS:

Marney B
2 hours ago
DNA testing??? Are they insane?

Gail
1 hour ago
Seconded. This can't be legal.

Stephanie
57 min ago
They are definitely trying to scare whoever is responsible out of the closet. It's probably not even really the girl's fault. Who knows what her life is like? Maybe her mom has to work three jobs or something. Bad parents aren't born, you know, they're made.

Mom22
52 min ago
I don't have a teenager, but if I did there is no way I would let them give a "sample." What is this? 1984?

LifeIsLiving
47 min ago
I would have my children give a blood sample if it would help find out who did that to their baby. Someone needs to send a message to these kids who apparently aren't too young to have sex, but think they're too young to be held accountable.

SaranB
45 min ago
Are you telling me you think that this was just some teenager who couldn't be bothered to put her child up for adoption? Do you really think people are that cruel?

246Barry
42 min ago
SHUT UP. AND FIND HIM. BEFORE HE FINDS YOU.

Carrollandthepups
37 min ago
Ugh, not this jerk again. 246Barry, no one wants you here.

Samuel L.

25 min ago

Just called you in to the police 246Barry. How you like that? Turns out they already know about you. It's all fun and games until you get arrested for harassment and your name is plastered all over the place. Because then it won't matter if the police don't do anything about you, because the rest of us will.

JENNA

JUNE 11, 1994

The Captain is coming at 8 p.m.! He said he's totally up for meeting my parents, too. I just hope they don't mess it up for me by acting like they think I'm a total nut bag. At least my dress is so cute. It's red and has this deep V that totally shows off everything. My mom didn't even give me crap about it.

It's because she knows who the Captain's family is. I think she hopes I'll snag him for good. Then maybe she'll stop spending all her free time praying for my mortal soul.

And I'm just not going to think about Tex being at the party. Because he will be. And he's totally going to try to kill my buzz. Telling me to be careful and whatnot. Like THAT's the real point and not that he wants me putting out for him instead of the Captain. But I'm not going to let him make me feel bad for getting the guy I always wanted. The kind nobody, not even my own parents, thinks I'm good enough for.

It would be a lot easier if I just hated Tex, though. If I didn't kind of also like that he cares about me. Then I could tell him to get the hell away from me forever. But it's not that simple. Nothing ever is.

Sandy

Sandy sat in a sticky booth at the back of Pat's Pancakes, waiting for Molly. The place was practically empty, unlike on weekends, when a line snaked out the door. A half dozen mostly old people were in the booths, eating their omelets and pancakes so slowly it was like they were being paid by the minute.

"What can I get you, hon?" The waitress snapped open her pad. She was pretty, or used to be. Now she had a fuzzy ponytail and a super-wrinkled face, but didn't seem *that* old. That was what Jenna would look like eventually. If she got the chance. *Someday*, Sandy thought, *I'll probably look like that, too.*

"Can I have coffee?" Sandy asked.

"*Just* coffee?" The waitress wasn't trying to be a bitch, Sandy knew. She was just trying to pay her bills.

"Yeah, for right now," Sandy said. "I'm waiting for somebody."

She'd have to hope that this Molly woman would order some food when she got there. Sandy couldn't afford to waste money eating when she wasn't hungry even to keep a fellow waitress happy. And she hadn't been hungry in days. Of course, that hadn't stopped Aidan from trying to stuff her like some overprotective grandmother the night before.

"I got crap for a sandwich, and some chips and cookies and an apple," Aidan had said, tossing a bunch of food into a pile on his bed.

He had been right about it being easy to sneak in the back door, and Sandy felt almost safe now that they were upstairs in his bedroom, behind his locked door. She looked down at all the food Aidan had swiped from the kitchen. There was even lettuce and a tomato and some pretty little jar of something that might have been mustard, because people who lived in houses like Aidan's didn't make ham and white bread sandwiches with French's mustard, the way Sandy always had. Aidan was staring down at the pile like he'd never made his own sandwich in his entire life. Like he had no goddamn idea where to start.

"Thank you," Sandy said, keeping her eyes on the food. Because she couldn't handle looking right at Aidan. "For letting me come here."

Because where the hell had she been planning to go? She hadn't been planning, that was the bottom line. She'd just wanted to get away from Hannah's dad, lurking outside Ridgedale Commons. And so she just kept pedaling until she was sure no one was following her. She didn't realize until too late that it was getting dark and she didn't have a plan. Despite what she'd been thinking, she couldn't sleep outside. Amazing how something like that could seem like a legitimate fucking option—*whatever, I'll just sleep outside if I have to*—until you started working through specifics. Where outside? In the woods? On the sidewalk? To begin with, it was too cold. And it wasn't like people in Ridgedale wouldn't notice *another* person sleeping on the street. There *weren't* any other people on the street.

Sandy was hoping Aidan wasn't going to make her eat. She wasn't sure she could make herself swallow anything. But she was thirsty as hell. Couldn't remember the last time she'd had something to drink. Felt like never. Sandy polished off two of the fancy glass bottles of lemonade Aidan had dropped on the bed, one after the other, before she looked back up. When she finally did, Aidan was staring at her with wide, freaked-out eyes. For the first time, he was getting just how fucked she was. She must have seemed like some kind of animal, drinking like that. She sure as hell felt like one.

"Sorry," she said, wiping at her dirty mouth with the back of her dirty hand.

"Nah, it's cool," Aidan said quietly as he sat down on the bed next to her. He was looking down at his own perfectly clean hands, probably wishing he'd never invited Sandy over. He'd said he wanted to help, sure. But it was one thing to play at the edges of her fucked-up life. It was another thing to take up center stage.

"I can take off, you know," Sandy said. She felt bad, putting all this shit on him. "No hard feelings. I don't want you to feel, like, necessary."

Aidan took the bottle of lemonade—Sandy's third—from her hands, took a sip, and handed it back to her.

"Oh, I'm not necessary," he said, turning to look at her. "I'm fucking essential."

In the morning, when Aidan kissed Sandy goodbye on his way to school, she knew it might be the last time she'd see him. That maybe it should be. But the plan was for Sandy to slip out later, after Aidan's mom and little brother had gone; she was supposed to meet up with Aidan after he was out of school.

"See you later," he said. "I'll text you."

It had made a difference, Aidan being there. But when you lived in the middle of a shit-storm, the question wasn't whether things were going to fly apart, it was when. The least Sandy could do was keep Aidan clear of the shrapnel.

After he was gone, Sandy pulled her mom's journal out of her backpack and lay on the floor, tucked behind his bed, praying his mother didn't charge in to toss the place for drugs or something while she was there. Jenna had already told Sandy some of what

was in the journal, enough for Sandy to have known the exact place
where the whole fucked-up story ended. Enough that Sandy would
have sworn nothing she read could make it worse. But she should
have known better. With Jenna, things could always get worse.

What if Jenna had decided that she couldn't take the memories
anymore? That was all Sandy could think once she was done reading the journal. What if coming back to Ridgedale had been about
Jenna finding an ending instead of a fresh start? No, Sandy didn't
believe that any more than she believed that Jenna had taken off.
And maybe that made her as stupid as anyone else who fell for Jenna's shit. But she didn't—wouldn't—believe it.

Sandy had a flash of a memory then: her and Jenna dancing. She'd
been barely ten, and they'd been in their shitty apartment in Camden, the one with the gas stove with only one burner that worked
and that wack-ass blue-green mold streak on the living room wall.
That day the sun had been so bright in the window that the place
hadn't looked so bad, especially with Jenna trying to teach Sandy
how to cha-cha. Jenna had her black hair piled on top of her head, a
cigarette pinched between her red lips, as she swung her hips back
and forth in her worn, skintight leggings, trying to get Sandy to
match her steps.

There wasn't much that Sandy remembered from her childhood,
but the particular bump in the road that came before that dancing
stood out because it had rolled right over her tenth birthday. Her
welcome into double digits had been totally forgotten in the three
straight days Jenna hadn't gotten out of bed and wouldn't stop crying even though Sandy brought her endless Diet Dr Peppers and
wine and Cheetos. Some guy—another guy like all the other guys—
had broken Jenna's heart. But by that afternoon—when Sandy was
ten years and four days old—they were dancing. And Sandy knew
once again that they'd make it. At least this time.

"You're getting it! You're getting it!" Jenna had squealed with delight when Sandy had been able to follow along. "Look at you! That's it!" Jenna had looked so happy as they'd danced to the blasting Kid Rock that was definitely not meant for the cha-cha. So happy she might burst. Because that was Jenna: so bad and then so, so good.

Jenna wouldn't kill herself. It wasn't possible. She always rebounded. And she rebounded hard. She might have come back to Ridgedale looking for something or someone, Tex, maybe. If he'd looked out for her back then, maybe Jenna thought he'd do it again. *That* Sandy could see Jenna doing—dragging them here because she had some twisted idea that her knight in shining armor would still be hanging around all these years later, waiting to rescue her once and for all.

"Sandy?"

When she looked up, there was a woman standing next to the booth in Pat's Pancakes. Pretty, with pale skin and long curly reddish hair. Molly looked nice and normal. Like a regular mom, but not in a bad way. It had been Aidan's idea to text her the night before. She was a reporter, his mom's friend. Somebody who might be able to help.

"Yeah." Sandy nodded, feeling a lot more nervous than she'd counted on.

"I'm Molly Sanderson." The woman reached out a hand as she sat down in the booth across from Sandy. "I don't know if you remember, but I actually called you a few months ago when I was doing a story on the Outreach Tutoring program. Rhea gave me your number."

"Oh, right," Sandy said, even though she didn't remember. At least that explained how the hell Molly had tracked her down so fast.

"Jenna is your mom, I'm guessing?"

Sandy nodded, then shrugged. "But she's not your usual kind of mom."

"I'm not sure there is such a thing," Molly said, which was nice. She didn't have to say that. "So you said she's missing?"

"She left Blondie's after work a couple days ago and never came home," Sandy said. "She's kind of a screwup. Totally a screwup. But not like this. She would call me."

"I believe you," Molly said. And it actually seemed like she did. "It sounds like you went to the police already."

"I did. The chief of police, Steve. He was nice and everything, and he said he would help. But then I found this in his house." She put the necklace on the table and slid it across. "It's my mom's. She never takes it off."

Molly reached forward to take it. She looked concerned. "Why were you in his house?"

"I didn't break in or anything." *I was just looking through his shit to steal drugs.* "I know his daughter."

"Would your mom have any reason to know Steve?"

"I don't think so, unless he arrested her. That could be, except she never mentioned it. And she would have. She tells me everything. But he definitely had this weird look on his face when I said her name."

"Did you ask his daughter?"

"Ask her what?"

"If her dad knows your mom."

"I can't really ask her anything right now." Sandy shook her head, tried not to notice how raw her throat felt. "She's kind of checked out."

She'd been lying when she'd texted Molly that she would tell her what happened to the baby. Sandy was going to get what she needed from this reporter, and then the woman could go to hell—no offense. What had happened to that baby was a secret Sandy would take to the grave. She hadn't even explained it to Aidan, who'd been nice enough not to ask how the hell she could have known what had happened to the baby's head.

"You could go to other police, you know," Molly said, like she was really trying to help. "The state police, maybe."

"I can't." Sandy shook her head. She had to hope this woman would drop it. "I mean, I *really* can't. Trust me."

"Okay," Molly said, backing off the way Sandy had wanted her to. "Let me just think for a minute." She stared at the table. When she looked up, she crossed her arms, her face tougher. "I'll do it. I'll ask him why he had the necklace. And if he doesn't have a good answer or he hasn't done enough to find your mother, I'll go to the state police myself. One way or another, we'll find out what happened to her, Sandy. I promise."

Then Molly leaned forward and put her hand over Sandy's. And there were the tears in Sandy's eyes again—seriously? Was this all it took? For some nice, normal-looking woman to be a little bit kind to her, and she totally fell apart?

"Okay," Sandy said, and that was all she could manage. She nodded and turned toward the window.

"But, Sandy, whatever happened to the baby—and I'm not saying it was you—whoever, whatever was involved. These things don't just go away, no matter how much you hope they will. And the harder you try to force them down, the harder they push their way back to the surface. I'm saying that from personal experience." Molly looked sad. "It can help if you tell someone what happened. I can be that person for you, Sandy. And I'm a lawyer—or I used to be a lawyer. I can be *your* lawyer for the purposes of this. That way no one can make me tell them what you told me. All you have to say is that you want me to be your lawyer."

"I want you to be my lawyer," Sandy said.

But that wasn't what she was thinking. She was thinking: *I want you to be my mother.*

===

Sandy hadn't wanted to go to Hannah's house for their tutoring session. She'd been hoping she'd never have to see where Hannah lived, never have to feel all that cozy love pouring out from the walls. But Hannah had said she was stuck home, watching her brother. She offered to reschedule, but Sandy wasn't ready for her math quiz, and if she wasn't prepared, if it didn't seem like she'd tried, Rhea would be crushed.

The house was basically the nightmare Sandy had dreaded. Nothing fancy, like Aidan's, but cheerful as all fuck. To-do lists and chore charts and newspaper articles labeled with Post-its and highlighting. There was one of those personalized calendars, with pictures of Hannah and Cole and a big red circle around March 31: "Hannah's Recital!"

"My parents won't be home for at least an hour and a half, and Cole's watching TV. If it's okay with you, could we study here at the table? In case he needs anything?" Hannah moved a stack of place mats and a little vase of flowers, then dropped her books in the center of the table. "Do you want something to drink or anything?"

"I'm good," Sandy said. She just wanted to get the whole thing over with and get the hell out of that house. Because it was so fucking hard to breathe in there. It was how Sandy always felt whenever she was anywhere too normal for too long. Like someone was crushing her chest in a vise.

They were about half an hour in when Hannah went to check on her little brother. "I'll be right back," she said. "Do these problems while I'm gone."

But Hannah was gone *forever.* Long enough for Sandy to do all the problems and then wait and wait for her to come back. Sandy listened to see if she could hear Hannah talking to her brother, but there was only the sound of the TV. It wasn't until Sandy checked her phone that she realized more than fifteen minutes had passed.

They needed to finish before Hannah's parents got home. It was one thing for Sandy to deal with being in Hannah's house, but she wouldn't be able to cope chatting up her parents.

After a few more minutes, Sandy didn't have a choice. She had to look for Hannah. Though it wouldn't be some kind of disaster if Cole saw Sandy, she was hoping to avoid talking to the kid, too.

When she peeked out into the living room, Hannah's brother was sprawled out asleep on the couch, light off, TV on. Hannah was nowhere in sight. Where the hell had she gone? Sandy made her way around the rest of the downstairs looking for her, wanting to call out but not wanting to wake the kid. And she hated the feeling of going somewhere in the house she hadn't specifically been invited. If something got stolen, guess who would be to blame?

At last Sandy spotted a door with a light on underneath it. The bathroom. "Are you okay?" she called through the door, knocking gently.

Hannah didn't answer, but Sandy could hear this noise inside, a steady *thud, thud, thud.*

"Hannah?" she called again. "What the hell are you doing in there? I'm going to have to take off soon."

Thud, thud, thud, quiet. *Thud, thud, thud.*

"Hello?" Sandy called more loudly when Hannah didn't answer. "Jesus. I'm going to open the door, okay?"

Sandy turned the doorknob, waiting for it to be locked. In which case, she'd just go, before Hannah's parents got home. But the door wasn't locked. Sandy pushed it slowly, waiting for Hannah to shout for her to stop, to say that she needed privacy. That she would be out in a minute.

There was no shout. No Hannah. Nothing except *thud, thud, thud.*

Sandy saw the puddle of bright red paint first. It was on the white tile floor, coming from behind the door. She saw it on the toilet, too, as she pushed open the door. More paint. On more of the floor. What the hell was paint doing all over the place? Hannah was painting something?

Not paint. It's not paint. Sandy was thinking those words before she could figure out what they meant. *Not paint.* She was still pushing open the door. And there was more and more of it, there was red all over everything.

Blood.

It's blood.

And then there was Hannah, crouched on the floor in the corner behind the door, naked from the waist down, rocking so hard that her elbows kept whacking against the tile wall behind her, *thud, thud, thud.* Her face was snow-white and still. Her hands were clenched into blood-covered fists. And there on the floor next to her was a pile of lumpier blood and something else coiled.

Attached to it was something that looked like a baby, except it was grayish-purple. Covered in blood and white waxy-looking stuff, too. And not moving.

"Holy fuck!" Sandy said, rushing over, slipping on the blood-slicked floor. She grabbed the towel ring, almost ripping it off the wall. "Hannah, what happened?"

Hannah just kept rocking.

"Are you okay?"

"I tried to get the cord off her neck," she whispered finally. "I did it. I did. But it was so . . . my fingers kept . . ." She stared out. "Slipping. But she was alive for a minute." Hannah gazed up at Sandy, her face equal parts wonder and horror. "She opened her eyes. She looked right at me."

"We have to call an ambulance." Sandy looked down at her blood-soaked shoes.

"She's going to kill me." Hannah clamped a hand over her mouth suddenly. Like the thought of her mother had only just occurred to her. "She's going to kill me. She's going to kill me. She's going to kill me."

"But you're bleeding." Sandy pointed toward the floor. Her hands were trembling. "And the——" She was going to say "baby." But one look at the gray-purple skin and it was obvious that if she'd ever been alive, the baby was long past saving.

"She's going to kill me." Hannah lurched toward Sandy, wrapping her bloody hands around Sandy's wrists. Her eyes were huge. "Please, you have to help me. She's going to kill me."

All Sandy had was questions. Did Hannah know she was pregnant? Did she hide it on purpose? Did she invite Sandy over because she knew she was going to have a baby? Who the hell was the father? What about that saving-herself-for-marriage bullshit? All of it, lies.

But then, Sandy knew about lies. The weird way they had of seeming just like the truth. And she knew about being scared and feeling so totally alone that you pray you'll disappear. Sandy looked around at the bloody floor. And again at Hannah, a girl who'd never been anything but nice to her. Who'd tried to help her when most people never bothered. Hannah wasn't a strong person. She wouldn't be able to do this alone. And she was right about her mother——she was going to kill Hannah.

But Sandy could do this. She could sweep up all these broken pieces. She could clean up somebody else's mess, like she'd done for Jenna a thousand times before. And so Sandy sucked in some air and swallowed down all of it——the fear, the blood, the actual dead human baby on the floor, inches away from her.

"We need some towels that your mom won't notice missing. Show me where they are," Sandy said. "And a bag you can get rid of. Paper towels and cleaning supplies. You should go take a shower." She checked the clock on her phone, already smeared with blood. "We don't have much time."

It wasn't until Sandy was almost done cleaning all of it up that she saw Hannah's little brother standing there behind her. She had no idea how long he'd been there or how much he'd seen.

"Sorry I made such a mess," she said to him. Because she had to say something.

But he didn't say a word. He just faded back into the darkness, then disappeared.

Sandy had raced out of Hannah's house with all that death around her neck. She jumped on her bike and she rode like the fucking wind. What she hadn't factored in was the rain. Or the way the duffel bag Hannah had given her—way too big for her back and heavier than she would have thought—would leave her so off-balance on the bike. It wasn't like she could go slow either. Not if she was going to get through this. Because there were things Sandy had seen and done in her life, things that a girl like Hannah would never survive. Not this, though. Never anything like this.

But Sandy had learned a long time ago that you could put a box around the things that you didn't want to become a part of you—seeing your mom naked on top of some drunk, the popular kid in your eighth-grade class telling everyone you had AIDS, holding your mom's head over the toilet while she puked. You couldn't get rid of those things completely, but they didn't have to seep out, mix with the rest. They didn't have to become a part of you.

So Sandy put her head down and rode as fast as she could. And she tried not to notice how her back seemed extra wet under the bag, she hoped not from the blood seeping through. Ten minutes, maybe fifteen, and she'd be there. And this would be something she'd be on her way to forgetting.

At least Sandy had known where to go. A place she knew from Jenna was dark and quiet and kept all its secrets. A place where no one could see a goddamn thing.

It was pouring by the time Sandy made that last turn toward the Essex Bridge, but her bike felt steady and her legs felt strong and she was almost there. It was almost over. And then she would make it like none of this had ever happened. She started pedaling even harder down that last hill, even though it was pouring rain, like maybe if she pedaled hard enough, she would take flight.

The animal came out of nowhere—a chipmunk, a squirrel, a possum. A shadow, maybe. It was too dark to know for sure. Too late to stop. Definitely too late to recover. Too late to stay on her bike. The rest happened in slow motion, the bike flying out in one direction, Sandy in the other. And the whole time her thinking only one thing: *Hold on to the bag.*

And she had, despite the burning pain in her knee and her arm. But the bag had gotten tangled beneath her as she fell and slid, her full weight crushed against it. And the baby inside. It wasn't until Sandy stood up, covered in blood—hers and maybe the baby's—that she knew: There are some things too horrible for even the strongest box to contain.

There had been one good thing about all that rain. It had made it easier to dig. Not a hole big enough for the bag or the towels. Just the baby. Because all Sandy had was her bare hands. Looking back on it now, the ground being so soft and loose, so easy to move, right up there near the edge of that creek, made it the last place she ever should have put a thing she wanted to stay buried.

Molly must have gotten up and come around the booth to sit next to Sandy while she was talking.

"It's going to be okay," she said, reaching forward to wrap her arms around Sandy. "I promise."

It wasn't until Molly was hugging her that Sandy realized she was shaking. Or how hard she was crying.

JENNA

If I had a gun, I'd shoot myself. But I don't have a gun. And I don't have any pills. And I can't stand the sight of blood.

Because all I keep seeing over and over again is Two-Six ripping off my underwear. And all I keep hearing is the Captain saying "Go ahead, you take it" after he lifted my skirt to show my ass to Two-Six like I was some kind of cow.

The Captain wasn't holding me from behind yet. I guess he thought maybe I'd be okay with it. Maybe even into it. Two guys at once, out there in the woods.

He'd been hinting about me screwing Two-Six all night, said he was depressed and that he deserved a good time. And they were fucked up out of their minds. We were all so wasted.

Then the Captain was like "No, I'm serious, I want you to let him do it." And when I said, "Fuck no," he said, "How many guys have you banged? What's one more?"

And I thought about saying, One—YOU. You're the only guy I ever banged. But I didn't want to give him the satisfaction.

Instead, I slapped him. And maybe that was what did it. Because this thing happened to the Captain's face. Like the lights went out. Like his insides died right in front of me.

Then he grabbed me from behind and lifted my dress all the way up so that even my tits were hanging out there so anybody could see. And I kept waiting for the Captain to come to his senses. And say: No, man, let her go. Especially when I started to scream and then started to cry. And you could still hear the noise even though the Captain had his hand smashed over my mouth.

But he didn't say stop. No one did. No one said another word.

Molly

"Can I give you a ride somewhere?" I asked Sandy once we were outside Pat's.

"I've got my bike," she said, motioning to it leaning up against the side of the diner.

The bike. I'd been trying not to picture the scene, but now there it was in my head—Sandy's body flipping off the bike, the bag strapped to her back with its unimaginable cargo. Her falling explained everything about the suspicious "condition" of the baby's body. And here she was, *still* riding around on that bike? She probably didn't have a choice. There surely wasn't an extra car sitting in her driveway. But my God. It was hard to believe she was upright after what she had been through. After what she was still going through, with her mom missing.

I had been thinking about Steve, too. And Barbara. I would have thought I'd feel some sort of satisfaction where Barbara was concerned—look at what all your judgment hath wrought. But what I felt for all of them was pity.

"I could drive you home?" I offered, still staring at the bike. "We could put your bike in the back of my car." *Or we could throw it out.*

"Yeah," Sandy said, but not like she was agreeing. She was staring out into the distance at the cars racing up and down Route 33. "We're, um, kind of in between places at the moment."

"Oh." That didn't sound good. "Where did you sleep last night?"

"My friend Aidan's house," she said, then her eyes got wide. "Shit, I forgot, you know his mom. Please don't tell her. I don't want to get Aidan in trouble."

"I won't tell her," I said. "Of course not."

I saw it then when she turned to get her bike, peeking down from the left sleeve of her T-shirt: the thorned stem of a rose. *The flower girl.*

This was the person Stella had been hiding—Sandy. And not because she was the mother of the dead baby or to protect Aidan. But because Stella was ashamed that her son had picked *this* girl.

"Why don't you come to my place for now?" I said. I wasn't going to let her go back to Aidan's. God knew what Stella would say if she found Sandy there. "Later I can take you somewhere else if you want. Do you have any other stuff you need to pick up?"

All she had with her was a little backpack. "There's a couple boxes," Sandy said after thinking about it for a minute. I was relieved she hadn't argued, but she didn't look thrilled. She shifted around uncomfortably, wouldn't meet my eyes. "I left them back at our old apartment. I guess I should probably go get them."

"Come on, let's go, then," I said, hoping that forward momentum might keep her from changing her mind.

Sandy was rolling her bike toward my car when she got a text. I watched her face tense, reading it. "It's Hannah's dad," she said finally. "I guess he texted me a couple times overnight. I didn't read them because they were from Hannah's phone. I thought they were from her and I just—I needed a break. But they can't find Hannah."

"Do you know where she is?"

"I'm not sure *Hannah* knows where she is. A day or two after the baby was born, she started talking about how it was mine, and she's been acting like that ever since." Sandy was still staring at her phone. "Wait, I might— Maybe she went down to where—to the creek. I called her that night, not until after I got rid of the bag and the towels in a dumpster behind that tanning salon Highlights. It was the only place that was closed." Her voice drifted as she looked off, like she was remembering. "I didn't tell her that I fell or anything, just that the creek was where I—where her baby was." Sandy shook her head. "Anyway, I think there's a chance Hannah went down to the creek before. I got this weird text from her once about 'how beautiful it was.' She didn't say what she was talking about and I didn't ask. I got so many weird messages from her. I didn't want to know anything else. I just wanted her to re-member."

"Maybe she finally has. You need to tell Steve where she is, Sandy."

"I know," she said, already typing out a response.

Sandy showed me the way to Ridgedale Commons, a depressing two-floor rectangle that looked like a motel you'd drive all night to avoid. I pulled up alongside the curb in front, having a hard time believing we were still in Ridgedale.

"I'll be right back," Sandy said, opening the door before the car had fully stopped.

"Are you sure you don't need help?"

"Nope." She shook her head as she rushed from the car. "It's not much."

I watched her walk, wiry and strong, across the browning side yard toward a staircase on the side. She looked around guiltily before squatting down and reaching beneath the stairs. Her boxes weren't "at" her old apartment, they were hidden under the building stairs. It was excruciating. I swallowed the lump in my throat. Things had been bad for me when I was her age, but not bad like that.

"Do you think, um, I could take a shower?" Sandy asked once we were at my house. We were standing in the little guest room with its excessively fluffy, overly fashionable blue-and-orange-hued bed.

"Of course, yes." I was relieved for the time her showering would buy me to collect my thoughts. It had been so easy to want to rescue Sandy. Now that I had, I felt overwhelmed and unprepared. "Let me get you some towels."

When I returned, Sandy was standing right where I'd left her, arms crossed like she was afraid of being blamed for breaking something. I handed her a stack of overly fluffy towels. Everything we had suddenly seemed outsize and unnecessarily inflated. Like I was overcompensating.

"There's shampoo and everything in the bathroom if you need it."

"Thanks," Sandy said, stuck in the center of the room, gripping my towels. "I'll be quick."

"Take your time. I'll call some more of the local hospitals." I planned to call the ME's office, too, to be sure there weren't any Jane Does, but there wasn't any reason to tell Sandy that. "Can I ask you one last thing?"

"Yeah, sure," Sandy said, looking like she was bracing for me to set fire to the bridge I'd so carefully built between us.

"You don't have to tell me if you don't want to," I said, leaning against the doorframe. "But did Hannah ever tell you who the father was?" It seemed unfair that he should be getting out of all of this scot-free, especially if he'd known that Hannah was pregnant.

"No." She shook her head. "But I think maybe he was a college kid."

"Why do you say that?"

Sandy shrugged. "Hannah always wanted to go to the Black Cat to study. Sometimes it was like she was waiting to see somebody. Looking out, you know." She shook her head again, seemed almost angry. "Before it happened, she told me she was saving herself until marriage. But I think that was more what her mom wanted. She took classes on campus last year, too. Part of some super-smart-kid program she was in. Maybe she met him then."

Shit. The Ridgedale University high school exchange program, supervised by Dean of Students Thomas Price.

"The night she had the baby—before she forgot it was her baby—she gave me all the stuff he'd given her, cards and whatever. In case her parents found out, I guess, and searched her room. I didn't look at any of it, but I still have it." Sandy motioned to her boxes, stacked along the wall in the guest room. "She never asked for it back. Maybe she forgot the guy when she forgot about it being her baby. I probably should have tried to shake her out of it. But I was afraid. You know how they tell you not to wake somebody who's sleepwalking?"

"You did the right thing, Sandy," I said without hesitating. "You did more than anyone could possibly have expected you to do."

According to Sandy, Aidan had already checked for Jenna at the Ridgedale University Hospital, but, knowing Aidan, I called again, just in case. I had expected the process of inquiring there and at the four other nearby hospitals to take a while, with multiple transfers to the relevant parties, followed by long periods on hold while nurses referenced what their unidentified patients looked like. Matched them with my description of Jenna. But within ten minutes, I had established that only two of the hospitals had any unidentified patients at all—both male, both elderly. Apparently, actual Jane Does weren't nearly as common as I'd assumed. When I called the ME's office, they had no unidentified victims, either. Maybe it would have been different in New York City, but in Ridgedale, people evidently didn't go unidentified for long, not even a baby. Soon everyone would know whom she belonged to.

When I ended the call with the last hospital, my eyes settled on Jenna's journal, sitting on the edge of the dining room table. Sandy's hand had lingered on it for such a long time before she left it for me.

She said that I should read it, that there was a chance it would help us find Jenna. But I could tell that part of her also didn't want me to. That she probably wished she'd never read it herself.

It didn't take more than a couple pages to realize what would be the worst part of the story laid out in the journal: Jenna's hope. By the time I'd finished, I knew why Sandy had picked that spot in the woods. And I knew that Harold, for all his obvious instability, had been right about what he'd seen. He'd just been wrong about the visions climbing out of the creek being the *same* young woman—a ghost separated by nearly twenty years. In fact, they'd been mother and daughter.

The bracelet I'd bartered from Harold. I'd forgotten all about it. Still in my coat pocket, I hoped. I was so glad I hadn't thrown it out, which was all I'd wanted to do after I'd hung up with Steve in an embarrassed huff.

I went out to the coat rack near our living room door to dig in my pocket. Sure enough, the bracelet was still there—and there was that inscription: *To J.M. Always, Tex.*

"Um, hi." When I looked up from the bracelet, there was Sandy wrapped in a towel, black hair wet and brushed back smoothly from her face. Standing there like that, she was even more striking than I'd realized. Truly beautiful. Her mother must have been, too. "Could I, um, borrow something to wear? I think I need to wash my clothes. If that's okay."

"Of course." I jumped to my feet. Clothes: something tangible and straightforward. Simple. That was something I could help with. "Come to my room and we'll see what might work."

Sandy looked like any other affluent Ridgedale teenager in my expensive jeans and T-shirt as we drove to the public library in search of Ridgedale High School yearbooks. A yearbook seemed like our best chance—maybe our only chance—to figure out the actual names that corresponded with the nicknames mentioned in Jenna's journal. It was a long shot, but it was the only one we had.

And I wanted something more before confronting Steve. I had promised Sandy I would ask him about Jenna's necklace, and I was still planning on it. But I'd be implicitly accusing him of something. And while I was willing to stick my neck out for Sandy in that way, part of me was hoping I wouldn't have to. That we'd figure out who those boys were in Jenna's journal. That we'd find them, now grown men, and that they would somehow lead us to her without me having to ask Steve a thing.

Sandy and I sat down at a long table in the back with the yearbooks the librarian had collected for me. The room was crowded with mothers and young children waiting for story time. I caught Sandy watching them with a mix of amazement and longing that I knew too well myself. Maybe even a little anger because I knew that, too. *Is that the kind of childhood other kids get? Yes*, I thought. *Yes, they do.* And after raising Ella, I knew that much was true.

"Why don't you start with these?" I said, handing Sandy the earlier and more likely irrelevant years. "Look for anything that mentions any of the nicknames. Here." I pointed to a spot under one senior's name in *The Ridgedale Record Class of 1994.* "Some of them put their nicknames right with their pictures."

But no one else seemed to have a nickname listed anywhere. My plan was starting to feel decidedly hopeless until I reached the team pictures at the back of the book—runners, hockey players, football players. Each had a formal group shot with several candids under it. The formal portraits had only players' full names, but the candids had nicknames, lots of them.

My eyes slid over the wrestling team and then swimming and then the varsity football players. No Captain, no Tex, and no Two-Six. I moved on to basketball, searching the faces of the assorted teenage boys, the skinny, acne-spotted ones and the ones who looked like they got all the girls. There were buzz cuts and mullets and one or two Mohawks. Aside from the snug, dated shorts and all that hair, they were the same kind of boys who could have been found in any current yearbook, in any town, anywhere in the country.

I looked down at a blurry, overexposed candid beneath the basketball team photo. It was impossible to make out the figures clearly—their faces fuzzy and indistinct—but there were two boys, close up against each other; one was shorter, clean-cut, with a square jaw and a flattop, and had his hand on the shoulder of a taller boy with longish hair and maybe a handsome face. In the background, a few feet away, was a much bigger guy, his back to the other two, shooting a basket. And beneath it a caption: *Tex showing up Two-Six and the Captain.* Even though the boys' faces in the candid weren't clear enough to compare to the group photo, their numbers were clear as day.

My heart was pounding as I scanned the team photo. And there they were, standing in a row, right above their names:

The Captain, Number 7, was Thomas Price. The boy Jenna had loved so much and who had brutalized her so.

Two-Six, Number 26, was Simon Barton. The one boy who hadn't made it out of the woods that night alive.

And Tex, Number 15, was Steve Carlson. The boy whose love had scared Jenna most of all.

Barbara

The doctors were back. They had work to do, and they wanted space to do it. But Barbara wasn't going anywhere. She was sure the final blow would come the second she left Hannah alone. That her daughter would slip away for good and there would only be Barbara to blame.

Or so Steve would think, apparently. Because he was already punishing her. He'd barely spoken to her since he'd rushed from the house to find Hannah. Had hardly looked at Barbara since she'd arrived at the hospital four hours earlier to find him standing gray-faced and soaking wet at Hannah's bedside.

How easy it must have been for him to make the whole thing Barbara's fault. Never mind his sins of omission.

Barbara had since learned the details of what had happened, prying them from a distant Steve one by one. Hannah had been in the water when he finally found her at the creek, flat on her back, her filmy light blue nightgown floating around her like a cloud. Steve actually said that, "like a cloud," describing it for Barbara as if seeing it all over again. Her eyes had been closed and she'd been dead white. In fact, Steve had been sure his daughter was dead when he'd leaped into the creek—with superhuman agility, one of the other officers had said—to rescue her.

Luckily, Hannah had gotten wedged up against some rocks on the side of the bank; otherwise, they might not have found her in

time. Hypothermia was her official diagnosis, and she hadn't re-
gained consciousness yet. Time would tell the extent of the damage,
the doctors said. In the meantime, they were warming her slowly
and saying their prayers. It was all they could do.

The only thing that mattered now was that Hannah got better. But it was hard not to think about what else the doctors had
quickly discovered upon examination: She'd delivered a baby recently. There would be a DNA test—assuming Hannah didn't wake
up and confess—but Barbara and Steve didn't need that to know the
truth: *That* baby had been Hannah's, not Sandy's.

"I don't think she was trying to kill herself," Steve had said
straight off. Like he wanted to keep anyone from even hinting at
suicide.

"Then what was she doing in the water, Steve?" Barbara had
pressed anyway. Because how blind was he going to be?

"Maybe she wanted to be close to her—to the baby."

"Well, isn't that romantic?" Barbara had said. "Too bad that didn't
occur to Hannah *before* she dumped her out there."

Barbara was supposed to be worried, frantic. She wasn't supposed
to be angry at Hannah. But she was. She was furious.

"For Christ's sake, Barb," Steve had snapped. "Let it go."

How was Barbara supposed to "let it go" when it made no sense?
When had it happened, and with *whom?* How had Hannah hidden
some boy so completely—and her pregnancy? It was true that many
people had not known Barbara was pregnant right up until the end.
Carrying small was probably genetic. And those stupid sweatshirts.
How convenient for Hannah, that that was the way she'd *always*
dressed. It was as though she'd been planning it from the start.

"You two should take a walk, get some coffee," said the older, gray-
haired doctor with the big clunky glasses. Barbara had been told

several times that this utterly underwhelming man was head of the ER, but she was having a hard time believing it. "It's important that you take care of yourselves. Stay fresh. Hannah will need you once she wakes up. Right now she's stable, I can assure you of that."

"Sorry," Barbara said, but like she wasn't very sorry at all. She was gripping the arms of the chair she'd been glued to since she'd arrived. "But I'm not leaving."

"Really, Ms. Carlson, it would be much better for Hannah if you and your husband could give us some space," the gray-haired doctor repeated. "Just five minutes or so and you can come right back."

They were going to do something they thought Steve and Barbara shouldn't see, change the colostomy bag, move around Hannah's floppy arms and legs. Something that made their daughter seem much worse off. The doctors had been optimistic but vague. What did "recover" and "regain functioning" mean? That Hannah would be 100 percent back to who she had been? Whoever that even was. In any case, the doctors needed her body temperature up before they would venture guesses.

"Come on," Steve said to Barbara. His voice was hoarse. He'd been screaming—one of the officers at the scene had told her that, too— screaming Hannah's name. "Let's get out of their way for a minute. I could use some coffee." He put a businesslike hand on Barbara's shoulder. That was how he'd been the whole time at the hospital: all business.

"Okay, fine," she said, for Steve's sake, though, not for the doctors'. "But only for a minute."

She followed Steve in silence down the hall toward the elevators. Instead of pressing the button for floor two (and the cafeteria), Steve pressed G for the ground floor.

"I thought you wanted coffee?"

Steve was avoiding eye contact. "Let's take a walk instead."

And so Barbara followed Steve off the elevator without arguing, even if the last thing in the world she wanted to do was take a walk. Her doing what Steve wanted was a peace offering, though she hardly felt like it was her responsibility to be holding out olive branches.

The hospital doors snapped open and they walked into the bright sunshine. It was warm for mid-March, the sky an unearthly blue that felt so terribly wrong under the circumstances. Steve was walking a bit ahead, more briskly now, as though trying to avoid her potential objections. And he was headed for those awful benches facing an inset patch of grass. It was a peaceful space for quiet contemplation. As far as Barbara was concerned, it was just like the dismal hospital chapel: too funereal.

"They said five minutes, Steve," Barbara called after him. Anywhere but those benches. "I don't want to go far."

"We won't," he said. But he didn't slow down, didn't look back at her.

We have to talk, he'd said hours earlier. Before the river, before his wet clothes, before Hannah and all those doctors. Barbara had managed to completely erase it from her memory, until now. There was nothing good about Steve saying *We have to talk*. Barbara knew that from personal experience.

It had been unseasonably warm that night, more like August than June. There was only a week until graduation, and just when Barbara and Steve were about to start a life together, all of a sudden he was pulling away.

More and more Barbara had caught Steve looking at Jenna.

Worse, he was trying to hide it less and less. Almost like he wanted Barbara to get so mad that she'd break up with him. It wasn't just his looking at Jenna that was the problem either. It was the *way* he was looking—love, that was the look on his face. Which proved how *not* about Jenna his distance was. Because there was nothing to love about Jenna Mendelson. She was a whore, plain and simple. And now poor Steve was another one of the stupid boys who'd fallen for her wares.

Ignoring his wandering eye had seemed to be working until that night, when Steve had said he wanted to "talk" to Barbara. What teenage boy ever wanted to "talk" to his girlfriend about anything other than breaking up? But *that* wasn't happening. Barbara was sure of that much.

"Hi there," she called sweetly as she climbed into Steve's beat-up Chevy truck.

"Hey," he'd said, already unhappy.

Barbara was going to ignore that, too. She'd ignore everything if she had to. Steve was trying to sabotage what they had because he was scared, and Barbara wasn't having it. They were perfect for each other. And they were going to be together, especially now. Steve would snap out of it once she told him. He was a good guy. He would do the right thing.

Barbara leaned over to kiss Steve in the driver's seat. She'd worn an extra-short skirt and one of her tighter T-shirts for the occasion, and they both rode up on purpose when Barbara tipped herself over. Steve hesitated but turned and kissed her quickly, more like a lip bump.

"I know I said I didn't want to go to the woods tonight," Barbara said. "But it's the last party, so let's go!"

"Yeah, maybe." Steve rubbed at his forehead with his thumb as he stared down at the steering wheel. "I think we should talk first, though." He shifted in his seat. He wasn't *really* going to do this, was he? Break up with her on this night, of all nights? Barbara had to head him off at the pass. Otherwise, they'd be stuck knowing forever what he'd really wanted.

"Okay, Steve, but there's something I have to tell you, too." Barbara turned to look out the open window toward her parents' big, beautiful house, which would someday be their big, beautiful house. "Can I go first?"

"Okay," Steve said after a long pause. Then he reached over and squeezed Barbara's knee in a weird "let's be friends" way. "Shoot."

Something in him had already switched off, Barbara could feel it. But that didn't mean it couldn't be flipped back on. It would be, she was sure of it. She forced a smile, even though her throat felt raw. She hadn't pictured it this way. But she refused to be sad. What did a perfect moment matter compared to a lifetime of happiness?

Barbara swallowed hard and smiled. "I'm pregnant!" she squealed, grabbing Steve's hands and pressing them hard against her flat belly, ignoring the way the color had left his face. "Isn't it amazing, Steve? Six weeks. I know we wanted to wait until we got married. But we can get married right now, there's nothing stopping us. I don't need a big wedding. I don't even need to be a bride. I just want to be your wife."

Steve stopped near that clutch of awful benches, motioning for Barbara to have a seat—*across* from him. Not next to him, where he could wrap an arm around her. No, *facing* her. Barbara perched on the edge of her bench, watching Steve stare down at his hands clasped in front of him, as if he was trying to decide where to begin.

"Wait, you don't actually think this is *my* fault, do you?" Barbara asked, her voice rising. That couldn't be what this was about, but it bore stating. Because Barbara *refused* to be made responsible for Hannah's insane choices. "I have done everything right, Steve. I have given my *life* for my children."

"I don't blame you for what's happened. No, of course not," he said, though he sounded like he was considering it for the first time. "We made mistakes with Hannah, that's obvious now. But that's on both of us."

So he wasn't letting her *off* the hook, he was putting himself *on* there with her? "What about the father? Are we going to find out who he is? Isn't it statutory rape?"

Steve shook his head. "Hannah would have been sixteen."

Barbara crossed her arms and blew out a breath. "But you'll keep on trying to find him. Right?"

When Steve looked at her, his eyes were glassy. "Of course I will."

"Good," Barbara said. "Because crime or not, he's accountable."

Steve was nodding, but his attention had slipped away again. Barbara sensed it. He was thinking about something else entirely.

"How long have you known she was back?" he asked finally.

Barbara should have prepared better for this moment. She'd known it would come. But all she'd wanted to do was forget the whole sordid mess. A mess, mind you, that she had no hand in creating.

"Who was back, Steve?" Barbara held herself tight, resisting the way her body had begun to tremble. "And before you answer—is this *really* what you want to talk about, with your *daughter* upstairs in a hospital bed?"

Steve didn't blink. "Tell me what happened between you and Jenna, Barbara. I need to know all of it or I won't be able to help you."

And there it was: the truth. This was what he thought of her.

"Help me?" She laughed icily. "Why would I need your *help*, Steve? What are you suggesting?"

"I know you were at Blondie's. Jenna's daughter came to see me. She told me that there was some blond woman with her mother during her last shift. They recognized your picture at Blondie's, Barbara. You were with her the last time anybody saw her."

"Yeah, and so what? I talked to Jenna, Steve." Barbara could feel her temper rising. "I wanted to know why she was back. I wanted to make sure she understood."

"Understood what?"

And he looked so *worried*. Unbelievable. Was he still *this* pathetic after all these years? It was infuriating. Barbara was so angry, her cheeks were burning. So angry that she could have spit—at Steve. How dare he sit there and make her explain herself when all she'd done was protect them.

"I asked her to leave us alone, Steve." Barbara fluttered her eyelashes and smiled viciously. "That's all I've ever wanted. We're a family, that's what I said. A happy family. I told Jenna she couldn't just come back here after all these years and ruin that."

Steve was supposed to say that Jenna never could have done that anyway. He was supposed to tell Barbara that he loved her and the kids far too much for anyone to threaten what they had. Not even Jenna. But he didn't say that. Steve was not a man who lied.

"Barbara, whatever happened, I'm sure you didn't mean to—"

"'Mean to'?" Barbara snapped. "'Mean to' what, Steve?"

"Barbara, please just tell me what happened."

"*Jenna* happened, Steve. That's what happened." Barbara stood calmly. She took a breath, steadied herself. Because she wasn't going to give him—to give Jenna—the satisfaction of getting upset. "If you want to know the truth, our nice talk inside the bar did turn a lot less nice in the parking lot. And you want to know why?"

"Yes, Barbara," Steve said. "I want to know everything."

"Jenna said she wasn't agreeing to anything until she talked to *you*," Barbara said. "She's been here for months, trying to work up the courage. Pathetic."

But that's all Barbara was telling Steve. She wasn't about to recount how Jenna had then started talking all this nonsense about what Steve had done the night Simon Barton died. Barbara hadn't listened to her lies, because that's what all of it was: lies. Barbara

remembered that night—when she was still blissfully, stupidly unaware of just how many pregnancies never made it past week twelve.
She'd been the one riding home in Steve's truck after he spoke with
the police. He told her all about what had happened with Simon.
He'd been standing there when it happened. They'd been stupid and
drunk and horsing around. To this day, Steve felt awful about it.

But the more Barbara didn't listen, the more hysterical Jenna got
in Blondie's parking lot, shouting about how the necklace she was
wearing was some kind of proof of something. Something about
Steve. She just would not shut up. And so Barbara tried to make her.
She hadn't meant to rip the necklace off. She'd only meant to shake
it, and Jenna.

It hadn't hurt Jenna, no matter what she'd acted like. The necklace had snapped right off like a piece of string. Because it was cheap
crap, just like Jenna. But Barbara wasn't going to tell Steve that
part, either. He didn't deserve to know.

"And then what happened?" Steve asked, looking at Barbara like
some kind of gap-mouthed spectator. "After she said she wanted to
talk to me first?"

"And then, Steve, I reminded Jenna of what she is: a sparkly piece
of trash. Something you pick up from the sidewalk because you
think it's worth something, but once you take a closer look, you
realize: Nope, the garbage is actually the only place it will ever be-
long. Then I got into my car and went home to my children—to *our*
children, Steve. Who the hell knows what happened to Jenna after
that? That's the thing about people like her, Steve. It's the truth that
lights the fuse."

MOLLY

JUNE 17, 2013

Justin took the news pretty well. I'd thought he'd fight me when I said I wasn't going back to Dr. Zomer. But he agreed that I really did seem better. It probably helped that I lied and told him that Dr. Zomer thought I was ready to "transition out of therapy."

Besides, he's been so distracted by all the interviews at Ridgedale. That's academia for you—they practically want you to move in and start teaching before they're willing to give you a job offer.

Maybe Dr. Zomer is right. Maybe being angry at Justin is better than blaming myself. But I have to believe there's a better way. A better way to save myself than hating the man I love.

Molly

Steve was at a table near the back of the hospital cafeteria when I got there. It was mostly empty, too late for lunch, a little early for dinner. Steve sat motionless, staring down at a paper coffee cup gripped in his big hands. He was wearing a T-shirt and dark jeans, which should have made him look young, like he did the last time I'd seen him out of uniform. But he looked ancient, and sunken, as though his bones were liquefying.

"Hi," I said when I made my way over to his table. I was bracing myself. The fact that I was willing to have this uncomfortable conversation did not mean I was looking forward to it.

Steve blinked up at me as though he had no idea who I was. When I'd called him after Sandy and I left the library, I hadn't known about Hannah. But as soon as I heard the broken cadence in his voice, I guessed. I had wanted to tell him never mind, that our conversation could wait. But Jenna had already been missing three days. There was no telling how much time she had left.

"Molly, sorry," Steve said, a hand drifting to his forehead. "I was a million miles away—remembering teaching Hannah to ride a bike, of all stupid things." He motioned for me to sit. "She would stick out this little bit of her tongue when she was concentrating really hard. I spent half the time trying to be sure she didn't accidentally bite it off." He smiled sadly. "Simpler times."

"How is she?" I asked as I sat down on the edge of the chair across from him. I wanted to be able to spring away quickly when things turned south.

"Off the record?"

"Of course," I said, even though I could hear Erik's voice in my head. *No. Never. No special favors. Never off the record.*

It hardly seemed to matter now. I wasn't there as a reporter. I was there for Sandy.

"She was awake for a little bit, which the doctors say is encouraging," Steve began. "She doesn't have any memory of what happened down at the creek. But she remembers us and herself and the baby. Hannah says the cord was around the baby's neck. I don't think the baby ever had a chance." He shook his head, wiped at his nose, and sniffled. "The ME's official report will confirm that. I know it will. Hannah won't say how the baby got down to the woods or why she was, well, in that condition. The father, maybe, I don't know. I'm hoping we can get her to come around and tell us everything."

I wanted there to be a way to tell him about Sandy's fall from the bike, to give him that last piece of the puzzle. But I couldn't, wouldn't do that. "I'm sorry to have to bother you now," I said. "If it could wait—"

He lifted a hand. "Honestly, it's a relief to think about something else for a minute."

I felt queasy. "Sandy Mendelson, Jenna's daughter, came to me for help. She's really worried about her mom."

"I know," he said without flinching. "She came to me, too. Poor kid. I've had officers out canvassing. I'll be able to send out more, now that the baby—"

"Do you know where Jenna is, Steve?"

His face tensed, but only for a split second. He could tell there was something wrong in the way I'd asked the question. That I wasn't just asking the chief of police for an update.

"Like I said, we'll have more resources now." He was still acting as though he didn't personally know Jenna. As though she were any other missing person. "I've looked around some myself, seeing if I could pick up on her trail. No luck."

I'd been hoping he wasn't going to do this, make me draw it out of him. I sucked in some more air and pulled Jenna's bracelet out of my pocket and put it on the table between us.

Steve stared at it for a long time. Then he smiled sadly, reaching forward to smooth his fingers over it. "A lot of gas station shifts to pay for this."

I pulled the necklace out and put it on the table, too. "And this one?"

"To replace the bracelet when she lost it. Where'd you find that?" This time he looked genuinely confused and concerned.

"In your house."

"*My* house?" But then I watched it flicker across his face: recognition. He had an idea how it had ended up in his house, no matter what he wanted to pretend. "Well, that doesn't make any sense."

I just wanted him to explain on his own. To make it all less suspicious: *Oh, yes, I knew Jenna in high school and I had a crush on her and she was also seeing Thomas Price, whom I also know even though I've pretended not to.* There was nothing good about having some kind of gotcha moment with Steve. But he was leaving me no choice.

I pulled the Ridgedale University yearbook out of my bag and opened it to the page I had flagged, the one with the basketball pictures. I spun it around and slid it in front of Steve. He stared down for a minute at the picture of Thomas Price, Simon Barton, and himself. When he met my eyes, he almost looked relieved. Like he'd been waiting for this moment for a very long time.

"I ran into Jenna about a year ago, in Philadelphia of all places, when I was at the International Chiefs of Police Conference. We only talked for a minute or two on the street, you know, a 'how you doing' kind of thing." He shook his head, smiled sadly. "All those old feelings came right back—I mean, it's different, of course. I'm a married man now. But I remembered exactly the way I'd felt. And Jenna was the same live wire she'd been all those years ago. God, was that kind of thing amazing to be around when I was seventeen. I never felt so alive." He glanced up, looked uncomfortable. "If you're thinking— I was glad to see her, yes, but I haven't seen or talked to her since that day. I didn't even know she was back in Ridgedale." He looked straight at me, like he wanted to be sure I knew that part was the truth. Still he was leaving out something. Maybe not about where Jenna was, but something. "We'll find Jenna now, I can promise you that. And when we do, her daughter will be the first to know."

"There is something else," I began. There was so much that he needed to explain, but there was even more that he needed to know. "I read Jenna's journal. I know Thomas Price assaulted her in high school. And I think there have been other girls on campus since. Several."

I watched Steve's face stiffen. "No one ever reported anything like that to me." He didn't sound defensive, exactly, but almost. "We would have investigated, obviously. Was that what was in the files?"

"There wasn't proof of anything. But it tells a story that fits. All of it does."

He picked up the bracelet, smoothing his fingers over it again. "I was the one that night who told Jenna to run, as soon as I got Simon off of her. When I grabbed him, the ground was wet. We slipped, both of us. His head hitting that rock was an accident." He paused. Stared at the table for a long minute. I wondered for a second if he thought I knew all of this already. But it seemed more like he wanted me to know. Like he needed the world to. "At least it was an accident the first time. But the second time his head came down?" Steve shook his head. "When the police showed up with the am-bulance, everybody just assumed it was an accident. It was wet, we were all drunk. Stupid kids, you know. Teammates. They came back the next day to interview me, but they'd already spoken to Price, and he'd lied and told them the whole thing was an accident. He knew it wasn't that simple. He was standing right there. He probably figured if he lied for me, I'd lie for him. By then he'd already threatened Jenna, too. She and I never talked about Simon specifically, but I'm guessing she figured out what happened between him and me after she ran. She never told me what Price said to keep her quiet, but man, was she terrified. And then she was just—gone. Left town. Went to live with her aunt, that was the rumor. She never came back, and I never heard from her. And Barbara was pregnant. She ended up losing that baby a few weeks later, but by then I—if I'd known there had been others, though . . ." He shook his head. "But I could have done *something* about Price, that's the truth, isn't it? No one was threatening me."

Hannah still had not occurred to him.

"You know, I think Hannah might have met the father of her baby on campus," I pressed on, because we had to finish. He had to know. "Thomas Price was in charge of the high school exchange program she was part of."

In agonizing slow motion, I watched Steve connect Price and Hannah. When he did, he closed his eyes and hung his head. After that, he didn't speak for such a long time. When he finally looked up, his eyes were glassy and stunned. A second later, they were filled with rage.

"Go to the state police now," he said. "Tell them what you just told me. I don't want any investigation of Price getting derailed because I was involved. And tell them to pick both of us up. Because if they don't, I swear to Christ, I will find Thomas Price, and I will kill him with my bare hands."

A young female officer with a petite curvy frame strode purposefully into the cafeteria, then headed straight for us with her hand resting on her radio as if it were a gun. She had a concerned but determined look on her face. For a second, I wondered if someone had already reported Steve. She stopped a few feet short of the table and pointed her chin in his direction.

"Excuse me one second," he said, composing himself admirably as he stood. He walked over to the officer, and the two of them exchanged a few clipped sentences. "Thank you," he said to her, then stepped back over to my table.

"They found Jenna's car," he said, sounding surprised and relieved. "Or rather, the owner of Blondie's, Monte, spotted it way down an embankment out near the Palisades Parkway, tucked under some brush."

"What about Jenna?"

"Don't know yet. It was too steep for him to make his way down. Hard to say when the accident even happened. Officers and fire department are on their way."

When I got home, Justin, Sandy, and Ella were playing Candy Land at the kitchen table. They were laughing, even Sandy. She seemed so much lighter and brighter. Like she was aging backward. Seeing her that way, the last thing I wanted was to tell her about her mother's car accident—an accident that we could only hope hadn't happened the full three days earlier. Then again, maybe knowing something, even something bad, would be better than knowing nothing at all.

"Hi," Justin said, with a "this has been an experience" expression as he crossed the room to kiss me. He'd offered to get Ella from school and to keep Sandy company until I got back. He probably hadn't realized what he was signing up for.

He whispered in my ear, "Everything go okay?"

I nodded and mouthed: *I'll tell you later.* "How are you guys?"

"We've been having a great time, right, girls?" he called to them, his eyes on mine.

"Yes," they said in unison.

"Mommy, I want Sandy to sleep over," Ella said, running over and grabbing on to my legs, her puffy mouth wobbling between a pout and a smile. "I want her to sleep in *my* room."

"Well, she is sleeping over, I think." I glanced at Sandy, who didn't object but kept her eyes on the Candy Land cards, sifting and resifting them into a careful pile.

"Yeah!" Ella cheered.

"But in the guest room, Peanut," I said. "Your bed is too small."

"Boo!" Ella called, but she looked thrilled as she ran back over and grabbed Sandy's hand. It was sweet seeing them together, and I had to will myself not to think about the sister Ella never had.

"Ella, Daddy is going to take you upstairs to get you ready for bed. I have to talk to Sandy for a minute." I tousled her hair and kissed her cheek. "I'll be up to say good night."

"Boo!" Ella went again, giggling as Justin scooped her up onto his shoulder and headed for the stairs.

When I turned back, Sandy was stacking the Candy Land cards meticulously back into the box. As if her life depended on it. She was smiling a little bit. No, not smiling. Grimacing. I pulled a chair out and sat down across from her. When I reached over and put a hand on hers, still gripping some of the cards, Sandy's fingers were ice-cold.

"Is she dead?" she asked. Quiet, matter-of-fact, as though she'd been waiting to hear that all along, maybe her whole life.

"They found her car, that's all we know," I said gently. "It looks like maybe she had an accident near the Palisades Parkway."

"The Palisades?" Sandy looked up at me. "But that's not on her way home. That's nowhere near anything. Where was she headed?"

"I don't know," I said. "I guess no one does yet."

"Can we go?" She stood up and looked around. "To where her car is?"

"Oh, they didn't tell me where exactly." Even if they had, I never would have taken Sandy out there to possibly watch her mother's dead body being dragged from some ditch. "They promised to call as soon as they know something. And then we'll go right away, okay?"

"Okay," she said reluctantly, lowering herself back down on the chair.

"Let me just run upstairs and say good night to Ella. She'll never go to sleep otherwise. If you haven't heard from the police by the time I get back down, I'll call them again."

"What about Hannah?" Sandy asked. "How is she?"

"They think she's going to be okay," I said, though that was a bit of an overstatement. I put a hand on Sandy's shoulder as I stood. "Right now you need to focus on taking care of yourself. I'll bet you haven't eaten. I'll send Justin down to make you something."

"Okay," Sandy said, though it was obvious she wasn't about to eat a thing.

Justin was in Ella's bedroom, snuggling her deep into her sea of stuffed animals—an ice cream sandwich with big goofy eyes, three dogs, and a panda bear in a flowered sundress. Her eyelids were heavy with sleep.

"I'm going to go change," Justin said, kissing me as he headed out of the room.

I crouched next to Ella's bed and pressed my forehead against hers. She hugged my head with her hot hands, so hard that she almost pulled out some of my hair.

"I missed you tonight," I said. A mother wasn't supposed to say that. I'd heard that once. But I didn't care anymore. Because it was true. And true had to matter more than right.

"I love you, too, Mommy," Ella said. "To the dinosaurs and back."

"Good night, Peanut." I kissed her face again and again until she giggled, then I pushed myself to my exhausted feet. "Light on or off?"

"Off," Ella said sleepily. "Bye-bye, Mommy."

I lingered in the doorway, watching Ella fall asleep. She was so perfect right now, just like that. I couldn't be sure of how things would turn out, but I could be sure of that much. And that was something.

I headed to the guest bedroom to pull the shades and turn down the bed. To get the room ready for what would likely be Sandy's long and terrible night to come. The police would call any minute, almost certainly with bad news. That would be followed by the long drive to the hospital and the heartbreaking identification of Sandy's mother, the gathering of her personal effects. It would all be tragic, devastating, and it would likely be the middle of the night by the time we got home. Sandy would be wrecked and exhausted, and I didn't want to have to be fussing around her then.

I turned on the small bedside lamp and rearranged the pillows twice. As if any of that could make the inevitable awfulness better. I was so distracted by my handiwork as I walked around the end of the bed that I crashed right into Sandy's boxes stacked against the wall. The top one tipped over, its contents spilling out into a sad mess on the floor. I kneeled down, quickly gathering up the photos and papers, some plastic cups and silverware, hopelessly trying to put it back the way it had been. I didn't want Sandy to think I'd been invading her privacy or, worse, to feel embarrassed that I'd seen what was left of her world.

I was about to toss in the last thing: a plastic bag filled with some scraps of paper, ticket stubs, a take-out menu—a sack of mementos—when I saw a long smudge of brownish red on the corner. That wasn't blood, was it? I held it up to take a closer look. It did look a lot like blood. God, blood from *that* night. Thinking about it made me feel sick. I peered at one of the notes inside. It was a thank-you from Rhea, addressed to Hannah. It had an address written in a girlish hand in a blank space at the bottom. These were the things Hannah had given Sandy for safekeeping: her memories from the baby's father. I was about to put the bag back in the box when a smaller slip of paper at the bottom caught my eye.

I pressed my face closer to the smudged plastic, my heart already beating hard.

No. I snapped my eyes closed.

That hadn't been—couldn't be.

I was tired. I was seeing things. I had to be. I squeezed my eyes tighter.

But when I opened them again, they were still there at the bottom of that blood-streaked bag. Little scraps of paper. Lots of them. And on them, lines of poetry written in Justin's familiar hand.

I didn't feel my feet moving, but they must have. Because soon I was standing in our bedroom, staring at Justin, gripping the blood-streaked plastic bag in one hand. The fingers of my other hand clenched into a fist. I was deep underwater, the sound roiling and bent against my ears. Justin was sitting there on the bed, pulling on a sweatshirt like it was any other day. As I watched him, the pressure around my head felt like it was going to crush my skull.

And there was Justin, saying something to me. Talking like the world had not just been incinerated. Like we were not reduced to embers.

When I put Hannah's bag of notes on the bed next to him, he fell silent. Froze.

He stared and stared and stared at that bag. And all I wanted him to do was look confused. For him to say "What?" or "Why?" or "I don't understand." But he didn't say anything. He didn't say a word. Instead, he dropped his face in his hands and kept it there for a horribly long time. I must have backed up, retreated to the wall, because all of a sudden my back was pressed against it.

When Justin looked at me, his eyes were wide and terrified. "Molly," he began, shaking his head.

And then he crossed the room to me. His arms soon locked around me like a cage. All I wanted to do was break free. To break him. To run. Except I couldn't move. I couldn't even breathe.

"I would do anything to take it back, Molly," he breathed into my rigid neck. "It was such a stupid, selfish mistake. I just—and this isn't an excuse, because it's my fault—I just missed you. I loved you and I missed you and I wanted you back. And I couldn't— I didn't know how to reach you."

"No," I said. The word sliced the back of my throat.

But it wasn't a yell. Or a sob. Or a scream. Just a statement: No. No, what? No, it didn't happen. No, you didn't miss me? No, you didn't love me. No. This. Cannot. Be.

"It was so long ago, too, Molly. Months," he said, rushing on with his panicked explanations. Like he was only now realizing the awful enormity of what was happening. "It ended before we ever moved here, I swear. Things were so much worse then. And I swear to God, I didn't know how old she was. We met on campus when I came to interview—I thought she was a college . . . Molly, I am so sorry."

"The baby," I heard myself say.

"I didn't know, not until after you—until just now, really, when Sandy told you. And even then, I mean, do we know for sure? There could have been other guys."

Justin went on, said other things, they rebounded off me in echoed shards, tearing at my skin. *She was the only one. Never again. I am so sorry. I love you. I am so sorry. I love you.*

I am so sorry. She reminded me of you.

I tried so hard to get you off the story. I wanted so badly to protect you.

"No," I whispered. My whole body had gone numb. But my lungs were on fire. "No."

Q: You seem extremely aggravated, Molly.

M.S.:   I am aggravated. I don't see why you're trying to get me angry at Justin.

Q: I'm just trying to clarify where Justin was that weekend. You told me that you couldn't reach him when you were at the doctor's office. But I didn't realize he was away that whole weekend.

M.S.:   Yes, at a conference in Boston. I told you, he had two conferences.

Q: But you're not angry at him for being away?

M.S.:   Why would I be angry at him for going to a conference?

Q: For being unreachable.

M.S.:   He was *working*. I was the one who freaked out.

Q: You had just received horrible news. Understandable that you were upset.

M.S.:   Except *I* was upset way before the appointment. Oh yes, I freaked out long before then. And if you want to know why I *really* feel guilty, it's because of *that*. Because Justin told me he would be busy. That he had three different panels and colleagues to meet with. He gave me a number where I could reach him if it was an emergency. But it wasn't an emergency. So I just kept calling and calling his cell phone. And I don't know if it was the hormones or what, but I got myself all worked into a panic—like maybe he was *dead* or something. I mean, it was so stupid. Because he was there *with* someone. She would have called me if he'd been hit by a car.

Q: She.

M.S: Oh God, seriously? Yes, Justin was traveling with his research assistant, and yes, she was young and pretty and blond.

Q: Did he often not call when he was traveling with her?

M.S.: Oh my God, this is ridiculous! You are desperate for me to be angry at him, aren't you? Yes, Justin was away in Boston at a conference with a pretty young colleague, and yes, I couldn't reach him at hours when I should have been able to. And yes, I was suspicious! Because I wasn't thinking clearly! So, I freaked out and kept calling his cell phone over and over and over again. Then I started calling his room in the middle of the night, and he didn't answer there. And I got so upset that it—that *I* probably made the baby's heart speed up. All while I should have been resting and staying calm. And so, *yes*, that's probably why I feel so guilty. Because *I* killed her! So there it is. Are you happy now, Dr. Zomer?

Q: But you don't blame Justin?

M.S.: Blame him? She was inside *me*, Dr. Zomer. *I* was her mother. I'm the one who was supposed to take care of her. I'm the one who was supposed to keep her alive.

Sandy

Molly hadn't been gone two minutes when Sandy's phone rang. A Ridgedale number that she didn't recognize—the police department, probably. Now that they were finally calling, she couldn't get herself to answer. Instead, she let it ring, four times in all. Sandy was sure it would have gone to voicemail by the time she answered it. But it hadn't.

"Is this Sandy Mendelson?"

"Yes?"

"This is Sergeant Fulton of the Ridgedale Police Department. Your mother, Jenna Mendelson, has been in an automobile accident."

"Is she dead?" Sandy heard herself sounding like she wanted that to be true. Even though she didn't. Even though nothing could have been further from the truth.

"Um, no, miss," he said, sounding confused about her jumping to that conclusion. And maybe a little suspicious. "Looks like she'll be okay. Doing pretty well, considering."

When Sandy got upstairs, Molly and Justin were in their bedroom, the door closed. Sandy sat on the edge of the guest bed for a minute, hoping they'd come out so Molly could offer, with that nice smile of hers, to take Sandy to the hospital *right now*.

Sandy would have headed out on her bike, but they'd taken Jenna to Bergen County Hospital, probably close to an hour by bike, and on a highway, and she didn't have money to call a cab. She had no choice but to knock.

Justin opened the door a crack, his body filling the doorway. "Hi." He was trying to sound friendly, but there was definitely something wrong. His eyes were all red, and his hair was all fucked up. "What's up?"

"Oh, sorry to bother you," Sandy began, and she seriously hated this shit—asking people for help. Like any bad habit: Do it once, and it got way too easy to do it again. "The police called. My mom is at the hospital. They said I could come down. I would ride my bike, but she's at the Bergen County Hospital and—"

Sandy heard Molly say something behind Justin.

"Wait, hold on." He ducked back into the bedroom, resting the door shut without pulling it closed.

There were more voices. Maybe they'd changed their minds about helping her. They had a kid of their own to worry about, and Molly had already helped Sandy a lot, more than most people did.

"You know, actually, it's okay," Sandy began as soon as the door opened again. She couldn't deal with being let down easy. But it was Molly this time, car keys already in her hand. "I'm just going to ride my—"

"No, no, I'll drive you." Molly's eyes were red and shiny, like Justin's had been. "Please, I insist." She smiled and waved Sandy forward. "What did they say?"

"That she's going to be okay," Sandy said, not sure she believed it herself.

"I'm so glad, Sandy," Molly said, and it looked like she meant it. "Come on, let's get you to her."

"You can go ahead on in, hon," said the nice nurse, standing to the side in her pink flowered scrubs, holding open the door to Jenna's hospital room. "You were the first person she asked about before she went into surgery. She'll be so happy to see you when she wakes up."

Sandy shuffled inside. But she hung back, near the door. Eyes on the ground. She was afraid to see how bad off Jenna was. When Sandy turned her gaze up, she saw that Jenna didn't look great, but maybe not as bad as Sandy had been afraid of. Her eyes were closed and her skin was a grayish blue that matched the hospital bedsheets. She had bruises all over her arms, a bandage on one cheek, her leg raised in a brace.

It was a miracle that Jenna wasn't worse, everyone at the hospital had said. She'd passed in and out of consciousness, severely dehydrated, hanging upside down, her leg pinned, bleeding internally—something surgery had corrected—for days, maybe. They couldn't be sure how long, because Jenna didn't remember when or how the accident had happened. But everyone had been convinced she was already dead when they pulled her out. If it hadn't been for Monte, she probably would have been.

"Let me know if you need anything." The nurse pulled up a chair next to Jenna's bedside and motioned for Sandy to sit. "She just had some pain medicine, and she's still sedated from the surgery. She'll probably sleep for a couple more hours. But if she wakes up and you need anything, just push this." She motioned to a call button on the wall. "My name is Terry."

Once the nurse was gone, Sandy kept on standing there for a while with her arms crossed, watching Jenna sleep. Eventually, she did rest on the hard chair a few feet from Jenna's bed, the whole time trying to figure out how the hell she could have ever thought, even for a second, that she might be better off without her. After a while, Sandy let herself relax a little, sinking lower in the chair as the minutes became hours, and the hours stretched on toward dawn.

=====

"Hey, there," Jenna said when Sandy woke up. "You've been out like a light in that chair for I don't know how long. They kept coming in and offering to wake you, but I told them to leave you the hell alone." Jenna half smiled with her bandaged mouth. "I like watching my girl sleep. Reminds me of when you were little."

The sun was up, streaming in through the curtains. Jenna looked pale and tired but much better than she had the night before. Makeup-less and with her hair pulled back, she looked like a totally different person. A little older, but more beautiful, too.

"Are you okay?" Sandy got up and stepped closer to the bed. "Does your leg hurt?"

Jenna smiled and shook her head, squeezing Sandy's hand. "They have me hopped up on so much shit, I feel better than I have in years."

"That's good." Sandy smiled, but she felt her mouth pulling hard the other way. She didn't want to cry. She hadn't cried in front of Jenna since she was— She couldn't remember the last time. And if someone was going to cry, it should be Jenna. She was the one who'd been in the accident. "What the hell happened?"

Jenna shook her head with a quivery smile. "The last thing I remember real clearly is going in to work. I was drying glasses by myself behind the bar, watching Judge Judy rip in to some prick with this ugly-ass barking dog, and you know how much I love when she does that."

Only Jenna.

"Yeah, I do," Sandy said, smiling. "But nothing else?"

"I've got some flashes of being in the car after the accident. My fucking leg was on fire, and I was so goddamn thirsty. That and the fucking quiet. You know how I hate that shit. Can you imagine

me with all that time on my hands, all by myself, just to think?"
As Jenna shrugged, tears filled her eyes. "I do remember hearing my phone ringing and ringing, up until the battery kicked.
And I knew it was you. I swear, you calling was what made me
hold on."

"You really don't know how the accident happened?"

Jenna frowned, shook her head. "I was definitely fucking sober by
the time they found me. But before that, who knows?"

"The Palisades Parkway?"

She shrugged. "Buying drugs, I guess. I know a guy who sort of
lives out that way. But not really. I got to be honest, I don't have a
clue."

"So you don't remember some woman you were talking to before
you left work? Laurie said she had blond hair."

"A woman?" Jenna looked as confused as Sandy had been. "Nah.
But like I said, I don't remember anything after Judy."

Sandy was trying to stay focused on Jenna being back, but it
was hard not to let her mind wander. Because even with Jenna
found, there were plenty of other things to worry about—no place
to live, no emergency fund. And now Jenna wouldn't be able to
work, and there would be medical bills. Jenna had insurance at
Blondie's, but only if they stayed in Ridgedale. Sandy wasn't sure
if the coast was clear for her after what had happened to Hannah.
To say they were screwed was a fucking understatement. But then
they'd always lived on the razor's edge. And so far they'd managed
to survive.

"Can you come here?" Jenna patted the bed next to her. "Closer."

Sandy pushed herself up onto the bed, which was a shitload stiffer
than it looked. Jenna reached forward and tucked Sandy's hair behind her ear, staring at her the whole time, like she was drinking
Sandy in, filling up on her. "You know, when you were a real little
girl, you were so afraid of the dark. I mean blind-ass terrified."

"Was not." But how would Sandy know? There was a reason she'd blocked out so much of her childhood. Jenna wasn't easy to live with now; for a little kid, she had been kind of a nightmare.

"I know, you're not afraid of anything anymore. But you'd cry yourself to sleep every night lying there. I told you a million times that you could leave the light on. You know me, why beat something when you can wriggle around it. But you were like 'Fuck, no.' Only five or something, and within weeks you'd cured yourself." Jenna's voice was breaking apart, her face melting. "You are so much stronger than I ever was, Sandy. Than I'll ever be."

Sandy rolled her eyes.

"I mean it, baby." Jenna's voice was serious. "There is so much in this world you could do. Anything you want. That's why I need you to do something for me, Sandy. But you have to promise you'll do it. Even if you don't want to."

That did not sound good. Not at all like something Sandy wanted to agree to. God fucking knew what Jenna was going to ask—buy her drugs, sell her extra pain pills, steal some hospital toilet paper.

Sandy shook her head. "Um, yeah, I don't think—"

"Sandy!" Jenna shouted. "I'm serious."

"Okay, okay," Sandy said, raising her hands. She could always pretend she'd done whatever Jenna asked.

"There's an envelope in there that belongs to you." Jenna pointed toward a hospital-issue plastic bag sitting on the little table near the windows. "All of it's in there. I counted. It's not worth saying, but I am more sorry about taking that money than I've ever been for anything in my entire life. I'd like to say I changed my mind before the accident. That I realized that only an asshole would spend her kid's money getting high. But let's face it, you and I both know that's probably a lie."

Sandy pulled out the envelope, and sure enough, there were all her twenties. Thank Jesus. Finally, something breaking in their favor. Enough for food while Jenna was in the hospital and at least a week in some shithole motel after she got out. In the meantime, the hospital would probably let Sandy sleep in the room, and if they didn't, she could go back to Molly's.

Jenna waved Sandy back over. "You know what I thought about out there when I knew it was you calling me over and over again?"

Sandy shook her head as she sat back down on the bed, trying not to cry. It wasn't working. All that fear, all that worry, she'd been holding back all these days was rushing in. Soon there would be nowhere left for it to go.

"I thought: *There's Sandy, taking care of* me *again. When all I've ever done is mess things up for her.*"

"That's not—"

"Yes, it is true, baby." Jenna stroked Sandy's cheek. "And I have to live with that. But you don't, Sandy. You have a choice. That's why I need you to take that money, and I need you to go." There were tears on Jenna's cheeks, rolling down in big fat streams. "You need to leave this town, and you need to never come back. You need to get away from me."

"Mom, what the hell are you—"

"Do it for me if you have to." Jenna's voice cracked, but she was trying hard to keep it together. "And I don't want you to call or write. You need to start a new life, Sandy. A life as beautiful as the person you are. And you need to do it without me."

"Without you?" Panic flooded Sandy's belly. "What are you talking about? That's crazy. I'll miss you. I can't go somewhere *alone*." She was starting to cry. She didn't want to be, but she was. Because she already knew that Jenna was right. She had to go.

"I love you, baby," Jenna whispered. "But if you stay, you won't stand a fucking chance. I'll destroy the both of us."

Then Jenna pulled Sandy's face close, kissing her on the forehead— just like the mom Sandy had always wanted her to be.

Sandy was numb when she pushed herself out into the busy hospital hall, doctors and nurses and patients moving this way and that. Life and death keeping on.

In tears, Sandy started toward the front doors of the hospital, waiting for someone to stop her. Waiting for someone to tell her that she wasn't free to go. That she needed to go back. But no one did. No one asked her to slow down. No one stood in her way. And before long, Sandy was outside, the sun in her face, the town to her back, trying to figure out which way to go.

But forward was all there was. That was the only way to go.

Molly

I was finishing cooking dinner, Ella coloring on the kitchen floor next to me, when there was a knock at the front door. When I looked out the window, Stella was on our front stoop, arms crossed, a determined set to her jaw. I'd been avoiding her since our last awkward coffee date a week earlier. I considered ignoring the door. Stella hadn't seen me look out, but surely she had spotted my car in the driveway. And I knew her well enough to know: If she really wanted to talk to me, she wouldn't go away until she did.

Apart from necessities like bringing Ella to school, meeting Stella at the Black Cat had been the first time I'd emerged from hiding in the six weeks since I'd found out about Justin and Hannah. It wasn't as though their involvement or the baby had gotten extensive coverage in the local news. Thanks to Erik, the *Reader* hadn't mentioned it, but people in town knew. At least I felt like they did.

Luckily, Barbara had left town with Hannah and Cole, one less horrifying interaction for me to contemplate. They'd gone for Hannah—whose prognosis was apparently good, and Cole was much better, too—to get her rehabilitation treatment at the University of Pennsylvania Hospital. Or so Barbara was telling people. There were rumors that Barbara's parents, humiliated by Steve's arrest and what had happened with Hannah, had insisted she leave for an extended summer at the family beach house in Cape May, New

Jersey. Steve was in Ridgedale, awaiting sentencing. He'd confessed to killing Simon Barton in exchange for a reduced, voluntary manslaughter charge. Given the circumstances, which Jenna had come forward to corroborate, the prosecutor seemed loath to pursue much jail time.

Five minutes into that first coffee with Stella, and I was glad I'd agreed to meet her. As always, I got lost in Stella's silly color commentary on life in Ridgedale. And I was impressed by her restraint. She didn't even mention Justin's name. We'd never talked about what had happened between him and Hannah, and I was sure Stella was dying for details.

Ironically, I was the one who ended up mentioning Justin, offhandedly repeating a joke he'd made recently about the Black Cat barista whom Stella couldn't stand. A joke I thought she'd appreciate.

"Wait, you've been talking to Justin?"

For weeks, I had hated Justin so much it frightened me. I wouldn't have thought it was possible to hate another human being that much. The detailed fantasies I'd had about ways to inflict suffering on him—physical and mental—were so elaborate, they were alarming. But eventually, my hatred had given way to sadness and then to resignation. Justin had betrayed me in the most horrifying way, exactly when I needed him most. And I had been lost to him for so long, caught up in the worst of my depression for over a year. Both things were true. That made me sad, mostly for me and Ella, but occasionally for Justin. After all, his life was ruined, too.

He'd left Ridgedale, fired immediately by the university, and moved back to Manhattan. With the help of a loan from his parents, he was trying to get a freelance career off the ground, editing a well-respected political blog. He and I talked, but not much.

"He's the father of my child, Stella," I'd said that afternoon at the Black Cat, already wishing I hadn't brought him up. "I have to talk to him."

"Yeah, I know. But the way you mentioned him." She looked sickened. "It seemed like you'd forgiven him. I hope you're not blaming yourself or something. It doesn't matter if you were depressed when he did it, Molly. That doesn't excuse it."

I felt a hard wave of anger that pushed me right to my feet. I was not going to sit there and be judged by Stella, of all people. "Okay, I think I'm going to go."

"I'm sorry, Molly. I'm not trying to be a bitch here. But I am your friend." Stella had pressed her lips together as she looked at me. "I—I just don't want to see you make a bad situation worse by trying to pretend it's okay."

"Well, thanks for that," I said, though I was pretty sure Stella's motives weren't nearly that altruistic. "But trust me, Stella, when I need your advice, I will let you know."

Now I peered at Stella, standing there on our stoop. She looked awful. She had on worn jeans and an ill-fitting, unflattering shirt. Her skin was blotchy. Maybe she was there to apologize. She had sent me some texts that I'd ignored. I owed it to her to hear her out.

"Can I come in?" she asked when I opened the door. Even her voice was deflated, no trace of her usual bravado. But she didn't sound all that apologetic. "There's something I need to talk to you about. It's been bothering me ever since we met last week. Longer than that, really. I just— It will only take a minute."

"I don't need another lecture, Stella," I said. "I know you think you're helping, but honestly, I'm fine."

She didn't say anything else as she took a couple of steps into the living room. She also didn't sit down. Instead, she looked toward the kitchen, where Ella was conducting an elaborate play with paper bag puppets. Like she wanted to be sure that Ella was safely out of earshot before she said whatever inappropriate thing she was about to say.

"For the record, I'm not forgiving Justin, Stella." I hated myself for launching into yet another explanation to which Stella was not entitled. I didn't need to explain myself to anyone. But I was hoping it would keep her from saying something else that would aggravate me. "And I'm sorry if I don't hate him the way you hate Kevin. But that's not what I want for myself. I don't enjoy it the way you do."

She winced but didn't argue. How could she when it was true?

"Maybe you could hate him just a little," she said. She was holding out her phone to me. "You never saw these, did you?"

"Saw what? What is it, Stella?" Reluctantly, I glanced down at the screen, long enough to see that it was a comments page from the *Ridgedale Reader*. "I don't read the comments on my stories. You know that."

"Now I do. But I didn't at the time." She was still holding out her phone. "Please read just this one. Then I will go. And you never have to talk to me again."

Never talk to her again? This time I squinted down at the screen, trying to make sense of the message. *This baby belongs to you.* And from a user name, 246Barry, that had Justin's office number in it— 246 Barry Hall—posted at the time I'd written the story, long before anyone knew about Hannah, much less Justin. "That doesn't make any sense."

"I know," Stella said ruefully. "I was too cryptic. Too clever for my own good. For anyone's good. I wanted you to figure it out without me ever having to tell you."

"Stella, what are you talking about?" I had the most terrible feeling. Not anger, fear. I wanted to be angry again.

"I saw a text someone sent to Justin, Molly. He went to the bathroom, left his phone there on the bar. I wasn't snooping or anything. It was just right there. And I didn't know who it was from at the time. It didn't even say anything that specific—just 'I really need to talk to you now, please,' that kind of thing. But it was the way it was written, you know? I just *knew*."

"Stella, 'knew' what? What are you talking about?"

"I made a joke about it to Justin when he got back from the bathroom: *You get her pregnant and leave her by the side of the road?* And there was just this look on Justin's face, Molly. Like he wanted to kill me. It was obvious: There *was* someone out there that he'd gotten pregnant. Then after they found the baby and you told me how he was acting about the story—I just—" Her voice caught. "I couldn't be sure it was his baby, except I was. But I was too much of a coward to tell you, so I posted some stupid messages that you never even saw. I would have told you if you hadn't found out yourself. I swear."

"What?" It was all I could think to say. None of what she was saying made any sense at all. "Wait, how would you— When would you have seen Justin's texts?" The three of us hadn't had dinner together in months, and even then they hadn't been alone together. "What bar?"

Stella took a deep breath as her eyes filled with tears. "It was just *one* glass of wine, Molly. *One* time. Nothing happened. But if Justin hadn't gotten the text that night? If he and I hadn't argued right after, would something have?" She shook her head. Shrugged. "I can live with you hating me for that. I'll have to. I can even live with you not hating him. Just don't forgive him, Molly—not all the way. He doesn't deserve that. And neither do you."

Erik came in while I was clearing out my desk. He was carrying coffee and a muffin, with several papers tucked under his arm. He looked tired but happy, like the parent of any new baby. I was so happy for him that it had all worked out at last.

"You don't have to do that, you know," he said as I gathered up the last of my files. "I've already said this a hundred times, but I'd love for you to keep a desk here. You can even freelance for whoever else you want."

Erik had said this many times since I'd given my notice two months earlier, five long months since Justin had moved out, three and a half months since I'd spoken to Stella. I'd seen her, of course, Ridgedale was small, but she'd kept a respectful distance.

"Can I leave it as a maybe?" I said, even though I knew it was a no.

"Of course," he said. "I understand, you've got a lot on your plate. And I can't wait to read it, truly."

I smiled. "Me, too. Now I just need to go write it."

"Well, the article was excellent, I'm sure the book will be, too," Erik said, referring to the *New York* magazine cover piece I'd done on Thomas Price, as well as the book deal I'd gotten in its wake. "I never had any doubt what you were capable of."

In the end, the assaults had spanned two decades and three universities, starting with Jenna Mendelson, who'd agreed to be interviewed for my article as long as I referred to her only as JM. I told Jenna about my connection to Sandy. It would have felt dishonest otherwise. But I didn't tell her that we were still exchanging emails. Sandy had asked me not to.

Sandy had gotten her GED with honors the first day she was able—on her seventeenth birthday—and was already taking classes at the New School while waiting tables and making plans to apply for a scholarship to attend college full-time in the fall. She and Aidan were in touch, as friends only, Sandy had been quick to clarify. She wasn't in the market for a boyfriend, not until she got where she wanted to go.

"Steve's allocution is today," Erik went on. "You want to cover it for old times' sake?"

He was joking, at least I was pretty sure he was, trying to make light of my very public situation. And I appreciated his kindness. It was a relief to have someone not ignore whom I'd been married to like it was some kind of shameful disease. In the end, Erik and Nancy had become the close friends I had always hoped they'd be. Right when I'd needed them the most.

"Thanks for the offer," I said, "but I think I'll pass."

I never could have passed up writing the story on Thomas Price, though. He'd been fired swiftly, then arrested shortly thereafter for sexual assault. Finally, he was no longer in a position to threaten anyone; further violence was apparently his threat of choice. Four women, some not so young anymore, planned to press charges. Not Rose, at least not yet. She hadn't resurfaced.

"I had a feeling about Price from day one," Deckler had said when I'd finally caught up with him for my article. A supervisor at Ridgedale University now, he was allowed to wear khakis and a button-down shirt, which, even I had to admit, looked a little better on him. He'd been hired back, and given the promotion, after threatening to sue for wrongful termination. "Guys like that don't bother to cover their tracks very well."

"Why did you give me the files?"

He'd shrugged. "You were new to town. I could be sure you weren't connected to anyone. Price had made real clear that he knew the chief of police from high school. That Steve would protect him no matter what. Same kind of lies he probably used to keep all of those girls quiet. After we found the baby and then you came around asking about Rose Gowan." He'd glanced away, uncomfortable. He knew about Justin—that was obvious. "Turns out they're not related, but I thought they might be. And I felt like that was enough. I had to do something, even if I lost my job."

At least Price would finally pay for something. He'd never again work at a university and would likely see real jail time. And the publicity had thrown Ridgedale University's procedures for handling sexual assaults under the microscope.

The door to the *Reader*'s offices opened again. It was Nancy, pushing a stroller. She looked elated and exhausted. Maybe a little more exhausted than Erik but also a little more elated. They'd fought so hard and so long for a baby that they seemed to be wasting not a second complaining about the less enjoyable parts of new parenthood. It was a wonder that Erik had been able to hold it together as well as he had during those first few days when I was working on the story about Hannah's baby. The birth mother of Erik and Nancy's baby had been having second thoughts. She'd taken off for her sister's house, and Erik had gone after her, hoping to change her mind. Apparently, since absolute secrecy had been the birth mother's prerequisite, Erik had been afraid to say anything to anyone about where he was or why. In the end, she'd decided to go through with the adoption.

Unable to resist, I went over to see Delilah, their impossibly chubby now-seven-month-old girl. "She keeps getting cuter and cuter," I said, touching her little toes as she broke into an enormous toothless grin. "How is that even possible?"

"I don't know," Nancy said, beaming cheerfully. "But I have to say, I agree. She certainly has opinions, though." She shrugged and smiled some more. "Like her birth mother says, I guess you've got to let go or be dragged."

Let go or be dragged. It bounced in my head like the ringing of a bell. And then I remembered where I'd heard it before, in Rose's hospital room. Stella had been the one to say it, but the words had belonged to Rose.

Ella and I went outside after dinner. The August night, fresh off a storm, felt cool and electrified. As I sat on our front steps, breathing deep the smell of grass and rain, I watched Ella race back and forth in the darkness, a long wand in her hand leaving enormous shimmery bubbles in her wake.

I was still watching her giggling in the fading light as my phone vibrated on the steps next to me. *Justin*, it said when I looked down at the screen. Calling again, as he did so often despite my repeated requests for emails only, and only about Ella. We'd told her the basics—Mommy and Daddy would live apart from now on, but that they both still loved her just as much. And no, Daddy wasn't coming home soon. He wasn't coming home ever. Civility, I was committed to that. But that was all.

I couldn't change how slow I'd been to see the truth about Justin or how much longer it had taken me to accept it. But I could do now what needed to be done for Ella and me. And I could do it without turning our lives into a torrent of rage, the way my own mother had. Without looking at the phone again, I silenced it and turned it facedown on the steps next to me.

Because Justin had been right about one thing: Not everything about where you're going has to be about where you've been.

"Mommy, look!" Ella squealed. When I turned, she was sprinting barefoot across the grass, pointing to the glow of fireflies, sparking and then disappearing in the darkness. "Can we catch some, Mommy?"

I looked over at our picture-perfect front yard, at our white picket fence and pretty white house, watching the glow of all those fireflies, so lazy and random and beautiful. Did capturing them require a special jar or a net? What happened if you gathered them in your hands? I had not the faintest clue.

"Yes, sweetheart. Of course we can," I said when Ella had run, full speed, back to me. I brushed back her curls from her sweet upturned face. "Come, let's go get a jar," I said, grasping her hand as we made our way inside. "And then I'll show you how it's done."

Epilogue

They're asleep in the blue vinyl chair pressed up against the wall, a couple of feet from my bed. I've read enough books—and I've read all the goddamn books—to know that I should wake them. We're never supposed to fall asleep holding her. But just for a minute I will let myself watch them. Let myself marvel at how impossible it is that they exist, so perfect like that: my newborn daughter wrapped tight in her hospital-issue blanket, cradled in my husband's arms.

Lucas's blond hair is sticking up, his long face covered with a few days' stubble. His soft plaid shirt unusually wrinkled. Unshowered and exhausted and disheveled, this man who wiped my forehead and held my hand and whispered in my ear and then shouted over my yelling—all at exactly the right moment and in just the right way— is more handsome than he has ever been. More handsome than any man could ever be.

Despite all my careful preparation, my labor eventually took a sharp turn and headed way the hell south. Forty grueling hours of drug-free (thank you very much) labor with hardly any progression and then the baby's heart rate suddenly fell off a cliff. General anesthesia and an emergency C-section were the only way to go. And so I wasn't even awake for the moment of her birth. Will never know what her first cry sounded like, can't tell her about her first seconds on Planet Earth. It is not the way I wanted it. It's not what I pictured. None of it is the way it was supposed to be.

But I won't take that as a sign. Some dark harbinger of doom. I will not manifest that which I am trying so hard to avoid. I heard that in yoga. Or in the one pre-natal yoga class I took. Yoga's just not for me, but that idea? It's worth keeping.

"We don't need perfect," Lucas said when it was all over. When I woke up already a mother and burst into tears. He was crying, too, as he kissed me, still visibly traumatized by my nearly fatal post-partum hemorrhage. He forced a smile, wiping at his face with his sleeve. "Besides, now this parenting thing can only go the fuck up from here."

The way he said *fuck* had made me smile. Lucas's fading accent was always most obvious when it got stuck on the unfamiliar swears. French. I never would have believed I'd end up married to some fancy French lawyer who I met when he accidentally knocked me off my bike. Lucas had passed too close early one Saturday when we were both doing high-speed laps around the loop in Central Park. He even had on one of those dumb skintight biking outfits and tight wraparound sunglasses, and he was riding the kind of flashy racing bike I liked to mock.

The day Lucas and I met was the last time we were in the hospital together. He'd come with me to have my elbow X-rayed. He joked when he finally met my friends at the New York City Administration for Child Services—where I'd worked for ten years after getting my master's, the past two as a deputy commissioner—that he'd never have gotten that first date if my elbow had actually been fractured. But he was wrong. I'd already fallen for him after an hour in that waiting room together.

Still, Lucas is nothing like the person I had pictured as my husband. Mostly, I had pictured no one. Had seen myself living out my days as an island, happily alone with friends and boyfriends and my great career. And yet, now that Lucas was here, it was obvious: he was the person I didn't realize I was waiting for.

Lucas startles awake suddenly, eyes wide as he realizes he's fallen asleep holding the baby.

"It's okay," I say. "I was watching. I wouldn't have let you drop her."

"Oh, good," he says, relieved.

"Can I hold her?"

"Of course," Lucas says, standing carefully, as though he is cuddling a bomb. He gazes down at her. "Ready to go to Mommy, Jenna Mendelson Mason?"

My daughter will never know her namesake. Jenna died three years ago. Stomach cancer that she never told me about, despite the fact that we'd started exchanging e-mails a couple years ago. It explained why she never wanted me to visit. Monte told me after the funeral that she couldn't stand the thought of me giving up one more minute of my life taking care of her.

But someday I will tell my daughter about her grandmother. I will share what really matters: that she was named after a woman brave enough to accept her shortcomings. A woman strong enough to set me free.

Acknowledgments

My deepest gratitude to the brilliant and insightful Claire Wachtel. Thank you, thank you, thank you. Sharing this creative process has been a true gift. Thank you for seeing this book's potential, then sticking with me in the trenches until it was all the way there.

Many thanks to Michael Morrison and Jonathan Burnham for your generous support and incredible enthusiasm. Thanks also to Hannah Wood, Leslie Cohen, Katie O'Callaghan, Amy Baker, Mary Sasso, Leigh Raynor, Kathryn Ratcliffe-Lee, and everyone else on the HarperCollins team. It's a pleasure to work with such warm and wonderful people.

To Marly Rusoff, the very best agent and most lovely friend, I am so lucky to be the beneficiary of your wisdom and grace. Thank you, Michael Radulescu, for your foreign rights and associated genius, and Julie Mosow, for always dropping everything to read another draft. Thank you to the fabulous Shari Smiley and the wonderful Lizzy Kremer.

Many thanks to the experts who patiently answered my questions, including Dr. Barbara Deli, Dr. Gerald Feigin, Karen Lundegaard, Dr. Ora Pearlstein, Maureen Rush and Kelly Smith. I am also indebted to the work of Pam Belluck and Dr. Carl P. Malmquist.

My endless gratitude to my fantastic friends and family, a.k.a. the country's most ferocious grassroots marketing team: John McCreight and Kim Healey, Diane and Stanley Dohm, Rebecca Prentice and Mike Blom, Stephen Prentice, Catherine and David Bohigian, Alanna Cavaricci, Sidney Cavaricci, the Cragan family, the Crane family, Larry and Suzy Daniels, Bob Daniels and Craig Leslie, Kate Eschelbach, David Fischer, Tania Garcia, Jessica and Jason Garmise, Sonya Glazer, Yuko Ikeda, David Kear, Merrie Koehlert, Hallie Levin, Brian and Laura Mayer, Brian McCreight, the Metzger family, Jason Miller, Sarah Moore, Frank Pometti, Jon Reinish, Maria Renz and Tom Barr, Julie Schwetlick, Maxine Solvay, Bronwen Stine, the Thomatos family, Meg Yonts, Denise Young Farrell, and Christine Yu. Beware: if you get too near any of them, they will make you buy another book.

A special thanks to Joe and Naomi Daniels for the help and the many years of friendship.

Thank you, Megan Crane, for promising me it would be worth it. To Victoria Cook, for simultaneously being the world's best spin doctor and one of the most honest people I know. Thank you to Elena Evangelo for lending your creative genius. And to my ladies: Cindy Buzzeo, Cara Cragan, Heather Frattone, Nicole Kear, Tara Pometti, and Motoko Rich. My life would be so much less without you in it.

To Martin and Clare Prentice, words can't express how grateful I am to, and for, the both of you.

To my husband, Tony: you are all things, always.

And to my daughters, Harper and Emerson, my heart and my soul. You are, and will always be, the most important story.

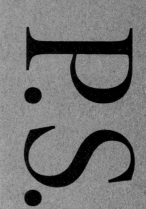

Insights,
Interviews
& More . . .

Meet
Kimberly McCreight

Beowulf Sheehan

KIMBERLY MCCREIGHT's fiction debut
was the *New York Times* bestseller
Reconstructing Amelia, which was
nominated for an Edgar Award for Best
First Novel as well as an Alex Award.
Named *Entertainment Weekly*'s Favorite
Book of the Year, *Reconstructing Amelia*
was one of CNN's Reader Favorites for
2013, a finalist for Goodreads Best
Mystery of the Year, and a Book Club
pick for Target, Books-a-Million, and
Indigo. *Reconstructing Amelia* has also
been optioned for film by HBO and

Nicole Kidman's Blossom Films. McCreight's second novel, *Where They Found Her*, was a *USA Today* bestseller. McCreight's teen trilogy, *The Outliers*, has been optioned for film by Lionsgate, Mandeville, and Reese Witherspoon's Pacific Standard. McCreight lives in Park Slope, Brooklyn, with her husband and two daughters.

www.kimberlymccreight.com ∽

Reading Group Guide
Discussion Questions for *Where They Found Her*

1. In what ways is Molly prepared, or not prepared, to report on the tragic discovery in Ridgedale?

2. How does Molly's job as a journalist compare with her previous one as a lawyer? In what ways are the skills required the same? Different?

3. In what situations might a newspaper editor be justified in not publishing certain facts of a story? What are a paper's social responsibilities?

4. Examine the many different experiences of motherhood in the novel. What are the various challenges of each?

5. How does shifting between several narrative voices affect the novel? Why do you think an author might use this technique?

6. Consider the use of newspaper articles, readers' online comments, Molly's counseling transcripts, and text messages in the novel. What does each bring to the story? How are these sources of information different?

7. After her initial shock, Molly comes to believe that covering the story of a baby who has died will help her recover from the death of her own

baby. Why does she feel this way? What's a healthy and effective way to respond to grief?

8. Erik cautions Molly that it's human nature for even good, honest people to "support . . . a self-serving narrative," even to the point of excluding facts. Why is this so?

9. What are some examples of lying in the novel? Are they all equal? When is lying justified?

10. Steve, Ridgedale's chief of police, has a very complicated position in the case. What different forces and loyalties are at work within him as he investigates?

11. How has the technological ability for readers to offer immediate online comments about articles changed the nature and effect of reading the news?

12. Barbara says that her husband, Steve, and daughter, Hannah, have "compassion [as] their strength" but suggests "all this caring for strangers came at a cost." What might she mean? What is a healthy amount of compassion?

13. Molly wrestles with the idea that "not everything about where you're headed . . . has to be about where you've been." To what extent does a person's past influence or define his or her future?

14. Both Molly and Sandy had very troubled mothers. What are the ▶

emotional or behavioral results of this poor parenting? What does it take to overcome such a start in life and become healthy and happy?

15. Sandy shows incredible strength throughout the novel. What qualities does she possess? Did her strengths develop *because of* or *despite* her difficult childhood?

16. In a discussion about Cole, Barbara yells at Rhea, claiming that she cannot understand the situation because she does not have children. To what extent is this true? ෴

Have You Read?
More by Kimberly McCreight

RECONSTRUCTING AMELIA

In this instant *New York Times* bestseller, a harried single mother is shocked when her daughter's exclusive private school calls to tell her that Amelia—her intelligent, high-achieving fifteen-year-old—has been caught cheating. But when Kate arrives at Grace Hall, she's blindsided by far more devastating news: Amelia is dead. Despondent, she supposedly jumped from the school's roof. Then Kate gets the anonymous text: Amelia didn't jump. In this powerful story of secrets and lies, friends and bullies, Kate sifts through Amelia's e-mails, text messages, and Facebook posts in a quest to vindicate the memory of a daughter whose life she could not save.

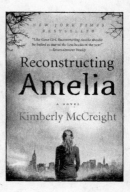

"Like *Gone Girl, Reconstructing Amelia* seamlessly marries a crime story with a relationship drama. And like *Gone Girl,* it should be hailed as one of the best books of the year. . . . A."
—*Entertainment Weekly*

Discover great authors, exclusive offers, and more at hc.com.

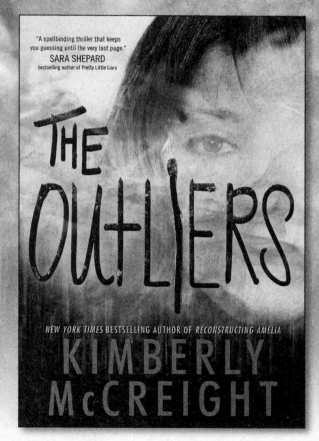